PRAISE FOR BOB BOAN'S

Williams Lake
Was Once
The Center Of The Universe

"In addition to telling stories about his characters, the author provides us with brief histories of Williams Lake, some of the bands that performed there during the 60's and their brand of Beach Music; it is a journey down a path that provides the reader with an opportunity to re-visit the adventurer in each of us."

– Christopher Biehler,
president Forevermore Records.

■ ■ ■

"I get a lot more pleasure from talking about Williams Lake now than I got from it then."

– Robert Honeycutt,
Williams Lake operator 1965 – 1969

■ ■ ■

"Bob takes me back in the day to a time when I felt in-vincible."

– Robert Jacobs II,
25-year-professional shagger and
1988 National Champion; actor in Shag: The Movie

ABOUT THE AUTHOR

BOB BOAN has been an active member of the space community for over a quarter of a century. He has worked on a variety of manned and unmanned space programs at different levels of responsibility over that time. Prior to his space experience, he was a member of academia. He taught primarily chemistry. He taught courses from high school through graduate school in several states.

Dr. Boan helped develop Communications, SIGINT, IMINT systems and concepts. He also has significant MASINT experience. He has multiple relevant patents and technical publications in his field.

He has attended a variety of colleges and universities. He received his BS from Campbell University, then Camp`bell College. His Master's was awarded by the University of Mississippi. He earned his doctorate at the Florida Institute of Technology.

Dr. Boan has authored a number of technical publications. He coauthored An Introduction to Planetary Defense: A Study of Modern Warfare Applied to Extra-Terrestrial Invasion, Brown Walker Press, 2006. He has written two other novels, Bobby Becomes Bob, Twilight Times Books, 2009, and Don't Tell Brenda.

Dr. Boan has been featured in Marquis Who's Who in the South and Southwest and in Marquis Who's Who in America.

ALSO BY BOB BOAN
An Introduction to Planetary Defense:
A Study of Modern Warfare Applied to Extra-Terrestrial Invasion
(With Travis S. Taylor),
BrownWalker Press, 2006

Bobby Becomes Bob
Twilight Times Books, 2009

Don't tell Brenda
Forthcoming

WILLIAMS LAKE WAS ONCE
THE CENTER OF THE UNIVERSE

Bob Boan

VERBAL PICTURES PRESS

This is a work of fiction. It is based on real and imaginary events as told by people who enjoyed Williams Lake during the second half of the sixties. People take actions. As a result, I needed names to associate with events. I used the source best known to me. I used names that belong to people I know; otherwise, I would have spent my time making up names – they would have been unrecognizable, therefore uninteresting. There are real people who may have been associated with episodes like some of those in the book. I have permission to use their names. If I do not have permission to use your name, its use is random and any relationship to an event(s) is purely coincidental. The selection of names is divorced from the story. To the best of my knowledge, there is no town named St. Umblers in North Carolina. St. Umblers is a product of my imagination. I took liberty with North Carolina's geography to place it there.

A Verbal Pictures Press original
Verbal Pictures Press
P.O. Box 302
North Myrtle Beach, SC 29597
Verbalpicturespress.com
ISBN: 978-0-9817332-0-3 (hardcover)
ISBN: 978-0-9817332-1-0 (paperback)

Front Cover Art: Painting, "Dancing on Water" by Becky Stowe, copyright 2008, is based on a photograph from Robert Honeycutt and commissioned by Bob Boan. Use of the name "Dancing on Water" is courtesy of Robert Honeycutt. The silhouette of shaggers – Bob and Judy, is by Bob Boan, copyright 2007.

Back Cover: The Williams Lake Pavilion, May 05, 2007, is courtesy of Timothy Lee.

Preface: The bust of Fat Harold is by Bob Boan, copyright 2007.

Jacket Design: Dorothy Clark, The Printing Port, Inc., Myrtle Beach, SC.

First Printing: July 2008.

Printed in the United States of America

DEDICATION

THIS BOOK IS DEDICATED to all those that we have known who were influential in our lives before they preceded us, especially: *Stacey, Mike, Bobby* and *Phil*. They loved us and we love them back.

We miss them. We will as long as we exist. However, they will stay with us forever through their impressions which they left upon us. We can conjure up their actions and attributes at any time. We can see them smile and enjoy life whenever we desire to do so. I hope that it is a shame that they did not get to see the impact that they have had on us. We can only hope that they would be as proud of what we have become as we are of who they were.

ACKNOWLEDGEMENTS

I OWE MUCH TO MANY for their contributions to this book. First, there were those who went to Williams Lake and helped forge the lasting memories. They went to have fun being with their friends while listening to the bands and dancing the Shag. Then there were those who were involved in the episodes that those took place in Ocean Drive, SC. That's where we met Fat Harold.

Thanks to Robert Honeycutt for opening and operating the pavilion at Williams Lake. He brought in the bands that provided the backdrop for many of the events described here. He provided information on some of the events at Williams Lake that helped to shape our lives.

I am deeply indebted to Fat Harold for the Preface.

Renowned artist, Becky Stowe, painted the front cover art. Thanks Becky, you created a masterpiece. Robert Honeycutt gave me a photograph of the circa late Forties Williams Lake Pavilion which was adapted into Becky's work. The title of Becky's painting, "Dancing on Water," is courtesy of Robert.

Wyman Honeycutt provided some of the information used to develop this book.

Donnie Ray Naylor provided important information.

Thanks to Timothy, Joe, Cherry, Connie Sue, Neil, Ah Me

and Reese for their memories and the details they added to the stories that I have recounted. I couldn't have done it without you. Deborah and Walt added some details.

I appreciate the opportunity to include snippets featuring people such as Judy, Jan, Page, Jerry and Melanie, Howard and Debbie, Tim and Deborah, Boonie and Lisa, Donnie and Kathy, Larry and Patrice and Walt. They are displaced in time and often in place. Thanks to these special people. Anyone would be fortunate to call them friends.

Timothy Lee has served as a sounding board and critic in addition to providing story lines. Timothy is responsible for the picture on the back cover which shows what remained of the Williams Lake Pavilion on May 07, 2007.

Ricky Pittman has served as editor and writing coach. His comments and guidance helped make the book better. It would no doubt be written better had I followed all his suggestions. Sometimes the story objected. Thanks, Rickey. I hope I did you proud.

I appreciate Jason Cordova's assistance in editing the book.

Grace Gustafson thanks for your comments, especially on fashion and style.

Judy Smith and I are the models for the silhouette shaggers. Thanks, Judy.

A special word of appreciation is due Fat Harold for being one of the stewards of Beach Music and the Shag. His endeavors have helped to preserve these treasures. Thank you, Fat Harold. Keep up the good work.

TABLE OF CONTENTS

PREFACE

Fun is timeless. Fun is the magnet which attracts us more strongly than any thing this side of love. Fun is probably the dominant component of love. This is a story about some of the adventures and misadventures of a group of adolescents who were seeking fun.

The events detailed here are a unique mix. These stories have been filtered and attenuated by time. They appear to be a combination of fact, fiction, legend and lies. The main characters were certainly real. Their search bought them to OD. I met them when they came to Ocean Drive, now North Myrtle Beach. They came seeking fun.

These events happened in the Sixties. The Sixties were unlike any other time in the history of the United States. The Sixties were a time of uncertainty. They were in a time with Woodstock, the peace movement, flower children and hippies. This group prepared to remain preppy. Style and dress were important to them. They were of a time social and political change. They were of a time with misunderstood geopolitical happenings.

I opened the Spanish Galleon in 1962. I started seeing some of the characters from these tales about 1964 or 1965. They were much like the other youth who frequented the Spanish Galleon. They came looking for a diversion from the harsh realities and uncertainties of life. They came to drink. They came looking for the fallen debutante. They came to shag. Most of all they came for fun. They began their quest for rosy futures at Williams Lake and at other venues for the same purposes that brought them to Ocean Drive.

There are only two sure things in the life of the human species. Change is one of those. Death is the other. These guys were out to cheat death. Lamentably, some of the characters in the story were unable to succeed in that goal over the long term. They were going to cram as much fun into the unknown amount of time they had available to them as was humanly possible.

I still see some of the characters from these episodes at Fat Harold's Beach Club. I see them at other places I go such as the Winter Boogie in Hickory, North Carolina, Twister's Fall Cyclone in Mooresville, North Carolina and Southern Comfort in Columbia, South Carolina. Some of them are still haunted by the Sixties. They still come looking for the fallen debutante. They are still come to dance the shag. They still search for all the fun humanly possible.

There was a kindred spirit among us then. Today that spirit is healthy and alive as ever within those of us still shaggin'.

Fat Harold

PROLOGUE

THIS IS A STORY that *must* be told! No — make that a story that is worthy of being told after waiting far too long. It's telling *will* wait no longer. I entrust it to the most worthy, most qualified person I know — you.

The events which are chronicled here took place in the second half of the Sixties, perhaps the most tumultuous period in the history of the United States. It was a time of great social change driven by an awakened social consciousness among the nation's youth. Those were the days of the Vietnam War — or Conflict — or whatever it was. It was the period that gave us flower children, VW microbuses, communes, the advent of drugs as a major player in our society and political change. The "Youth" of the country rebelled against the "Establishment." Their peers were being sent to die in Vietnam for causes that were not well understood. They demanded a voice concerning the political direction of the country, and the country's mores and values were changing in response to that rebellion.

It was a time like no other. Young men and women were coming of age. It was true in rural in North Carolina just as it was in the remainder of the United States.

The plan these young people adopted was to fortify themselves with enough alcohol to feel invincible and at the same time feel cool to the highest degree possible. They had to surround themselves with equally fun-loving friends to survive. Their group was in love with the music of the time and the bands that performed it. Those bands played for audiences that seemed to grow ever larger over those years of transition from youth to adult.

I will tell the story as though it were as fact. This is *perhaps* the way it was. This is *perhaps* the way some people want to remember it. However, it is probably not the way most people would *prefer* to remember it, nor, for that matter, the way they do. Much of the story has been forgotten. We might be best served if other parts were forgotten as well. However, we remember those profound events which were life altering during the period when Williams Lake was the center of the universe.

The main characters would probably wish that some of the fiction as told to be true. They are equally likely to wish that some of the truth were fiction. It is not the absolute accuracy of the story that is important. It is the story *itself* that is important.

The principal characters in this story made everyone happy with their visits. Some were happy with their arrival and others, perhaps the majority, were happy because of their departures. Most of the main perpetrators are still alive at the time of this writing. However, as sure as the sun sets in the evening, the relentlessness of time will eliminate their memories.

We cannot hold on to the past. It is history. It is fleeting, and it is changing at a rapid rate in our imperfect memories. We need it to change with us as we grow to make it all right — to make *us* all right. Though the past is always with us, the recordings of the past have a curious way of changing and reshaping themselves over time to suit our purposes. The past is never quite as kind or grand as our fondest recollections of it. Neither is it as bad as our worst remembrances and regrets regarding it. Therefore, with that in mind, I will tell this story only as distant memories recall it before those memories become even fuzzier than they already are after the passage of forty years or so.

This story is about something far more significant than Williams Lake. Williams Lake just happens to be the backdrop. These are tales of maturation or lack thereof in a group of youth from Small Town USA. That brings on the question, "Which is the better path to mature or not to mature?" It does not ask, "Which is the more socially accepted path?"

Williams Lake was once the center of the universe to at least some of the principal characters. It was a touchstone for all of them to a greater or lesser degree. However, make no mistake — it *was* a touchstone for *all* of them. It *is* part of the fabric of the survivors. They can still smell the freshness of the night air around Williams Lake and the heavy gray smoke inside. It contributes to a significant part of our memories of those who died unfulfilled.

In 1965, Robert Honeycutt, assisted by his brother Wyman, opened a dance hall in rural Eastern North Carolina. Honeycutt hired locals such as Donnie Ray Naylor and Graham Dixon Jackson to help run the facility. It was in a plain white wooden building sitting on the edge of Williams Lake.

The Lake's opening was fortuitous to some, and an unlucky break for others. The lives of all who went to Williams Lake were altered as surely as if they had been "taken" by some alien faction. There were some for whom it was vitally important. Their experiences in those few rapidly fleeting years marked them for life. Looking back, those years of invincibility marched through their lives faster than a tornado through a rural trailer park. It caused as much damage and revealed as much strength of character. Those experiences defined the principal characters and the others who went to Williams Lake. Those experiences continue to help define them today.

This is the story of Cosmo, Dion, Tea and their friends. It is about the adventures and equally importantly, their misadventures. For those comrades at that time Williams Lakes was the center of their universe.

I can see it clearly. It started in the early part of summer in 1965. It was a hot, muggy summer day typical of those of Eastern North Carolina. Dion, Tea and Cosmo were looking for something to do that night.

CHAPTER ONE

HALF AND HALF

Early summer 1965

"LET'S GO TO THE DANCE at the Armory tonight," suggested Cosmo. Tea and Dion nodded their agreement.

"We can ride over to the ABC store on the way and buy some liquor" Tea said. "I'll drive."

"It's a deal," Cosmo agreed.

Dion, the quiet and studious member of the group, merely nodded and asked rhetorically with a faint laugh, "You mean the Alcoholic Beverage Control store?"

Tea nodded. He laughed and started to answer before he caught on to Dion's dry joke.

Cosmo continued. "What time do you want to go? I can go anytime after six. The dance doesn't start until eight."

"I'll pick you up at six thirty and we'll pick Dion up on the way to the ABC store," Tea said. Tea explained his plan, "I think Mr. Wilson will sell Dion liquor now. He has not seen him in four or five months since we the last time we were in there. And do you remember he demanded to see our licenses before he threw us out? He will think that Dion must have turned twenty-one to come back in there trying to buy liquor again. The Wilson's have always had great respect for Dion because he's so smart and so highly regarded around here. Besides, the combination of his being tall and skinny and the early thinning of his hair leaving that little peninsula on his forehead make him look older than he is."

"If not," Cosmo commented, "we'll find someone going in who'll buy it for us if we pay them fifty cents to a dollar."

"I'm certain I can pull it off," Dion said authoritatively. "Just know what you want and give me your money before we get there. I'll come back with the goods."

At a little after seven, Tea, in his little green two door Tempest, stopped in front of Dion's house with Cosmo riding shotgun. Cosmo was decked out in a light blue shirt.

"You're late," Dion challenged them.

"We are right on time   Tea time that is! That means we are indeed late. As usual, Tea was late getting to my house. You know Tea is always late." Cosmo said.

"I know Tea is habitually late. Cosmo, did you know that no matter how hard you try, you can't baptize a cat?" Dion said.

"What does baptizing a silly cat have to do with Tea being late?" Cosmo asked. A puzzled look came over his face.

"It's like that with Tea. Try as you will, you can't make Tea be on time and he is proud of that fact. Tea has never owned a watch. It wouldn't matter if he did; he'd still be late. Time is just a vague concept to him. Look at him beaming with pride because of our discussion of his tardiness. He would miss out on a million dollars if he had to be on time to collect it. He has the crazy thought that always being late will postpone his funeral. He missed out on several inches of height and a lifetime with hair because he was late for both when they were being passed out at birth. He would probably be six foot six inches instead of five nine if he had been on time that day. Those missing nine inches tell you how late he was. I'm certain that his height was diminished by an inch for each increment of tardiness. Those inches of missing height were relegated to his ample waistline instead. He was given the trait of being late instead of brains on that day. He could have been a tall genius instead of a stunted late guy who is the same height as you, Cosmo. But you are skinny; therefore, five nine must have been your intended height."

"You're no giant yourself. You're only two and a half inches taller than me," Tea replied.

"He musta been on time cause look, he's as skinny as me, and he sure didn't miss out on no brains. He's the smartest person we know. Nobody else we know in these parts comes close to being as smart as Dion. And besides being smart, he is very athletic." Cosmo jumped mouth first into the verbal sparring match.

"Hold on! Wait a minute! Bobby is as smart as Dion. What do you say about that Dion?" Tea said.

"He is my alter ego. It is true that we are very much alike. You could say we are interchangeable except for the fact that I'm much better looking and considerably more suave," Dion answered.

"Yea, right?" Tea said.

"I just wish I were as smart as him," Dion said.

"You and everybody else," Cosmo said, modifying his position.

"Dion, I remember you said once you would you would never drink beer, coffee or whiskey. What happened, huh? Did you forget or did you give up?" Tea said. He winked at Cosmo.

"I still have not had any coffee or beer. Besides, I have done nothing to deserve to taste the special flavors of coffee and beer. Two of three is a great record. If I were a major league baseball player and averaged hits two every three times at bat, I would the richest player in the majors, maybe the richest man on Earth. I would be making over a hundred thousand dollars a year. I would be rich beyond your imagination if I made two out every three shots in basketball."

Cosmo and Tea could identify with Dion's discourse. Sports were among the few things they were interested in other than girls and having a good time.

So the conversation went during the ten minute ride to the ABC store in a neighboring town. If there had been one in St. Umblers, they would have gone to the next town anyway as everybody knew them in St. Umblers and their parents would have received three or four phone calls reporting their purchase within ten minutes from well-intended neighbors.

St. Umblers was in a dry county. The state of North Carolina left the decision of whether to sell alcoholic beverages or remain dry to the voters in each of its one hundred counties. There was an unusual social marriage in the county between the churches and the bootleggers. There were plenty of both and both were opposed to legalizing the sale of liquor. The preachers and churches were opposed to the sales based on their concept of high moral principles. They were interested in the preservation of the community's souls as drinking spirits would surely condemn one to hell or worse. They were motivated by one of the two universal motivators. They were motivated by the fear of loss. They did not consider themselves as being in concert with the bootleggers. The opposition by the bootleggers on the other hand was driven by the other universal motivator. They were fueled by the desire for gain — greed. Many bootleggers made a significant amount of money by being paid handsomely for the risk they took to sell their wares. They would be largely, if not completely, out of business if liquor were legal. They consciously and actively pushed a united opposition through the churches.

The three shared energetic, clean fun during the ride as they razzed and bashed each other. Each enjoyed the company of the other two. Those were relaxed carefree days. They were young, vivacious and invincible. They were off to have a party. What more could one have asked of life?

"Park around the corner from the store," Dion ordered Tea. "I don't want Mr. Wilson to see you two outside."

"Okay," Tea said.

"What do you want?" Dion asked.

"I want a pint of Calvert," Cosmo said proudly.

Tea elbowed Cosmo. "Are you gonna stay sober tonight? You gone sissy on us or what? Dion, how about you and I get some real liquor? Why don't we get a fifth of Smirnoff and a fifth of Calvert? We can split the fifth of Smirnoff as usual before we go in and have the fifth of Calvert for drinking later during the breaks."

"Suits me. We'll have to get the red label because I only have enough money for that. I guess you will want to ruin the Smirnoff by chasing it with a can of Coke, huh? None of that sweet stuff for me. A drink of water will do just fine for my chaser, thank you." Dion answered.

"Actually, I meant that I want a fifth of Calvert. Maybe I should get a pint too for when I empty the fifth. I wouldn't want to run out on a Friday night. I have to get warmed up for tomorrow night." Cosmo said. "Here's my money." Cosmo said. He extended his hand with some bills in it toward Dion.

"I'm in too," Tea said. He handed over his money.

Dion collected the money from each. They had the correct change as they knew exactly what the various liquors cost.

"Cosmo let me out," Dion said.

Cosmo dismounted the car.

Dion quickly unfolded himself as he leaped from the back seat onto the sidewalk. "I'll bring back the goods in a few minutes," he said confidently.

Tea and Cosmo watched as he disappeared around the corner.

"Hello, Mr. Wilson," Dion said. He sloughed slight at the shoulders in an effort to appear nonchalant to the cashier as he strode into the store. He tried adding to the air of nonchalance by adopting what he thought was the same mix of bravado and shyness possessed by his favorite actor, Jimmy Stewart. He flashed a big confident smile and thought, *John Wayne would have trouble pulling this off any better than I am.*

"Hello, Dion, how are you doing tonight? I have not seen you in a while," Mr. Wilson said.

"I'm doing great thank you, Mr. Wilson. I have just been going to Campbell and working. Between the two, there has been little time to be out and about. I need to get some whiskey for a party."

He walked over and picked up the two fifths of Calvert and the fifth of red label Smirnoff. He sat three bottles down on the counter. "How much do I owe you?"

Mr. Wilson studied him for a few seconds without answering. Dion did not flinch. Finally, Mr. Wilson said, "That will be $10.80."

Dion knew he was home free and would never have trouble buying at that ABC store again. He handed over $11.00 and waited triumphantly for the change. "Thank you, sir. Have a good night," he said to Mr. Wilson as he picked up the bag with the whiskey in it.

Cosmo jumped with excitement as he reported to Tea,

"WOW! That's a big bag under his arm. He did it! He did it! We won't have to pay nobody to buy booze for us again. Dion can buy it!"

"I'm going to really enjoy drinking this liquor," Dion said. His pearly white grin that was as wide as his face gave away that he was so proud of his accomplishment that felt ten feet tall. The youngest of the three had pulled of the "Miracle of the Liquor Store" as they would later call it. It was perfect. "How many twenty year olds do you know who could have pulled that off?" Dion asked. "I can't wait to taste that liquor; it will be a celebration."

"I reckon you are it. You are the Man!" Tea responded. "But no drinking until we get to the Armory. I want to stop and pick up a can of Cocola on the way."

"I knew that was coming! Cosmo, Tea just can not stand to have a drink without ruining it with all that sweet Coke. He has to have a girl's drink. It has to be sweet."

"I need to get some 7Up and ice to mix with my Calvert. I don't like the taste by itself, unless it's cold enough, then I can drink it straight." Cosmo said.

They stopped at the Quick Stop, where Tea and Cosmo purchased their sodas. Dion filled a cup with ice and water. They were soon in the little green Tempest headed for the Armory. The dance had started before they arrived a little after eight.

They found a place to park in the darkness between a car and the field at the end of the parking lot.

"I have started drinking," announced Cosmo who had mixed a drink on the way from the Quick Stop. "I guess you two will have to catch up."

"Cosmo that'll happen quickly," Tea said.

"Lets just show him. Tea, draw a line at the halfway point on that Smirnoff bottle and hand it here. It is my turn to go first. Then I want a swallow of my water," Dion said.

"What are you going to do? Are you going to chug that fifth?" Cosmo asked. "I heard that you and Tea have done it before but I didn't believe it."

While Cosmo was talking Tea took a pencil and drew a line near the middle of the Smirnoff bottle. "Here you go," he said. "Cosmo, just watch and learn how to drink."

While Tea spoke to Cosmo, Dion took the bottle and started draining it. "Dion! Stop! You have had your half!" Tea yelled frantically to Dion who drank half the bottle without pulling it from his lips.

Dion reluctantly pulled the bottle from his lips to check the line. He made a terrible, scrunched up face as he said, "Ooooooooh, my, that's awful. I think you had better not drink that. Since I have already been afflicted by it, you had better let me finish it."

"Hand it over!" Tea insisted. "I'll take my chances."

Dion took a swallow of water and said, "It's close to the line. You finish it." He then handed the bottle to Tea who turned it with the red label faced up and polished it off. He took several long pulls on the Coke can he threw the empty bottle into the field.

Tea said to no one in particular, "That dead soldier served the cause well. A moment of silence for the dead soldier please."

They sat without speaking until Cosmo said, "I saw that and I still don't believe what I saw. That was awesome. Unbelievable!"

"Let's go commit the ultimate Baptist sin. Let's go dance. I'm ready!" Dion said.

They alighted from the car and started toward the Armory where they could hear the band already playing. They paid their dollar and went into the dimly lit building.

"There must be seventy five to a hundred people already in here. They are dancing and having fun without us" Tea said.

Since St. Umblers was a small community of less than three thousand, people they knew everyone there including a few from several neighboring communities who came to cruise town on Sunday afternoons.

The situation was different from the sock hops in high school. At the sock hops the boys all lined up along the wall nearest the exit. They were afraid to ask a girl to dance for fear of rejection. They were afraid even though they all knew the unwritten etiquette of shag required a girl to graciously accept a request for a dance. At sock those hops, the girls lined up along the other wall waiting and hoping a guy who was a good shagger would come ask her to dance. The sock hops had a DJ who played only Beach Music and the Shag was the only dance on the floor.

There was a live band at the Armory. A local favorite, The Entertainers, were providing the music that night.

The boys and girls mingled in small groups. In was more common to find small groups of boys and small groups of girls. The dance floor had been corrupted by such the Twist and various unsynchronized butt-shaking dances. The majority of those stuck with the Shag. Beach Music definitely still ruled. Those other dances except occasionally the Twist had to be done to Beach Music. The other dances were tolerated by all because they were easier to learn and accomplish. They were even admired by some.

The group was more relaxed than at the sock hops. They were louder. In addition, many of them, most in fact, had had at least a little to drink before entering. They were having fun and they were having on it their terms. They were having fun at their pace.

Cosmo went over to The Gator. He excitedly spouted out,

"It's a miracle! It's a miracle! You should have seen Dion and Tea. I thought they would die right there in their car seats. They each chugged down a half of a fifth of red-label Smirnoff without taking the bottle from their mouths. If you had told me that some one did that, I would have told you that it wont possible. It's a miracle! I would have gagged and thrown up."

The Gator sagely advised Cosmo, "Dick, those two are wild. There ain't no telling what they might do. That probably won't even make them drunk. Dick, I drink a little myself, but I'm telling you, you had better not try that trick. I know I sure won't. You and I can't hang with those two when it comes to drinking. I won't even try. You can try if you are of a mind to, I'm telling you, you can't drink with them. Don't even try it, Dick. You can bet I ain't studying doing that."

"You are absolutely right; I can't keep up with those two." Cosmo said. He nodded to acknowledge his acceptance of The Gator's advice.

Cosmo was still wide-eyed with amazement. He told everyone he talked with about the miracle he had just witnessed. The story gave Cosmo a reason to fit into any group.

Dion was off to dance. He and Bobby were considered by many to be the best shaggers in the area. Most of the girls silently hoped he would ask her to dance. Some probably considered rushing over to ask him to dance. However, that was inappropriate since it was not a lady's choice dance. Being asked to dance by Dion or other accomplished shaggers was an accepted sign that the girl was at least a respectable dancer. It was a stamp of approval and provided an ego boost for the girl.

Dion was coming of the dance floor after he and Debbie danced a rendition of a Temptations' song when Jan approached him. "Dion, it is true what Cosmo said about you and Tea?" She asked in awe.

"I don't know the answer to your question as I do not know what Cosmo said. What did Cosmo say about us?" Dion said.

"Cosmo said you chugged a half a fifth of red label vodka without stopping. And then Tea chugged the other half the same way," Jan said. Impressing Jan took some doing because among the girls Jan was the one who could handle her liquor the best. Jan could party with the best. She could drink long and strong. Everybody liked Jan. The boys liked her. Even the girls liked her. That was a major accomplishment as sometimes the girls in that area were a little jealous of other girls, particularly if they thought the other girl was good-looking. Most often the other girls really disliked girls with big boobs. Jan had them. The other girls liked her because she genuinely liked them and Jan was unpretentious.

"I don't know if I drank a half a fifth," Dion replied. He answer in his normal analytic and precise nature that reflected his desire to be accurate. Jan looked like she wanted to interrupt. He, ever the gentleman, politely continued his answer before she could speak. "It was close to a half fifth."

"Didn't it burn your throat something awful?" Jan asked. She made a contoured mouth as she sought information. Her curiosity gave away that she be inclined to try such a feat herself.

"It does burn a little, but you have to concentrate on the task at hand. You hardly notice that little sting. You get used to it pretty quickly."

"Does it give you a hangover to drink it like that?" Jan continued her inquiry.

"No more than any other approach to drinking. Oxygen deprivation is after all oxygen deprivation. However, it is a much more efficient way to drink than to sit and sip it. Jan, if you are considering trying it, start with a little and work up to a larger amount if you want to chug. I don't necessarily recommend chugging." Dion said.

Dion excused himself and walked over to talk to Donald.

"Heard about your preparation for the dance," Donald, who did not drink, greeted him. Donald pointed to Bill who was doing one of those butt-shaking dances. "Look at that Bill dance; he sure can shake his behind."

"I for one think he has fine skills for such a dance. Anybody, including you, can easily do that. You might not be as good as Bill, but you can do that," Dion replied. Donald did not shake his butt to the music or shag, but he loved to watch. Donald wanted very badly to dance to impress a certain young lady who was a shagger. He was sorely afraid she would turn him down or that he would embarrass himself. He wanted to ask her for a date; alas, he was afraid to do that for fear of rejection. He thought that dancing would afford him an opportunity. And, it would have. Those who knew of her crush on Donald knew she would have jumped at the chance to say yes.

"He is not nearly the dancer you are. He sure can shake his ass. There are girls here who don't shag but like to shake their ass. He gets to dance with all the girls in that group whereas you don't," Donald responded.

"You are right about that, my friend. I don't get to dance with them. However, on the other hand I do not wish to do such a dance. If that's the price of dancing with a particular girl, then I am unwilling to pay it. I'm not looking for a girl to date; I just want to dance and have fun. There are plenty of attractive girls here with whom one can shag."

"I hear you are something of a "Snow Man," Donald said changing the subject.

"I don't know anything about that. I could entice my share of the women I guess." Dion answered.

"Let's see you go out there and snow Priscilla. She's dancing with Vance." Donald said. He hoped to watch in order to
learn how to pursue the lady of his desires.

"Now, just why would I want to do that? I plan to leave this
area after college. Snowing Priscilla could be a mistake. She
might snow me, then what would I do? It would be like a dog
chasing a car. Once he has caught the car, what is he going to
do with it? I would have that same problem. If that happened,
she might want to stay here to be near her family. She's pretty
enough and it's tempting, but I know Vance has his eye on her.
I think they would make a better couple than she and I. I have
to go away to follow the path down which life will lead me.
No thank you. I think I'll stay away from attempting to snow
any of these young ladies for the moment, I have places to go
and see and things to do." Dion said. He had an air of great authority in his voice. "I see those moon-eyes you have for Helen.
I think you should just go and approach her. I would be happy
to intercede and approach her for you; however, if I where her,
I know I would have little to no respect for someone who em-
ployed a surrogate to open the door as opposed to having the
courage to come straight to me and profess his interest. Just
go over and talk to her. I wish you well in that pursuit."

Dion joined Tea and Cosmo who were talking to Mike,
Gator and Reese. He arrived as Reese was telling them about
a place to which he had been the previous Saturday.

"I went to Williams Lake last Saturday. It is on Mr. Clayton
Williams' property out in the country in the Mingo Community between Dunn and Salemburg. They had Gene Barbour
and The Cavaliers playing. There were people from all over
eastern North Carolina there. There was shaggin', nothing but
shaggin,' going on there. None of that butt shaking stuff was
happening at Williams Lake. There must have been over six

hundred people there and everybody looked like they were having a good time. I'm going back tomorrow night. The band starts at eight and plays till midnight."

"Gene Barbour is a classmate of Dion, Cosmo and myself at Campbell. I love to hear them do "Ain't No Big Thing." That's their best song." Tea said.

"Did you do any shaggin'?" Mike asked.

"No, but I sure did do some fine drinking. I left feeling good. Most everybody there was at least a little tipsy," Reese said. His great big white toothy smile made him look like the cat that stole away the owner's prized golden bird.

"Knowing you, I bet you were knee-walking Dick," teased The Gator.

Dion merely laughed softly knowing that the greatest truths are said in truth. Reese was known to be the number one boozer in town among their age group. Dion and Tea could only moderately challenge Reese when it came to consuming alcohol.

"Why you have already took drunk tonight, Dick," The Gator continued.

"Gator, Reese not only took drunk. He never lets drunk go. He has taken drunk and kept drunk," Dion said.

Reese gave his best Elvis imitation as he always did when intoxicated. He first pushed up the left side of his thick black framed glasses. Then through his big white toothed smile he roared in his best Elvis voice, "Thank you! Thank you! Thank you very much!" Without another word, Reese walked away.

"Do you know how to tell if Reese is drunk?" Dion asked The Gator.

"No Dick I reckon I don't." The Gator said.

"You see, north of Vancouver there are two mountains called the Twin Lions. They say the way to tell the weather there is look toward the Twin Lions. If you can see the mountains, it is going to rain. If you can't see the mountains, it is raining."

"Dick what in the hell does the weather in Vancouver have to do with Reese taking drunk?" The Gator said, a hint of agitation in his voice.

"It is sort of like that with Reese. If you see him drinking, he is going to take drunk. If you don't see him drinking, he has already taken drunk." Dion said.

"We need to go to Williams Lake tomorrow night," Mike said with a sense of urgency without speaking to anyone in particular. "Who's for going?"

Tea was first to answer. "I'm in," he said. "Cosmo, can you drive?"

"I don't know. Why should I drive?" Cosmo whined.

"You have ready access to a car. That's something the rest of us don't have," Tea answered.

"I would like to go if I can get a ride. Right now, I'm leaving for the car to get a drink. Tea, Cosmo are you coming? We can work this out later," Dion said.

Mike asked with his usual mischievous smile, "Do either of you have a drink you could spare? I'm all out."

Dion scolded him. "Come prepared, Mike!"

"I can spare one," said Cosmo who had only slightly dented his fifth and was not going it by himself that night.

They went out and sat in the car drinking and making the classic guys small talk for about thirty minutes. They talked about sports for a few minutes. Then the conservation turned to liquor for a minute or two. The last twenty-five minutes or so turned to serious guy talk. That time was occupied by talk about girls. Most serious guy talks were discussions of the fairer sex. Their testosterone driven conversations always lead right to the issues of curves. They concluded that curves were what first attracted them to a member of the opposite sex. That meant T & A were the highlights of these conversation. Some thought tits were the curves of choice. Asses were the attraction for others.

"Who has the best looking tail in the building tonight?" Tea quizzed the others.

"That's easy. Priscilla has the by far the best looking butt in the group," Mike answered.

"I say Belinda. I believe the sexiest part of a girl's body is right where the butt and legs converge. Belinda's spot is exquisite." Dion said.

"I'm a boob man," said Cosmo. Faye has the biggest, best looking boobs in there," Cosmo said.

"On that score, I agree with Cosmo. Jan is close behind her though," Tea said.

"Don't you realize that anything more than a hand full or a mouth full of tits is wasted?" Mike lectured them.

The group continued their analysis as they would many times in the future. There were no losers. There were only winners in that discussion. How could you lose regardless of your position on such a delicious topic? There only winners even though none of them had had hands-on experience so to speak; however, not a one of them was going to acknowledge that fact to the others. No need to. Such an elegant topic of discussion did not require such an admission. Each was allowed to speak as an expert on the topic. Each of them suspected the others were in the same situation as themselves. None of them, however, wanted to force such an admission as he was afraid he would be the next to be coerced to come clean. It was best to let amateur/pro status alone at least for the moment.

CHAPTER TWO

SO THIS IS WILLIAMS LAKE

SATURDAY MORNING COSMO called Tea. "I can drive tonight. I'll pick Mike up at six. We will pick Dion up at six fifteen and we will be at your house at six thirty. We will have to go by the ABC store on the way to Williams Lake. You'd better be ready because we are not going to wait for you. We are going drinking with or without you. I've already talked to Dion and Mike."

Cosmo was good to his word. He arrived for Mike and Dion as promised. They were at Tea's house at six thirty. As usual, Tea failed to be ready. "Let's go!" Dion ordered Cosmo. "It is time to get to our drinking."

"I'm for that." Mike added.

"Let's give him five minutes," answered Cosmo. He was forever the peacemaker.

Dion shouted over his left shoulder as he leaped from the from the right rear door of the white Impala. "OK. I'll go tell him."

"Hey Tea, this is serious. You are cutting into our drinking and partying time. That is unacceptable. Cosmo is willing to wait five minutes. Mike and I are commandeering the car if you are not in it when the five minutes are up. We will leave you here!" Dion said. He explained the situation with an air of urgency and authority that Tea immediately recognized as representing a final position on the matter of time.

"I'll be ready in two minutes," Tea answered. He feverishly combed at his hair.

"Then, that's your new deadline," Dion informed him. "See you at the car in one minute and forty-five seconds flat." Dion said. He turned to start to the door.

"Wait!" pleaded Tea. "I'm ready." They quickly made their way to the car and joined Cosmo and Mike.

"You deserve a medal for getting Tea out here so quickly." Mike said.

"Actually, you probably deserve to be elected President for such an accomplishment. How did you pull that one off?" Cosmo's said.

Dion picked up on the political theme, "My campaign promise which swayed Tea's vote was that Mike and I would mutiny and commandeer the car. We, with Cosmo in captivity, would immediately depart for fine drinking and partying."

"You should have heard the conviction in his voice as he told he about this change in plan. I think he would have done it," Tea whimpered.

"Oh, I'm sure he'd have done it and I would have helped him. I think it was a brilliant plan," Mike said.

"Leave it to Dion to come up with the solution to the problem. He always does," Cosmo added.

Tea became the critic when the topic left his slow preparation. He didn't want the conversation to go back there. "Dion, why are you wearing that yellow shirt? You think yellow looks good on you. Well, let me tell you. It doesn't! And you wear your pants too tight."

"You know I do not begin to work hard enough at finding things that are wrong with other people! To Criticize! I must make a note to myself to work harder at that," Dion said.

"Now cut it out and let's do some partying," Cosmo said in an effort to broker peace.

Tea's effort to deflect the conversation from himself had worked.

They were approaching the ABC store. "We had better decide what we are going to get before we get to the store. We don't want to sit outside too long as that will draw undesired attention to us." Dion said in an attempt to focus them. "I'll go in and get the merchandise. Tea, do you want to split a fifth? We'll have about thirty minutes to drink it before we get to Williams Lake."

"How about a fifth of George?" Tea responded.

"I want a fifth of the Yell myself," Mike added.

"I want a fifth of Calvert," Cosmo boosted.

"I'm going to get a pint of George to supplement my half of the fifth. I think you might want one too, Tea," Dion said.

"I'll have two pints of Old Mr. Boston," Cosmo said. He chose a less expensive beverage since he was going to buy two pints.

"I guess I had better have two pints of the Yell," Mike said. "I can't run out and leave you three drinking. I have to keep up."

"Get me a pint of George too. I'll not get left behind you two," Tea said.

They each handed his money to Dion. They knew what each bottle cost from their previous visits. There was no room for error for Dion and Tea as they came from poor families. Cosmo had a little more room for error while Mike came from what by comparison was a wealthy family. None of them cared. It was not a contest and no one was keeping score. They would be drunk soon and the price of the liquor was not a big factor. Drunk is drunk; the price of the liquor was never a factor though it might influence how each would feel the next day.

Dion walked into the liquor store with all the confidence of a man three times his age.

"That's quite a haul you have there Dion," Mr. Wilson observed.

"Oh. This has to last for quiet a while. I might as well get it while I am here and have the luxury of a little money." Dion said. He paid the bill. He had the price to the penny for the purchase.

"Thanks, I'll see you soon," he said to Mr. Wilson with a sincere politeness. He turned efficiently toward the door.

"Mike was especially glad to see Dion carrying his load as he had not been there to see the performance the preceding night. "Dion, you are the man," Mike made his signature look that was a combination of scrunching of his shoulders, reverse coupling of his hands and a mischievous smile.

Cosmo ordered with great urgency. "Get in. We need to stop at Hardee's and get some cups of Cocola and some ice to mix our drinks. Get in and let's get going!"

They stopped at Hardee's. Dion went for a large cup of ice. The other three each bought a large cup of Coca-Cola. They pulled into one of the customer parking spaces in the dark area of the lot to mix a drink. Dion and Tea mixed a half a fifth each for the road.

Cosmo nosed the car onto the road and started toward Spivey's Corner. They were nice, fun-loving white guys. However, suddenly they were breaking the law. There was drinking. Worse yet, they were drinking while driving.

"We are going to have to establish a maximum safe drinking speed for when we are enjoying a drink," Dion said. "My mother told me, "You were too hard to raise to get killed doing sometime stupid." I suggest we adapt forty-five miles per hour as our maximum drinking speed. Besides, it will give us more time to drink on our way to where we are going and we will be less likely to spill liquor on the car or on us."

"I agree," added Cosmo.

"Me too," said Mike. "Great plan."

"Gentlemen, we have a drinking speed. Any one may invoke drinking speed and it must be heeded. After all we are a civilized group and must act with proper decorum." Dion said.

"Yes, your majesty," Mike bowed. "You have my word of undying gratitude. Long live the "King of the Lake."

"Drinking speed will be our secret," Cosmo said. "Each of us must swear an oath of allegiance and secrecy. We will tell no one unless they are on a journey with us."

They were under way to Williams Lake at last. They were driving through the country at drinking speed. They were drinking as they cruised along the lonely dark back road. That was the life. They sparred verbally as they went. Each was getting prepared for the unknown adventure that Williams Lake would present.

When they arrived at Williams Lake, they were ready. "Dion, our fifth is gone," Tea informed him.

"How are you doing with that first pint?" Tea asked Mike.

"I'm about done," Mike responded.

"I've almost done mine in," Cosmo added. "I was drinking fast while I drove."

The other three knew Cosmo had not finished a pint or anything close to it. Nevertheless, they were not going to embarrass their friend by asking to see his bottle. He was too good a guy for them to do that to.

"We had better put our pints behind a tire so we can get to them easily and not have to get into the car. Put your pint behind the tire closest to where you are sitting. Just do not tell anyone here about this plan." Dion said. His scheme was to allow any of them to be able to come out and have a drink without Cosmo or any of the group having to be along.

"We all need to be here at the car ten minutes after the band stops playing to go home," Cosmo sounded off worriedly.

"Let's get in there and see what's going on," Mike said, impatient to join the fun.

Off they went toward the pavilion. They paid and went in. The place was full. Mike estimated that there were over seven hundred people in the building. Some they recognized from Sunday afternoons spent "cruising Main." However, most of these kids they had never seen before. They were dancing the Shag. They were shaggin' to the music of the Monzas. The Monzas were not spectacular that night, but they were good enough. They didn't put on a great floorshow as did some of the groups. Nevertheless, they played good solid Beach Music. The audience spent its time shaggin' instead of watching the band.

Reese was there and was, as usual, tipsy. Mike went over and almost reverently called the fact to Reese's attention. "You are looking mighty fine and very inebriated my man."

All Reese could return was his Elvis impression although it was a little labored as he worked hard to reply "Thank you! Thank you. Thank you very much," while pushing up the right side of his Ben Franklin glasses. Reese, like many of their peers, wore big, black-framed granny glasses, as they were also known, as a fashion statement that became popular in

1965. Reese just happened to hang onto them long after most others had abandoned the look within two years because of the serious political attitude of the youth of the day. After he finished his appreciation speech, Reese slowly and unsteadily wandered away into the crowd.

"Dion, there is a guy whose dancing style is very similar to yours and he is almost as smooth as you. Though he doesn't move his feet nearly as quickly," Tea said. He pointed at a slight young man dancing with a beautiful young lady with huge breasts.

"What guy? All I see are boobs," Mike said.

Dion studied the couple. "I think we should call her Lungs because she sure can breathe with that rack. That's Charles from Four Oaks. I'll get him to introduce me to her. Then I can dance with her."

He walked over to the couple, "Charles, how are you doing? Your dancing is looking good. I didn't know you had it in you."

"I hear you are pretty good yourself. Are we going to get to see your show?" Charles answered.

"Maybe, I have not seen any women I know yet." Dion responded. "When I see one I'll dance some. The woman you were dancing with is a good shagger."   Both of them knew that it was not necessary to know a woman to ask her to dance. The etiquette of the dance dictated that a girl accept the invitation to dance from any guy who asked her unless she was with a date. It was then incumbent on the guy to ask the date's permission to ask the girl to dance. It was polite enough for the date to say no. They both also knew this was a polite means of asking to be introduced unless there was a thing between the guy and girl to be respected.

"Dion, you need to meet Joan. She is a good dancer,"

Charles said. He pulled the young lady over to where he and Dion stood. "Joan, this is Dion. Rumor has it he is the best shagger around. He dances like his feet have batteries in them. He just told me that he thinks you are pretty good too," he said by way of introduction.

When the next song, "Sixty Minute Man," started, Dion extended his left hand gently toward Joan and said, "Would you like to dance?"

"Yes, I would like that very much," Joan replied. She took his left hand in her right hand. Dion led her to a vacant spot on the dance floor. He positioned them for the start of the dance. When the beat came around, he started them off into that wonderful dance called the Shag. Joan was a good shagger. Dion was spectacular. Together they were electric and rhythmically sexy. They sparkled as they moved back and forth to the beat of the music.

Many of the other young people in attendance gathered around to watch them. The ice was broken at Williams Lake; they were no longer strangers. They were accepted; they belonged. They were right at home. For a fleeting moment, Williams Lake was to become the center of their universe. They would never be the same again. The bar for the level of adventure required to satisfy them was forever raised by their experiences at Williams Lake starting that hot, quiet summer night. They went to Williams Lake that night. They left the Lake.

After he had danced several more songs with Joan, Dion said to Tea, "I have a drink waiting behind the right rear wheel of Cosmo's car and I am going to go get it. Are you interested in joining me?"

"Hold on, I'm coming. Wait while I get a Cocola," Tea replied. As soon as Tea had his Coke, he started out of the building behind Dion. They walked across the road to the parking lot without another word. They arrived at Cosmo's car which was in the fourth spot on the right; a spot they had been lucky to get as its previous occupant was inexplicably leaving as they arrived. The rest of the parking lot closest to the pavilion had been full when they arrived.

"I think you really like Lungs, Tea broke the silence after they had each poured a drink and had been slowly sipping on them for a few minutes.

"Yes, that girl can breathe! I think she's pretty. She's fun to boot. I would like to get to know her much better. I think she might like that too. I'm far from certain about that. There were a dozens of young men acting like moons orbiting her planet. We will just have to see how that works out. I certainly enjoy dancing with her; a number of people gathered around to watch. I know all the guys were watching her. I don't blame them for that. She is incredibly sexy when she is dancing and that cute behind is in motion. I watched her myself while she was dancing with Charles."

"All the girls who gathered around were watching you very intently. A bunch of the men was watching you as well trying to learn. Many of them are like me, they have not been able to figure out how you dance the way you do. How do you do that?" Tea rambled with true admiration.

Dion decided to tutor Tea on the Shag. "All you do is listen to the music and move your feet to its rhythm. I mean really listen. Let your feet listen to the music. Let your feet hear the music and respond. One of the secrets to the dance is small slide steps taken by having the knees driving the ankles. It is also important to stay on the balls of your feet so that you never have to sift your weigh to make a move. When you shift your weigh to the rear, you lose at least a step to the beat and to your partner. While the guy leads, he must learn to adjust his speed backward and forward to allow his partner to keep up. There are only two positions that are important – those are the distal and the proximal positions. When you dance the Shag, you must adjust as necessary to accommodate your partner. You must sometimes follow to really be able to lead. Never let them know. Remember the music is not perfectly symmetrical; it is important to vary the size and shape of your steps to remain with the music and your partner. Always be thinking at least eight steps ahead of where you are. Just be sure to complete one step before starting the next. Finish a step in position to start the next."

"That all sounds great. How do you do it I ask?" pleaded a confused Tea. "I want to learn to dance myself. How do you do the things you do?"

"Dancing is just second nature to me. I make it up as I go. There is no way that I know to teach instinct. I wish I could teach you. I just do what I do; I have never watched me or tried to figure it out," Dion answered.

"You look like a bug out there skimming across the water. It's like you're sliding on glass or something. Your feet never look like they leave the floor; yet they are never on the floor. You just seem to float. You're always in such great control. You're so confident out there. I hope I figure it out one day." Tea said.

"Give it a try. Girls are very tolerant of those who are willing to try to dance. They don't care if you have two right feet as long as you do your best and treat them with respect. They will help you. Just remember that in general only very good things happen while you dance. You get to meet a wide assortment of women by dancing and they are already favorably disposed to you because of the fact that you dance. Dancing creates a nonthreatening environment for the lady where she is able to evaluate you."

When Tea didn't respond immediately, Dion continued, "Don't try to be me. I hope I'm a better me than you could ever be. Be yourself. I'm sure you are a better you than I could ever be. I could never out Tea Tea. Don't try to out Dion Dion. Be the best Tea you can be. The worst Tea you can be will be far better than the best Dion you can be." Dion said. He concluded what he thought was excellent advice to give to Tea or anyone else for that matter.

"You have this one move where you are dancing backward that looks like you should be going forward instead. It is like you're on the moon or something. What do you call that move?" Tea asked.

"I don't have names for my moves. I didn't even know that I did such a thing," Dion answered. "You might try to learn to dance with a doorknob. You can learn shaggin' with a doorknob. I have heard others say they did." Dion said.

They sat in silence and calm again while they consumed their drinks. The only sounds outside were those of frogs around the lake. They could hear the band playing inside. Occasionally they heard a loud applause. They finished their drinks and went inside.

Tea watched and listened to the band. Tea loved to hear a band; almost any band would do. Tea had company as there others in the group who did not dance the Shag. They too watched. Many, like Tea, wanted to learn. They enjoyed being a part of the Shag scene. Some, like Tea, would learn in time; others would just continue to watch and enjoy the dance from afar. Still others would make their way in life without shaggin' be a part of it.

Boy, the Shag doesn't seem so hard after hearing Dion explain it. I'm going to have to try it. Tea thought to himself.

Dion did dance when he returned. He danced almost every song. When the band stopped playing, the little group of friends left.

"That was some fun. Reese was right; this is a fine place to be. It's great," Dion said.

"We need to bring as any of the people we run around with as possible to experience this environment. They would enjoy this too," Tea said. "I'm sure Gator, Cherry, Connie Sue, Toney, Neil, Harry and Dare among others would love coming here. We just have to tell them about it to get them to come. This is some fine party." Tea was trying to organize a party.

"The Lake! What a place to be!" was all Cosmo could muster. "What a place to be! What a place to be!!"

Hence following Cosmo's commentary and consistent with the regular use of abbreviations for standards and physical constants such as 'c' for the speed of light and 'OD' for Ocean Drive in South Carolina, Williams Lake would be thereafter the Lake to those who were in the know.

Mike knew there was nothing more he could add. He just grinned his sneaky grin as he reached forward and stretched his arms with his fingers intertwined and flexed backward while his shoulders fell. He was contented; he was feeling no pain and he had had a great time.

The Lake was an integral part of their lives. They were to become a rich portion of the lure and of the lore of the Lake. They would recruit others to join them as members of the Williams Lake society.

CHAPTER THREE

CRUISING AND RECRUITING

THE COMRADES WERE newly invigorated by their outing the previous night. They pulled into the Gas Company parking lot at one fifteen. Dion and Tea were with Cosmo. Mike drove up in his dad's car. They were on a mission. They were going to recruit others to go to the Lake. If they didn't see them cruising Main and that would be unusual indeed, they would catch them during the week. They were determined to have reinforcements at the Lake the next Saturday night.

The four of them approached Cosmo's father's white Impala. "Shotgun!" yelled an exuberant Tea. Other than that outburst, they quietly climbed into the car and rolled down the windows in very a workmanlike fashion. That was a great car for cruising because it had no center post to interfere with their vision. They were off to do a job. It was time to put on the style. It was time to join the Mobile Society. They were out to be part and parcel of it.

They "cruised the loop" on Sunday afternoon. You were not really a driver until you had cruised the loop. You had to be been seen in your mobile splendor. That brought on an air of accomplishment and satisfaction. That was a high point of life in and around St. Umblers. The vehicle was totally unimportant. Being seen behind the wheel was what mattered.

St. Umblers was in a strategic geographic location. It was the center of three rings of towns. It was like a sun orbited by its planets. The inner ring was a group of small towns and communities all approximately seven miles away. Most were smaller than St. Umblers. The second was a less populous ring about fifteen miles from St. Umblers. Those communities were larger than St. Umblers. The third ring was a group of towns about thirty miles from St. Umblers. They were far bigger than St. Umblers. It appeared that the gravity of St. Umblers was like that of a sun in that it compacted growth nearby and allowed for freer growth as one traveled farther from it.

Young people from all three rings transitioning to adulthood came to St. Umblers to join in the Sunday afternoon cruise with the mobile society.

Every car was like a float in a parade except that no added decoration was required. It was a come-as-you-are event. Many of the floats in the parade stopped at Herbert's to get something to eat.

The whole loop was only about two miles round trip. It took about thirty minutes because there were so many cars cruisin' the circuit. It was necessary to go slow to make sure you were not just seen, but recognized. That was both an art and a science.

"I think we will be able to talk to people better if we park at the Gas Company and get out of the car and talk to others passing by," Tea said after they had cruised Main twice. "We are seeing people alright, but we need more time to talk to them. We can get them to stop and we can tell them about the Lake."

"You have a plan there," Mike added.

"I can park right there," Cosmo announced as they turned into the drive that the Gas Company shared with Herbert's. He did and they exited the car.

As cars came by with people they wanted to recruit, they stopped them and told them of the Lake.

Neil was the first person they actively recruited after he alit from the car in which he was a passenger. "Neil, you should have been with us last night. Man, we had the best time anyone ever had. Son, you missed it!" Tea literally jumped off the asphalt with exuberance as he extolled the wonders of Williams Lake to Neil. "We are going back next Saturday night. You have to come with us. It was great. There were over seven hundred people there dancing and partying. You've gotta come with us."

"That sounds like fun," replied Neil. "I'll see if I can go."

Soon Reese drove up in his red Corvette and parked to join them. He too was a recruiter telling people about the splendors of the Lake.

Next, The Gator came along with Vance. Everyone converged upon The Gator. "Gator, you and Vance need to join us at the Lake next Saturday night. We are going to have a big time," Cosmo sounded off before the others could speak.

"Dick, I don't know about that. You may be too wild for me. I cannot drink with Dion and Tea. Nor Reese. Dick, I don't know about you and Mike," Gator said. "I'll think about it." The Gator was hooked.

Vance was a good-looking, impeccably dressed young man. People liked Vance; he was a man's man. He was decisive. He had a plan for where he was going in life and it did not include dancing. He stated flatly in his most stoic rhetoric, "I ain't studying going to no Williams Lake. You can count me out right now!"

They talked to others later in the day. They recruited Cherry, Carol, Luray and Connie Sue to go the following weekend. The girls were easy to recruit because they wanted to dance. They were going to drink very little. They hoped they would dance every song.

Toney came driving into the Gas Company parking lot while they were busy proselytizing to Carol and coincidentally to Luray because she was riding with Carol. He parked and walked over to Carol's car. He listened to some of the conversation before saying, "Hey, I'd like to go. What time are you going? Can I get a ride with someone; my father will not let me take his car."

Tea was delighted to have another recruit. Especially one who could party the way Toney could. He responded immediately, "We will find you a ride." He was volunteering others as he was sometimes prone to do.

They managed to find a few other recruits during the week. Harry agreed to go as did Glenn. There would be other recruits in weeks to come.

CHAPTER FOUR

BACK TO THE LAKE

SATURDAY'S ARRIVAL SEEMED to creep because if the building excitement. The group which was planning to go gathered in the Gas Company parking lot. They worked out transportation arrangements. Cosmo was driving that white Impala. Dion, Tea and The Gator rode with Cosmo. Glenn drove a car full as did Harry. They headed straight for the ABC store.

"You know how this works," Dion said to Tea and Cosmo. "Gator, the deal is that you give me your money and tell me what you want before we get there. I go in and buy the goods."

"Dick, I don't know how much things cost," Gator replied.

"You tell us what you want and we can probably tell you how much it cost or you can just give Dion more than enough to buy what you want," Tea informed him. "Dion, I'm having the usual."

"Me too," Cosmo said. "Gator, you need a fifth and a pint."

"I like Jack green label. How much is it?" Gator responded.

They told him and he gave his money to Dion before they reached at the ABC store.

Mr. Wilson greeted Dion will a bright, warm smile, "Hello

Dion. How are you today?"

"I'm just great thank you, Mr. Wilson. How are you? How are Mrs. Wilson and the boys? It has been a couple of weeks since I have seen either of the boys."

He gathered up the liquor for the evening.

"You are sure enough buying a large quantity of liquor recently. You aren't trying to be a bootlegger are you? I know you come from a dry county and there is a lot bootlegging going on over there. I can't sell it to you to bootleg you know," Mr. Wilson said.

He maintained his calm as he paid Mr. Wilson. He went back to the car. "Mr. Wilson was testing me tonight. He asked me if I was bootlegging since I was buying so much."

"Were you scared? How did you handle that?" Tea asked. "Are we going to lose our ability to buy liquor straight from the ABC?

"Are we going to have to pay people to buy it for us again?" worried Cosmo.

"It was easy enough to handle," Dion answered. "I just told him a story about how my father would be upset if I were bootlegging and that I try to avoid making my father upset as that is generally bad news for me."

"Did he buy that story?" Tea asked.

Dion recounted the episode to the eager ears. "Yes, he did. I said. No, sir. I'm not bootlegging. I would have no place to do that. You know my father would skin me alive if I did that on his property. He would be awfully embarrassed about anyone in his family breaking the law. I would fail to enjoy that at all.' Mr. Wilson said 'I know that's true enough. I guess you are not a bootlegger after all.'" I said thank you and quietly walked out the door."

"I need some Cocola," Tea said. That broke the ensuing silence caused by their reflection of the significance of the event.

"I do not need a Coke for my chugging pleasure. I'll stick with water," Dion said.

A wide-eyed Gator asked in anticipation, "Dick, are you two idiots gonna chug that fifth? Dick, you are crazy! That stuff will kill you. I've gotta see this for myself! I've never dreamed of it and if it was told of anybody except you two, I'd never believe it."

They stopped at the convenience store and made their purchases. As Cosmo drove, Dion said to him, "Drinking speed, please, sir." He turned around to Tea and ordered, "You mark it. I'm going first tonight."

Tea obliged. He marked the bottle and handed it to Dion saying, "I guess you earned it tonight." Dion took it without a word and turned it up. Tea made no effort to stop him. Dion stopped just past the line. He handed it back to Tea still without a word. Tea took the half-full bottle and quietly finished it.

The first sound after Tea threw the empty vodka bottle out the back window was Gator saying, "Damn Dick, you two are totally crazy. Just plain paper-bag-ugly crazy! I still don't believe it after sitting right here watching it. Dick, I hope you don't die from that. I need a big drink myself after seeing that." The Gator took that big drink.

Cosmo sipped quietly as he drove toward Williams Lake.

The conversation resumed when Cosmo asked no one in particular, "Do you think we will find some good looking women there tonight?"

All three answered in unison, we will, or something to that effect. They talked about girls attributes and which were their individual favorites. They talked about who had the best looking butt, who had the biggest boobs and who was the prettiest. The one thing they all agreed on was that redheads were the most alluring. There was some mystical power in that red hair. The brighter red the woman's hair, the more intrigued with her they were. Yes sir, there was something about red hair on a woman that carried an undeniable mystique.

They arrived at the Lake. "Looks like we are going to park in the back of the lot," Cosmo informed them as he turned in. "The place is packed tonight. I'll bet it is full of women."

"That sounds good to me. I am ready to go," Dion said. "Are you ready? Cosmo, are you still sipping on that first little drink? You ready Gator?"

"Dick, The Gator's ready! Are we going in or are we sitting around here all night? Come on Dick lets go. Tea and Cosmo can catch up later," he growled in reply as he displayed his sneaky grin.

"We are ready. I'm coming right now," Tea said. "Have you put your reserve where you will know where it is later. Gator put some liquor behind that tire beside you so you can have a drink later without needing anybody to come out here with you."

"Dick, I can do that," Gator answered.

"There's Donnie Ray taking up money at the door," Tea said referring to the bouncer. "That big ole boy plays football for East Carolina. He's a good one."

They paid Donnie Ray their admission fee as they entered to join the festivities. Gene Barbour and the Cavaliers was the band that night. Since they were from a nearby town, the place was packed. The Cavaliers were charged up by the audience and were at their best.

Dion went right to dancing. He danced with a variety of young ladies before the break. Cosmo danced a few times. Tea was roaming and talking to anybody who would talk to him. The Gator merely stood around wide-eyed watching the women with his sheepish grin on except for the couple of minutes he talked to a ripped Reese.

At the break, all four went out to the car for a drink.

"Dion, there is a guy in there who shags a lot like you. He is about as good as you too. His name is Ricky. His date is one good-looking black-haired woman. Here name is Grace. Man they are great. I'll show them to you when we go back in." Tea said. He boiled over with excitement at having met Ricky and Grace.

"I saw most of the other people from St. Umblers in there but I didn't talk to them," said Cosmo. "Did any of you see them?"

Gator spoke up. "Dick, I saw Cherry, Glenn and Reese. Dick, Reese was barely able to move he had taken so drunk. I talked to Cherry and Glenn. They were having a good time."

"Any of you boys have a spare drink?" A voice behind the car asked.

"Why it's Neil," Tea said.

"Neil, come on over her and join us. Dion and Tea might be out. I can give you a drink," Cosmo encouraged Neil to join the group.

"How are you boys doing?" Neil asked as Cosmo poured him a drink.

"I know you have to be having a good time," Tea said looking dead at Neil.

"Oh yeah this is great. Thanks for inviting me. I'm having a large time!" Neil said.

Bill joined the group. Then others including first Woody followed by Cherry and Connie Sue together found them. They were followed by Lamar and Glenn. A couple of moments later, Reese staggered up. They had a St. Umblers reunion right there in the parking lot.

"Reese you have not just taken drunk. You are blind drunk tonight," Woody teased. He elbowed Glenn and Tea who were on either side of him. There was another piece of evidence that the greatest truths are often told in jest.

"Dick, you sure enough know Reese." The Gator said to Woody.

The conversation continued for a few more minutes. "I'm going back in to do some shaggin'," Dion said.

"Boy, you save a dance for me," Connie Sue said.

"That would be my pleasure indeed. You can bet I'll come find you soon," Dion replied. He went in.

"Dick, you can bet he will dance with you tonight. Dion is good to his word," The Gator grinned as he spoke to Connie Sue. "Hey Dick, wait for me. I'll go with you." Gator said to a departing Dion. He hurried to catch him when he slowed to oblige the request.

"Dion, I have been looking for you. You need to come see Ricky and Grace," Tea said. He pulled Dion's right arm to lead him in the direction of Ricky and Grace.

"OK. Show them to me," Dion said as they started for the area to the left of the bandstand. There Ricky and Grace danced to what else but the Cavaliers rendition of the Tymes song "Ms. Grace." Ricky was a slightly built guy about two or three inches shorter than Dion. Grace was almost the same height as Ricky. They were probably a year or two older than Dion and Tea. "They are great," Dion said after watching for thirty to forty seconds. "He is the best I have ever seen. Did you notice that he dances on the girl's foot?

"No. I had not noticed that," Tea said.

"It seems to work for him. See how gracefully he slides those feet. That is doing the Shag. He doesn't do the up and down footwork which you see many people do because it is far easier. She's very good too," Dion said.

"They told me they come here all the time. They always dance right in this area. Their friends are always over here with them." Tea said with great pleasure as he told their tale. They watched Ricky and Grace shag to one more song. Dion was not impressed enough to keep him from enjoying the dance himself.

True to his word, he went over and extended his hand to Connie Sue at the beginning of "Fine Brown Frame." "May I have this dance?" She accepted. Dion danced two more songs with Connie Sue.

Connie Sue was a petite young lady who wore her short black hair in a Piquant Pixie coif with tousled curls and curved bangs. Dion enjoyed dancing with her. After the third dance, Dion excused himself and went to dance with others. He was particularly looking for Joan, or Lungs, as she was known to Dion and his friends. He did not find her.

He danced with Susan whom he thought to be the most beautiful woman he knew. If there was a female he was attracted to, it was Susan. Susan was a tall, slender lady who was from a town about seven miles from St. Umblers. She had long shoulder-length shiny straight black hair and a slightly oval face covered by radiant skin. She was blessed with a perfect complexion. Unfortunately, for Dion she was going steady another guy from the country toward Raleigh from St. Umblers. She came to St. Umblers on Sunday with that young man to "cruise Main." Susan was there without her beau that night. Dion danced with her several times; he was not going to press his presence on her. That would be inappropriate and it might be awkward for Susan.

Tea was wandering meeting and talking to people all over the building. He talked to anybody who would talk to him.

Cosmo danced with a few of the ladies. He even managed to dance with Carol a time or two. Cosmo was stricken by Carol. So were most of the other males in the building. She was tall and pretty with a good-looking butt and big boobs. She had a winsome personality. As Hollywood would say, she had "It." She would flirt with any guy who approached her which drove most of them crazy. She was a fine dancer. She was asked to dance every song and did shag to almost every one. She had the opportunity to dance her feet off.

Carol had come with her friends Patricia and Luray. Patricia was almost as popular as Carol. She too was very attractive. She also had a fine body. Patricia too could dance; she was actually a better dancer than Carol; however, the members of the opposite sex were unconcerned about the difference in dancing ability. Luray was a little younger and not as well favored as Carol or Patricia. She was cute, not a raving beauty like Carol and Patricia. Luray was a beginning dancer and was unable to attract the attention on the dance floor that Carol and Patricia did. However, Cosmo and Gator both noticed her. Cosmo spent a fair amount of time talking to her. The Gator just watched and grinned his normal mischievous grin.

The Gator came to life on the way home from the Lake. The Gator was a funny man. He just knew how to say things so they were funny. He could make saying "Hello" funny. He would use a deep voice to say, "He, he, he, Hello Dick!" The Gator called everyone "Dick" except his mother when he addressed them. He, like all the kids of St. Umblers, was taught to use proper decorum and respect when addressing his elders. He, like all the kids, exercised that decorum.

The Lake closed at midnight. The band stopped playing at ten till to allow time for the facility to be emptied by closing time. As soon as the band stopped, staff members were yelling that everyone had to vacate the premise. "You have to get out of here – now! It doesn't matter to us where you go. But you have got to get out of here!"

Several people stopped outside the door and carried on a spirited conversation for about twenty minutes. The group dwindled rapidly until only Tea, Woody and The Gator were left. Woody finally left. Tea and The Gator staggered over to Cosmo's car. Cosmo and Dion were engaged in talking about the women they had seen and those with whom they had visited.

"Hey Dick, lets go to the truck stop for a bite of breakfast," Gator said as soon as he sat down in the back seat.

"Gator, that's a good idea," Tea said.

"I like it myself. It would help me sober up," Cosmo said.

"Dick, Tea is the one that really needs sobering up," The Gator replied. "We can get some coffee in him. Look at him slumped over there."

"Did you know that coffee does not really sober a person up; it just gives you a wide awake drunk. Food does slow down the rate at which alcohol is absorbed in the digestive system." Dion said.

Cosmo changed the topic of conversation, "I thought Carol was the best looking woman in the place tonight."

"That's a highly personal and arguable topic. I agree with you that Carol is beautiful, stunning in fact. I know that Susan was far and away the most attractive woman there. It was no contest." Dion said authoritatively.

"Dick you are really hung up on that girl aren't you?" The Gator said.

"She is beautiful alright. But, why do you waste your time thinking about her? She is not the least bit interested in you. She is going with a rich guy with a fancy car and you with no car or money have no chance," Tea said. The other three thought he was asleep.

"You are correct about the rich guy. You are also right about having no chance as long as he is in the picture. She was still the best-looking woman there tonight. Maybe another night will produce another answer, but tonight was Susan's night," Dion said.

"I still say it was Carol. What an ass that woman has. I'll bet it as soft as a way under inflated balloon. And she has big old beautiful boobs," Cosmo said.

"I thought there were several dozen best looking. I prefer variety and avoid picking just one," The Gator said.

"Man, Patricia was hot. She was the best looking I ever saw. So was Grace. And, Queenie. And, how did you like Belinda? Wasn't she the best-looking woman you ever saw? And, that Debbie; *wow*, was she something else or was I looking at the wrong person? And, Sara? And, the other Debbie." Tea shot gunned options.

"Dick, you don't cull nothing do you?" Gator teased Tea with a big white grin.

"They were all looking mighty good. They were all too good to cull. They were the best looking women I ever saw," Tea rebutted.

"You are right that they all looked real good, but Carol won the contest," Cosmo told Tea. "Even you have to admit that."

"She is a fine choice, Cosmo. I think Carol was the most beautiful woman I ever saw. You should have seen Betty Jean. Now there was a beautiful woman," Tea said.

So the conversation went until they pulled in to the truck stop. They had to wake Tea up when they were ready to go in. Tea ordered went around to various tables talking to the inhabitants. As usual, he was a social butterfly.

"Look at that Tea. He is always looking for the next woman. The one he is close to is never good enough. He has to worry them all. He has to be seen and heard." Cosmo volunteered his assessment of the situation. Finally, a few minutes before their orders arrived, Tea wandered back to the table and sat down.

"Dick, Tea is liquored up. His face is about to fall on the table. You two are spiffed too, but not that bad."The Gator said.

"Gator we didn't take drunk by ourselves. You were right in there with us," Cosmo said.

"When his food comes . . ." It did before The Gator could complete the sentence. The server sat down their plates. It was necessary to wake Tea so he could eat. "Look his face is gonna fall right into his grits Dick."

They ate quietly and paid. They were pretty much partied out for one night. They needed something in reserve for another night. They planned to return to the Lake on Wednesday night. In fact, they were planning to go on most Wednesday and Saturday nights.

CHAPTER FIVE

A WAD

A FEW WEEKS LATER on a Saturday night they were preparing to go to the Lake. Dion, Mike and Cherry were riding with Cosmo. They went in the opposite direction to pick up Debbie and one of her girl friends before procceding to the ABC store. They came back through St. Umblers to meet Toney, Tea, CJ and Patricia. Toney followed Cosmo. They made a stop at the ABC. They parked around the corner behind the building housing the ABC store. As usual, Dion went and bought the goods.

As the guys decided on their orders and straightened out their money, Debbie asked, "Would it be okay for us to have a couple of sips of your liquor? We are only going to drink a little bit. We are afraid of getting in trouble when we get home if we go in unsteady on our feet."

"You can have some of mine," Cosmo quickly replied. He was relieved to have someone to help him so he didn't look like a wimp.

"Sure," Dion and Mike answered, "You can have a sip or two."

Dion and Mike started drinking from their bottles on the way to the convenience store.

In the other car Tea, Toney and CJ also had started. They went in to get soft drinks and cups of ice. Toney shouted out in a deep, scratchy voice for every one to hear, "I got a wad! I'm buying the sodas." Everyone looked around at him. Some had annoyed looks on their faces.

The store clerk said, "sir, would you please be a little quieter? You are disturbing the other customers."

A nicely dressed gentleman and his wife were standing a few feet away. The gentleman looked at Toney and said, "It is nice that you have a large sum of money and it is extremely kind of you to offer to buy sodas for your friends. However, it appears you have been drinking something stronger than soft drinks and that is causing you to be loud. Would please be quieter because you are offending my wife?"

Toney was wired for a fight. Toney had a style of his own. His personality, his dress and his moppy head of shaggy peroxide-blond hair were all unique among his peers. He had the Beatles look before the Beatles came on the American scene. He had a smile a mile wide. His laugh was infectious. The girls thought he was the most beautiful guy around. In fact, Becky has been quoted as saying that she had her first wet dream over Toney. That was Toney in brief.

Toney looked at him and responded, "Or would you rather bite me?" He said in the same loud, scratchy voice, "I got a wad!"

Debbie and her friend went to his aide. They were able to get Toney to leave before there any more trouble.

CJ turned to the couple offering an attempt at restoring the peace. It turned out to be a backhanded apology at best. "You'll have to forgive him. He ain't originally from the South.

Bless his little ole heart, he moved here as fast as he could."

Toney handed CJ his car keys and sat down in the back seat. He grabbed his fifth and shouted out the window at the top of voice, "I got a wad!" He then took a big gulp from the fifth. He repeated his yell as they past an oncoming car, "I got a wad! Have you got a wad?" He pulled a roll of bills from his left front pants pocket, indeed a wad, and shook it out the window at a car sitting beside them at a traffic light while it was red. "I got a wad! Have you got a wad or would you rather bite me?"

Toney proceeded to get drunk on the way to the Lake. He appeared to say in his deepest voice to everyone with whom he came in contact, "I got a wad! Have you got a wad?" his voice becoming hoarser each time he repeated his mantra.

They arrived at the Lake before the entertainment started. Maurice Williams lead The Zodiacs that night. In an interview with Wyman Honeycutt in July 2006, Honeycutt said that Maurice Williams was a fine man to deal with. Honeycutt spoke of their overpaying Williams once because of confusion over the amount paid in advance. Williams returned the over-payment.

That was another great night and fun was had by all. They enjoyed being with the youth from other nearby towns such as Dunn, Clinton, Fayetteville and Erwin. There were friends from Benson, Coats, Cleveland, Meadow, Four Oaks, Buies Creek, and Lillington. There was laughter. There was singing along with the band. Some were on the stage trying to perform with the band. Others pulled them down. Most of all there was shaggin' and more shaggin'.

Another night was ready to be added to their chest of war stories. So they thought. The Lake had closed and it was time to gather in the parking lot and check behind each tire as all the bottles had to be accounted for before a car moved and ran over one. That night felt the same as any other night. But no, that feeling was wrong!

"Where's Toney?" Patricia asked as she paced around the empty car. Toney was missing and of all the nights, he had Patricia riding home with him. Patricia's mother had imposed a strict curfew on her that particular night. Tea and CJ were also riding with Toney.

Toney and his passengers had planned to leave a little sooner after closing than normal because of Patricia's curfew. They had searched the parking lot, the dance floor and the restrooms. They checked each car with steamed up windows to see if Toney had taken up with a honey for a little loving before going home.

They went back inside to check the pavilion again. They went behind the bandstand. They had managed to borrow a flashlight which allowed them to see things they had not seen before. They found an olive London Fog topcoat. It bore the initials MLB embroidered in black on the left lapel. There was also a gallon jug with a few drops of what appeared to be PJ.

"That can't possibly belong to anyone other than Mary Lemuel. The word is that she routinely brings in a gallon or two of various punches and sometimes moonshine under her coat. It must be true because there is the jug right beside the topcoat," Tea said.

"She has three or four of those London Fogs. She wears one every night. They all have MLB on the lapel. I know she smuggles a pint of Calvert through the door in each pocket." CJ said.

"Did you know that Reese and Larry gave her her first beer, a Schlitz? She sure took it from there. You know her father is a teetotaler, but she can put it away with anybody. She more than makes up for him," Tea said.

"I have a hard time seeing how she carries those jugs under the coat without them showing. She'd look pregnant or deformed. Maybe she puts a string through the finger hole and around her neck," CJ said.

"That would be heavy, especially, two of them. You would think the strings would show." Tea said.

"Well, it's a fact that she has them. I guess she gets the empties out the same way she gets the full ones in," CJ said.

"Yeah, she must get them in another way," Tea said.

"I heard that one of the girls in her group never brought anything to drink and bummed off Mary Lemuel. One night Mary Lemuel had a gallon of virgin grape juice. The young lady drank on it all night and was as drunk as anyone at the end of the night from that grape juice. She was sprawled across the back seat nearly passed out," CJ said.

"Pretty clever, huh? Did Mary Lemuel tell her later?" Tea asked.

"I don't know. I'll bet you she did. That would have been half the fun." CJ said.

"Still no Toney. Let's go back to the car," Tea said.

They went back and asked everyone still there where Toney was last seen. They determined that he was last seen at the front right side of the stage. They started toward the stage. As they were walking toward it, a hint of something in the tiny gap below the red curtain at the bottom of the stage reflected the flashlight's beam.

They lifted the curtain. There was Toney. He was lying on his back with his feet crossed and his hands folded over his chest. He had a huge smile on his face. He must have thought he was in heaven while he was awake listening to the music from the band and the shuffling of feet as people danced. Waking Toney was difficult. He was more than a little annoyed over the fuss being made about his being lost and the ensuing searching to find him.

Toney made his standard commentary. "All of you go to hell! Kiss my ass. I got a Wad!"

They loaded into the car. CJ was driving. Patricia was in the front passenger's seat. Toney and Tea were in the back seat. On the way home from the Lake, Patricia ragged hard on Toney about "sleeping" under the stage. "Toney your antics are going to make me late get home. My mother will kill me," she said.

After a few seconds of silence she continued, "Toney, you jerk, why did you do that?"

"Leave me alone. It is bad enough that y'all woke me up. This nagging is too much," Toney finally said. He was getting mad. Or, should we say he was getting pissed-off?

"Toney you could have let somebody know where you were going," CJ said.

"I didn't even know where I was going," Toney said.

"I'm going to get in so much trouble when I get home," Patricia said.

"Leave me alone! Kiss my ass!" Toney said in an irritated voice.

Patricia and CJ continued bombarding Toney with questions and comments about his actions and the subsequent search. They were over halfway to their destination. They were about ten miles from their homen when Toney demanded, "CJ and Patricia have to get the hell out of the car."

"It is unsafe to leave them out here on the highway alone. CJ is far more able to drive than you or I. Besides, Toney they are not bad people," Tea pleaded their case.

Toney's response was always predictable. He shouted, "The hell with them! They have to get out! They have to get out now!"

"You can't leave us here. I have to get home," Patricia said.

"Just who will drive if they get out?" Tea asked.

"You will dammit!" Toney shouted,

"I can't drive," Tea said.

The answer was the same, "The hell with them! They have to get out! They have to get out right here! CJ stop the car right now!"

CJ and Patricia were also upset by then. CJ slammed on the brakes. He stopped the car in the middle of the highway. He opened the door and stepped onto the highway. "One of you can drive this piece of crap. Drive it to Hell!" CJ shouted at Toney and Tea.

Patricia joined CJ on the highway. She slammed the car door so hard that the car shook from the blow. "Go to Hell!' she yelled. "Don't ever speak to me again."

Tea reluctantly slid behind the steering wheel. He put the car in drive. As he pulled away, CJ and Patricia were sitting on the ditch bank waiting for a car to come by which would give them a ride home. To their good fortune, one came within five minutes and picked them up.

There was only one "small" problem left for Toney and Tea. "Toney we have a small problem. I can't see well enough to drive," Tea said as he was driving down the road at a snail's pace.

"That's no problem. Keep going. You are doing fine," Toney said.

"Toney we need to stop because the line in the road is double. Worse, those double lines are getting further apart. I have to stop," Tea said.

He stopped the car without waiting for Toney to answer.

Toney opened the car door and looked down at the white line on the edge of the highway. He thought he saw that the car was still on the road. He was hoping that that was what he saw in his blurred vision. He said, "You are doing fine. You are on the highway. Keep driving."

Tea put the car in gear and moved along the highway. He weaved along the road going off first on the right. He turned the steering wheel hard to the left. Then he crossed the road and went off the road on the left. He reversed the turn of the steering wheel. He went back to the right.

"Now the double lines are crossing each other," Tea said.

"We're doing fine. Keep driving. We'll be home soon," Toney replied.

While Toney was making that response, the car carrying CJ and Patricia drove past Tea and Toney. The driver had to judge when to pass Tea in his rhythmic weaving left and right. CJ and Patricia gave Toney and Tea the single finger salute with which the British longbow men had mocked the French out their respective windows as they passed. Toney and Tea did not see the act.

As it turned out CJ and Patricia were home earlier than Tea.

Tea continued to fight the steering wheel first to the right and then to the left. It was a good thing for them that no traffic came from the oppose direction. Tea managed to make it to the front of his house.

"We are at my house," Tea said.

Toney did not answer. In fact, he had not spoken in the last ten to fifteen minutes.

Tea stopped the car and turned off the ignition. He looked over and saw Toney slouched over with his head against the car window. He was asleep.

Tea laid his head against the doorpost beside him and went to sleep himself. They woke up early in the morning after sleeping in the car for several hours. Tea went into his house and Toney drove home.

CHAPTER SIX

A MUSTANG WITH PANTIES

THE NEXT SATURDAY NIGHT, as usual, they went to the Lake. The Catalinas provided the music that evening.

The men met some new young ladies who lived in the country about ten miles from St. Umblers. There were six girls planning a slumber party at Linda's house. The guys were invited to drop in at Linda's for a while. Tea, Cosmo and Dion were riding with Harry in his red sixty-five Mustang. The young hostess gave them directions to the house. Harry, Cosmo and Dion went to the car. They had to wait for Tea who undoubtedly was talking to someone.

Harry was like a little elf. He was about five foot six with a Pillsbury doughboy body and fully flushed cheeks. He had a full-bodied laugh. The most prominent feature of that laugh was the bouncing of his belly. He His arms were slightly short for his body. Harry was funny with his deep gravelly voice because he knew how to deliver a comment in a fashion that would make people laugh. Anybody laugh.

"It is a shame that I am out of liquor," Dion lamented as they sat in the car. "Cosmo, I bet you have some left. Is that true? If you do, I want some of it."

"You know better than that. I drank it all," answered Cosmo from the other side of the back seat.

"Harry, let me out for a minute," Dion asked.

Harry obliged the request. He stepped out in order to allow Dion to exit the car. Dion alighted from the back seat as Harry held the back of the driver's seat forward. Dion walked around the car and looked behind the right rear tire of the car. Then he looked a few feet behind the car in the nearly empty parking lot. He walked over and bent down at the waist to pick up something. He walked back to the car and repositioned himself in the back seat while concealing his prize.

"Look what I found. It is an almost full pint. It's Cosmo's brand. It must have been left for me by someone else since Cosmo drank all of his liquor."

"Hey, could I have some of that?" Cosmo asked with a red face.

"Me too," pleaded Harry.

"Save me some," Tea chimed in.

"After I have a good pull on it, I will see if there is any left. If so, Harry gets first dibs," Dion answered them. "Tea, we are out of Coke. I am uncertain how you could drink this."

"Just give it to me and see," Tea replied as Harry eased the car onto the road and started for the slumber party.

"Cosmo, I have reconsidered and you may have the first drink." With that Dion handed the bottle to Cosmo who took a swallow and handed it back to Dion with a grimace.

"I don't think that is Lord Calvert. It doesn't taste right," said Cosmo in an effort to hide the fact that he had thrown away almost a pint.

Dion took the bottle and took a large pull on it. "The taste is close enough to Lord Calvert for me; whatever it is does the trick." He handed the bottle to Harry saying, "Have some and pass it to Tea. Tea you make sure there enough left for me."

Harry took a drink and handed it to Tea. Tea took a big drink and returned it to Dion who promptly finished it off. "Sure was nice of some stranger to leave this for us."

The subject of conversation soon turned to the women who had been present at the Lake. The natural progression was to talk about who looked the best and who had the best butt and who had the best boobs. Cosmo, Tea and Dion stuck to their previous assessments. Harry was new to that topic of conservation with the group.

"That's an easy choice. The best-looking woman there was Toney's cousin, Debbie. She looked way better than anyone else," proclaimed Harry.

When they pulled into Linda's yard, Mike and The Gator were waiting for them in Mike's father's car. To their surprise, Cherry was waiting with them.

They dismounted the cars. All except Harry went to the door. Mike opened it and they went in unannounced. The girls were running around in their undies. The presence of boys did not seem to be an issue with them; they merely continued moving about with ease. They turned on the phonograph and played music. Linda had only a few Beach Music songs. They played those repeatedly. The male shaggers took turns dancing with the girls on the heart pine floor.

Harry and Tea took up a collection. They then went down the road to a bootlegger's house after one of the girls gave them instructions. They came back in twenty minutes with two quarts of white lightning.

"He didn't have much, but we were able to get this home brew," Tea proclaimed while holding up two Mason jars.

"Dick, let's give 'er a try," Gator blasted. He grabbed one

of quarts and hoisted it to his mouth. "Dick, that's smooth!"

"Let me try that hooch," Dion said as he reached for the other quart. He took a long pull and said "That will be fine. That is good sipping whisky. This tastes like something Jerry's dad makes. It tastes like his nectarine brandy. That's his specialty. Since I know, Melanie drinks this stuff or something close to it, ladies, I am certain you can drink it if you want to. She drinks in what she calls tippy taps. You'd probably call them very small swallows," Dion said.

"Or sips," Tea said.

Cherry looked at Dion and said with a shy, sneaking little smile, "Dion you are such a gentleman. You are always kind and considerate of me and the other girls."

Cherry was a pretty girl. She wore her black hair at a moderate length reaching past the mid-point on her neck. She typically pulled it behind her ears. At other times, she wore it swept to one side and secured with a band or a ribbon. That night she had it flipped up at the ears. She was average height for a girl. She was about average size. She was neither skinny nor fat. She was, however, intelligent. She was extremely observant. She came across as quiet, but that was simply the result of her intense interest in learning about people which she accomplished by watching. Cherry refrained from the use of profanity. Cherry preferred others behave likewise. She was good for the group because she would always say good things about others.

Gator lowered his voice and growled looking at three of the girls standing near him. "Yeah, Dick, Wayne might have made this; it's that good. Dick, he makes good stuff. Don't he live out in the country? Dick, The Gator says you can girls can handle this. Take small sips."

They did. The girls took turns sipping the hooch right along with the men.

They drank, danced and talked mixed with some making out until about three-thirty. "I have to go home. My old man will be getting up by five-thirty and I had better have the car back or he will be furious. He will stay grumpy all day if he gets up and the car is not there," Mike informed them. "Gator, Cherry are you ready to go?" With that they left.

The four who arrived in the red Mustang stayed another hour. They continued to dance and talk. There was some serious making out, however, none went to completion. Before they left, the four collected trophies to take back to St. Umblers.

"Hey, Dion, can you drive? I'm a little messed up," Harry asked as they approached the little red car.

"Sure. I need the keys," Dion answered.

They were off to St. Umblers.

When they arrived in St. Umblers, Harry said, "I'm not ready to go in yet. Let's cruise around town some."

"Count me in," Cosmo said.

They rode up and down the streets of St. Umblers with their trophies proudly displaced. Unfortunately, there was no one to see them. Then as they drove out the residential area toward the north on Main Street Harry decided people needed to notice them. He leaned out the window and yelled, "Wake up St. Umblers! It's almost time for us to go to bed." He even yelled the phrase as they passed his house.

"Dion turn around here at the fork and go back down Main Street. Let's wake them up," Cosmo said.

Dion turned the car back down Main Street.

Cosmo joined Harry yelling out the window. They were almost yelling in stereo, "Wake up you people. It's almost time for us to go to bed." After they shouted their refrain a time or two, Tea woke up enough to join them. They circled Church

Street still yelling. When Dion turned backed down Main Street, he started blowing the horn to add some more noise.

As they reached the commercial district, a North Carolina Highway Patrol car was approaching the intersection from the west. He turned on his flashing blue lights and motioned for Dion to pull over in front of the hotel and movie theatre. Dion did so and the patrol car pulled in behind them.

"This could be trouble," worried Cosmo.

The patrolman left his car and slowly walked up to the driver's side of the Mustang. He was observing the Mustang's occupants as he walked. He noticed strange looking hats on their heads. "Men, you are letting your party get a little out of control. You are making too much noise. You must cut that out or I have to take you to the police station. Can you cut it out?"

"Yes, sir, we can be quiet. We will be silent. We were just having a little fun," Dion answered soberly.

"Good!" The patrolman leaned over to see the passengers better. "Been on a panty raid have you?"

"No, sir, we took these from the girls a short while ago," Dion answered. "We took two spares in case we lost some." Dion held up the other two pair for the patrolman to see.

"You have had quite a night. Do any of you have anything to worry about afterward or did you use protection?" asked the patrolman who was acting more like a friend than a law enforcement officer.

"No, sir, we didn't do anything like that. We just took the panties. We have nothing to worry about. The girls are also free from worry," Tea said.

"Who has the ones with blood on them?" The patrolman inquired.

"Cosmo has a pair with a red racing stripe. He could take those out to the dirt track for a lap or two." laughed Harry

pointing toward Cosmo in who was sitting right by the patrolman.

"You have had quite a night. Why don't you go on home
and get some rest? Good night and remember to keep it quiet,"
the patrolman said as he started back toward his car. He
turned off the flashing blue lights and drove away.

"Let's go home," Cosmo said.

They did just that. That was the end of another fine
Williams Lake night.

CHAPTER SEVEN

LAMAR AND THE QUEEN

IT WAS A SATURDAY NIGHT and to no one's surprise, a large percentage of the youth of St. Umblers was at Williams Lake. For some of them Williams Lake was indeed the center of their universe. There were Cosmo, Dion, Tea, Harry, Lamar, Gator, Neil, Glenn, Woody, Cherry, Connie Sue, Debbie, Jan, Judy, the other Debbie, Dare, Sue among others. The place was packed. Word of the Lake had reached more people and more were coming.

Dion, The Gator and Tea had ridden with Cosmo. They had to park at the back of the main parking lot across the highway from the entrance. They had come to like to park there and would do so even when they were early. They found that hiding their stores was much easier in the darkness. That did not really matter as their stash was the worst kept secret at Williams Lake. Tea and Cosmo made a point of telling almost everybody they talked to. Harry too had told people. Dion and The Gator were stoic about and never mentioned it. Mike was also quiet about the subject. It was okay because they were fun-loving kids; they had no interest in or need to steal someone else's liquor. They would not mind someone who thought he or she really needed a drink taking one, they expected to be informed, or better yet, asked in advance by the perpetrator.

Arthur Alexander was there singing his rhythmic style of music that night. His music had a cadence which was great for dancing the Cha-Cha. Wyman Honeycutt had had to drive to Fayetteville to pick him up at the airport making him a little late getting there. However, the Cavaliers who were the backup band performed well prior to his arrival.

Dion had been dancing with Queenie that night. She had been asking him to help her with the Cha-Cha. Dion thought she was attractive and fun so he was trying to help her. They became cozy and developed some chemistry while dancing. When they were not dancing, she would snuggle up real close to him and rub her left breast against him. That proved a bit awkward and embarrassing to Dion as he was unaccustomed to such attention. There was only so much of that a guy could take without responding. Dion was not going to demean Queenie by responding in public.

"Would you like to accompany me to the car so that I may obtain a drink? You may have one as well if you would like," Dion offered at the end of a dance shortly after the break as they walked off the dance floor.

"I would like that very much," she promptly relied. They started out to Cosmo's car.

"Hey, Dion would you and your friend like a drink? I have a variety here and plenty of chasers and mixers," Bill Warren asked as they approached his car. Bill was known to have a well-stocked bar in his trunk. Bill was from the next county but was frequently in St. Umblers on Sunday afternoon. As a result, the people of St. Umblers were fully acquainted with him.

"Would you like to stop and have a drink with Bill? He has a variety of choices and I only have one," Dion asked Queenie.

"If you think that's a good plan, then yes I would. I just want to be with you right now. Let's have one and go on over to the car and have one of yours," she replied.

"Queenie, this is Bill Warren. Bill, this is Queenie," Dion introduced the two.

"Help yourselves to whatever you would like," Bill said politely, pointing toward the trunk of his car.

"What would you like?" Dion asked Queenie.

"How about some vodka and 7 Up? I like it better than brown liquor; it is just prettier," was her answer.

Dion mixed her a weak one. He handed it to Queenie. He turned toward Bill and said "I think I would like some of that Jack. You have the black label too! I'll have some of that on ice if I may!"

Bill handed him the Jack Black on the rocks. Dion then remembered his manners and asked "Bill, what are you having?"

"I think I'm going to join you in the Jack Black," he replied and fixed himself a drink.

"Queenie and I have been dancing almost nonstop. She's good and getting better all the time. She just needs mileage. Arthur Alexander is on his game tonight. The Cavaliers are also doing a fine job. Are you having a good time?" Dion said. His shotgun delivery resulted from his nervousness over his novice with the expected upcoming encounter.

"I am. I have not done much dancing, I have enjoyed the music and the people. I was preparing to go back in after the break when y'all came along."

When Queenie finished her drink, Dion said, "Thanks, Bill we are going to move along. Thanks for waiting and talking with us." He guided Queenie away from Bill's car.

"Do you still want to have that drink we came out for?" Queenie asked as she continued to press against him as she had all the time they were at Bill's car.

"Yes, I do. Would you like to join me?" he asked hoping she would say yes. Even though he was a virgin, he was consumed with new sensations because of her rubbing against him.

"Yes, I would like that very much," she answered in a silky, sexy voice.

Dion led her toward the back of the parking lot where Cosmo's car was parked. They met The Gator a few steps into their journey. "Dick, I'm going back in. I had to have me a big 'un." He said. He looked at Queenie and asked, "Dick, do you need a big 'un?"

"No. But a small drink would be nice. That's what I'm going to have," she said.

"Dick, have fun!" he grinned with a knowing HE, HE, HE, as he walked away.

The Gator went inside and found Lamar. "Dick, did you know Dion's out in Cosmo's car with your old girlfriend?"

"Gator, I don't think he has any idea what he's getting into," Lamar answered.

Meanwhile Dion and Queenie had become comfortable in the back seat of Cosmo's car. Dion had retrieved the remainder of his spare pint and they sipped on it as they made small talk. They began to pet lightly. Their passions were flaming. They kissed more urgently and with greater longing. They began to explore each other with their hands. At first, the hands stayed off taboo terrain. They were becoming consumed by their mutual desires. Dion was first to stray from the socially acceptable realm of petting. He reached his left hand under Queenie's navy skirt to feel her leg. She merely purred louder instead of objecting as Dion had expected. He lifted her skirt slightly and reached higher. There was still no objection.

He brought his hands around her and started nervously unbuttoning her crisp white shirt. "May I?" he asked.

"Oh, yes!" she responded. He was clumsy because he was in foreign territory. He had no experience and no knowledge of what he was doing. Never the less, those new sensations felt great. His hands were hot to the touch. It felt good to her. His brain was on hold. She was on fire inside. She had relinquished control of her body and her delights to him. Carnal instinct had possessed both of them. They did not need previous knowledge; their bodies, not their minds, were telling them what to do. It was all natural action and reaction. They were no longer conscious of the world surrounding them; they were only conscious of each other and the pleasure they were enjoying.

Again he asked "May I?" as he touched her bra strap.

To which she replied "Hurry, I'm on fire. I want you to touch me all over."

Awkwardly he fiddled with her bra until he figured out how it was fastened. He then quickly removed it. He put his mouth over her left breast and licked, sucked and nibbled gently on it. He felt her nipple grow hard against his tongue as he continued to probe it. He heard her moaning in a low voice. She was writhing in a fit of pleasure. As he moved his mouth to the other breast and pleased it in the same fashion, he reached up her dress and found her lacey panties. He took his mouth of her breast long enough to ask politely as he tugged ever so slightly to signify his intentions, "May I?"

"Oh, yes. Oh, yes," she panted.

Dion pulled harder on her panties. She arched her back upward to take pressure off the panties to assist him in removing them. He then slipped them off as she dry hunched the air. As soon the panties were off, he was exploring her hot, wet forbidden secret zone. First, he began by rubbing it with his finger, then entering his finger into her to her delight. "He only faintly heard her repeating "Oh, Oh, Oooooooooh." They were both about to explode.

She whispered, "Hurry and get your clothes off! I want to feel you inside me. I want you to put out my fire with your hot, white cream. No one has ever made me feel this good. No has ever made me as hot as this. I want you now." It was all she could do to maintain her sanity in the face of her razing desire.

Dion unbuckled his belt as she was reaching to explore his secret male part. She rubbed his pants as he was working to get out of them. As she sat partially up to reach for his groin area, her skirt had fallen back down to over her secret. He had pushed his pants to a little below his waist.

"Dion, I wouldn't do her with your instrument," boomed Lamar who had his head stuck in the window. "She ain't worth it," added a wobbly Lamar.

Dion and Queenie both sat up. Queenie grabbed her shirt and rapidly and skillfully pulled it in front of her bare breasts. "You never did do me, and you never will!"

With that admonition, Lamar left shouting only one word, "Bitch!"

The moment was gone. The passion was lost. They quietly redressed. Dion said politely, "I'm sorry about that. I'll escort you back in. I hope that you are not too embarrassed. I am certain Lamar will not say anything. I know no one will ever hear of it from me. Your reputation will remain intact."

"Thank you. Cherry is always talking about what a gentleman you are. She's correct about that. You did and do treat me with such kindness and politeness," was all Queenie said on the way back into the dance area.

Donnie Ray was at the door as they walked back in. "Hello Dion," he said. He appeared to be fishing for an introduction.

Donnie Ray, how are you?" Dion replied.

He escorted Queenie back to the floor without another word. "May I have this dance?" he asked with his left hand extended. They danced a few more times. He acted as though nothing had happened. She was nervous at first but his calm became contagious. Once she was calm, he left her. He would never be in her company again. After all, *If Lamar would not do her, I will not do her* he thought to himself.

Lamar's night still had excitement in store for him. He was among the last to leave. He had come with a full car. "Lamar, I need to find a ride. I came with Harry but I was late getting out here and I guess Harry either forgot me or left because I was late," a nervous Cato said as he approached.

Even in his impaired state, Lamar could tell Cato was frantic and desperate. "I have a car full already. I don't know where we would put you."

"Put him in the trunk," Mike joked.

However, Lamar took Mike seriously. "OK we can get you in the trunk if you need a ride that badly."

"Thank you! That's better than being left out here or asking you to call my father to come and get me. Either way he would kill me when I did get home. I'll be glad to ride in the trunk. Just don't leave me here. Please don't leave me here," Cato pleaded.

Lamar unlocked the trunk and said to Cato, "Get in!"

Cato started to climb into the trunk. An impatient Lamar and Mike were watching. Before Cato could get all the way in Lamar slammed the trunk lid. "OUCH. Oh that hurts!" rang out of the trunk.

"I don't understand why the trunk lid didn't close," Lamar

said as he slammed the lid down again only to feel it stop with a loud THUD again.

Again they heard "Oh that hurts! Let me get my arm in before you slam it again," Cato moaned in pain. Lamar waited and when they could not longer see Cato's arm, closed the lid again to a pleasing CLICK.

Lamar deposited Cato at home. "Thanks," Cato said as he rushed into the house. Fortunately, Cato did not sustain a broken bone. He was however sore and badly bruised for a couple of weeks. His father asked him, "Cato, how did you get such bad bruises on your arm?"

All Cato could think to say was, "I was in an arm fight."

"With just your right arm? His father asked.

"Yes, sir," was the reply.

"That's the dumbest fight I ever heard of," said Cato's father in a voice full of incredulity.

"We made up the rules. We allowed only the right arm to be used to hit each other," Cato dodged.

"Did the other guy use just his right arm?" questioned his father assuming that the fight was with a right-handed person.

"Oh, yeah. Sure," Cato said quickly hoping to end the interrogation immediately. He was lucky to escape as his father walked away shaking his head in amazement. "What will these kids come up with next? One armed fight. They are all just plain wacko."

CHAPTER EIGHT

PLEASE PASS THE GIRLS

THERE WERE NIGHTS WHEN they went to places other than
the Lake. One such occasion was a Friday night when Joe Pope
and The Tams were in Fayetteville at the National Guard Armory. They, like most shaggers and Beach Music fans, loved
to hear the Tams perform. They decided to go as soon as they
heard about The Tams. Cosmo was the first to know. Dion, his
brother Lado and Tea immediately said they would go with
Cosmo on that Friday night. When Friday came, Cosmo was
unable to drive so Tea brought out the Tempest and they were
off to the ABC store and beyond to Fayetteville.

The Tams were playing when they reached the Fayetteville
Armory. The Tams were hot. They played all their well-known
songs. They played "What Kind of Fool (Do You Think I
Am?)", "Standing In" and others from their repertoire.

At the break, Joe Pope walked up to Dion and Tea. "It's
good to see you. I see you two show up fairly often when we
play. You always look like you are having a good time," he
said with a great big laugh. His approaching the guys was not
unusual as Joe Pope routinely talked to members of the audi-

ence and tried to make them feel special.

"We are doing fine and having a big time as usual, Joe." Tea answered reaching out to shake Joe Pope's hand.

"Man, you and the band are on fire tonight. I think this may be the best we have ever seen you play. You are really good tonight. Joe, would you play "Silly Little Girl" for me? It is an awesome song. I think it is your best. Hey, it is as good a song as there is," Dion said to Joe while shaking his hand.

"I'm going to play "Silly Little Girl" for you right after the break. Now I had better catch the rest of the band. I'll tell them what you said; they will be delighted to hear it," Joe said.

After the break, it was time for some more dancing. The Shag was contagious. Tea had caught the fever and had started shaggin' some times. He joined Dion and Cosmo on the floor at times.

Tea and Cosmo were out dancing while Dion set out to survey the women in the crowd. He was standing with Lado and a couple of young ladies when he spotted a stunning young lady standing all by herself some fifteen or twenty feet away. She was about five-four. She was wearing a long-sleeved white shirt and meticulously pressed blue jeans. She wore her light blonde hair about shoulder length was his analysis since her hair was magnificently frizzed. The frizz fit her. It framed her face beautifully and added a great deal of energy to her already alluring face. He could see she was special. She looked strong yet was quite fragile underneath everything else. She was beautiful. She looked incredible. Dion was intrigued.

When the next song started, she was still standing alone. He waited through more than half of the song before he walked over to over to her and did something that was a serious departure from his normal behavior. He put his right arm around her shoulders and said "Would you like to come over and talk with us?"

Without saying a word, she snuggled ever so slightly under his strong arm. She started walking with him. They stopped in front of the friends he had been with without exchanging another word.

She said to one of the girls, "Hello Ann, do you remember me? I'm Alan's friend Judy."

"Of course you are, hello. It is good to see you. This is Sara. You have met Dion. This is Dion's brother, Lado." Ann replied.

They each offered their salutations.

The next song started and Dion was about to ask Judy to dance. Tea swooped in out of nowhere, grabbed her by the arm and said to her "May I have this dance?" as he was leading, more accurately pulling, her off to the dance floor without waiting for a reply.

After the song, Tea staggered back over to the group. "I'm having the best time I ever had tonight."

At the beginning of the next song, Joe Pope announced, "We are going to play this next song for my friends Dion and Tea." He motioned to where they were in the middle of the floor in front of the bandstand. "Dion requested it. He said it is his favorite song by The Tams. We appreciate knowing that. You two gentlemen get your ladies and get on the floor to start the dance. Then, everyone else join them on the dance floor."

Dion asked Sara, "Would you like to dance with me?"

"You bet," she answered pleased to be in the spotlight.

Tea asked Ann, "Dance with me?" She accepted with a single nod of her head.

The Tams started playing "Silly Little Girl . . ." and the dance was under way. The two couples were dancing side by side with the lines in the hardwood floor. Shortly after they started, others joined them, Dion made a move to his left and reached over Tea and dropped his hand and Sara's down to

Tea and Ann's hands. He took Ann's hand and left Sara's for Tea to catch. They continued dancing without missing a beat. In about twenty seconds, Dion said to Tea, "Time to switch back." He repeated the move with the hands. The second time was even smoother as all four knew what was going on. The song ended and they walked to where Lado was standing. Cosmo had joined him by then.

"Wow that was some move. How did you do that cross and keep up with the beat?" Cosmo drawled in amazement.

"It wont easy. You have to ask Dion. He's the one who came up with it. But it was wonderful. I'll bet you no one has ever done that," Tea responded in a loud, excited voice.

"Dion, you amaze me. Where did you come up with that move?" Cosmo said as he turned toward Dion.

"I made it up there on the floor. It seemed natural so I did it. I didn't think anything about it. Joe gave me the license to show off and I used it. That's all," Dion answered with sincere modesty.

"It looked complicated enough to me. I don't think I could do it without you guiding me," Cosmo countered.

"I don't know if I could do it again without you," Tea said.

"That is enough talk about that. I'm off to the car to finish my liquor. Is anyone else up for a drink?" Dion said as he started toward the door.

"What and miss The Tams?" asked Lado who drank very little.

"Only for a few minutes," Dion answered. "Ladies, would you be kind enough to join us?" Dion asked Ann and Sara before turning toward the door.

"I would love to," Sara answered.

"Why not?" Ann added.

The entire group went to the car and drank the remaining liquor.

"Cosmo let me have a pull on that bottle," Dion said after he and Sara had finished his bottle.

"Okay, just a little one," Cosmo said.

"Sara, would you like a swig?" Dion asked holding the bottle out to her. "I'll pour you some in your cup before I drink from the bottle."

She nodded.

He poured some. He poured some of Tea's Coke into it before handing it to her.

When they had finished the liquor, they went back to the dance. They stayed with Ann and Sara most of the night. Dion or Cosmo would go dance with someone else periodically. They always came back to Ann and Sara. Dion looked for Judy the remainder of the night without seeing her again.

"You know that Judy had the best looking behind of anyone out there tonight. That girl is absolutely gorgeous. She can wear a pair of pants and she can wear them better than most. That girl is a spreight!" Dion ignited the conversation in the car. "She was special! Thanks for scaring her off, Tea."

"It was my pleasure. I thought she was the most beautiful woman I ever saw. At least, I danced with her," replied Tea.

"She was some kinda fittin'," Lado said.

"If I'm lucky, I'll see her again. I have not seen her at the Lake. If she had been there, I would have seen her," Dion said.

"Does she measure up to Susan?" Cosmo asked.

"She rivals Susan quite well," Dion replied.

"I'm hungry," Tea said. "There's a Waffle House. I'm going to stop there."

They went into the Waffle House and had breakfast. Tea again was about to fall in his plate.

"Do you want me to drive? Lado asked as they exited the Waffle House for the car.

"No, that car would be too hard for you to drive. I'll drive and you keep me awake," Tea answered.

"I'll let you and Lado get us home while I play Tea and sleep in the back seat. Lado, you had better ride shotgun," Dion said.

"Me too," Cosmo added as he pretty much fell into the back seat.

Tea had turned onto the Instate Highway before Dion and Cosmo went to sleep. They were awakened about fifteen minutes later by a series of repeated sharp THUD, THUD, THUD, THUD, noises which sounded like metal hitting metal.

"What was that?" asked a startled Dion as they felt the car swerve to the left and rise over the edge of the payment back onto the highway.

It was repeated by an equally startled Cosmo.

"What in the hell was that?" screamed an excited, half-awake Tea.

"It was just the mirror hitting those little green reflector posts. Tea handled it well. He only hit four or five before pulling back onto the highway," Lado informed them as calmly as a person could.

"Lado, you were supposed to keep me awake! Did you see I was going to hit those reflectors? What in the HELL were you doing?" yelled a shaken Tea.

"Yes. I saw you were going to hit them, but you looked so peaceful sleeping that I didn't want to wake you up. Besides you wont really hurting anything. It was just reflectors. It wont serious. If it had been important, I would have woke you up right then. I would have woke you right up if it had been a truck or something. You know they are on the other side of the highway divider," Lado continued his calm defense.

"Tea, keep it between the ditches and keep the noise down.

I am trying to sleep here," Dion said as he repositioned himself to go back to sleep.

"I was trying to sleep too," Tea answered. "I'm awake now."

"Good, stay that way till you get me home," Dion finished the conversation before going back to sleep.

Tea did exactly that ending another fine night. He had fully understood his instructions.

CHAPTER NINE

SHE'S NOT THAT KIND OF GIRL!

THE FOLLOWING SATURDAY night it was back to the Lake. Tea, Dion, Mike and The Gator rode with Cosmo. The back-seat was packed. They made their obligatory stop at the ABC store. They were eager to return to the Lake as they had missed the previous Saturday night. They arrived early and took up a parking space in the back of the main parking lot as usual. They sat quietly in the car drinking until there was a sizable crowd assembled in the pavilion.

"Gentleman, I am ready to go boogie," Dion informed them as he opened the rear door.

"I'm coming with you," Mike said with a devilish grin as he stepped out the other rear door. The Gator slid out of the middle of the back seat without saying a word. Tea and Cosmo left the front seat.

Cosmo informed them, "Wait. We need to hide our pints before we go."

As they returned to the car, The Gator thought out loud, "Dick, you know there ain't a wheel in the middle of the back seat. Where am I going to hide mine?"

Tea was first to speak, "How about behind that tree right in front of the car?" The Gator put his pint on the other side of the tree as suggested.

Then they went in without further conversation. They Wyman paid at the door. Donnie Ray stamped their hands as they entered.

The Mighty Tassels were playing. They were one of the most charged up and exciting bands to play at the Lake. They were lead by Kenny Helser who was an enormous talent as the premiere voice.

The entire St. Umblers group except The Gator danced most of the night away. At some point late in the evening, Cosmo wound up dancing with Carol. Cosmo asked Carol, "How did you get here tonight? Did you drive?"

"I rode with Patricia, Kay and Luray," she answered.

"May I give you a ride home?" asked a sexually aroused Cosmo. He failed to tell her that there were already four guys riding with him. He kept that little tidbit to himself as he was afraid it would cause her to decline his request. Little did he realize that such information would have made her more likely to accept his invitation.

"Sure. I guess that would be a good thing. However, Patricia is spending the night with me and will also need a ride. Kay and Luray may come spend the night. My parents are away," Carol answered after a slight hesitation.

"Good! Do you want to meet me at my car or do you want me to pick you up at Kay's car?" Cosmo asked with an air of anticipation.

"I know where you park. I'll have Kay drop Patricia and I off at your car," Carol told him without any emotion at all.

The Lake closed at its regular time. That seemed like forever to Cosmo who felt trapped by the dragging passage of each laborious song. Cosmo was primed to score. That would be his night of conquest; there was no stopping him. Cosmo was the first to the car. Dion, Mike and The Gator came along shortly afterward. Tea as usual was the last to show because he was talking to someone. Even Tea beat Kay and her passengers to Cosmo's car. They could see Kay's white Chevrolet sedan approach as they stood outside Cosmo's car.

"You guys are going to have to get another ride home. I'm taking Carol home and she is hot for me. I just know it." Cosmo said after he saw Kay's car coming. He had waited until then as he secretly had reservations about Carol showing. The wait allowed him to build courage. Seeing Kay's car moving their way gave him the bravado to make his proclamation.

"Cosmo, why did you wait until everybody else from St. Umblers had left to drop this information on us. In fact, almost everyone has already left. The parking lot is virtually empty. There is no one for us to get a ride with! You should have told us before the band stopped playing." Dion said in exasperation.

"There's no way for us to get a ride now," Mike added. "Everybody's already left."

"Dick, we came with you and we are going home with you. You can drive Carol home and we will chaperone" Gator said somewhat angrily.

At that moment, Kay pulled her car beside Cosmo's. The girls had apparently seen the situation as they droved. The group started talking.

"Kay and Luray are coming by my house, but they are not staying overnight," Carol said facing Cosmo. "The girls and I decided that it would good for us all to have a party. We can do so in my yard. Some of us will ride with you, Cosmo. And some of you guys ride with Kay"

It was decided that Tea and The Gator would ride the Kay and Luray. Carol and Patricia would ride with Cosmo. Carol in the front with Cosmo and Patricia in the back seat between Dion and Mike. They talked a little longer before they left the Lake.

"Carol, Cosmo is all hot and thinks he is going to get some tonight," Mike said.

"For two dollars apiece, I'll do you all," Carol answered with a serious laugh. The greatest truths are said in jest.

"She wont serious. She wouldn't do that. She not that kind of girl," Cosmo defended Carol's honor.

"Oh, I meant it. Two dollars each and I'll do all five of you tonight," Carol reiterated.

"Here's my money. He, he, he," Mike said holding out two crumpled one dollar bills toward Carol. He followed that act by assuming his signature scrunched body posture with his hands flexed backward toward the ground. He was laughing a sneaking whole body laugh.

"You can be first," Carol said to Mike in a business like tone.

"Here is four dollars; I'll go twice," Dion laughed holding out four folded green bills.

"You can go whenever you would like. Perhaps Mike would let you go first and you could go again later," Carol responded.

The other three girls, Tea and The Gator joined in the laughter.

"Dick, if I give you ten dollars do I get all the opportunities? Can I go as often as I would like?" Gator said

"Give me the ten dollars and get ready," she responded. Everybody other than Cosmo, who had visions of having Carol to himself, was having a good time. The evening just wasn't working out the way Cosmo had planned. It was plain to see that Cosmo was losing control of the situation. Far worse, he was losing control of Carol. It was equally as obvious from his serious pacing that Cosmo did not like that twist of events.

"Stop talking about it. You know it wont going to happen. She's not that kind of girl," Cosmo scolded them in an effort to regain control. He took Carol's arm and said, "Why don't you slid right in here beside me."

The cars left single file with Kay leading.

Every time Carol tried to move away to talk to the passengers in the back Cosmo pulled her back close to him. She wanted to participate in the spirited conversation going on back there. Dion, Patricia and Mike were busy talking about nothing in particular. "Cosmo stop pulling on me! I want to be involved in that conversation," Carol shouted at Cosmo. She thought for a moment before saying in a cooing voice, "Save it for later, Honey." Her intent was to assuage his wounded feelings.

"Dion, can you drive without wrecking us?" Cosmo asked. "I want to be with Carol."

"You know I can," Dion replied. "You had better pull over."

"You can't stop! We have to stay with Kay. They will be worried about us if we stop," Carol interrupted.

"Cosmo, hold the wheel and slid over. I'm going to come over the back of the seat. You keep us straight until I get over and get seated," Dion said.

"You are going to wreck us," Patricia said grabbing Dion by the arm. "Please don't try this. It is scaring me."

"If anybody can pull it off, it's Dion. I want to see this. This could be fun," Mike egged them on. "This will make a great story to tell later. Go ahead and do it." Mike said in his most mischievous laugh.

First Carol followed by Cosmo slid to their right.

"Cosmo, hold on the steering wheel to keep us straight. Here I come," Dion said as he put his legs over the seat back in front of him. He pushed off the rear seat to help himself get over the seat back. He was wadded up in the front seat with his shoulders parallel to the windshield and the rear surface of the red trimmed seat. He suddenly whipped his body to the left and pushed by legs under the steering wheel while gaining control of the car from Cosmo. There was relief in the air from the other four passengers. No one spoke for the next few minutes; none of them had any idea how long it actually was.

Mike broke the silence, "That was incredible! How did you know how to do that?"

"I had no clue what I was going to do. I made it up as I went," Dion answered.

Cosmo was trying to kiss Carol for the remainder of the trip. "Carol, let's you and me get away from the rest of these people when we get to your house. We can go to your room and make out." He tried to be quiet, but Cosmo had one of those voices that carried. It was loud enough for everyone else in the car to hear.

"I have a better idea. We can go into the top floor of the barn. No one will know where we have gone. Now be quiet about it," she whispered in his right ear so no one else could hear.

They arrived at Carol's house. Dion, Mike, Tea, Patricia, Kay and Luray were in the yard talking.

"Hey, where are Cosmo and Carol?" Mike asked the others.

"I have not seen them in a while," Patricia said. The others noded.

"We need to find them," Tea said. "Let's go. We need to split up and each look in a different location."

"I'll go in the house," Patricia said.

"I'll look down the road," Tea said. "Mike, you take the barn."

"Dick, I'll look under the house," The Gator added.

"I'll look behind the hedge rows in the front," Dion added. "Kay and Luray should stay together. You two look in the cars."

About a minute later Mike heard soft rustling sounds coming from the second floor of the barn. He climbed the ladder without a sound hoping to see Carol in the buff when he peeked into the upper level. He was disappointed to see a fully clothed Carol in the dim light. He also saw a fully clothed Cosmo. "Hoozinair?" Mike said to announce himself in spite of the fact that he obviously already knew the answer.

"It's just Cosmo and I," Carol said.

"Okay, you've been found," Mike said while laughing. He dipped his shoulders but was unable to flex his hands backward because they were busy at that moment holding him on the ladder. "Come on out and join the rest of us. Unless it is that you want to earn that two dollars now, Carol."

"Okay," was all she said.

"I told you she wont that kind of girl," Cosmo persisted.

All three of them climbed down to go join the rest of the group.

Soon thereafter Kay said, "It is getting late. It is two-thirty. And I don't think I'm going to get any sleep here tonight. I'm going home."

"Can you drop me at home? I think I should go too," Luray asked.

"Yes," Kay responded. They left in Kay's car.

About half an hour passed with various verbal sparring occurring as the party continued. Carol's boyfriend drove up and alighted from his car. Small talk ensued.

"We had better go," Cosmo said to the others.

"Yeah, let's go," Mike said.

They started walking to the car. "I'm going to sneak in the house and hide under Carol's bed. I don't think he is going to have to pay two dollars. I'll bet that I will find out shortly. Cosmo, drive about half a mile toward town. Pull over and wait for me with the lights off. I'll be there soon regardless of what happens," Dion said. With that, Dion slipped into the house and hid under Carol's bed.

In less than five minutes, Dion heard footsteps coming toward the bedroom. A few seconds later Carol and her boyfriend had removed their clothes and climbed in bed. The bed sank and was almost against his chest as he lay there. Soon the guy must have rolled over on Carol as the bed sagged more in one area and made contact with his flattened chest. He decided it was time to come out. "Surprise! There are more of us in here than will fit conveniently," he shouted as he sprang from under the bed. "Did he pay his two dollars?" Dion asked. Then he bolted from the door without waiting for an answer.

The startled boyfriend tried to give chase but Dion had too much of a head start. It would not have mattered anyway. He was not going to catch Dion that night or any other. Dion continued to the waiting car. "Let's get out of here," Dion shouted. He was laughing as hard as he could. They left the premises.

Dion had a hard time recounting the episode. He managed to get it out through his laughter. "You were right, Cosmo. She's not that kind of girl," Dion said.

CHAPTER TEN

STEVE AND THE DRYER

"THERE'S STEVE. He would probably like to join us," Cosmo said while he was driving down a sparsely populated Main Street. "Let's ask him if he would like to go us. Steve, get in quickly. We're off to take drunk," Cosmo said proudly. "We are on the way to the ABC store to get the goods." Steve joined them in the car.

"You trying to attract bulls or what?" asked Harry in his deepest hoarse voice before he broke into rolling laughter.

"What do you mean?" a puzzled Steve asked.

"I think Harry is referring to that bright red shirt you're wearing," Dion interpreted for Steve.

"My grandmother is coming tonight so I have to be home by eleven. And I have to be sober," Steve informed them.

"Thursday night at eleven is a strange time for your grandmother to come to visit, especially when she only lives a few miles away." Tea mused. "We are going to take drunk anyway."

"I'm not going to drink because I can't go home staggering. I'll just ride along and talk to you and enjoy watching y'all drink," Steve responded.

They went to the ABC store. Dion retrieved the liquor for the four who had planned to drink. They went to the convenience store to get mixers and chasers. Cosmo drove them back to St. Umblers where they stopped at the park. They went over and sat on a picnic table. They talked as they drank.

Steve was sitting there squirming. He was sorely tempted. He was getting thirsty watching the others turn up their cups. They were starting to get a little tipsy. Finally, he blurted out, "Hey, I guess I could have one little drink."

"You can have a drink of mine," Cosmo responded. Cosmo held out his bottle to Steve. The others agreed that they too could spare a little.

"Thanks," Steve said as he poured a drink from Cosmo's bottle. Steve finished it quickly. Harry handed his bottle to Steve. Steve poured another drink. He finished it in short order. He took a drink from Tea and then one from Dion. Steve was catching up to them in rapid fashion. Steve was drinking right along with everyone else by then. Before ten-fifteen, they were finishing their liquor. All of them, Steve included, had taken drunk.

Steve reminded them of his situation. "I'm dead. I have to be home at eleven. I have to be sober. My mother will kill me if I come in like this."

"We could try pouring coffee into him," Cosmo offered.

"Good try bad idea. We would just have a wide-awake drunk then. Who could drink enough of that foul-tasting stuff to force out the liquor?" Dion said.

"Let's go get him something to eat," Harry said.

"That would only keep him drunk longer. It would slow the absorption of the liquor," Tea said with an authoritative air, a pleased look on his face.

They were driving around in Cosmo's car trying to find a

solution to their dilemma. They rode past the Laundromat. Dion looked inside as they passed. It was deserted.

"Cosmo pull into the Laundromat. We could put him in the dryer and speed up his sobering," Dion said. Cosmo obeyed.

Mike drove up at that time. Robert, perhaps Steve's best friend, was with him as a passenger. Mike parked right beside them. They alighted from the two cars at the same time.

"He is too big to go into the dryer," Cosmo objected.

"Oh, we can get him in," a sober Mike said. Mike was enjoying the thought. He contorted into his mischievous posture and laughed under his breath.

"It the best idea I have heard," Tea added.

"Will it hurt?" Steve asked.

"Would you rather take your chances with your mother or with the dryer?" Dion queried Steve.

"I'll try the dryer. But, I don't like it," Steve answered.

"Let's get it over with so we can get you home, hopefully sober. Come on." Dion said. He turned to go into the Laundromat. "Does anyone have any quarters?" he said, realizing that quarters were required to operate the machines. They had only two quarters among the entire group. Steve anted up one and Harry the other.

"Pick him up and we will stuff him in," Tea ordered. It took some pushing and shoving. Eventually, they did get him in and closed the door. The two quarters were inserted into the slot. The dryer was started. Steve started rotating in the chamber. The rotation was very slow at first. The dryer gained speed.

Mike giggled. "The temperature must be rising in there. He is starting to sweat."

In another minute, Harry laughed and observed, "His face is contorting. Look at him. He is trying to say something but I can't hear it over the noise of the dryer."

"He's yelling, 'Let me out! Stop the dryer! Let me out!'" Mike said as he dipped into his classic move and laughed out loud.

"If we stop him now, he will still be drunk. Let him dry out in there." Dion said.

Yeah, he is OK," Tea said. "Leave him alone. I think this might be working."

"The dryer is burning him. He will have burn marks all over his body. We have to get him out," Cosmo the peace-maker pleaded.

"You, sir, are outvoted," Harry said assuming a statesman like posture and voice which he tried to mimic from a radio or television announcer. "We will let him stay, sir!"

They left Steve in the machine for what seemed to him to be hours although in reality it was a few minutes. Once the dryer stopped they immediately opened the door, pulled the frantic Steve from it, and placed him on the floor feet first.

"How do you feel?" Dion asked.

"I'm hot. My throat is dry. I'll die from all these burns!" Steve whimpered.

"Are you sober or do we need to put you in a while longer?" Dion asked.

"Now that I think about it, I think I am sober!" Steve answered.

"Do you think or do you know?" Dion asked.

"I'm sober enough to go home. My mother and grand-mother will never know that I was liquored up a few minutes ago. I'll do anything to avoid in that dryer again."

Robert who had been silent during the whole episode asked "Mike, can we give Steve a ride home?"

"Sure," Mike replied. The three of them hopped into the car and were gone. The others left right behind them.

"Steve, did you have any trouble with your folks last night?" Robert asked him the next day.

"Not at all. I was as sober as my grandmother when I walked in that door. Do not, I mean DO NOT try that tactic for sobering up again! I have bruises all over my body and they hurt!" a relieved Steve said.

CHAPTER ELEVEN

THE HAZARDS OF SEX IN A FULL CAR

COSMO'S CAR WAS FULL on the way to the Lake. The Lake had become so popular with the youth of St. Umblers that it was difficult for everyone to obtain a ride. That night there were six in the car; there was Cosmo, and as usual Dion and Tea, Mike, The Gator and Jimmy who was a newcomer to the group. Three were in the front seat. Dion, Tea and Mike filled the backseat. They arrived early and parked in their usual spot in the back of the parking lot. The Men of Distinction were scheduled to provide the entertainment that night.

When The Men of Distinction started playing, they went in and joined the other youth. They were as usual having a high old time. They were enjoying the band and their peers. They were also enjoying shaggin' the night away. Dion's instructions and demonstrations had paid dividends. They were all able to shag at some level, a least enough that the women were delighted to be asked to dance with them.

After a few songs, Harry Driver walked on stage and took the microphone. He instructed The Men of Distinction, "Fellas, please play "Happy Birthday." Continue until I tell you to stop."

He turned toward the crowd and said while "Happy Birthday" was played in the background, "Audience we have a very special young lady out there who as you may have guessed by now is having a birthday today. She is having that important eighteenth birthday. Let's help her celebrate her birthday. Please give Deborah a big hand to get her up here on the stage to recognize this important occasion."

Deborah did not go to the stage. While the band continued to play "Happy Birthday," Harry Driver tried to coax Deborah to the stage. "Deborah, come on up here so we can all celebrate your birthday with you. For those of you who don't know her, Deborah is Betty Alberty's niece. So you know she is a natural dancer."

Deborah continued to shy away from the stage even though her friends in the audience were encouraging her to go to the stage. At Harry Driver's instruction, the band finally started singing "Happy Birthday." Harry Driver who still had the microphone pumped his open palms upward indicating that he wanted the audience to join in and sing along. Soon almost everyone in the building was engaged in singing "Happy Birthday" to Deborah. They finished the song with a rousing round of applause.

They never did get Deborah on the stage. The Men of Distinction resumed their normal routine of songs. Deborah's birthday was soon forgotten by the majority of the audience. The audience had fun the remainder of the evening without ever seeing Deborah mount the stage.

Cosmo had spotted Luray and Patricia. He had gone over to talk to them. Cosmo did not know Luray. He had never seen her before. Luray was a young lady with a little residual baby fat. She had long reddish-brown hair that appeared too big and heavy for her body. Cosmo was still intent on losing his virginity and in his estimation thus passing into manhood. It wasn't particularly important to him who it was with which he accomplished his mission. Initially, he had had his eye on Patricia. Much to his dismay Patricia was interested in another guy. He quickly turned his attentions fully to Luray in hopes of finding a conquest. He kept Luray dancing all night long. He had heard that dancing could often lead to romancing. According to what he had heard, the dancing lubricated a woman's sex pot.

Cosmo's intentions were to pickup Luray and take her home. He had in mind a detour with a romp in the hay as part of the process. "Luray, may I drive you home after the dance?" Cosmo asked. He would not have asked the question except that he was fairly certain that she would accept his offer. He just knew that was the night he was going to get lucky. He was going to become a man.

"Oh Cosmo, that sounds wonderful. I'd really like that. However, I have to go straight home because my parents will be waiting up for me. I would get in really big trouble if I show up at home after one-thirty. And you know Patricia and I came here together so I have to go back with her." Luray said with an adoring look in her eyes.

Cosmo was slightly deflated by that response. He was still hopeful of achieving success in his mission. "That will be fine. You and Patricia can ride with us. We will be kind of cozy in the car because they're a group of us," Cosmo said without telling her how many of "us" there really were. He was quietly scheming to figure out a way to make the situation work to his best advantage.

As was invariably true, the shaggin' ended. The Men of Distinction had put on a fine show. They stopped at the usual time. The youth streamed through the door on their way out. As usual, Donnie Ray was there to squelch possible trouble.

He bid goodnight to those whom he knew while remaining vigilant. Cosmo escorted Luray and Patricia to the car. The other five soon arrived.

Cosmo was grinning from ear to ear as he greeted the others. None of them had seen a grin that big and white in a long time. "Gator, can you drive?"

"Dick, you know The Gator can drive. Why do you ask, Dick?" Gator said in his deepest voice.

"Because Luray and I are going to be in the backseat and somebody has to drive. You look like you're the most sober," Cosmo responded. "The rest of you just have to figure out how to get into the car without disturbing us," Cosmo continued with an air of confidence and victory.

"Patricia and I can sit in the trunk," Dion offered. "Are you willing Patricia? That will leave room for one more in there. It had better be Mike or Jimmy so we don't get too crowded."

Mike quickly offered, "I'll join you in the trunk. It sounds like we would have a good time."

The only thing left to resolve was who would sit in the middle of the front seat. For some reason Tea, who was the biggest of the group, slid into the center of the front seat. Jimmy, the smallest one of the group, slid in beside him in the front passenger position. Cosmo and Luray took the backseat. The car doors were closed. They were off. Dion and Mike were sitting on either side of Patricia each was using one hand and to hold up the trunk lid to prevent it from closing on them.

"You know I think I know how we can make some more room," Mike said grinning while holding up the car's jack. He threw it out. It hit the highway with a loud metallic CLANK and bounced several feet in the air as they drove away from it.

"We can make some more room if we throw the spare tire out," Dion said.

Mike was coming as close to jumping with excitement as he could while continuing to hold up the trunk lid. "That's a heck of a good idea. Let's do it! Patricia, can you hold up the trunk lid?"

They had to squirm around and maneuver. After several efforts, they were able to get the tire elevated to even with the top of the trunk. The three of them gave it a final push. Patricia used her feet to help push. They sat and watched while giggling in self-satisfaction as the tire hit the highway and started bouncing along following the car. The car was moving too fast for the tired to catch up. After a couple of minutes, the tire was overcome by gravity and fell rattling onto the highway. The trunk was much more spacious and the three of them were able to sit more comfortably. They were laughing, grinning and giggling. A good time was being had in the trunk. They were totally oblivious to events occurring in the passenger compartment of the car.

Meanwhile things were becoming hot and steamy in the backseat. As soon as the car was out of the parking lot Cosmo began to plant kisses on Luray's mouth. He was all over her. He soon became bolder and let his hands begin to roam over her body. He was relentless. She was accommodating. They were both lost in the passion of the moment. They had completely forgotten that there were other people in the car. It probably wouldn't have mattered to them any way. They were hungry for each other and they were going to satisfy their hunger. They were each going to have their fill of the other.

Cosmo was becoming bolder and bolder. In a rare moment, Cosmo was taking charge of the situation. Cosmo reached up under Luray's skirt and with her assistance pulled her panties off. He was filled with excitement and anticipation. He was moving in for the kill. She was positioning herself on her back to make sure the kill happened. She threw her feet high into the air with her legs spread apart. Cosmo was fumbling desperately to get his pants off. They were both breathing hard and panting. They were both too excited to wait. That was to be Cosmo's magic moment.

Tea was sitting in front the heater vent. He was bombed and the heat was making him nauseous. That nausea became worse as they continued to travel. It finally reached the point of near explosion. He looked to his right where Jimmy was sitting between him and the door. He thought to himself, *there is not enough time to pull over.* Then he looked to his left at The Gator behind the steering wheel. *I can't throw up on my buddy The Gator. Throwing up on The Gator would cause him to wreck the car.* He abandoned the option of throwing up on The Gator holding back the river of vomit as long as he could.

His next and final move was to turn his head toward the backseat. He saw Cosmo and Luray about to satisfy their lust. He tried to turn away. It was too late! He let out a loud "Ralph"! Vomit issued from his mouth into the backseat. Before Cosmo and Luray could respond he went "Buick" throwing another heavy load of bile and stomach contents upon the backseat passengers. Luray threw Cosmo upward with enough force that he hit the roof. He had extinguished their passion as efficiently as a fireman putting out a small grass fire. Cosmo and Luray had been brought back to reality in a harsh manner. Tea called for the "Buick" one more time. That forced another heavy rain of vomit on to Cosmo and Luray who were screaming.

The Gator pulled over onto the shoulder as quickly as possible. Jimmy scurried out the passenger door to allow Tea an exit. Tea staggered out with Jimmy holding him the best he could. Jimmy wasn't doing a very good job because Tea was considerably bigger than him.

"Dick, why didn't you tell me earlier that you needed to throw up? I could have stopped the car. It wont necessary to throw up all over Cosmo and Luray. Who's going to clean up the mess in Cosmo's car?" Gator scolded Tea who had emptied his stomach.

Cosmo and Luray were still moving around in the mess in the backseat trying to orient themselves properly. They were trying to get their clothes back on. Luray burst out crying with big sobs. She started to put on one of her shoes. She stopped when she put her toe in because it was full of liquid. She opened the rear door and held her shoes outside. She poured the retch out of them. She couldn't get out of the car fast enough.

Cosmo jumped out of the car. He was furious at Tea for two reasons. First, he had ruined Cosmo's pending conquest. Second, the car was an absolute disaster. "Tea, why in the world did you do that? There wont any reason for that! My car is just ruined! How am I going to get all this cleaned up tonight? No, you're going to have to clean it out! You're going to sit in the backseat in your mess on the way home."

There had been a party going on in the trunk when the chaos began. The party never slowed. While the five who had been in the passenger compartment were frantic, the three in the trunk continued their conversation. It was as though they were five hundred miles away from the activity. They tuned out the speeches and lectures. After all, in their estimation they were not involved and saw no reason to get involved at that time because there was little if anything they could do to help.

Eventually, some order was restored. They carefully poured the vomit off of plastic floor mats. They took all the paper products that they could find and wiped the backseat out as much as possible. That still didn't do a very good job because there was just too much volume. The Gator reclaimed the steering wheel. Luray and Cosmo sat in the front seat with him. Tea sprawled on the backseat. Poor Jimmy, who had been just an innocent bystander, was relegated to being cramped into backseat. The remainder of the trip to Luray's house was packed with silence in the passenger compartment.

The merriment in the trunk continued. Once they arrived at Luray's house, Luray and Patricia went inside. Dion and Mike chose to remain in the trunk.

Cosmo's initiation into manhood would have to wait for another time. He was nearly there before the upset occurred.

CHAPTER TWELVE

THE AZALEA FESTIVAL

DURING THE DRIVE to Campbell one morning Cosmo informed Tea and Dion, "I've never been to the Azalea Festival. It's coming up in a couple weeks. I think we ought to go. What do you think?"

"I have never been either. If I'll bet we could have a good time," Dion answered.

"Let's go. I'm there," Tea chimed in. "Where would we stay?"

"They tell me you can find a place once you get down there," Cosmo answered.

"You know I have a still in my lab. I could make some drinking liquor; actually it would probably be more like sipping whiskey. I'll distill it multiple times so it will be really strong stuff. It will be about 180 to 190 proof. I have a five gallon jug. That will be enough that we can get a small army of people drunk," Dion informed them.

"You make the liquor and I'll drive," Cosmo said.

True to his word, Dion filled the five-gallon container over the next couple of weeks.

"What proof is it?" Tea asked in anticipation at lunch one day.

"I don't see any reason to check what proof it is," Dion said. "We are going to drink it anyway. So it really doesn't matter what proof it is."

"You're right. But it would be nice to know what proof it is," Tea said playfully.

"Just be in the car tomorrow ready to leave as soon as classes are over," Cosmo told the two of them. "We have room. We might as well see if we can get somebody else to go."

"How about The Gator?" Tea asked.

"He'd be fine," Cosmo said. "We should see him in the parking lot of The Gas Company tonight. We can ask him if he wants to go."

They did see The Gator The Gas Company that night. "Do you want to go with us to the Azalea Festival tomorrow? We have plenty of alcohol," Cosmo asked.

"Of course," Gator muttered.

"We are all out of class at eleven. What time are you available?" Cosmo tried to establish the departure time.

"I can be ready at noon," Gator said.

"That should be fine. Because we have to go get the jug from the lab anyway and get it loaded in the trunk," Dion said.

"We'll pick you up at five minutes past noon. Be ready to go," Cosmo told The Gator with authority.

They were excited on their way to the campus the next morning. They were each eager and ready to go to the Azalea Festival. Each of them had a difficult time focusing on their classes. Eleven 'clock finally came. Cosmo, Tea and Dion met in the parking lot at Cosmo's car. They drove around to the back of the science building.

Cosmo parked and stayed with the car while Dion and Tea

went to get the bounty. Cosmo was grinning with excitement when he saw them coming with the jug loaded on a cart. "I didn't realize just how big that thing would be. We sure can do some drinking during this trip."

Tea and Dion secured their prize in Cosmo's trunk. Dion took the cart back into the science building. Then they drove back to St. Umblers to pick up The Gator.

The Gator came out of his house and jumped in the back left. Dion had the other rear seat. Their plan had been not to drink anything until they reached Wilmington. However, by the time they made it to Newton Grove they were revisiting that strategy. "Hey, let's stop here and get some BBQ, and we will see if they have one of those big mayonnaise or ketchup jars that we can have. If they do, we can mix of PJ," Tea said unwilling to wait any longer before having a drink.

"Yes there's a grocery store right across the circle from the grill. We can get grape juice there," Cosmo said.

That was the new plan. They stopped. They had barbeque for lunch. They asked the owner if they could have one of his big mayonnaise jars. He was kind enough to give them one that had been cleaned. They drove around the circle and went into the grocery store. They bought four half gallons of grape juice. They added some of the grain alcohol Dion had distilled to the mayonnaise jar. They filled the rest of the jar with grape juice. Everybody poured some into a cup of ice and started drinking.

They were only a few miles down the road when Tea said, "That's not very strong. I don't think it has enough liquor in it."

"We can fix that easily enough. I'll just add some more al-cohol to it if Cosmo will pull off the highway," Dion said. Cosmo stopped the car on the shoulder of the highway. Dion

went to the trunk and poured more alcohol into the mayonnaise jar. Each refilled his cup and started drinking again.
They were off once more.

After about thirty miles, it was Cosmo's turn to say, "Why
not put in some more alcohol. This is weak stuff." With that,
Cosmo pulled the car over onto the shoulder of the highway
again. Tea added more alcohol to the mayonnaise jar. Cosmo
started the car down the road again with each of them drinking the very stiff PJ. They were getting a little tipsy at that
point.

By the time they reached Wilmington, they were scorched.
They finally found their way to Carolina Beach. They set out
to find a place to stay. Eventually, they found a house where
three rooms were for rent. They took the rooms because they
were expecting Mike and Harry to show up later. They moved
their stuff in and continued to drink.

When the owner of the house realized how drunk they
were, she had second thoughts about having rented the rooms
to them. "I bet you will get a good deal trouble. If I have any
trouble from you, I'm going to throw you out," she said indignantly to them. "You keep real quite. I don't like noisy
renters." Then she flounced away with a righteous air.

Around six that afternoon Cosmo passed out. The Gator
was nowhere to be found. "I'm going to walk down to the
Boardwalk to get a hamburger and maybe some French fries,"
Dion said to Tea. "Do you want to go?"

"Yeah. Let's go," Tea responded as he slurred his words.

They left the house staggering toward the Boardwalk.
When they arrived at the Boardwalk, they encountered Lado,
Phil and Thomas. The three younger men were running at
them on the boardwalk. Two policemen who appeared to be
running after them.

"Lado, why are you running?" Dion asked as they approached.

Lado answered, "There was some asshole back there who tried to steal my wallet. I hit him. Then Phil hit his buddy. After that the police started chasing us and let those assholes get away."

"Quick! Duck under this building. Those police are not going to follow you there," Tea instructed.

The three of them ducked under the building. Dion and Tea followed them. They crawled a long way under the building. They each found a concrete support pillar to hide behind. The police came and shone their flashlights under the old building.

They heard one of the policemen say to the other, "I don't see them under there. If they were crazy enough to go under there, I'm ready to let them go."

"Fine with me! I don't want to crawl under there with all those rats and spiders," the second policeman said. The policemen left.

The five of them waited a little while under the building.

"I think it is safe to come out," Tea said. When they crawled out onto the street, they were covered with dirt and spider webs.

"We made this time. You'd better lay low. Those cops are still going to be out looking for you. I'm getting hungry," Tea said. "Let's go get that hamburger and those French fries."

They walked a street further from the beach and turned to the right in search of a place to get something to eat. In the second block, they found a little café. Four of them of them ordered hamburgers and French fries. Dion was the dissenter who ordered onion rings instead of French fries. They ate quietly and left. Tea and Dion went one way while Lado, Phil and Thomas went the other.

Neither Tea nor Dion remembered exactly what happened after that the remainder of the night. Bill and Larry brought Dion back to the house where the guys had rented rooms about three in the morning. "We found him standing in the middle of the highway with his eyes hanging on his cheeks too drunk to move. He had no idea whether he had walked or if someone drove him there. We don't either. You had better be a little calmer here or you are going to get into real trouble. Dion, you are just lucky that a car didn't come along and hit you. Stay here and get some sleep so you can sober up," said Bill. Bill and Larry left.

None of them knew how Mike and Harry found where they were staying. Nobody knew what time Mike and Harry had arrived.

Cosmo, who had been in bed all night, was up at nine shouting, "Y'all have gotta hurry up if you want to go to the parade with me. I'm not missing the parade."

The Gator, who had gone unaccounted for before six the previous night, dragged himself out of bed to join Cosmo.

Dion and Tea had more difficulty getting going than the other two. They were both still drunk sporting the onset of major hangovers. "I'll be ready to go as soon as I have a shower and a hair of the dog," Dion said.

"Me too," Tea said. "Gator, where have you been boy?"

The Gator had no ready answer. He said, "I don't know anything about what happened between yesterday afternoon and now. I don't know where I went or how. I don't know when or how I made it here."

"You go ahead and take your shower because it takes you so long to do your hair. I can take a shower and get dressed while you're doing your hair. I'll have a hair of the dog while you're taking that shower," Dion said. "Cosmo, what did you do with that alcohol? Do we have any grape juice left?"

Cosmo answered, "I'll get it out of the car. I don't think we have any grape juice left though."

"I guess I will have to drink it over ice and add some water to it," Dion said. He did.

By that time Mike and Harry had been awakened by all the noise. "We're going to the parade too," Mike said.

"I'll be ready to go soon. I'd like to see the parade," Harry said to all in the room using his best deep, gravelly voice.

Once they were all ready, they loaded into Cosmo's car. They left to go see the parade. They had some difficulty finding a parking place as they were somewhat late arriving before the parade. They found one and managed to find a spot on the street corner from which to watch the parade. A number of cars passed in the parade as did floats; they were talking to the occupants of most of the cars and floats. Then along came a brown convertible with Little Johnny the Philip Morris man sitting on top of the back seat. Little Johnny yelled out, "Call for Philip Morris!" When he came nearer, he repeated his statement, "Call for Philip Morris!"

"Dick, you'd better stop smoking those things. Those weeds are going to kill you," The Gator yelled at Little Johnny. Dion and Tea joined The Gator in admonishing Little Johnny to stop smoking.

The car Little Johnny was riding in slowed almost to a stop in front of them. They entered the street. Little Johnny said, "Why? Don't you smoke? I have some Philip Morris here for you to try." They struck up quite a conversation. Actually, it was more like an argument.

After the argument had ensued for a few minutes, Little Johnny motioned for them to come farther out into the street. "Ride with me in the parade?" Little Johnny said.

They did. Or at least they did for a few blocks until the police came and ordered them out of the car. They obliged the
police and the parade continued.

After the parade was over, Cosmo informed his passengers,
"I promised my mother that I would go and see the azaleas in
the park. All I have to do is ride through the park and look
then we can be out of here and go back to the house." There
was no objection from any one. Cosmo drove to and through
the park. It would have been a much quicker drive except for
the fact that there was a continuous line of cars driving slowly
through the park so the occupants could admire the azaleas.
They endured it and went back to the house where they were
staying.

They arrived back at the house to see all of their possessions
in a heap on the front porch. There was no sign of anyone else.
They went into the house looking for the lady who owned it.
They found her in the kitchen. She grabbed up a knife and
started shaking at them. "I told the lot of you that if you gave
me any trouble, I'd throw you out. I knew you are trouble
when I rented you the rooms. I saw you fools on TV. You were
out there in the street bothering everybody and interfering
with everybody's opportunity to see the parade. I want you
out on here! I want to out of here right now! You're just trouble!" She was becoming more agitated with every word she
said.

"We're only going to leave if we get our money back," Dion
said quite boldly. He said it even though he knew that they
had not paid in advance. They should have some compensa-
tion for their inconvenience. After all, they had done no
damage to her or her property.

The lady gave the money begrudgingly. "Now get out of
here quickly so I can rent those rooms to respectable people!"

They gathered up their things. They tossed them haphazardly into Cosmo and Harry's cars. They set out to find another place to stay. By the middle of the afternoon, they had found new accommodations. That property was several blocks farther from the beach, at least they had a place to stay.

"Let's have us a drink to celebrate finding a new and better place to stay," Tea said. That was all the encouragement that group needed. They found a grocery store and bought some more grape juice, some vegetable cocktail juice and some ice. They went back and sat on the front porch drinking PJ. They drank quite a bit. In fact, they drank until they became intoxicated. They were fortunate the new location was just around the corner from a café that served fried chicken. They went there for chicken, coleslaw and baked beans. The day was still young so they went back and sat on the porch to drink some more waiting for dark to come.

"Some of the girls are staying just a few blocks from here. I suggest we go there and see what they are doing," Tea said.

Dion was the only taker. "Who are you talking about?"

"I know that Connie Sue, Dare and Sue are there. I don't know if anybody else is there or not," Tea responded. "Let's go."

The others decided they would stay at the house and go to the Boardwalk later. Dion and Tea were off for a four block walk or stagger as it turned out to be.

The girls were staying at a motel that was owned by their aunt. The three of them were in their room adjacent to the office. Connie Sue and Dare's mother and their aunt were in the office which had sleeping quarters.

Dion and Tea could hear the girls in the room so they knew which door to knock on. They thought they were knocking quietly so that their mother and aunt did not hear them. What was quiet to them was loud to most of people. Connie Sue opened the door and invited them in. All three of the girls almost in unison said, "You have to be really quiet because Mother has already told us we couldn't have boys in here tonight."

Dare continued, "We can't let them hear us or they will be over here for sure. And if they come over, they will make you leave. Afterward, we'll be in trouble."

"The two of you are really liquored up tonight! I'll bet you've been drinking all day," Connie Sue said. "We haven't had a drop. It's too bad you couldn't bring us some. But we would get in trouble if you did."

More conversation among the group followed. The girls kept trying to keep the tone down. Tea and Dion kept getting louder; especially Tea. They were too wasted to understand how loud they were.

Shortly there was an insistent knock on the door. They heard a voice, "Girls, are there boys in there with you?" It was Connie Sue and Dare's mother.

"No, ma'am," answered Connie Sue as Dare was trying to usher their guests into hiding or out the bathroom window.

Tea was closest to the bathroom and started there to climb out the window. He climbed onto the commode lid and took a powerful jump in an attempt to go through the window. He encountered resistance and flew back into the bathroom with a loud CRASH. He climbed back on the commode lid and tried again. That effort had the same result. He was determined so he tried one more time. Once again he came back faster than he had tried to go out. He had cuts and scrapes along with a trickling red flow on his face.

In the meantime, Dion had found the perfect hiding place. At least in his drunkenness he thought so. He went over and stood in front of the clothes in the open closet. There was no door on the closet. He was easily seen by the girls' mother and aunt when they entered the room.

"Dion, what are you doing in here? Girls, you know you know that you are not supposed to have boys in here. Dion, are you by yourself?" Dare and Connie Sue's mother said.

"Yes, ma'am, I think I am. You can't see me I'm hiding. I'm drunk and you are not so you can't see me," Dion said amazed that the ladies could see him in his hiding place. He thought that Tea had successfully jumped out the bathroom window.

"I heard banging noises in the bathroom. What's going on in there?" The Aunt said. At that moment, she looked into the bathroom to see Tea with a bleeding face that had been scratched raw by whatever was on the other side of the bathroom window.

"The two of you get out of here and don't come back. These girls are grounded for a week. It's a good thing that you both are so intoxicated you couldn't do anything if you tried. Go on and get out of here. Girls, you are to stay in this room!" The girls' mother said.

They left and the girls stayed. The next day the reason for Tea's cut and bleeding face became obvious. They sneaked back by and looked out the bathroom window. There was a gray concrete wall just one foot beyond the bathroom window. When Tea had jumped, he had hit the wall and flew back into the room. So much for that great escape!

They staggered their way back to the house in which they were staying. They had another drink or two. Then JW came by for a visit.

"Let's go and do something," JW said.

"Why don't we ride down to where the Bill, Larry and John are staying?" Dion responded.

"Do you know where that is?" Tea asked.

"Yes. Well, not exactly. It's down at the other end of the beach; we can find it by looking for their cars. We'd better take along some alcohol or we will have nothing to drink there." Dion answered. Dion poured a quart of the grain alcohol into a Mason jar.

JW was jumping at the bit, "Let's go." They jumped in JW's car and he drove them to the other end of the beach. As they drove to the other end they were looking intently for Bill and Larry's cars. They finally spotted three familiar cars in the front yard of a house on the oceanfront. They pulled in to go join the party.

They went into the house where there were a number of people they knew. Bill and Larry were here. John and Glenn were also in the house. They were acquainted with two of the young ladies. Dion poured a drink for each of the people who were already in the house. He poured one for JW and one for himself. That left a little less than a pint.

Tea reached grabbed the Mason jar from Dion's hand and said, "I'm going to show you how to drink this stuff." Before anyone could react, he had turned up the jar and chugged it.

In about forty-five minutes or so Tea was suddenly missing. They went looking for him. Bill called out, "Here he is," from the bathroom. He had taken off his shirt and pants and laid down the tile floor to keep cool. He was passed out.

Larry said to the group, "He is slap wasted. You know a person could die from chugging grain alcohol like that."

"Let's just let him lie there where he is cool and sleep. Hopefully he'll sleep it off tonight," Bill said.

After a while JW and Dion left. JW drove Dion back to the house where he was staying.

Tea slept off his liquor. Dion, Gator and Cosmo picked him

up late in the morning. They went back to the house where the four of them packed up their belongings. They stopped at a café, had lunch and headed back to St. Umblers.

CHAPTER THIRTEEN

NO SLEEPING ALLOWED

It WAS A HOT SUMMER NIGHT. The night was made special by the fact Dion was able to drive. He picked up Cosmo first followed by Tea and then Harry. By six-thirty, they were on their way to the ABC store.

Dion pulled the little mint green car into their normal parking space at the Lake. They were each filled with the excitement of anticipation of an adventure about to begin. As he drank, each was thinking about his prospects of hooking up with the right woman that night. When the band started playing, they followed their ritual of stowing their reserves. They could have put the bottles anywhere because nobody was going to bother them. Practice makes permanent, not perfect, and each would know where to find his bottle even in his drunkest state.

They paid Donnie Ray and went in. It was a small crowd for the Lake. However, more people started pouring in and in a short time, the place was almost full. Billy Stewart, who was affectionately known as the "Fat Boy," was the featured artist. He was backed by The Cavaliers who were without Gene Barber that particular night.

The Fat Boy was at his best. And, that was good. He was smoking. He put on a show dominated by his fare of Fat Boy standards. He sang "Summertime" twice. It was mandatory that he sing his personal anthem, "Fat Boy." As he sang, he danced. Periodically, he would do a 360-degree spin. At the beginning of the spin, he would squeeze his hand-held microphone into the air and turn around to catch it as it dropped toward the floor. The Fat Boy could sing; he was also quite a showman, a crowd favorite. There were as many people watching the Fat Boy perform as were shaggin'. That was unusual as most of the people normally came to shag. Tea and Harry were among the group watching the Fat Boy put on his show. They were swinging and swaying with the remainder of the group.

Cosmo was dancing with Joan Dale. He has been dating her during the previous weeks. He was busy trying to entice her into allowing him to partake of her delights. He was putting forth his best effort on the dance floor. However, Joan Dale was having no part of going to the car with him. Cosmo was still on his mission to lose his virginity. Tonight was going to be just another long night of frustration in accomplishing that mission. He continued to try right up to the end.

It was one of those occasions when boyfriend was not there. Dion seized upon the opportunity to dance with her repeatedly. They were good together, real good!

Charles from Four Oaks was there. Lungs was also there for the first time in many nights. Charles monopolized Lungs' shaggin' time.

Ricky and Grace were there as they normally were. They were as always shaggin' very smoothly. As usual, they only danced with each other. They were a little closer to the water than their normal position because of the crowd that was watching the Fat Boy.

"Charles, let's go over and dance with Ricky and Grace," Dion said.

"Yeah. We can show off tonight. Let's go they will see if Ricky and Grace will join us." Charles said.

Dion, Susan, Charles and Lungs walked over to where Ricky and Grace were dancing. At the end of the song, they approached Ricky and Grace.

"Hello Grace, Ricky. I think you know Susan, Joan and Charles. You two are dancing beautifully as usual. You are doing the Shag the way it's supposed to be done," Dion said calling Lungs by her name as that was the proper thing to do.

Charles asked Ricky, "Why don't we show off some tonight? The four of us are all game for it."

Ricky was his quiet and reserved self as he answered, "I don't know. I don't do much of that. I just shag the best I know how. You two are awfully good. You might embarrass me"

"It's more likely that we would get embarrassed. I have a hard time seeing how we or anybody else could embarrass you. We might not be able to keep up with you is the simple truth," Charles answered.

"I hope I live long enough and get to the point that I can shag well enough to embarrass you. That would be a sight worth seeing. I'll bet people would pay good money to see that. Let's just dance and have some fun," Dion said.

"OK, let's shag our best. We will let it happen naturally. I think I'll pass on trying to show off though," Ricky responded to the challenge. That was his way, nothing flashy, just plain good old shaggin'.

"You look stunning tonight! Do I have permission to show off my lady?" Dion said. Susan was radiant. She was a dazzling beauty.

"Maybe. You know I can't keep up with you when you really turn it on. Your friend Page is probably the only one who can. Let's see what Ricky and Charles do. Then decide if you need to show off," Susan answered.

The three couples were there to shag. Shag they did. They were on the dance floor almost every song. Weejuns were flying. They all enjoyed it fully. None of them really needed to show off nor did they. They just did some of the most beautiful shaggin' ever seen at the Lake. Many of the others present gathered around them to watch. The group of on lookers varied from song to song. These three young men were considered by many to be the best shaggers at the Lake.

The evening ended. To his lament, Dion said goodbye to Susan who had ridden with friends. "I have had a most wonderful time dancing with you tonight. Thank you so very much for making my day," he said to her.

"I too enjoyed it very much. You were a real gentleman. You never made an improper advance although I think you wanted to. If I weren't going steady I would be more interested in you. You're handsome and you're charming. You're a wonderful dancer too. You seem to be an around good guy," Susan replied in her silky smooth voice.

Dion said to Susan, "The French have a saying that goes something like, 'In water you see your face. In wine you see another's heart.' I think that I should buy you a bottle of fine wine so that you could see inside my heart."

"I don't need a bottle of wine to see what's there. I already know what's there. However, my heart is full of another. If that were not true, I would choose you. I am flattered by your attention and affection. I think you are the nicest person I ever met. I feel I could trust you with my life or my fondest possession. You are very tempting! I will always treasure your friendship," she replied.

She turned and walked to the car in which he was riding. She had some hesitation over the need to depart. Nevertheless, she did.

Dion walked by Cosmo on his way to the car. Cosmo was still working hard to prevail upon Joan Dale to come with him. Joan Dale was obviously interested in Cosmo but had no intention to be labeled a cheap girl.

The car was loaded. They left the Lake at the end of one more beautiful evening. Tea and Cosmo were sitting in the backseat. A few minutes after they were on the highway Tea said, "I'm going to go to sleep now."

"It will not be long before I join you," Cosmo said just before he yawned.

Dion answered them, "that would be a bad idea." He looked over to his right and saw that Harry was already almost asleep. "If you sleep, I'm going to sleep too."

"You can't do that. You have to drive," Tea laughed.

"I have some bad news for you. If you all go to sleep, I'll go to sleep too." Dion insisted.

The three of them did indeed go to sleep. Dion drove for a few miles thinking about how to handle the situation. He recognized an area of the road ahead of them where there was a high embankment and a very shallow ditch. He talked to himself, *I know how to cure them of sleeping when I'm driving.* As he eased beside the embankment, he slowed the car almost to a stop. He slowly and carefully edged the car along the embankment so that it just made contact with the loose soil. Moist dirt came flowing into the windows of the passenger side. It mounded up on Tea and Harry. He brought the car to a complete stop. He quickly laid his head back pretending to be asleep.

"What is all this wet stuff all over me?" Tea squeaked as he came out of his drunken sleep.

"We're in a ditch! There is wet dirt all over me!" Harry growled in the deep voice.

The noise Tea and Harry made woke Cosmo up. "What do you mean we're in a ditch?"

"Dion, there is wet dirt all over me and Harry! We're in a ditch! How are you going to us get out of here?" Tea said.

Dion smiled a sly smile. "I'm going to drive out. I told you that if you all went to sleep that I would go to sleep too. You didn't think I would do it. Do you think you can stay awake? We're going to go to the car wash and wash down the passenger side of the car and vacuum out the dirt."

They drove into the car wash at about two A.M. There was no one else there so they had the place to themselves. They quickly washed the car. The vacuuming job took considerably longer however. When they had finished cleaning the car, Dion drove each of them home. He then went home and parked the car in the carport. He went in and went to bed.

CHAPTER FOURTEEN

THE TRUCK

COSMO PICKED TEA and Dion up on his way to the college campus. They were unusually quiet on the ride the class that Friday morning.

Their classes came and went. They saw each other periodically during the breaks between classes. They typically saw Dion infrequently because he had many hours in labs in addition to regular classroom time. They glided into the car which was parked under a big, verdant oak tree.

"This is going to be quite a day," Cosmo said. "It will be the first Friday that I have missed going to the Lake or to someplace else to shag since we started going to the Lake. I have a date with Joan Dale tonight; she doesn't want to go to go dancing."

"We are going to enjoy shaggin' for you Cosmo. We are going to the Armory tonight," Dion said. "I hope you have a really good time. Joan Dale is a very attractive woman and she is very much into you."

"You should tell her that the two of you need to go to the Armory. Just because you have a date wont no good reason to miss going to the Armory. It wont possible that you couldn't talk her into going to the Armory when you made the date. You know she likes to go too. You didn't try very hard because you just want to get laid. We know you hope you are going to get lucky tonight," Tea said.

"I sure do hope I get lucky. I really like Joan Dale. I don't think of her that way. She's not a loose girl. She's beautiful and she's a lot of fun. I plan to go out with her whenever I can. When we do go out, we may go to the Lake and we may not," Cosmo informed them. His commentary revealed what Dion and Tea already suspected. Cosmo was smitten by Joan Dale's beauty and charms.

It was a short eight miles to the next town. They were full of banter as the car rolled along.

"Hey, there's where The Gator's new honey lives," Tea said pointing at a red brick house set back from the highway on the left.

"How do you know that and we don't?" Cosmo asked.

"Because I rode over here with him on Tuesday evening. He started to stop to visit, but he chickened out at the last minute. He has been going out with her recently. I think The Gator is hooked," Tea answered.

"She seems to be fine person. She laughs with her whole body the way The Gator does. I think they make a good couple," Dion said.

"Over there in that white house on the right is where Jerry lives," Dion said a mile or so further down the road.

"That GTO he has is real fast," Tea said.

"This is an interesting little town," Cosmo announced. "You know this town took its name from the family that started a cotton business?"

They came to the intersection where the traffic light was located. The light was red for them so Cosmo stopped the car.

They were the only car stopped at the traffic light. They sat there for what seemed like an hour to Cosmo because he was anxious to see Joan Dale even though that was hours away. The traffic light turned green.

Cosmo started to move the car into the intersection. They all looked to the left and saw a old dirty brown truck loaded with logs flying down the highway toward the intersection. Cosmo didn't hit the brakes.

"Cosmo stop! That truck is going to hit us. He'll kill us for sure," a worried Tea said.

As soon as it was clear to him that Cosmo did not intend to stop the car Dion yelled, "Stop!" Cosmo was not stopping! Dion quickly reached over to his left to the steering column, turned off the car and pulled out the keys.

"Cosmo that truck would have killed us! It would have flattened us right there in the middle of the intersection! He would have run over us! He would still be going leaving us a greasy spot in the road! This car would not have even slowed him down!" An excited, nervous Dion yelled.

"We almost died there! Cosmo, you almost killed us! What could you have been thinking? You're acting like one of those no driving sons-of-bitches! Did you get your driver's license at Sears and Roebuck?" Tea said his voice full of animation.

Cosmo was totally unfazed by the event. He calmly said to them in his dry sense of humor, "We would've been alright. If he had hit us it would have been his fault. It wouldn't have hurt us because it was his fault."

"Cosmo, do you have any idea what you just said?" Dion asked.

With that, the severity of the situation finally hit Cosmo. Suddenly, he became a nervous wreck. He started ranting and raving uncontrollably.

Dion handed Cosmo the car keys. Cosmo took them with his shaking hands.

"When the light turns green go on through the intersection and turn to the right on the street past the railroad track. We'll stop there and get ourselves calmed down," Tea ordered.

When the light turned green, Cosmo started the car again. He crept through the intersection then over the railroad track and turned right onto the next street. He pulled onto the shoulder and stopped the car immediately. All three of them leaped out and walked around for a few minutes without speaking.

Cosmo was the first to speak. "Okay. I'm ready to go on home now." They silently reentered the car. Cosmo cranked it and turned toward St. Umblers.

They rode in silence for the next three or four miles. With the episode a few minutes behind them it became a funny reflection. Dion and Tea both chided Cosmo for the rest of the way home. Each time they would meet a car on the highway one of them would say, "If he had hit us and killed us, we will be alright because it would have been his fault." Each time one of them said it both of them would break out laughing. Dion and Tea had that horse saddled and they were going to ride it.

The first few times he heard it Cosmo sat quietly. He was seething a little bit because the other two were poking fun at him. After that, it became funny to Cosmo too. As they pulled into St. Umblers, Cosmo was the last to repeat the phrase, "If he hits us and kills us, we will be alright because it would be his fault."

Dion and Tea recovered from the truck incident later in the day. Dion and Tea went to the Armory that night and to Lake as usual the next.

Tea drove to the Lake. Harry and Neil went with them. It was an eerie sort of the evening. Things just didn't seem right. That was the first time they had been to the Lake without Cosmo, Mike or The Gator. Both Cosmo and The Gator were off on dates with women about whom they seemed quite serious. Mike was out of the area. The Entertainers were playing that night.

They had a reasonably good time but it still seemed quite strange. The dynamics were beginning to change in their little group. Some new priorities were coming to light.

CHAPTER FIFTEEN

THE COUNTY JAIL

"COSMO AND THE GATOR are both going on dates tonight. I still want go to the Lake. I can't drive tonight. Do you want to go?" Tea said to Dion on the telephone late that morning.

"Why yes, you know I do. Unfortunately, I can't drive either. I have to work a while this afternoon. Do you think you could look around and see if we can find a ride?" Dion answered.

"Yeah. I'll do that. I think Glenn is going to go and if so we can probably ride with him," Tea responded. "I'll walk over later in the afternoon and ask him if he is going and if we can have a ride."

After he arrived at home from work about six-thirty, Dion called Tea. "Did you have any luck with Glenn?"

"He's going to pick me up at seven and will be to your house by about seven-fifteen to get you," Tea happily informed Dion.

Dion cleaned up and had a bite to eat. He didn't have much time to spare but he was ready when Glenn and Tea arrived at seven-thirty. They were right on time - Tea time that is. Tea held the back to the front passenger's seat forward so Dion could climb into the rear of the dark green two-door hardtop.

As soon as he was settled Dion said, "Glenn, I sure do appreciate the ride. I would have hated to stay home tonight."

"I'm happy to have you riding with me. Besides, I understand that you can get us some liquor at the ABC store," Glenn responded. "I guess we need to be on our way there, don't we?"

"That's the best idea I've heard all day," Tea said.

They were off to the ABC store. Dion went in and bantered with Mr. Wilson. He purchased the liquor for the three of them. They left the ABC store and went to the convenience store to get necessary supplies. Because they were a little late getting to the Lake, their regular parking spot was already taken. They looked around for a few minutes. Tea burst out, "Glenn park right here." Glenn backed up slightly. He turned the car to the right into a tight parking space. The three of them sat there and enjoyed their adult beverages for a few minutes before going in.

The Lake was packed. Martha and The Vandellas were playing that night. The Honeycutts paid the band the then unheard of sum of eleven hundred dollars for their appearance that night.[1]

Everyone seemed to be having a good time. At the break Dion, Tea and Glenn met at the car for a drink. Tea spoke up "There's certainly nobody here tonight. This place is dead. I don't know what's wrong"

Tea's statement brought a look of confusion to Glenn's face. "The place is packed," he said.

"I think Tea is referring to the fact that only a few of our friends who are regulars are in attendance tonight. It is interesting how our minds work. The Lake is packed and rocking yet to Tea there is no one here. I am on the other hand having a wonderful time," Dion said.

"Yeah, that's because you have been shaggin' with that big-boobed Joan or Lungs as you call her, all night. I might be having a good time too if I were dancing with her," Tea re-butted.

"Why don't you ask her to dance yourself," Glenn offered a practical solution to Tea issue.

"I think I will. I guess I'll have to beat Dion to it though. I have a plan. My night is looking up already," Tea answered.

"Be my guest if you can get her to dance, you should go for it. I'll shag with her later. I'll dance some with Connie Sue when we go back in to afford you an opportunity. I have wanted to dance with that petite little stick of dynamite any-way. That girl is a barrel of fun. She is so energetic. She can dance too. I enjoy dancing with her," Dion offered.

"Connie Sue is like our little sister. You aren't getting mushy ideas are you?" Tea said.

"You are right that she is like a little sister. No, I don't have any romantic ideas. You know I would hurt anyone who caused her trouble. I'm just planning to dance with her," Dion said.

When the break was over, they went back in. Dion did in-deed go find Connie Sue and danced four songs with her. He thought that would have given Tea ample time to make his move on Lungs if he were going to do so. After the fourth song, Dion went looking for Lungs. When he found her she was dancing with another guy. He waited patiently until the dance was over and for the next one to start. When the music began, he started to move toward Lungs. At the same time, she started toward him. He extended his left hand gently and politely asked, "May I have this dance?"

"I was wondering where you were. I'm glad you came back," Joan said as she extended her right hand to meet his left. They took to the floor. They finished that dance. In fact, they danced to every song the rest of the night.

Tea had not availed himself of the opportunity that Dion had presented. Instead, he became occupied with talking with Ann and Charlene. He danced some with them and then disappeared into the crowd looking for the proverbial greener pastures.

"Joan, you are more beautiful tonight than I've ever seen you. That's going some because you are normally dazzling. I want you to know that I really enjoy dancing with you and I hope we get to do it again," Dion said when the evening was over.

"I've enjoyed it too. I too hope we are going to get the chance to do this again," Joan answered.

Dion would never call Joan Lungs again. He retired that nickname. They shared a special attraction. However, as fate often does it interfered with the magic of the moment. They were never to see each other again after that night. That was truly a shame!

All three were wobbly from the spirits they had consumed. Glenn pulled into the highway. He started toward St. Umblers with the car weaving a bit.

Glenn had driven about five miles. He looked in the rearview mirror and exclaimed, "There's a flashing blue bubblegum machine coming up behind us. He's coming pretty fast. I'm going to pullover. I don't think he'd be going that fast if he were coming after us." Glenn guided the car onto the shoulder as smoothly as he could. He tried hard to keep the car steady but it still wobbled and weaved.

The sheriff's car pulled on to the shoulder right behind Glenn's car. The sheriff's deputy slowly walked up to the driver's window. "Stay in the car. Let me see your driver's license." He bent down and looked into the car to see the occupants' faces. He stuck out his left hand to get Glenn's driver's license.

Glenn fumbled with his wallet before he finally removed his license. He handed it to the deputy. "Officer is there a problem?"

"Glenn, I'm afraid there is. You were weaving pretty badly driving down the road. I need you to step out of the car very slowly. I'm going to give you some sobriety tests." The deputy responded. "You two stay in the car," he added looking at Dion and Tea.

Glenn complied with the order. He stood up and promptly stumbled against the side of the car.

"I want to see you walk the way I do," the deputy said as he demonstrated putting one foot immediately in front of the other for a few steps.

Glenn tried. As was to be expected, he could not maintain his balance in order to do so. "Give me another chance. I stumbled because of the darkness." Glenn asked of the deputy.

"I'd be glad to," the deputy responded. Glenn tried again with the same results.

"Son, I'm afraid that I have to take you in. You are driving under the influence," the deputy said. "Come over here and sit down in the backseat of my car. Is it okay for one of your friends to drive your car to the county jail if he is sober enough?"

"Yeah, it's okay. Dion would probably be the better choice," Glenn lamented from the backseat of the deputy's car."

"Stay here. I'll be right back," the deputy ordered.

The deputy walked back to the driver's window of the car. He bent down and looked in. "Are either of you sobered enough to drive this car to the county jail without wrecking it? I'm going to take your friend there. If neither of you is sober enough to drive you'll have to wait here until someone can come and get you. I'll be glad to take any names and phone numbers that you would like me to have and have someone from the jail call."

"I think I can do it," Dion answered. "I don't know where the county jail is sir. Can you give me directions?"

"I'm going to drive slowly. You follow me. You shouldn't get lost," the deputy responded.

"I'll be ready as soon as I get under the wheel." Dion slipped behind the wheel of the car. As the deputy was walking, back to his car Dion asked over his shoulder, "Tea, why don't you get up here in the front seat too?" Tea did so as quickly as he could.

The deputy kept his word and drove slowly to the county jail. Dion worked hard at keeping the car straight as he followed the deputy. He did do some weaving which wasn't too bad because they were going about 50 mph.

"How are we going to get Glenn out of jail?" Dion asked.

"I have no idea. I know don't have any money," slurred Tea. "The only thing I know is to go get his Dad to come get him. I'm not looking forward to making that trip."

"Me either. I'm not looking forward to having to go knock on that door and wake his Dad up. It's going be awfully late before we can get there. I'd rather do that than have somebody wake my Dad up with the same story," Dion said.

They arrived at the county jail. "Park in that lot," the deputy told Dion. He was pointing to a parking lot across the street from the jail. Dion complied with the deputy's instructions. The two of them alighted from the car and walked across the street into the County Jail. The deputy had preceded them taking Glenn with him.

When they were inside, they saw Glenn and the deputy at the front desk in the jail. They heard the man behind the desk ask the deputy who had stopped them, "What's he in here for?" in an agitated, impatient voice.

"I arrested him for driving under the influence," the deputy replied. "Book him. These two were riding with him; I ask them to come down too. We are not arresting either of them. They came voluntarily."

"You lack the authority to make such a decision," the man behind the counter grouched. "They must have been guilty of at least public drunkenness at a bare minimum."

"They may have been because I'm sure they were coming from Williams Lake. We can't charge them because I didn't see them," the deputy snapped back.

"They're drunk in here right now. That's public drunkenness if I ever saw it. We should lock them both up," the clerk persisted with a disdainful look on his face. "You boys been to Williams Lake, have you?"

"Yes sir, we have," Tea answered. Dion only looked on in silence.

"What's the matter with you? You gone mute all of a sudden or something? You and your kind are no good trouble makers," he snarled at Dion.

"Nothing sir," Dion answered.

"So you are a smarty pants. I'll show you. We are going to get you yet. You are going to do something and we are going to get you," he continued growling at Dion.

The deputy finally interceded with the ongoing inquisition, "Leave them alone. Let's get this young man booked before the sun comes up."

"Alright! Already!" the man barked at the deputy.

"What's your name and address? What your father's name?" he grilled at Glenn.

"My name is Glenn," He continued with his last name and address.

"Where are your driver's licenses? What is your father's name? I think we should call him and let him know where his precious piece-of-thrash son is spending the night. I'll bet he would be proud of you then, wouldn't he?" the man taunted Glenn.

"He might be," Glenn retaliated.

"Don't you sass me boy," the man roared.

"What are you going to do? Lock him up?" Dion asked.

"I ain't through with you brat," the highly agitated man said sensing that they were no longer afraid of him. He pointed at the officer behind the cell room door, "Lock him up!" referring to Glenn. "Now you two get of here," he ordered Dion and Tea. "I think I'll send an officer after you to catch one of you driving under the influence or both of you for vagrancy if you don't drive away from here."

Dion and Tea started to leave as Glenn asked the officer behind the cell room doors, "May I smoke in here?"

"You are allowed to smoke if you have your own smokes."

"Can you get my cigarettes out of the car and bring them to me?" Glenn asked as he looked toward Tea and Dion.

"No problem," Tea answered.

They crossed the street and found Glenn's cigarettes in his car. They returned to the jail. "I'll take those." The grumpy man said.

"These are Glenn's and we need to get them to him," Dion replied.

"I'll see that he gets them. Hand them over," demanded the man sitting behind the desk with a sneaky smile.

"No thank you sir. Glenn asked that we bring them to him. That is just what I intent to do. He's allowed to have visitors," Dion said.

"Hand them over and get out of here," the man growled one more time.

"I'll take them to him. Besides, I see they are the same kind that you smoke. You will keep them and smoke them yourself," Dion bristled.

The man was outraged, "I will not put up with your insolence. The only way you are going back there is a prisoner."

"If that's what it takes, let's go," Dion said.

"I'm placing you under arrest for public drunkenness in the county jail," he shouted at Dion with a laugh. "I told you I would get you, Mr. Smarty Pants."

The jailer had returned to the door and heard the end of the conversation. "Leave that boy alone. You have been out to get him since he walked in here," he said to the distraught man behind the counter.

"Nope! No, sir-ree Bob. He is under arrest. He's mine now. You take him back and put him with his buddy," commanded the man to the jailer.

Dion handed Tea the keys to Glenn's car.

The jailer lead him away saying, "I'm terribly sorry, son. It wont no reason for him to treat you that way. He's a real unpleasant trouble-maker."

"Glenn, here are your cigarettes," Dion said holding out the pack.

Glenn reacted with surprise, "What the Hell are you doing here?"

Dion recounted the story to him. Then they sat and talked for a little bit before Dion said, "Which bed is yours? Your roommate is ready to go to sleep."

They went to sleep. They slept until about eleven when the jailer came and said, "You can go home now."

Tea had driven back to St. Umblers struggling to stay awake

all the way. Only the excitement of the moment and his fear of facing Glenn's father made that possible. He went to see Glenn's father at nine. "What are you doing driving Glenn's car? Where is Glenn? Did he get drunk and thrown into jail?" Glenn's father, who had had a drink or two himself in his time, asked.

"I guess I should tell you the truth," Tea said. "Yes, sir, he was arrested for drunk driving. They threw him in the Sampson County jail. Dion went in to take his cigarettes and was locked up too because he refused to give the man at the desk those cigarettes."

Glenn's father chuckled. "That's about the beatenest story I've heard in a long time. Here is Dion an avid nonsmoker who has tried to talk Glenn into giving up smoking. He gets thrown in jail with Glenn because he insists that he is going to take those cigarettes to Glenn. Now that's a friend for you. I hope Glenn appreciates what a good friend he has in Dion and you too. I'll bet Dion had correctly pegged that man at the desk. He probably would have kept those cigarettes."

"You are correct. There wont many people who would have stood up to that man just because he gave his word that he would see to those cigarettes getting to Glenn. I would have done it myself if Dion had not. Besides, somebody had to be able to get the rest out of jail. I know that hateful man would have smoked those cigarettes himself."

"Tea, I have to be at the store. Can you go get them out of jail?" Glenn's father asked.

"Yes sir. I can go right away," Tea answered.

"Here's one hundred dollars that ought to get both of them out. There is no reason to tell Dion's father. He'd be just absolutely livid. It was worth every penny to hear that story. If there is any change, let Glenn keep it. You take Glenn's car and go get them."

Tea went back to the county jail. "How much does it cost to get Glenn and Dion out of jail?"

There was a different man at the desk that morning. He answered pleasantly let me look that up. He came back in just a moment and said, "One driving under the influence. Son, that is mighty dangerous. Don't let your friend do that again. The next time will be real trouble for him." He continued shaking his head in disbelief, "One locked up for public drunkenness in the county jail. Well, now don't that beat all! That's the first time I have ever heard that charge! That will be twenty dollars apiece."

Tea handed the man the required forty dollars.

The man signaled the jailer to go get Dion and Glenn. He did so immediately. The two of them walked with Tea to the parking lot across the street. They went home.

CHAPTER SIXTEEN

IF NOT SUSAN, SARA

IT WAS A WELL-KNOWN FACT around St. Umblers and the surrounding communities that Dion was crazy about Susan. It was equally well known that Susan had a steady boyfriend. In Dion's estimation, that was a shame. The truth of the matter is that that was probably the best outcome possible for the parties concerned. Her boyfriend had much more to commend himself to Susan than did Dion. Dion lacked a means of transportation to see Susan on a predictable basis had he the opportunity as Susan lived about eight miles away. That notwithstanding, everyone needs hope. Everyone has desire. Susan certainly embodied Dion's hopes and desires. Both of which were to go unfulfilled.

Susan's younger sister, Sara, had started going with the St. Umblers group to Williams Lake on occasion. Sara was a tall slender young lady. She was the prototype for Twiggy who came along as a super model some years later. She had long flowing yellow brown hair with a hint of red in it. While not as attractive as Susan, she was quite beautiful in her own right. She had an infectious laugh and smile. She laughed and smiled very frequently. Everybody liked Sara. She deserved to be liked. Sara loved to dance. She was a fair shagger though no threat to the best.

On that particular occasion, Cherry and Sara had ridden to the Lake with Cosmo, Tea and Dion. As usual Cosmo was driving. Tea sat shotgun. Dion was in the back with Cherry and Sara. The men were drinking. Cherry, as was her habit, only had a few sips. Sara who was almost a stranger to liquor was drinking what for her was a considerable amount of whiskey. The short of it is that Sara was taking drunk. That made her cuter than normal because she became giddy and funny. She laughed almost nonstop all the way to the Lake after she had had a drink or two.

They arrived at the Lake. They socialized for a short while before they went in to dance. The O'Kaysions provided the entertainment that evening.

The band took its break. The guys had been dancing vigorously. They went out to the car for some refreshment. Sara was doing quite a bob and weave as she staggered to the car with Cherry's assistance.

"I would like a drink too," giggled Sara as she approached the car.

"I'm not sure that's a good idea. Why don't you sit down right here in the backseat of the car and talk to us till break is over." Dion said.

"All of you are drinking. I want a drink too," Sara responded with a slight hint of a demand in her voice.

"Ah, it will be alright. You can have a drink of my liquor," Cosmo said as he put his right arm around her shoulders. Then he quickly moved his arm down around her waist. Cosmo appeared to be thinking here was his opportunity to lose his virginity. He appeared willing to at least give it a try.

Sara took Cosmo's cup. She took a big gulp from it and handed it back to Cosmo. As she did, she wiggled free of his grasp. She stumbled over and rested herself against the left rear quarter panel of the car.

Cosmo, even in his drunken state, recognized the rebuff. He took the hint and moved away from her toward the front of the car. "Tea, I'll drink all my liquor. Then I'm going to drink some of yours," Cosmo said in an attempt to remove attention from Sara's rejection.

"There wont no way you're going to drink any of my liquor Cosmo. I have already drunk it all," he responded with a great big grin on his face.

"I guess I'll have to have some of Dion's," Cosmo responded.

"I think that'll be too hard too. Looks to me like Dion's already finished his off also," Tea informed Cosmo. "I hear the band playing. I'm going back in."

"I'm going with you." Cherry said.

Cosmo closed his bottle and stowed it for safekeeping. He gave pursuit to Tea and Cherry.

Dion walked over to Sara. He gently took her right arm and open the left rear passengers door the car with his left hand. "Sara, I don't think you are in any condition to go back in at the moment why don't you sit right here and I'll wait with you a while until you sober up some. Then we'll go back inside."

Sara reached up and flung her arms around Dion's neck. She said to him, "I don't want to sit in the car. Can we walk some?"

Dion gently removed her arms from around his neck. He took her left arm in his right arm in order to properly escort her, "Yes, we can walk some." He started walking toward the highway with Sara in tow.

Sara protested mildly, "I would really like to walk into the woods over there."

"Do you think that's a good idea? It's going to be very dark and dusty in there. We might stumble over a root or something," Dion said.

"That's exactly where I want to go," Sara persisted.

Dion relented with resignation as a gentleman would do. "Okay. Even though I still think it is a bad idea, I yield to your wishes. We will give it a try." He turned Sara around and the two of them started walking into the woods. It was dark in the woods. They stumbled over a number of roots which were not visible in the darkness.

When they were deep enough into the woods that the cars behind were too far away to be seen in the darkness, Sara said, "Let's stop right here." She stopped abruptly and leaned her back against a medium-sized oak tree. She was quite wobbly.

"I guess if you can't have Susan then you'll settle for me," Sara said as she looked at him.

Dion was completely taken aback. "I would never consider having you as settling. You would be a great prize."

Sara sat down on the ground with her back still against the tree. Dion sat down on the ground beside her.

Without saying another word, Sara started unbuttoning her starched white blouse. She unzipped her light blue skirt. "Then why don't you do to me what you would do to Susan if she were here?" Sara asked in a very alluring voice.

"I'll do just that," Dion responded. He reached over and buttoned her blouse. Then he said, "Let me help you up." He took her hand and pulled her to a standing position.

When she back on her feet, she put her arms around his neck again. She started to lean forward to kiss him. Before she could complete the task Dion said, "Let me help you get your skirt back on properly." He held her skirt up as she put the blouse back into it. When she completed tucking the blouse in, he quickly zipped up the skirt and fastened the button.

"I'll bet that's not what you would do to Susan if she were here," Sara who was embarrassed said. "Nobody wants me! I'm just Susan's little sister!"

"I'm quite flattered at your offer. That is exactly what I would do to Susan if were here under the same circumstances. As attractive as I find both of you to be, I could not take advantage of either of you in a drunken state. I suspect that you would regret it when you sobered up. If you make me that offer sometime when you're sober, we'll see what happens. You are going to turn men's heads everywhere you go just by being you because you are beautiful in your own right," Dion said to her it his calmest voice. "I think it would be a good idea for us to go back inside. You should wipe the dust from the seat of your skirt before we go."

"I thought you'd want me since you can't have Susan. Thank you for the respect you showed me," Sara said as they walked toward the Lake.

Dion merely said, "I believe it's possible to always be nice to people. You don't have to give yourself away to be liked or accepted by other people. I should not have allowed you to get into that position. Please accept my apology."

Later when they were back inside after Sara had sobered some, she recounted the event to Cherry. "I'm embarrassed at my behavior. Do you think he's going to believe that I'm an easy girl?"

"I believe he meant exactly what he said. He would have treated Susan exactly the same way. Dion is always such a gentleman," Cherry assured Sara.

CHAPTER SEVENTEEN

THE FRAT HOUSE

SOME OF THE GROUP had started meeting at the Scout hut for social hour before the evening's adventure on Saturday nights. They also met there on some Friday nights. Their social hours became more frequent and longer as time passed. Some of them started bringing dates on occasions.

They would frequently cook steaks on Saturday night before heading to the Lake. Getting access to the Scout hut regularly was becoming more and more of an issue.

One night Vance and Woody came to the Scout hut with their steaks and potatoes in hand. They were beaming from ear to ear. It was obvious that they thought they had something on the rest of the group. Vance opened the conversation with, "We've found a house we can rent for almost nothing and turn into a fraternity house. We'll be able to use it whenever we want to. It's just four miles up the highway. It sits isolated in a big field so there are no neighbors to disturb."

"It's been vacant for several years. The owner says he be glad to rent it to us because it's not doing him any good just sitting here. He only wants ten dollars a month for rent. We would have to go and clean it. We would have to paint the inside before we can use it. It has a stove and refrigerator already. They work; they just have to be cleaned." Woody added.

Considerable discussion followed about the house and its location. In the end, it was thought it was a great idea and many of them were willing to contribute to the rent. There were about twenty who ultimately wanted to be members and agreed to pay a dollar a month each for the rent and upkeep. That was a momentous occasion.

"Let's all go out tomorrow afternoon and get the place cleaned up," Vance suggested. There was general agreement. On Sunday afternoon by one-thirty, there were about thirty youth from St. Umblers cleaning up the fraternity house. They worked until dark. They removed cobwebs, they dusted and they swept. They cleaned out the refrigerator. They cleaned up the stove. They cleaned the house from top to bottom including washing the windows inside and out.

"Since we have electricity, we can come out at night and paint the place. We can go to the hardware store tomorrow afternoon and get some paint and rollers. I'll be ready to come out right after dinner tomorrow night to get started," CJ said.

"I'll be ready to help if I can get ride," Dion said.

"I'll pick you up at six-fifteen," CJ responded.

"What color are we going to paint it?" Cosmo asked.

"We can paint it psychedelic colors - greens and pinks - that would be cool. I have some black lights I can bring out and put up to make it really glow," Woody said.

They spent Monday, Tuesday and Thursday nights working from about six-thirty until about eleven painting the house. It was ready to be christened at the Friday night social hour.

The fraternity house became a much more important part of

their life. It became a place for them to go to drink and socialize before going to the Lake. They would also go there frequently on weekday nights. They did not go there on Sunday nights as that would be frowned upon by the community in general and their parents in particular.

After a few weeks, they finished their work on the fraternity house. They had been able to find beds to put into the two bedrooms. One bedroom had bunk beds on one side of the room and a double bed on the other side. The other bedroom had two double beds. They had a beat up tan and green sleeper sofa in the living room. They had an RCA stereo record player. They didn't want any other furniture because they wanted to have space to mingle and perhaps even dance while there were partying. Some of them started spending nights out there during the week.

They had built a grill outside of the north wall. That grill was used frequently on the weekends. One Saturday night they had decided to grill out in preparation for going to the Lake. Most of them brought a ribeye or porterhouse steak for the grill and a potato to bake.

When Robert arrived, Harry growled at him in his deep voice, "Boy, what do you have there?"

"That'd be called a sirloin steak don't you know," Robert said with a giggle.

"I knew that was a sirloin steak. Is that all you brought?" Harry quizzed Robert.

Robert laughed. "That's all I brought. I'm going to have me some naked meat tonight," he said, using a term he had heard some of the black men use. "This is going to be some fine eating."

"The charcoal is ready. You can put your steaks on," Tea announced.

They jockeyed around the grill to put their steaks on. "I can

wait if there is not enough room. It doesn't take me very long
to cook my steak. I just like to strike a match and run the cow
by at about forty feet, cut the steak and eat it. I want to hear
the cow's last moo," Dion said.

The steaks were cooked. The meal was eaten. Afterward
everyone stayed around for a bit, continuing to drink and prepare for the trip to the Lake.

Dion walked over to Jennifer. Jennifer was a beautiful
young lady with brown hair that reached about three inches
below shoulder level. At about five foot eight she was taller
than most of the girls. She was looking splendid in her bright
green and white horizontal striped shirtwaist dress. She was
slender and very fit. Jennifer was also very quiet. She made
a habit of not calling attention to herself. He said to her, "Jennifer, I'm surprised you look a little tipsy."

"Scott's over there shooting tequila. He left me by myself
so I'm going to get tore up from the floor up!" Jennifer responded with a little bit of a slur in her rich Southern voice.

Jennifer had come with her husband Scott. To most people,
they were a lovely couple. Dion knew that as much as it was
unlike Jennifer to get drunk, it was unlike Scott to drink tequila
shooters. "I'm sure Scott will be fine. One of you needs to stay
sober enough to drive," Dion said.

Scott came over to talk to Jennifer and Dion. "Hi," he said
to Dion as he approached.

"Good to see you, Scott. How are you?" Dion answered.

"I'm doing great," Scott said.

"I heard you had a little run in with a lady in town about a
parking space," Dion said.

"I didn't even know what she was talking about. Before I
could speak she had blasted me with all kinds of four letter
words and worse," Scott said.

"What did you said back to her?" Dion asked.

"I didn't say a word. I was afraid it would get worse," Scott said.

"Did you think about retaliating?" Dion asked.

"Yes, I just decided if I was going to tote a cussing and I certainly did, I didn't want it to be any worse than it already was," Scott said.

"Scot, you are the man!" Dion said.

"No. This is your world and I'm just happy to be in it," Scott said.

"We're just a couple that things happen to," Jennifer added.

"Good night and stay safe," Dion said.

"No more tequila shooters for me," Scott said.

Jennifer accomplished just what she said she was going to do. As promised, she got tore up from the floor up. Scott quit drinking for the night. Consistent with being the good man that he was Scott managed to get the two of them home safely.

Some twenty yards away The Gator's date said in a loud agitated voice, "You never pay me enough attention! Why do you even want me around? You act like you are not with me." Then she turned and flounced away to the back yard.

Dion heard the commotion though the contents of her comments were inaudible. When he witnessed Gator's date stomping away in obvious anger, he walked over to the stunned Gator. The puzzled look on The Gator's face gave again the fact that he failed to understand or appreciate what had just happened.

"Gator, what was your lady so upset about?" Dion asked.

"She was making all kinds of noise about me never listening to her. I'm not certain exactly what it was about because I was busy watching Boonie stagger around. Dick, he has sure enough taken serious drunk tonight," Gator said.

Gator thought about the episode for a few seconds. "Dick, I don't get women." He added.

With that Dion walked away to find Tea and Cosmo. "Let's go do some shaggin'," Dion said to them.

"I'll be ready in about five minutes," Tea replied.

"That will give me time to go over to speak to Boonie and Lisa; then I'll be ready to go." Dion said.

Dion started toward the porch where Boonie and Lisa where talking. He passed Jerry and Melanie along the way.

"Where ya going?" Jerry asked.

"I'm going to speak to Boonie before I leave." Dion said.

"We'll join ya," Melanie said.

"Hey, Boonman, how are you doing?"

"Boonie is scalded." Slight, brown-haired Lisa said.

"No he's not." Melanie said to Lisa.

"Boonman, did you have a little much?" Dion asked.

"He sure did. He's pretty bad off, but he knows all his vowels. It's too bad one can't make many words from vowels alone," She contorted her pretty, tanned face to the right to mimic a drunk and strained as a drunk would do to slur "A". She contorted to the left and struggled to get out a distorted "E". Lisa continued with "I, O and U". The long laugh she added at the completion of the vowel recitation let her friends know that she was enjoying Boonie's impairment.

Boonie raised his head to its normal six foot one inch level. "Do you know anything about extratesticles?" Boonie asked Dion.

"The hell," Jerry said with a laugh.

"Uh, I mean extraterrestrials?" He asked looking at Dion.

Boonie stroked the well-trimmed hair on his chin and his mustache with his right hand while he appeared to search hard for what he wanted to say. He slowly craned his long neck forward and upward as far as he could. Boonie's face became whiter than normal. He lowered the pitch and level of his normal voice and said, "This is where I live." He lowered the frequency of his voice even further and through a satisfied grin said with emphasis, "In the dark!" Then he fell silent again as he hugged a pillar supporting the porch roof with both arms for support.

"Boonie, that corn you and Dion were drinking has whipped your poo poo." Jerry said.

"I think it was more that sweet, home remedy brandy than the corn. I didn't think he had much of the corn. He was hard into brandy," Dion said.

"They can't mess with me. I've been to the Claremont Café," Boonie said peering at the night sky.

"Boonman, hang in there. Excuse me," Dion said as he turned to go.

Dion found Tea and Cosmo. Ten minutes later, they were off to the Lake, but only after Dion and Cosmo threatened to leave Tea.

CHAPTER EIGHTEEN

PIG PARTY

THERE HAD BEEN A pig party or two in the past. There had not had one in some time. Both CJ and Dion noticed that Chuck was asking questions quite frequently about having a pig party. When he wasn't asking about a pig party, he was making comments about a pig party. They independently decided that Chuck had found himself a ringer.

Chuck was the kind of guy who always had to have the one up position. If you had two blue cows, then Chuck had at least three. If you thought you could play baseball, Chuck would tell you he could play better. No matter what you knew, he knew something better. No matter what you had, he had one better. No matter where you'd been, he had been farther and he had gotten there faster. Chuck was actually a pretty nice guy except for the fact he always had to be one up on everybody else.

"Have you noticed how Chuck keeps asking about the next pig party?" CJ asked Dion one afternoon.

"I have been observing that for several weeks," Dion responded. "I wasn't sure anyone else had noticed."

CJ smiled a sneaky smile and said, "You know something is up here. I just know it."

"It looks to me like you are thinking along the same vein as me," Dion said. "I'm thinking that Chuck has found the ultimate pig for the next party. What about you?"

"That's exactly what I'm thinking. I think he believes he has found a ringer. What do you say we set him up?" CJ said.

They decided to set him up. "Let's have a by-written-invitation-only party. The invitation will state that anyone who discusses the party in advance will be denied admission," a mischievous CJ schemed.

"Good idea. You and I will be the hosts. As a result, we will be the only people who will know who is invited. We will write out the invitation with instructions, time and location," Dion said.

CJ thought for a minute. Then said, "Everyone other than Chuck will have an invitation that requests he bring his best looking date. The invitation will specify blazers and ties for the gentlemen and party dresses for the ladies."

"I guess it goes without saying that Chuck's invitation will be different. Chuck will be invited to a pig party. He will not want to discuss it with anyone else if he has the ringer that we think he does. We will invite enough people that the frat house will be too small. Let's get the Scout hut since it is just one big room and there are plenty of chairs that we can use." Dion said.

"Let's tell everyone else to be there at six and that the doors will close to them promptly at fifteen after. We'll tell Chuck the party begins at six forty-five and that doors will not open until six-thirty. That way we can tell all the other guys what is really happening at about six-twenty. That will give us all a chance to get our dates and be seated for Chuck's entrance," CJ said. He was on a roll and loving the plot.

"We need to pick a date for the party. How about two weeks from Saturday?" Dion said.

CJ grinned. He rubbed his hands together vigorously as he said, "That's a good day. It'll give us time to get everything organized. And we don't want to be too far in the future because someone else might try to organize a real pig party. If that happened, I'd sure hate to see Chuck win the prize. We would never hear the end of that."

"Let's get our list of invitees made out right away. Then we will split them up by who's going to write that particular invitation," Dion said.

"Okay. But I want to write Chuck's invitation," CJ said.

They made out their list. There were just over two dozen names on it. CJ took the first half of the names while Dion took the second half. Each had his list to which he was going to write invitations.

"Do you think we should bring a couple of the others in on the plan? They can help us to avoid having someone else plan a major event for that Saturday. We could get Woody, Donald, John and Vance. I think they all be happy to help pull this off," Dion said.

"If you think it's a good idea, I trust your judgment. It probably is a good idea. It'll be easier with some other people helping out," CJ answered.

Dion pondered the approach before saying, "I'll get to Woody and Donald tomorrow. Can you get in touch with John and Vance?"

The next day Dion and CJ talked with their assigned contacts. These recruits were willing volunteers who were eager to pull off such an event. The plan offered a chance to bring a little humility to Chuck. They were all up to that task. They were eager to see the look on Chuck's face after he was out of that green Pontiac and walked in the door of the Scout hut to see everyone else dressed in their finest with their best-looking dates.

The invitations were sent out two days later. They carried an RSVP date of Friday of the following week. The schemers were busy putting everything together to perfection.

Maintaining secrecy for two and a half weeks is difficult when just one person knows something that juicy. Maintaining secrecy for two and a half weeks when two people know the details is extremely difficult. When six people know, is a virtual impossibility to maintain secrecy. Nonetheless, the time passed and the secret was secure. The lives of the participants in a campaign often depend upon the success of the mission. And success frequently depends one hundred percent on secrecy. In truth, that was exactly the case here.

Chuck had been antsy and nervous all week. He too had his great secret and he was afraid someone would discover it. He was greatly relieved when Saturday came and no one had found him out. He was making sure that that would continue to be the case for the day. He secluded himself from the rest of the partygoers.

Chuck had told his ringer that he would pick her up at seven-thirty for the party. He had told her that even though he had planned to be there at six-fifteen. She had told him on the phone that she would be there by herself when he came to pick her up. How lucky could he possibly be? He was hoping that he would find her in the middle of preparing for his arrival. Just as Dion and CJ's plans had worked to perfection, so did his.

Chuck was beaming as he turned his car onto the dirt path leading to an old white wooden house. He was thinking to himself, *This is my time! I will show them! There will be no doubt who the winner is today! They will know that I'm the man!* His heart was racing with excitement as he stopped the car in the front yard. He was finally going to be the clear-cut winner. No one could stop him! He alit from the car and bounded to the front door at just past six fifteen.

His date heard a loud insistent KNOCK, KNOCK, KNOCK, KNOCK, KNOCK on the front door. The ferocity of the knocking startled her. She regained her composure and grabbed her faded purple and white striped robe. She pulled it on and went to the door. She opened the front door and was surprised to see Chuck standing there. "I don't understand. You said you would be here at seven-thirty and it's only six-fifteen. I'm not ready," she protested.

Chuck was pleased. His plan had worked; in fact, he could not have worked things out any better. She was standing there before him, five foot six inches tall, weighing approximately two hundred and ten pounds. She was dressed in her dingy tattered robe. She had a multitude of different colored Coke can-sized rollers in her hair and she had cold cream or some sort of white mask smeared over a portion of her face. Even with the white goop on her face, pockmarks which were probably the result of chickenpox were visible. Her glasses were askew over her eyes.

Chuck said scurrilously, "I'm sorry but the starting time for the party has been moved up to six forty-five. I just found out a few minutes ago. We have to go."

"Chuck I'm not ready. I can be ready in twenty minutes," she responded emphatically.

Chuck looked at her as if though he were a conquering hero and said, "If you want to go with me to the party, we have to leave right now. You look just fine. Let's go!" *You look perfect just as you are. I'm gonna win,* he thought to himself.

"Can I at least have five or ten minutes?" She pleaded.

"There's no time for that. There's a vote for an award at the beginning of the party and I don't want to miss it. I have to be there for that vote. If you are gonna come, let's go! If you're not coming, I'm going anyway. I don't have any more time to wait. Let's go right now! If you're goin', get your ass in the car now!" Chuck said as he turned and started toward the Pontiac.

She called after him, "Let me get my purse and lock the door. I'm coming with you."

She hurried to the passenger's side of the car. "Throw that baseball bat into the backseat so it will be out of your way," a smug Chuck ordered.

She did as he commanded. They were off to the party. They were each pleased with their individual accomplishment. Her accomplishment was that she was on the date with the handsome Chuck. His was that he had his prize pig for the party. They were off to St. Umblers.

While that was occurring in the country, CJ and Dion gathered the men together outside the Scout hut. CJ told them, "Chuck is going to come running in here shortly thinking this is a pig party. Dion and I had decided he had a real ringer so we thought it would be good to set him up. Perhaps he'll gain a little humility from this. Maybe afterward he won't always have to tell us how good he is and his are."

Dion continued." We want you all to be seated with your girlfriends when Chuck walks in the door. As soon as he gets inside John and Vance are going to block the door so he can't get back out. He is going to know he has been had. CJ is immediately going to ask everyone who thinks Chuck is the winner to stand up. If you think, Chuck has the prize pig please stand and ask your date to stand. We think it will be unanimous. Donald is going to hand him the prize money at that time. Please don't tell your dates what is going on until after Donald hands Chuck the money."

Everyone went inside and sat down to await Chuck's arrival. They had a short wait. Chuck came rushing through the door towing his date in his right hand. He was so eager that he didn't even see who was in the audience until he heard CJ say, "All those who think that Chuck is the winner please stand up."

He watched still filled with excitement as everyone stood up almost in unison. Only then did he see that everyone else in the room was dressed up and each guy had his best looking date with him. His excitement turned to horror as Donald handed him the prize money. He dropped the money and grabbed his date's left hand saying, "Let's get out of here. Some pig party this turned out to be! Y'all are awful!"

At that moment, his date realized what had just happened. She was supposed to have been and as it turns out she was Chuck's ringer for a pig party. She was embarrassed. As she started out the door behind Chuck, her embarrassment turned to full-fledged anger. Her anger only multiplied when she remembered how Chuck had tricked her into leaving home before she was ready. She realized he had wanted her to look as bad as possible. He had succeeded, but she was going to make him regret it.

When she reached the car, she opened the passenger's door. Instead of getting into the car, she pulled the back of the passenger's seat forward. She reached into the backseat and pulled out that baseball bat which Chuck had instructed her to put there. "Chuck I'm going to get you!" she shouted as she cleared the door with the baseball bat.

Some of the occupants of the Scout hut had already started to exit to watch Chuck's departure. When the others heard the shouting, they too came out to see what was going on. To their surprise, they saw Chuck's date chasing him with the baseball bat. She soon decided she was not going to catch Chuck as he was too fast for her. She was getting winded from the chase. She started walking slowly back toward the car dragging the baseball bat behind her. She never saw the group assembled outside the Scout hut.

When she saw Chuck's car, she was spurred by a new burst of energy. She put the baseball bat on her right shoulder. "Chuck, I think you're gonna wanta see this," she drawled with a deep rural southern accent.

Chuck did not respond. He just moved a little farther away from the baseball bat and the mad woman wielding it. He was surprised to hear a loud WAP behind him. Chuck then heard WAP, WAP, WAP before he could turn around. When he finally did turn, he was horrified at what he saw. There was his date, repeatedly slamming his baseball bat into the hood and fenders of his car. All of the people from the party were merely standing and watching instead of trying to stop her.

He shouted at the top of his lungs, "Stop that! You're ruining my car! There wont no reason to do that! Stop it now!"

She did stop. Her stopping was totally independent of his shouted command. She stopped because the baseball bat splintered in her hands. She had nothing left to continue her assault on the car. She was exhausted. She finally sat down in the passenger's seat and started crying uncontrollably.

The other girls gathered around her and made an effort to console her. They let her know that they did not know what was going on in advance. She knew from their respectful silence that they understood. More importantly, she knew that they really cared about her as a person. They finally comforted her to the point she calmed down.

Connie Sue gently reached over and took the shattered baseball bat from her hands. She asked politely, "Honey what is your name?"

The girl muttered an inaudible response, "#@$!%^& or some other phrase that was less than lady-like." It did not matter. No one was going to invade her emotions to ask again. They had bonded right then and there.

Cherry joined in using her typical understated wisdom saying, "I guess you just needed a better baseball bat."

"Chuck, you get your sorry ass over here and take this young lady home!" Faye said with compassion for her fellow female.

Chuck did as he was ordered.

As Chuck drove his badly dented car out of the parking lot, Connie Sue offered the ladies some sage advice. "Girls you had better stay away from Chuck. He will go straight from adolescence to adultery by way of marriage."

Only Chuck and his date know what happened on the trip to her house. No one ever inquired. Chuck remained out of sight for the rest of the weekend and to the extent possible the next week.

That event was over, never to be forgotten.

CHATER NINETEEN

OFF TO CAROLINA BEACH

REESE PULLED INTO the parking lot with the top down on his shiny new white convertible with red vinyl interior. He alit from his car and joined the conversation. "Tomorrow's Friday. Let's get a group together and go to Carolina Beach for the weekend," he said as he straightened his glasses on his face.

Tea was first to answer, "You know we've been planning a party at the Frat House tomorrow night and to go to the Lake on Saturday night." Tea's comment reflected the fact that he did sometimes not handle change well.

Reese said without recognizing that situation, "You know going to Carolina Beach would be a change. We would meet some new people. New women. We would do some different things. We could still go shaggin' there."

"That sounds great to me. I would love to go to Carolina Beach. Does anybody else want to go? What time do you want to leave, Reese?" Cosmo said,

"I'll be ready as soon as I get off work at three," Reese responded. "Who else wants to go?" It was soon established that Dion, Warren and Toney were ready to go. Once they joined in, Tea decided he would go as well; after all, he was not one to miss a party.

"We would have to take two cars. If you can drive, so can I. That would put three people in each car," Cosmo said.

"Will I guess we are set and ready to go then? Since Tea and Warren live close to each other, I'll pick the two of them up between three-fifteen and three-thirty," Reese said.

"I'll pick Toney and Dion and up between three and three-thirty. We'll meet you here at three forty-five and we can ride down as a caravan. I'll follow you," Cosmo said.

"Good. We'll go by the ABC store on the way. We should be able to be there by six-thirty or seven at the latest," Reese said. "I'll see you tomorrow afternoon. I'm going to go home and pack. Tea, you and Warren be ready when I get there" Reese said before he left.

The others talked for a little while longer. They too decided it was time to go home and pack. Toney said, "I'll take Tea and Warren home."

"I'll take Dion home. I'll come pick you up a little after three tomorrow," Cosmo said to Toney.

At three forty-five, the next afternoon the group met at the appointed parking lot. Without further delay, they left for the ABC store. When they arrived, Reese and Dion went in to buy liquor for their respective cars. They both carried on some small talk with Mr. Wilson as they collected and paid for their provisions. They drove to the convenience store. In keeping with their ritual, they bought cups, ice, mixers and chasers.

They were off to Carolina Beach. They broke open the whiskey as soon as they were out of town.

Warren was a big guy. He was about six feet, three inches tall. He was sitting in the backseat of Reese's new convertible where he could stretch out more than he would have been able to in the front. He was two years younger than Dion, Tea and Cosmo. Since he had recently graduated from high school, he had little experience with alcohol.

Tea looked back and saw that Warren was losing his coordination. Tea said to him, "It didn't take you very long to take drunk. Did it?"

"I'm pretty well on my way. I think I'm going to take commode hugging drunk," Warren responded.

Reese looked in the rearview mirror and said to Warren, "Just take it a little bit easy back there. Walk 'em slow for a little while. We don't want you to pass out before we get there; you are too big for us to carry."

"Don't you worry about me. I can handle it," Warren said, followed by a drunken giggle.

About twenty minutes later Tea looked back again and saw Warren turning green. About that time, Warren put his left hand in front of his mouth. He was still holding his drink in his dominant right hand. "Reese I think you'd better pullover pretty quickly. I think Warren is getting a little bit sick," Tea said.

Reese started to pull over. Too late. His lunch exploded from Warren's mouth. It came out as four discrete high-pressure streams between his fingers and one waterfall behind his palm into his lap and onto the seat. Warren was swimming in it before Reese could get the car pulled over. In fact, he had finished heaving by the time Reese had brought the car to a stop.

It was a good thing that Reese too was lit. As a result, he took the setback reasonably calmly. "Let's go on to the beach. Warren can clean up the car there. He can sit in it till then," Reese said calmly.

Cosmo had pulled off the highway right behind Reese. Reese informed them, "Let's go on. It's just Warren spewing in the backseat."

They reentered their cars and once again were off to Carolina Beach. Warren passed out in Reese's backseat.

They found a place to stay. They managed to get Warren out Reese's car and into a bed where he slept for a couple of hours while the others went out to dinner. They brought him back a chicken salad sandwich which he devoured in about two bites.

They, with the exception of Warren who was still drunk, sat around and had a drink or two each. By bedtime, they were all toasted again. Dion, Cosmo, Reese and Toney decided they were going shaggin'. Tea and Warren were just going to hang there at the house for a little while.

The shaggers left. Tea picked up a paper bag with his four bottles of vodka in it. He said to Warren, "Let's go for a walk and have a drink down on the beach. We just have to cross the street and walk between those houses over there to get on the beach."

"OK. I would like to do that. I don't know where my liquor is," Warren said.

"You can have some of mine tonight. But you have to repay it tomorrow," Tea said making a benevolent gesture. They started out the door. They crossed the street and walked out onto the beach. They sat down and sipped vodka from the bottle for several hours. As Warren had forecast, he got blitzed. Again, Tea was right with him. They were far from a pretty sight.

Tea finally said, "I think I need to go get in the bed."

It was all Warren could do to mutter, "Me too." They started their trek back to the house. They were stumbling and staggering along the way. They made it over the sidewalk on to the street and successfully crossed over the street. In front of the house when Tea went to step up on to the sidewalk, his step came up a little bit short. He tripped and stumbled but managed to avoid falling. He turned back into the street as he maintained his posture. However, he was less fortunate with respect to the paper bag that he was carrying. He lost control of the bag which fell into the street with a series of explosions resulting from the breaking of glass. Warren turned and sat down on the sidewalk beside the broken bottles. Tea dropped to his hands and knees and was feverishly trying to rake the flowing clear streams of vodka back into the bag which was filled with broken bottles. As he attempted to do so, he was cutting his hands on the pieces of glass that were lying in the streams of vodka. Those disparate streams were commingling into a single river at the curb. That river slowly ran off to Tea's left and under Warren's legs toward a drain at the corner of the street.

Warren sat with his hands cupping his chin crying. He was repeatedly saying through his tears, "I'm sorry Tea! Tea, I'm so sorry!"

That scene continued in the pale yellow light of the moon for several minutes before an elderly black gentleman came walking down the sidewalk. He had watched the events unfold from about one hundred feet away. He stopped and at first merely looked as Tea was still trying to corral the residual vodka most of which had escaped. "Son, I don't think I can help you. Tell me what the problem is?" He said even though it was obvious to him.

Tea looked up at him with Tears streaming down his face and said, "I can't get my liquor back into the bag."

The old man scratched his chin with his left hand and made

a sagacious proclamation, "I'm sorry but you might as well give it up. This is a lost cause."

When the old man's words sank in, Tea started crying. He sat down in the street watching the last of the vodka disappear and cried like a baby overdue for feeding.

After a while, the two of them continued to stagger toward the house. They were still crying when the other four came back. They were questioned as to why they were crying.

"Tea, let's go back out there. We may still be able to save some of that vodka. I think I can do it." Toney said.

"It's no use. The old man already told me it was a lost cause because it'd been a long time and the vodka had already run off. I'm just going to go to bed. I hope that I can get some more tomorrow. That will mean that I can't eat, but that's a small sacrifice to have something to drink," Tea said.

"I have never heard such a sad story in my life," Reese said.

With that piece of wisdom in mind, they all went to bed.

As soon as they were out of bed the next morning, Dion announced, "I'm having a hair of the dog that bit me for a remedy." He poured some vodka into a glass. He then added red vegetable juice cocktail, Worcestershire sauce and lemon juice to make a Bloody Mary. Cosmo gave Tea some of his vodka so he too could make a Bloody Mary. Warren found his bag of liquor and fixed himself a drink. They had officially started drinking for the day at ten-thirty in the morning.

Cosmo was serious about drinking that particular day. He took fully drunk by three in the afternoon. At that time, he decided he would take a nap. When he awakened, he had a major hangover and headache even though he was still under the influence. Everyone except Toney had gone out to the beach where they continued to enjoy matching their peers.

"Toney, I have a monster headache. I'm going to take a couple of those seltzer tablets to see if they will make it better. Do you see a clean glass anywhere?" Cosmo said.

Toney didn't answer. Cosmo looked for clean glass without finding one. He decided he had the solution. He plopped two of those seltzer tablets into his mouth and swallowed them using just a few drops of a caramel colored carbonated soft drink to wash they down. That was after all, water he reasoned. He looked at the bottle from which he had taken the tablets where the instructions said to use eight ounces of water. He drank what he thought was eight ounces of the soft drink. In a fraction of a second the seltzer tablets were fizzing and bubbling in his stomach. He started belching. He had absolutely no control of the belching as it continued. His stomach was feeling really bloated and tight from all the gas being released from the fizzing tablets.

"Help! This gas is just filling me up and choking me," Cosmo called to Toney.

Toney staggered in asking, "Cosmo what did you do?"

Cosmo tried his best to explain to Toney what he had done between belches. "All I did was plopped to those seltzer tablets into my mouth and drink eight ounces of soda to dissolve them like the instructions said. My stomach really hurts! You had to get me to a doctor! Hurry!"

"Where are your car keys?" Toney asked.

As Cosmo held them out he said, "Right here they are. You drive. I'm in too much pain."

Toney drove around for a short while looking for a doctor's office that was open on Saturday. As they were passing the hospital, Cosmo said through the belches, "Take me to the emergency room here. Hurry up! I'm in great pain. I hurt."

Toney turned into the hospital. He found an entrance and took Cosmo in. Toney explained the problem to the nurse on duty. Cosmo was fortunate that he only had to wait about ten minutes for a treatment room to open up. A nurse told Toney, "You need to wait here. I don't think you'll be waiting very long." She took Cosmo back for treatment.

Toney waited about forty-five minutes though it seemed like hours. The doctor came out and said, "Toney? Toney? Are you still here?"

"That'd be me," Toney replied as he walked toward the doctor.

"Son, we had to pump your friend's stomach out. He's pretty sore right now. He's also drunk. I have told him we need to keep in here overnight to make sure that he doesn't have any complications. You can come back and get him tomorrow morning after eleven," the Doctor said.

Toney said, "Okay," as he wobbled toward the door.

The doctor called after him, "Son, it looks to me like you need a driver. Do you want us to get you a taxi?"

"I drove in here so I guess I can drive back. And I'll drive here tomorrow morning to pick Cosmo up."

Cosmo's friends arrived at the hospital to get him about eleven-thirty the next morning. Cosmo was still having pains his stomach when he was released. He asked Dion and Toney "Can one of you drive? I hurt way too bad to be sitting under the wheel of the car. I want to get in the backseat and stretch out."

Each responded that he was capable of driving. Cosmo asked Toney, "How about giving Dion the keys and let him drive?"

Toney complied. He assumed the shotgun position. Cosmo stretched out on the backseat. Dion drove them to St. Umblers stopping only for lunch along the way. Reese followed close behind.

CHAPTER TWENTY

THE FRAT HOUSE RAID

ONE FRIDAY NIGHT a fine party going on at the frat house. The house was full. There must have been twenty to thirty young people partying in the yard. Everyone was having a grand time. The sound of Beach Music could be heard emanating from the record on the stereo in the house. There was dancing in the house. There was dancing on the porch. There was dancing on the grass in the yard.

The party had been going on for about an hour at seven-thirty. Someone called out, "Company's coming. It's a black and white car that I don't recognize as belonging to any of our group."

Another responded, "They will be welcome. I hope they have come to party." A number of the young people stopped and watched the dust flying up behind the car as it approached the house.

In a few seconds, the black and white car came to a sudden stop at the entrance to the front yard. A big man in a green sheriff's department uniform stepped out of the car. He was about six foot, four inches tall. He easily weighed two hundred and eighty pounds, maybe three hundred. He had a huge Billy stick slung from a strap on his wide black leather belt. He started ambling toward the house.

"Who's responsible for this place?" He asked in a deep gruff voice speaking to no one in particular as he did.

There was a muffled, "It's Hoss Miller!" coming from two or three people. Even without that information, most of them probably recognized Sheriff Miller. He was not an easy man to miss with his stature. Hoss Miller had a reputation of being a very tough lawman. He was the all-business, no-nonsense type.

Dion, Tea and Vance stepped forward. Vance said, "I guess we can speak for the group Mr. Miller."

"Now, I want you boys to listen very carefully to what I'm going to tell you. Especially, you Vance, because I know your daddy real good. I know your daddy would be real upset if he heard from me Dion. I can get you too Tea. Some of the people out this way have been complaining that there's too much partying and too much noise out here. They don't much like liquor being out here either," the Sheriff said.

He was poised to continue, when Vance interrupted him, "Sheriff, there isn't anybody who lives close enough to hear any noise here and we keep the partying right here in the yard and in the house. We don't bother anybody. There isn't anybody who lives with a mile of here."

The Sheriff's face turned brilliant red. It was clear he was upset at being talked back to. "Don't you sass me none boy. Your folks might put up with that, but I don't! I'll have you locked you up in a minute. I don't like me no smart Alec. You just say one more word and I'm taking you to jail right now! Tonight!" The sheriff looked around to see who was in the group. He stopped to see if he recognized each of them as he scanned. Then he said, "This is my last warning to all of you. If I have to come back out here, I'm taking the lot of you to jail. All of you mark my words carefully. At some time, you are going to screw up and I'm going to be back. I'm going to enjoy arresting you. You'd best not be a comin' back out here no more because I'm gonna git you shore as you do. You hear me now?"

He turned and strode slowly with a triumphant air back to the car. He had shown the group who was in charge. He turned the car around in front yard. He floored the car as he started out the drive its tires spinning and kicking up dust and dirt as it threw rocks back toward the house. Fortunately, no one was hurt. None of the cars was hit by the flying rocks either. Then faster than he had come, he was gone. He had come and gone in a span of about ten minutes. Hoss Miller had left his warning. Like the famous World War II General McArthur, Hoss Miller promised he would return.

Hoss Miller's visit put a temporary damper on the party. However, it only took five to ten minutes to get the party back to its previous level of activity and pleasure. The party continued for a short while and then started breaking up as the participants started leaving for the Amory and other venues.

"Boy, Hoss Miller was acting like some redneck sheriff tonight," Dion said.

"He was as red as a fire truck," Tea said.

Things returned to normal at the frat house as the days passed. The parties recovered to their former status as those who had been frightened away gradually returned when Hoss Miller did not return. Apparently, the youth of St. Umblers thought that the Hoss Miller episode was behind them and that they would not be bothered by him again.

One fine bright sunny yellow Saturday afternoon Dion

went out to the frat house with the two young men from Four Oaks. They picked Dion up around three-forty. Charles and George wanted a chance to do some early drinking because they had a mandatory family engagement that evening. They also knew that Dion had some fresh grain alcohol that he had made. They were certain that he would be willing to share it. On that score, they were correct.

They were drinking before four. Charles and George had picked up some clear citrus soft drinks to mix with their alcohol. Dion was drinking his over ice with a little water. It did not take very long for the three of them to show signs of their efforts. When that occurred, their conversation turned quite philosophical.

It happened that the three of them had the same favorite snack. That snack was those long crunchy irregular shaped almost pretzel-like baked sticks. They were a yellow orange color because they were cheese flavored. Or, were they orange yellow? The pieces were covered in a light yellowish orange powder that came off on the fingers when one picked up the pieces. They were simply delicious.

Dion pulled a large bag of the snack from a classic brown paper bag. "I see you have fine cheeses," Charles said.

George slapped his hands together as if applauding and said, "Those are fine cheeses indeed!"

Dion opened the bag and put it on the table. "Help yourself. Please have some. Just don't try to eat them all. I must have some."

Charles and George joined Dion in enjoying the magnificent snack. They continued drinking with their delicacy.

"About all a man needs is some good liquor and some fine cheeses," Charles said.

George nodded in agreement.

Dion looked pensive for a few seconds before he said, "Indeed, a man does need some good liquor and fine cheeses. Fine women complete the mix.   Speaking of fine women, Charles, where is Joan these days? I haven't seen her in quite a while. She hasn't been at the Lake in weeks."

George spoke before Charles could respond, "I hear you are goo goo-eyed over that girl. I hear you call her Lungs. Why is that?" He giggled.

"Because she has great big boobs," Charles said to George.

"Now that you mentioned it, she does have enough lung capacity to blow up a two man rubber raft," George responded with a big laugh.

Charles looked at Dion and said, "This guy that she had dated a few times a couple of years ago has come home from the Marines and has been occupying her time. It's a real shame because he is quite a redneck. However, he has a fast car and some money. I haven't seen her myself in several weeks."

"He sounds like a pretty lucky guy to me," Dion replied.

"Yes sir! Fine liquor, fine cheeses and fine women. That's the right prescription alright. I think that's what I want! We need to obtain all three. Here's to Lungs wherever she may be," George said.

By six, some of the other members of the frat house had begun to arrive. Charles and George were showing effects of the alcohol. They were reluctant to do so but they had to leave or incur their parents' wrath for missing their evening social.

Charles and George left saying to everyone they met on their way to the car, "Fine liquor, fine cheeses and fine women."

The party that night at the frat house was the best in weeks. There were about fifty to sixty revelers present.

At about seven-twenty, someone on the porch yelled out, "There is a whole line of cars turning off the highway and coming up the drive."

Some of them stepped on the porch to be able to see what was going on. "There are five Sheriff's Department cars coming up here," one male said.

"This is going to be trouble!" a girl yelped.

"I'm getting out of here," a young man said.

"Let's hit the corn field! They can't catch us in there!" Someone else yelled.

As soon as that statement was uttered, there was a steady stream of youth running into the cornfield through the tall bright green leaves. The corn was still a couple of weeks from having ripe produce. Nonetheless, it was tall enough to hide them.

Hoss Miller led his caravan of patrol cars into the yard. He surveyed the situation. When he saw only Dion, Tea, Vance and Little Whittington, disappointment claimed his face. "I told you I'd be back. I'm going to shut this place down. We are not going to have people like you in this neighborhood." He strode toward the front porch. Then it was like a bolt of lightning had hit him right on the pointed top of his head. He perked up a little as he asked, "Where is everybody else? There's way too many cars here for it just to be the four of you here. I told you I was going to get you. Now, you're mine."

Suddenly, it dawned on him there should more people. He took another look around.

"Where is everybody else? Whir's the rest of yore buddies? Hoozinair? Ya'll get'em on out here. You hear?" Hoss growled as he gestured toward the house with his head.

"What are you talking about, Sheriff Miller?" Vance asked.

"Don't you try to be smart with me, boy. I'm going to take

pleasure in calling yore daddy and tell him you're in jail," Hoss Miller replied. "Now whir's everybody else?" He demanded impatiently.

Little Whittington giggled. "You scared them so bad coming up her I guess they're all over the county,"

Hoss Miller turned to Little Whittington. "What do you mean?"

"When we saw your cars turning off the highway, everybody else took off running all directions," Little Whittington answered.

Hoss looked like the kid whose first new balloon had just been popped at the County fair.

Tea looked at him and asked, "Sheriff Miller, would you rather have us out there on the highway drinking or have us do it here where we are not harming anybody?"

One of Sheriff Miller's deputies who was standing behind him spoke up, "That sounds like a pretty fair question you know. What you think?"

Sheriff Miller looked at the deputy and growled, "You taking their side against me?"

"No sir Sheriff. I just think it's safer to have them here than to have them on the highway drinking," the deputy answered.

Hoss Miller looked defeated. He turned around and visually interrogated the other three deputies looking for support. When he didn't find any from them, he finally said in a low voice, "Let's get out of here." The five lawmen turned and walked to their cars without saying another word. There were no more harsh admonitions or warnings coming from Hoss Miller. He and his deputies just left slowly and quietly. They would never come to the frat house again.

CHAPTER TWENTY-ONE

SAVED MY LIFE

ON THURSDAY OF THAT week, Dion turned twenty-one. Tea had turned twenty-one some four months earlier; therefore, he had been buying the liquor. On Saturday night when they were on their way to the Lake, they stopped the ABC store. Dion went in with Tea to make the purchase. With that being, a special occasion Dion decided to buy some more expensive liquor then his normal.

When he walked up to the counter and put his purchase down, Mr. Wilson looked up and saw him for the first time. He said, "Dion, I haven't seen you in here in months. How have you been?"

"I have been doing just great thank you Mr. Wilson. How have you been? How are Mrs. Wilson and the boys?" Dion replied.

"You're buying some fancy liquor. Is tonight a special occasion?"

"Yes sir. I just turned twenty-one and I'm going to celebrate. I thought it would be nice to have something a little better than normal to drink,"

"I'm happy for your cause to celebrate. Happy birthday," Mr. Wilson said in a dry, emotionless tone. Mr. Wilson looked at Dion with disappointment in his eyes. He chose not to say anything about Dion duping him in the past. It was clear that it was on his mind because his expression revealed disappointment.

Dion said as he walked out the door, "Thank you, Mr. Wilson. Good night."

Mr. Wilson looked at Dion without saying anything. He made a feeble wave with his right hand. He had the look of betrayal on his face.

Tea picked up the supplies for himself, Cosmo and The Gator. Among the bottles, he bought was one for emergency use. After buying the regular stock, he only had enough money to buy a bottle of Cream of Kentucky. He bought it.

The two of them walked back to the car together. Tea told Cosmo and The Gator about Mr. Wilson's response to Dion's being twenty-one.

"I hereby invoke drinking speed," Dion announced.

"Dick, that's a real good idea," The Gator said.

"I shall obey your wish, sir," Cosmo said.

After they had each had a drink or two, Mr. Wilson's response became quite a cause for laughter among the group. In fact, the story was retold and laughed at again many times on the way to the Lake. Every time silence filled the car, someone would break the ice by retelling the story of the look on Mr. Wilson's face. Then they would all break out anew in laughter. It always seemed funniest the when The Gator would growl in a low voice, "Mr. Wilson, I'm celebrating my twenty-first birthday."

A few miles before they arrived at the Lake Dion said to Tea, "What was that emergency bottle you bought?"

"That is Cream of Kentucky," Tea said.

"I suggest that we go ahead and open it. We can drink some of it and save our better stuff for later," Dion said.

"I've never tried Cream of Kentucky before. It was the cheapest thing in the store and I had enough money left to buy it. Let's give it a try now and execute your plan to save our regular liquor for later," Tea said.

Tea opened the pint of Cream of Kentucky. He took a drink and handed the bottle to Dion. "This stuff is the most horrible tasting liquor I ever had," Tea said with a decided grimace on his face.

Dion had already taken a drink before Tea finished that proclamation. "I think you are way wrong, sir. This stuff is worst than horrible. It makes kerosene taste good. In fact, it could stand a good shot of kerosene to improve it. Moon shiners do it all the time," Dion said. Dion handed the open bottle back to Tea.

Tea took another drink. "This is truly horrible. It is the worst mess I have ever had. I think we should throw this stuff out of the car," Tea said.

"That would certainly go against tradition. It would be the first time we ever threw away any liquor. As you wish, sir," Dion said.

Tea started to throw the Cream of Kentucky out the window.

"Wait a minute! Don't throw that bottle out the window let me try it," Cosmo interceded.

"When you get that terrible taste in your mouth just remember you ask for it," Tea said as he handed the bottle to Cosmo.

Cosmo took a small sip. He nearly gagged from the taste. "You were right. This is terrible! You want me to throw the bottle out?" Cosmo said through choking and coughing which was partially for effect and partially the realistic result of drinking such a terrible beverage.

The Gator sat quietly with the big white-toothed grin on his face. "If you think it's that terrible, I know it wont no reason for me to try," he said.

"No, I should bear that burden. Hand me the bottle and I'll do the dastardly deed. I expect this to be only liquor that I ever throw away," Tea said.

Cosmo handed the bottle back to Tea. Tea threw the bottle out the window with great ceremony stating, "With this rejection I promise never again to buy or drink Cream of Kentucky. Be gone foul liquor. Be gone!"

The remainder of that pint of Cream of Kentucky was indeed the only liquor that any of that group ever knowingly threw away.

They arrived at the Lake and assumed their typical parking space. It was almost as though the space were reserved for them. They sat and finished their drinks while carrying on guy conversation which was usually centered on women. Before they went inside, they honored their tradition by placing their reserve bottles where they were easily retrieved. They went in and enjoyed the musical stylings of Mary Wells.

They danced the night away having a great time. While they were dancing, Neil, AKA Yard Dog, spent his evening sitting on the front edge of the bandstand holding on to the microphone cord and staring up at Ms. Wells as she sang. Neil did not move the entire evening. Nor did he speak; that was most unusual for Neil who was quite an accomplished talker. He was blitzed and mesmerized by Ms. Wells.

Sometime after the break, Cosmo went missing. "Dick, I don't know where Cosmo is. I guess he's laid out in the parking lot," The Gator said to Dion. He continued, "Dick, do you think we should go out there and have a look?"

"No. Cosmo can take care of himself. Let's wait a little while and see if we see him. If not, one of us can go out and have a look around the car," Dion said.

When another half hour to forty-five minutes passed without any sign of Cosmo, Dion went over to Tea who was dancing with Kristen. She lived farther from the Lake then did most of the people in attendance. She was about two inches shorter than Tea. She was perky and very attractive. Her blonde hair was just shorter than shoulder length. Her hair was a little thin and fine. She wore it straight without bangs. Dion and Tea had met her earlier at OD. They had occasion to make her acquaintance when they stopped another young man from driving off with her purse. After that episode, Dion and Tea danced with her the most of the rest of the evening. That was her first trip to the Lake. She had come because Dion and Tea had raved about how much fun it was. She had to see for herself.

"Have you seen Cosmo since the break?" Dion asked Tea.

"No. He was still out at the car when I left to come in," Tea said.

"He was still out there when I left to come in too. Cosmo was smashed. That's the drunkest I've seen him in a long time," Dion said.

Tea danced two more songs with Kristen. Then he said to Dion, "I think I'll go out and check on Cosmo." He turned to Kristen and asked, "Do you wanna walk out to the car with me to check on Cosmo?"

"I don't know Cosmo. I think I'll stay here because Paul asked me to dance with him. This is a good time for me to do that. I'm certain he thinks he's been waiting long enough for me. I'll see you when you come back," Kristen responded.

"Well, I'll see you in a few minutes," Tea said. With that, he turned and started toward the door. Tea walked up to the car. Cosmo had the engine running and was lying on the ground with the exhaust pipe stuck in his mouth. He was sucking on it as hard as he could.

"Cosmo what are you doing?" Tea asked.

"I'm going to keel myself. Then I'm going to keel you," Cosmo responded.

"What is the matter?" Tea asked.

Cosmo came as close to jumping up as he possibly could in his drunken condition. He managed to get on his feet. He took a swing at Tea. That swing missed by a couple of feet. "You SOB. I'm going to keel you." Cosmo said as he staggered around.

"Then go ahead," Tea said.

"You SOB. You drank my liquor. I know it was you that drank it because it's gone. It's not behind the wheel where I put it. It wont nobody else out here. Nobody else would have done it. You drank it! I know you drank it! How come you'd do such a thing to a friend? You will never do it again," Cosmo said.

Tea started looking under the car for Cosmo's bottle. Cosmo lowered himself back onto the ground and resumed sucking on the exhaust pipe. "I'm going to keel myself! Then I'm going to keel you! You drank my liquor," Cosmo screamed.

At that time Tea held up a pint of Lord Calvert saying, "Cosmo you put your bottle behind the wrong wheel. I have found a pint of the Lord Calvert! Here it is! Nobody has drunk any of it. It hasn't even been opened!"

As Tea came around to the rear of the car, Cosmo was once

again struggling off the ground. Cosmo looked at the bottle of Lord Calvert. Then he threw his arms around Tea crying, "You saved my life! You saved my life!"

Tea and Cosmo went back into the pavilion. Tea had time to shag to a couple more songs with Kristen before the evening ended. Cosmo spent the rest of the evening leaning against a wall for mutual support. He never did drink any of that Lord Calvert that night. He didn't need to.

Dion drove Cosmo's car home. "I'm seeing four lanes in the highway. I'm going to try an experiment. I wonder if it will work. June told me that she covers her right eye with her right hand so that she sees only two lanes when she is driving. I have to try it."

"You know it just might work, Dick," Gator laughed.

"If it works for you, then I'm going to have to remember to try that sometime," Cosmo said.

As Dion should have already known, the experiment did not work. He still saw more lanes of the highway than actually existed.

Dion dropped The Gator off first. He drove the few blocks to Tea's house.

When Tea alighted from the car, Cosmo opened the right front passenger's door and staggered out. Cosmo started crying again. Cosmo threw his arms around Tea's neck and said through his sobs, "You saved my life! You saved my life!"

CHAPTER TWENTY-TWO

ONE BIG 'UN

SOME OF THE ST. UMBLERS group decided to go to Durham to see James Brown on Friday night. Six of them crammed into Cosmo's car. In addition to Cosmo, there were Dion, Cherry, Connie Sue, Gator and Tea. They indulged in a libation on the way.

James Brown was performing in an old facility where he was at ground level. That was due to the fact that there was no bandstand or stage. James Brown lived up to his self-proclaimed reputation of being "The hardest working man in show business" that night. He was singing, screaming and dancing all over the floor. He was constantly moving through and interacting with the crowd.

He came upon the St. Umblers group and stopped to sing a few bars to the group. As he was singing, he broke into his one footed shuffles to the left which he followed by reversing that and going on one foot to the right. To his surprise and the surprise of most of the people around Dion immediately mirrored his dance. As James Brown went to the left, Dion faced him to his right. When James Brown went back to his right

Dion reversed to his left. Dion was as agile and quick as James Brown matching him step for step.

James Brown was so taken back by that event that he remained there and sang several songs for the St. Umblers group. They tried to join in and sing with him. Nobody will ever accuse them of putting on a great or even a good performance singing with James Brown. They knew the words but had a hard time singing on time or on key. Tea and Connie Sue were most vociferous with their singing. Tea was singing discordantly. Tea was just being Tea. Connie Sue actually sang pretty well. Her soft high-pitched voice produced an interesting contrasting harmony with James Brown's deep gravelly voice. Cherry sang along quietly so as not to be noticed. Staying behind the limelight was commonplace for her. Cosmo was the only one who refrained from singing.

As James Brown started to walk away, The Gator asked him, "Dick would you play 'Papa's Got a Brand New Bag?'" James Brown said yes. He did after "This is a Man's World."

It was not the Lake yet the group had a great time. That was a rare occasion to see James Brown in person. They spent the night shaggin' and singing. They knew how to party as James Brown had learned when he came upon them.

The following night they were back to their normal haunt. It was a hopping night at the Lake. It was the last Saturday night of the month. The party was enjoined. The dancing was great. There were kids are from all over eastern North Carolina. There were even some from as far away as Virginia Beach.

The group that traveled together from St. Umblers was different than the one from the night before. Whereas Cosmo and Gator went to the James Brown concert the night before, they did not go to the Lake that night. They were replaced by Glenn and Harry. Glenn drove the group to the Lake. The

SWINGIN' MEDALLIONS provided the entertainment that night.

The St. Umblers group knew most of the people present. After all, they had been coming to the Lake for some time. Jan was there. She was wearing a black outfit which was her fashion signature. Jan's friend Annette was with her. Howard was there with his beautiful red-haired bride Debbie. Jan and Debbie were great friends. Make that best friends. The four of them joined the St. Umblers group. They knew how to have a good time.

The evening ended without regret. They returned to St. Umblers in Glenn's car. They were quite satisfied with the evening.

Glenn was driving at normal highway speed. He was weaving a little on the highway. While he had been drinking, he was nowhere close to as gone as some of the group were on many nights on their way home from the Lake.

About five miles before they reached St. Umblers a highway patrol car appeared from nowhere. It fell in behind Glenn with its blue lights flashing. Glenn pulled over onto the shoulder of the highway. He waited in dread as the patrolman came up to the window.

"Oh no! This is not going to be good. We've seen this before. Haven't we, Dion, Tea? That turned out real ugly and I have a feeling this will too," Glenn lamented.

"We should least try to stay out of the county jail this time," Dion said.

"Son, let me see your driver's license," the patrolman demanded in a calm voice.

Glenn handed the patrolman his driver's license. Then he asked, "Officer I know I wasn't speeding."

"That's correct son. That's not why I pulled you over. You

were weaving back there on the highway. I smell alcohol on your breath. I pulled you over because I thought you were driving under the influence. I need you to step out of the car and come with me for a sobriety test. Actually, in your case I think it is a drunkenness test," the patrolman said.

Glenn did as he was told. He followed the patrolman to the back of his car. He knew what was coming. He had been through the drill before.

"Glenn I want you to walk the way I do," the patrolman said as he demonstrated walking placing one foot immediately in front of the other.

Glenn tried the exercise. He successfully made five steps before he faltered and staggered slightly.

"That's enough. You were definitely driving under the influence. Let's go back to the car. I'm going to have to write you a ticket. Is there anybody in your car you trust to drive it? If not, I'll have to call your folks to come get you. I can't let you drive home," the patrolman said.

"I'm sure Dion can drive us home safely," Glenn said.

The patrolman leaned over to look into the car. "Which one of you is Dion?"

"I am, sir," Dion answered respectfully.

"I need you to step out here," the patrolman said. Dion complied. He walked around the car to where the patrolman and Glenn were standing.

"Would you be comfortable driving Glenn's car to St. Umblers?" The patrolman asked.

"Yes sir. I would," Dion answered matter-of-factly.

"Are you willing to take a sobriety test to see if you are capable of driving?" The patrolman asked.

"Yes sir. I think I can pass that test," Dion said confidently.

The patrolman repeated his demonstration on the sobriety

test for Dion's benefit. As soon as the patrolman turned around, Dion followed without hesitation or stumbling.

"Okay I'll let you drive this group to St. Umblers." He said as he turned to go to his car, "Wait here. I'm going to write Glenn a ticket for DUI."

"Damn! I sure don't need that officer. Is there anyway that you would not write that ticket," Glenn pleaded.

"No. I have to write you that DUI," the patrolman dead-panned as he flashed his ticket pad.

"Officer may I at least have a drink while you write that DUI?" Glenn asked nonchalantly.

"Of course not!" The patrolman barked.

"Why not? He wouldn't be driving and you've already said he is under the influence," Dion said.

That seemed to fluster the patrolman a little bit. "Because it just wouldn't be right," the patrolman answered.

"What would you do? Would you write him a ticket for driving more under the influence if he did have a drink? That wouldn't be right because he wouldn't even be driving. Is there even such a thing as driving more under the influence?" Dion said, applying logic.

"You have a point there I don't know of a law about driving more under the influence. I just cannot allow Glenn to have that drink," the patrolman said.

"What real recourse do you have if he does take a drink? He'll be sitting in his private car and therefore will not be subject to public drunkenness," Tea said.

The patrolman turned to Glenn and said, "If it's that big a deal, get in your car and have that drink. Just do it so I don't see you. I'm tired of this discussion. I'm going to go sit down in my car to write your DUI. You'll have to go to court about this. The date and location will be on the ticket."

Glenn sat down and started drinking. Dion glided behind the steering wheel. The patrolman wrote the DUI ticket and brought it to Glenn's car. The patrolman passed a ticket through the open driver's window to Dion who handed it to Glenn.

"You drive carefully and get these people straight home."

"Yes sir. I'll drive drinking speed the rest of the way," Dion said.

"Drinking speed? What is drinking speed? I've never heard of such a thing," puzzled the patrolman out loud.

"Drinking speed is forty-five miles per hour sir," Dion said.

Dion started the engine. He put the car in drive. He pulled the car back onto the highway. He drove them to St. Umblers. There was much conversation about the ticket and supporting Glenn in court over the next five miles. Each of the other five vowed be a witness for Glenn.

Dion drove them home. After he had dropped off the other four passengers, he asked Glenn, "What would you like to do about your car? Would you like me to drive home and then you drive home from my house? Would it be better for me to drive you home? I can walk home from there or I can drive your car home and bring it back later."

"I'm pretty messed up now. If it's all right with you, why don't you drive me home and take the car to your house. You can bring it back later. I'll call you when I get up. Daddy is not going to be happy about this," Glenn answered.

"That will be fine if it's all right with you. I hope I'll sleep till about ten-thirty or eleven," Dion said.

Dion drove Glenn home. " Just come over after lunch. We will pick up Tea and cruise Main," Glenn said.

Dion arrived at Glenn's house about one-thirty. They picked Tea up and cruised main for a couple hours.

"Daddy says he's going to get a lawyer to fight the DUI.

Are you willing to be witnesses in my defense?" Glenn said.

"You know we'll be there," Tea said.

"You can count on us," Dion said.

"It looks like I'll need all the help I can get," Glenn said.

"You can count on us to be there to support you. I'm sure that Harry, Cherry and Connie Sue will be right there," Tea said.

Glenn's father did hire an attorney. The attorney met with Glenn and the other five who were in the car. He exposed them to his strategy for the trial. He listened to what each of their testimonies was going to be. He advised each of them not to add any information in response to a question. He told them that it was best to say as little as possible.

The day of the trial came. Glenn was understandably nervous. The only witness that the prosecutor called was the highway patrolman.

"On the evening in question did you have occasion to stop the defendant's car?" The prosecutor asked the patrolman.

"Yes I did," the patrolman answered solemnly.

"What was your reason for stopping the defendant?" The prosecutor asked.

"I stopped him because he was weaving on the highway."

"What happened after you stopped the car?" The prosecutor asked.

"I asked the driver to step out of the car to take a sobriety test."

"Who was the driver?" The prosecutor asked.

"Him," the patrolman answered while pointing at Glenn.

"How did he do on the sobriety test?" The prosecutor asked.

The patrolman looked at Glenn and said "He successfully made five steps before he faltered and staggered on the next one."

"What did that mean?" The prosecutor asked.

"I concluded that he was drunk. I ask if anyone else could drive his car. He said yes that young man over there could do so," the patrolman answered pointing at Dion.

"How did you respond to that?" The prosecutor asked.

"I gave him the same sobriety test and he passed it."

The prosecutor's last question for the patrolman was, "Did anything out of the ordinary happen after that?"

"Yes sir. For the first time in my life, I was asked if it would be OK to have a drink while I wrote the DUI. That young man, Dion, who drove the car argued that there really would be no violation for that because I couldn't give him a driving more under the influence citation and that he would not be driving in any event. I told the defendant that he could take a drink as long as I didn't see it."

"I have no further questions Your Honor," the prosecutor said before turning to take his seat.

"Your witness," the Judge said to the defense attorney.

"I only have a couple of questions Your Honor," the defense attorney said.

He turned to the patrolman asked, "Do sober people ever fail the sobriety tests? Isn't it possible that Glenn stumbled on a rock since he only faltered on one step?"

"I don't think I've ever had a sober person fail the sobriety test. I guess it is possible for someone to stumble on a rock."

"How many steps did Dion take?" the defense attorney asked.

"I don't know for sure but it was about ten or twelve."

"So if you can take ten steps, you're sober. Is that correct?" The attorney asked.

"Not necessarily."

"How many steps do you have to take to be sober?" The attorney asked.

"I don't know if there is an exact number that make you pass for sober. But I smelled alcohol on his breath too."

"Because you smelled alcohol on his breath and he stumbled after five steps you concluded he was drunk. Is that correct?" The cross examination continued.

"Yes, that's correct."

"Did you smell alcohol Dion's breath?" The attorney asked.

"I did."

"Did you conclude that Dion was drunk or sober?" The attorney asked.

"Sober."

"You smelled alcohol on Dion's breath just as you did on Glenn's. However, you didn't conclude that Dion was drunk? Why is that?" The defense attorney railed away at the patrolman.

"Because he didn't stagger in the sobriety test."

"How many steps do you think Dion could have taken before he staggered?" The attorney demanded.

"I have no way of knowing."

"Then are you telling us that you don't know if Glenn was drunk but that you wrote him the DUI because in your judgment he was drunk?" asked the attorney.

"In my opinion the defendant was drunk. I wrote him the DUI." the patrolman answered indignantly.

"I have no further questions of this witness your honor," said the defense attorney as he turned to go to his seat.

"The prosecution rests your honor," said prosecutor as he remained seated.

"The defense may call its first witness," announced the Judge.

"Thank you your honor. The defense calls Dion to the stand," announced the defense attorney.

Dion was sworn in. He was seated in the witness chair beside the Judge.

"Were you with Glenn on the night in question?" The defense attorney asked.

"Yes, sir I was," Dion said.

"In your opinion was Glenn drunk at the time the patrolman stopped him?" The defense attorney asked.

"If he was, I didn't know it," Dion answered.

"How far do you think you could've walked in that sobriety test before you staggered?" The defense attorney asked.

"Until I tripped on a rock or stepped in a hole," Dion answered.

"No further questions, Your Honor," the defense attorney stated.

"Did you know that Glenn was drinking that night?" The prosecutor asked Dion.

"Yes sir," Dion answered.

"How did you know that?" The prosecutor asked. One could see by the look on his face that he was thinking that he had Dion trapped and that he would show Glenn was clearly guilty of the DUI.

"Because I saw him take a drink," Dion answered the question as asked honestly and confidently without disclosing the whole truth.

"Did you see him take more than one drink?" The prosecutor asked.

"No, sir. I just saw him have one drink," Dion answered honestly.

"Just one?" The prosecutor asked with incredulity in his voice.

"Yes sir. Just one," Dion responded without hesitation.

"Let me remind you that you're under oath. Now is your

answer still just one?" The prosecutor pounded on Dion in an attempt to get him to change his story.

"Yes sir. I know I'm under oath. But I still saw Glenn have just one drink before the patrolman stopped him," Dion answered without wavering.

Tea and Connie Sue were called to the stand next by the defense attorney. The examination and the cross examination went substantially the same as with Dion. They were asked essentially the same questions about Glenn's drinking on the night he received the DUI. They gave essentially the same answers.

"Your Honor the defense calls Harry to the stand," the defense attorney announced.

Harry went forth to be sworn in. He was seated in the witness chair.

The examination was following exactly the same pattern of that of the three previous witnesses with respect to Glenn's drinking on the night that Glenn received the DUI until a new question by the defense attorney.

"Harry, do you think Glenn is as agile as Dion?"

The prosecutor stood up saying, "Your Honor! I object. This witness is no expert on agility! He can only provide an opinion."

"Your Honor my question deals with the determination of sobriety. The highway patrolman is also not a certified expert on agility and the prosecution introduced his unqualified opinion on agility as a determination of sobriety," the defense attorney argued.

"Objection overruled. The witness will answer the question," the Judge said sternly.

"There wont no chance of that happening. Dion is "Mr. Agile." Glenn is stronger but he is not nearly as agile as Dion," Harry said.

"Harry, do you think Dion could have stumbled during the sobriety test?" the defense attorney asked.

"If he had, his feet are so fast that no one would have seen it unless he fell down. Sometimes when he's shaggin' his feet are moving so fast that we cannot see them," Harry answered.

"No further questions Your Honor," the defense attorney said as he sat down.

"Your witness, Mr. Prosecutor," the Judge said.

The prosecutor stood up and faced Harry. He moved a few steps in Harry's direction. "Harry, did you see Glenn drinking on the night in question?" The prosecutor asked.

"I image!" Harry bellowed in a laughing response.

"Please, just answer the question," admonished the stern-faced Judge.

"Harry did you see Glenn drinking liquor that night?" asked a perturbed prosecutor.

"Yes sir you bet I did," Harry answered with a wink toward Glenn.

"Your Honor, please instruct the witness to refrain from gestures toward the defendant!" The prosecutor demanded.

The Judge turned toward Harry and said, "You are to avoid making eye contact with or gesturing toward the defendant."

"Yes sir, Judge," Harry said flippantly.

"What did you see Glenn drink that night?" The prosecutor asked.

Harry hesitated a moment then said, "I saw him have one drink." There was a momentary pause in the courtroom. Everyone could tell by his facial expression that the prosecutor was considering asking another question but he was trying to compose just the right question.

Harry became nervous with anticipation. Sweat popped out on his forehead. Not a good sign as Harry was normally very calm and cool. He was under pressure and it showed. Something had to give. It was Harry's cool.

"One big 'un!" He blurted out in a deep playful voice. As he spoke, Harry held out his hands out in front of himself and stretched them so that his right hand was about two feet over his left to demonstrate one big un.

Laughter broke out among the people in the courtroom. Even the prosecutor had to fight to suppress a giggle.

The judge slammed his gavel on the bench and shouted, "Quiet! Order in the court! This is a defense witness! I'm declaring a mistrial. Court is adjourned immediately. The defendant is to be released."

CHAPTER TWENTY-THREE

THE SHOTGUN

COSMO'S MOTHER APPROACHED him late one afternoon. She put her arms around him and addressed him by name, "Cosmo lets invite your friends to come here one night instead of everybody going out. It would be safer and cheaper. We could do it Friday night."

"Mama, most of them go to the Armory on Friday nights," Cosmo balked.

"Let's try it Friday night and see. I think it would be fun for your group. It would give me a chance to meet some of your other friends," Cosmo's mother argued.

"It's definitely too late for this Friday. Everyone already has plans and it's too late to change them," Cosmo continued to resist the idea.

"Okay. Let's try next Friday night. We'll send out invitations to the people you want to come," Cosmo's mother said adamantly.

Cosmo knew his mother would not be deterred from her plan. He relented, "Okay. I'll make a list of invitees by tomorrow night."

"Good. I'll send out the invitations to them right after I get the list," she said.

Cosmo made a list of invitees which he gave to his mother. There were about forty names on his list. He had hoped a long list would deter his mother. Actually, it had exactly the opposite effect from that he hoped to achieve. His mother filled out the invitations and mailed them.

The following Friday came soon enough. In fact, it came very fast for Cosmo who was worried that something would go wrong and his mother would get upset. Cosmo's mother laid out his clothes for him for the evening. She picked out a fine white Dobby striped shirt which she had starched and ironed. She paired that with a pair of heavily starched navy slacks. Cosmo looked like a page from a fashion magazine.

Guests started arriving at six-thirty consistent with the invitation. There were cars parked all up and down both sides the street outside Cosmo's house.

The invitation had requested that each of the invitees bring their own beverage. About ten minutes until seven Neil came to the door with four partial bottles of liquor held under his crossed arms. Tea happened to be at the door when Neil arrived. Neil was grinning from ear to ear. "Is this enough to get me in?" Neil said.

"Where did you get those bottles of liquor?" Tea asked.

"From my daddy's cabinet," Neil said with a laugh.

Neil was shocked at Tea's answer. "No. We can't let you bring your daddy's liquor in here. How would you feel if somebody stole your liquor? It's the same thing. You need to take those bottles back home. It's better you come with nothing than come with those."

"I understand. I'll take my daddy's liquor home. Do you think anybody here will let me have some of theirs?" Neil said.

"I'm sure there'll be enough liquor here for you to be able to get a drink," Tea said.

Neil walked home in dejection. He put away the liquor he had taken from his father's cabinet. He walked back to Cosmo's house uncertain if he would have anything to drink. He was back only a few minutes before he found he had nothing to worry about. There was plenty of liquor his friends were willing to share.

About nine, Cosmo approached Dion. By then, Cosmo was in full stagger mode. Dion took one look at his face and asked, "Cosmo what is wrong with your left eye?"

"What do you mean? There is nothing wrong with my eye," Cosmo slurred his response.

"It has bright red streaks and a dark red poodle in the center," Dion said pointing to Cosmo's eye. "What have you been doing?"

"I just went to the bathroom. I had kind of a hard time with my bowel movement. That's all."

"Did you strain real hard?" Dion asked.

"Only a little."

"Cosmo you must have strained so in that bowel movement that you ruptured blood vessels in your eye," Dion said.

"I don't know how I could've done that."

While all of that was going on Mike was busy pouring liquor into a small dish. He put the dish down to see if Cosmo's mother's cat would drink from it. When the cat did start lapping up the liquor, Mike decided he was going to try to find out how much liquor it would take to get the cat drunk. He was much more attentive to and diligent about his experiment than he had ever been in a classroom.

Since the cat was small, it only took a little liquor to get it drunk. However, because the cat lapped up the liquor slowly, it took over an hour for the cat to show the effects. The cat started staggering around the yard.

The cat went up to Cosmo and rubbed against his pants leg. Then it lay down on Cosmo's left foot. Cosmo had not even noticed the cat. He started to walk and almost tripped over the cat exclaiming, "Darn cat!" He pushed the cat aside with that left foot. That almost made him fall.

Cosmo watched as the cat staggered away a few steps then fell. The cat struggled back onto its feet. It barely navigated two steps before it fell again. As Cosmo watched the cat repeat the sequence several times, he realized what had happened. He became angry.

"The cat's drunk! Tea you made my mother's cat drunk! It wont nobody else here who would do that. Where are you? I'm going to keel you," Cosmo yelled though Tea was nowhere to be seen.

Cosmo set out on a search for Tea. He found Tea talking to Cherry beside the hedges at the back of the house. "Why did you get my mother's cat drunk? You just have to cause trouble, don't you?"

"Cosmo, I don't know anything about your cat being drunk," Tea said.

"We've been standing right here talking for over half an hour," Cherry said.

"He could have done it before that!" Cosmo barked. Cosmo paused to think for a few seconds before saying, "I'm going to keel you!"

"Cosmo, I don't know what you think I have done, but I didn't do it," Tea said.

Cosmo turned and walked into the house. He retrieved his father's twelve-gauge shotgun from the den. Cosmo didn't check to see if there was a shell in the gun. He headed back outside with the shotgun dangling from his right hand.

Cosmo's mother saw him as he walked out of the house and followed him.

Cosmo walked back to where Tea and Cherry were still talking. He stopped a few feet short of the two of them and said, "Cherry, stand aside so I can keel him!"

"Cosmo, you don't want to hurt Tea. He has been your friend all your life," Cherry said without moving.

"Cherry, please go ahead and move so I can keel him. He's needed it for a long time. I should have keeled him a lot of times before now," Cosmo insisted.

Jimmy, who had been standing a few feet away, came over and pulled Cherry away from Tea. Jimmy tried his luck at dissuading Cosmo, "Cosmo, you know you don't want to kill anybody. Why don't you put that shotgun away?"

Cosmo raised the barrel of the shotgun pointing it at Tea face, "Move out of the way Jimmy. It's time for me to keel Tea. He's had it comin' a long time and I'm not going to wait any longer. I shoulda keeled him a lot of times."

"I guess if you must kill me, then you should go ahead and do it," a spiffed Tea reasoned.

Jimmy stepped in front of Tea. "No. I'm not going to let you do it."

Cosmo's mother stepped in front of him. "You don't want to hurt Tea. He's your friend. He's been your friend your whole life. You certainly don't want to hurt Jimmy. Has Jimmy done anything to you?" She said.

"I don't want to hurt Jimmy. Jimmy's my friend. You're right. I don't want to hurt Tea. I want to keel him," Cosmo responded.

"How are you going to kill Tea without hurting him?" She asked.

"I'm going to shoot him with the shotgun. I'll shoot him right in the head. That will keel him without hurting him," Cosmo explained. Cosmo thought for a moment before saying, "That head is so hard that the shotgun might not hurt it so I'd better shoot him in the stomach. That belly is nice and soft. I know the bullets will go right in there."

"Go ahead and shoot me if you have to but I think shooting me in the stomach would hurt," Tea said as Cosmo lowered the shotgun to point at his stomach.

"Cosmo, you put that shotgun down. It will hurt Tea. You don't want to hurt Tea. He's your friend," his mother tried one more time.

"That's some friend that'll get your mother's cat drunk. He's always picking on me and causing trouble. He needs to be keeled. He's needed it a lot of times and I'm going to do it this time," Cosmo said.

Just after Cosmo made that statement Mike came around the corner and walked over to Cherry. "What's this all about?" Mike asked Cherry.

"Cosmo says he has to kill Tea because Tea made his mother's cat drunk."

Mike moved closer to Cosmo before saying, "Cosmo, I am the one who gave the liquor to that cat, not Tea."

"Y'all would say anything to keep me from keeling Tea. It doesn't matter. Tea's still got it comin'. He's had it comin' a long time. I'm still going to keel him." Cosmo would not be deterred.

Cosmo's mother walked over and stood in front Tea. First, Jimmy joined her. Then Mike moved in front of them. Then five or six other people stepped between Cosmo and Tea.

Someone grabbed the barrel on the shotgun and forced it toward the ground. In the excitement, Cosmo pulled the trigger. There was a metallic CLICK! There was no shell in the barrel so no damage was done. They took the shotgun from Cosmo and handed it to his mother.

It had not been Cosmo's finest night. The strain of thinking he had to protect his mother from being unset was probably too much for him.

"Let's go have a drink," Cosmo said to Tea.

They walked into the carport and poured themselves a drink each as a though nothing had happened. Tea and Cosmo were instantly friends again. The party resumed with no immediate memory of the event. There was no discussion of the event the remainder of the night or anytime soon thereafter. It was stressful as it occurred. When it was over it was over. It was almost as though it had never happened at all.

CHAPTER TWENTY-FOUR

WHY? OH, WHY?

THERE WAS GENERAL agreement by the youth of St. Umblers that Neil was by far the worst driver around. The standing joke went, "If it will move, Neil can have a wreck in it. If it doesn't move, Neil can run into it. Nothing or anybody is safe anywhere when Neil gets behind the wheel of a car."

To say that Neil had a poor driving record was an understatement. He had been having accidents as long as he had been driving. It was said that Neil ran into the highway patrolman's car after taking his driver's license exam.

A few days after getting his driver's license, Neil decided that he was going to go for a drive. He bounded out of the house and eagerly jumped behind the wheel of the car his parents had given him on his sixteenth birthday. He cranked the car and put it in reverse. As he started to back up he turned the car to the right. He backed a few more feet when he heard a loud metal on metal CRASH! He said to himself, *On my! What have I done?* He looked around to see the crumpled the driver's door of his mother's tan sedan.

He threw the car into drive. He slammed on the accelerator. He heard another loud metal on metal CRASH! He slammed on the brakes. Neil looked up to see that he had just crushed the passenger's door of his father's black truck. He thought, *You had better get out of here quick because otherwise you are in big trouble. You cannot be around here when Daddy finds out what you've just done.* He had not yet looked to see what damage was done to his car from either collision.

He put the car into reverse and managed to get by his mother's car. He was ecstatic. He had both hands off the wheel and he was laughing out loud at his success in getting past his mother's car. To his surprise, he suddenly heard another loud CRASH. That time he felt a jolt race through his body as the car came to a sudden stop. He had backed across the street and into his neighbor's brick restraining wall.

He put the car in drive again and hit the accelerator. Instantly he heard another CRASH. He had run into his family's mailbox.

Still the ever-undaunted warrior Neil backed the car up. He stopped the car. He put the car into drive and was off on his intended drive. He returned home that day without another accident but not without incident. He had on three separate occasions come within three inches or less of hitting other automobiles. Two of those cars had been parked where it appeared they would be safe in the owner's yards. Neil had on both occasions run up onto the sidewalk on the opposite side of the street from his lane and into the yards where the cars were seemingly safely parked.

Neil had driven some of the regulars to Williams Lake one night. They had been drinking, but only a little. Since they were early, the lot was wide open. Instead of taking an unbounded spot, Neil picked a narrow opening between two already parked cars. As he was pulling into the space, Connie

Sue yelled out from the front passenger seat, "Neil stop! You're about to hit that car on the right." Connie Sue had fear in her voice.

However, instead of stopping Neil turned the car hard to the left. Harry shouted from the left rear passenger seat, "Stop Neil! You are going to run into the car on the left." Fortunately, Neil did as commanded. He stopped only a few inches from the right rear bumper of an elevated pickup truck. The bumper of that truck was approximately the same height as Neil's face behind the steering wheel.

"Neil if you'll put the car in park and get out, I'll park it safely." Harry said.

Cherry sat mute in the center of the backseat with her knees knocking.

Neil stopped the car. He put the car in park and nonchalantly climbed out as Harry had suggested. Harry was not his normal jovial self as he stood beside the car shaking visibly. Harry composed himself enough to pull the car into the space three to the right of where Neil had been determined to squeeze in. Harry handed the keys to Neil who was oblivious to what had just transpired.

"Thanks old buddy," Neil said with a grin as he took the keys from Harry.

"Neil, you simply must pay attention when you're driving," Connie Sue said. Worry punctuated her sentence.

Neil laughed an unconcerned impish laugh in response to Connie Sue's admonition. "Aw! We were not going to hurt anything. And even if I did, you know Daddy would get it fixed."

"Neil, I'm with Connie Sue. You need to drive better for your sake and ours," Harry said.

At that point Robert entered the conversation, "Neil maybe

you should let Harry or I drive when we're with you. It would be much safer for all of us. It would save your Dad big bucks too."

Cosmo drove into a spot just to the right of where Harry had parked Neil's car. Dion, Tea and Toney were with Cosmo. They congregated with Neil and his passengers between the two cars having a few drinks and socializing.

They paid at the door and entered the pavilion together. Another man was collecting money that night since Donnie Ray had quit working there. Kenny Helser and The Pieces of Eight provided the entertainment.

Kenny Helser was putting on a fine performance. The band was especially wound up that evening. They were being cheered on by the audience which was enjoying the show. Late in the evening, the band became so energized that Kenny Helser and the band members except the guitar player were hanging from the rafters by their legs singing "Lonely Drifter." The band members played their instruments as they hung there. Even the keyboard player joined them. No mean feat.

Neil decided in an unusual move that he and his group should leave a little early. He informed each of them individually, "I think we'd better leave about twenty minutes before closing so that we don't have so much traffic to deal with. After all, y'all have been concerned about my driving."

Each of the other four conceded to Neil that they thought that was a really good idea. In fact, they showed up at the car up a full half an hour before the Lake closed in spite of the fact that they were really enjoying The Pieces of Eight. Neil came out to join them a few minutes later. Neil drove very slowly to the parking lot exit and turned left.

The crowd was especially large that night. As a result, cars were parked lining both sides of the highway for about half a mile beyond the dam. The drive started uneventfully enough. However, that soon changed.

Neil had passed between the first four pairs of cars when suddenly he veered to the right. He hit the car on the right in the driver's door. Before anyone could react, Neil had jerked the steering wheel to left and had gone across the highway hitting the car one position up in the right rear passenger's door. He ricocheted side-to-side until he had hit in alternating fashion five cars on the left side of the highway and six cars on the right.

Neil remained undaunted and unfazed by the series of events. He regained control of the car and drove on home as though nothing had happened.

The next day news of Neil's most recent driving calamity spread rapidly among the youth of St. Umblers. Harry, Connie Sue and Robert each told the story repeatedly to the other kids. Each of them put his or her special twist on the telling. But any way the story was told, it was obvious that Neil still had not learned to control an automobile.

Connie Sue talked about how Neil had a crazed look on his face and a stranglehold on the steering wheel as he went through the episode. She said, "Neil looked like an oscillating fan. He was bouncing to his right jerking the steering wheel. Then he was bouncing to the left jerking the car in that direction. Then he was bouncing back to the right again. Then back to the left. He continued that bouncing from one side of the road to the other through the whole episode." As she talked, she was demonstrating the fierce back and forth right to left motions Neil made while contorting her face to replicate his expression from the night before. "He had a really crazed look on his face. He looked as though he meant to hit those cars in the order he hit them, as though he were playing a pinball game."

Harry focused on the damage to Neil's car. "You should see Neil's car. Both front fenders are just demolished. It's amazing to me that they didn't cut the front tires up so that they went flat and he couldn't continue to drive. You should've seen that madman try to drive," Harry said to anyone who would listen.

Robert was all about the damage to the parked cars. He described where each car was hit and the extent of the damage done do it. "You should've seen the crushed metal lined up along the highway. Wars have been fought with less damage. There were about a dozen or more sick people out there that morning when they saw their cars and all the damage, don't you know?"

Cherry remained largely quiet on the subject. All she had to say was, "Neil looked like a kamikaze dive bomber yanking that wheel back and forth. It was like he was seeking revenge against those cars. Not the owners, the cars. I didn't think we were going to get out of that car alive. I don't think I will ride with Neil again anytime soon."

After listening to them recount Neil's episode Dion said, "Neil will never drive the road less traveled. That would mean that he would have significantly less potential victims to crash into."

To no one's surprise; however, Neil was never comforted with the results of his parade of damaged automobiles. He just seemed to lead a charmed life when it came to the personal deleterious results of his driving. If it had been anybody else behind that steering wheel, someone would have come and found him to make him pay the damages. But that was not Neil's fate. That would have been somebody else's fate.

Neil drove to the Lake on another Saturday night. On that particular night Connie Sue, Robert and Tea were with him.

Neil pulled into the same spot to park that his car that he had occupied on the night of his infamous ricochet crash ride. Cosmo was already parked in the same spot he had occupied on that night. Dion, Harry and Toney were with Cosmo.

True to her word, Cherry had ridden with Anne instead of Neil that night.

Toney said to Neil in his deep gravelly voice, "Be careful when you're driving here. If you hit this car, it's going to cost you a wad," as he pointed Cosmo's car. "I'm just real surprised it didn't cost you a huge wad the night you hit those eleven cars parked along the highway."

Neil laughed all over with his body rising and falling as he did. He also threw his arms askew about his body in random fashion as he laughed. That display indicated that he obviously thought Toney's commentary was quite funny.

"Instead of leaving early tonight," Connie Sue implored Neil, "Why don't we wait for most of the cars to leave the Lake in order to avoid traffic? I think we will be less likely to have an accident that way."

"I think that would be good too, don't you know?" Robert added in phase with Connie Sue.

"You know, I'm all right with that," said a laughing Neil. "We'll meet here at the car when the Lake closes. We will give everybody else twenty or thirty minutes to leave."

"They'll need every bit of that time as a head start to get out of the mad driver's way," Harry said with a chuckle. "I can see them now running for their cars when the Lake closes to get out of Neil's way. There wont no way any of them are gonna want to be the last to leave or even close to." Harry said as his short plump body did an exaggerated demonstration of a person running for his car in order to get a head start on Neil.

When the Lake closed, the two carloads of youth gathered

at the cars and talked for about twenty minutes while other cars left. When the parking lot was essentially empty Cosmo said, "Neil, I'll follow you. That way I can keep a good eye on you and avoid you hitting me in the rear. I think I can handle the challenge of keeping you from hitting me in the front."

They all laughed thinking that was really funny. Neil pulled out of the parking lot first with Cosmo giving him a wide berth from behind. Everything went swimmingly for the first two miles. Then Neil rounded a curve to see the flashing blue lights of a highway patrol car on the right side of the road. The highway patrol car's headlights were shining on a white car which the patrolman had stopped.

The patrolman had pulled off the highway at an angle behind the unlucky driver. As a result a few inches of the left rear of his car was over the asphalt of the highway.

True to form, Neil hit those few inches of the patrolman's car. The impact caused the patrolman's car to slide to the left and farther into the highway.

"Oh boy! This is going to be real trouble, don't you know?" Robert said.

As the patrolman turned and started to walk toward Neil's stopped car Connie Sue said to Neil, "It looks like you are going to jail this time." She laughed, "That will make the roads safer."

Cosmo had seen the event take place. He pulled his car over on to the right shoulder of the highway a couple of hundred feet behind Neil.

It was obvious that the patrolman was angry as he arrived at Neil's car. "Son can't you see something as large as that patrol cruiser? I even have the lights flashing," the patrolman asked in an angry tone. "Let me see your driver's license," he demanded.

Neil handed the patrolman his license. He said to the patrolman with logic uncommon to Neil, "Officer, your car was sitting out in the highway and there's a double yellow line here so I wasn't able to stay on my side of the road and get by your car. That's why I hit your car."

That seemed to diffuse some of the patrolman's anger. He turned and looked at his car. Then he turned back to Neil and surprisingly said, "You're right, I'm parked partially on the highway. Get out of your car and let's see what damage was done."

The event had sobered Neil up quickly. He and the patrolman walked to the front of Neil's car. The patrolman said, "You see all that water and anti freeze on the highway? It appears that you have a busted radiator. You are not going to be able to drive your car until it's fixed. I'm going to have to call the dispatcher at the station to see if we can get a ride for you and your friends."

The patrolman went to his car and made a radio call to headquarters. The anxious listeners could not hear the details of the conversation; however, they could tell from the officer's tone that he was not having a good conversation.

He came back to Neil and the others. "We will have to get the car towed in. The highway patrol will take care of the repairs," he grumbled.

"Thank you, officer. Let me tell my friends in the car back here what is going on,"

As Neil was speaking, Glenn, who was alone, came around the curve and spotted the stopped cars. He recognized the cars of Neil and Cosmo car. He stopped to help.

"Officer, we can get a ride home with my friends in the two cars behind us. There's no need to get a car to come and get us," Neil said.

The officer asked him, "Are you certain about that? Leave the keys with me and we will get your car fixed and get it to you."

Neil and his passengers were able to get rides with Cosmo and Glenn. They were off to St. Umblers to go home and to bed.

The highway patrol had Neil's car repaired. They returned the car to him the following Thursday.

On the following Sunday evening, a group was gathered at the Gas Company to chat. It was one of those rare occasions when Dion had his father's car. He had picked up Cosmo and Tea in the little mint green sedan. Neil and Harry were in Neil's car at the Gas Company.

Neil asked the other three, "Come on and get in my car we will ride around and drink some beer."

"Neil, are you crazy? What you have had, seventeen wrecks in the last fourteen weeks? You and Harry come on and ride with me. After all, it's a rare occasion that I get to drive the car. And I know it's safer than riding with you," Dion replied.

"Dion, you're making Neil's driving record sound better than is," Harry chuckled.

Everyone joined in the laugh.

"You're right, Harry. Dion was trying to make Neil feel better the best way he knew how," Cosmo said with a laugh.

Neil and Harry fell into the backseat of Dion's car on either side of Cosmo. They talked as Dion drove them around for a couple of hours.

"It's ten o'clock, I have to get home." Neil said.

"I can stay out longer if you can take me home, Dion," Harry said.

"I would be more than happy to," Dion said.

Dion drove back around to the Gas Company and stopped a few feet behind Neil's car. Neil, who was sitting behind Dion, jumped out of the car and raced to his car. He had left the left rear passengers door open on Dion's car in the process. Cosmo moved over and reached to his left to close the standing door. The door closed with a click. But before Dion could put the car in drive Neil had started his car and put it in reverse hitting the accelerator. Dion put the little sedan in drive but before it could move forward, there was a loud CRASH. The little car shook in response to being hit by Neil's car.

Both drivers put their cars in park. They turned off their engines. They stepped out to survey the damage. The other passengers in Dion's car joined them.

"Yard Dog, just look what you've done now. It's a new personal record. There's number eighteen!" Harry laughed.

Before anyone else could speak, Neil was jumping up and down waving his hands over his head crying, "Why? Oh, why? You know I can't drive!"

Neil went on to have another dozen or so accidents over the next couple of months. His driving record improved only after his father the car took way for a month. He reinforced that by telling Neil, "When you get the car back if you have another accident, you will be grounded with respect to driving for the next year."

Neil learned he had to pay attention to what he was doing when he was driving or face the prospect of walking frequently. He was far too lazy for that. Against all odds, the lesson had taken.

CHAPTER TWENTY-FIVE

FIRST BAND AT THE SPANISH GALLEON

RING, RING, RING, RING. Dion answered the phone on the fourth ring, "Good Morning."

"Hey, do you know that Glenn drove to South of the Border for breakfast this morning? Larry and Mike went with him," Tea asked Dion in a voice filled with mild excitement.

"No, I knew nothing of it. They were parked out with the rest of us this morning when I left at around two-thirty to go to bed." Dion replied.

"They did it. Jerry just told me," Tea continued. "There wont no way I would drive one hundred miles for breakfast. Those three are just plain stupid to do such a thing. To a better subject, I can take tomorrow off from work. If you can take tomorrow afternoon off, we'll go to OD for the weekend!"

"Sure, I can take off tomorrow afternoon. I'll work late tonight and then go in early tomorrow morning to get my work done. I'd love to go to OD!" Dion answered.

"Let's dress up and look as though we are young sophisticates," Tea said.

"We will act like we have there before," Dion said.

"Let's wear ties to show off," Tea said.

"Okay," Dion said.

"That settles it. I'll pick you up at one tomorrow and we will drive down." Tea said.

"Great, I'll be ready," Dion ended the conversation.

Tea was so excited that he showed up at Dion's house at eleven forty-five the next morning. That trip had to be important because Tea he was early. That was the same Tea who was always late! There seemed to be a natural law prohibiting Tea from being on time let alone being early.

"Hurry up! Time is wasting! We need to get on the road," Tea said to Dion as soon as he arrived.

"I'll be ready in five minutes," Dion answered. He was true to his word and the little green Tempest was off to OD.

They stopped along the way and picked up their necessary provisions. In their excitement, they had not taken time to eat lunch. They had been saving that treat for OD. They proudly walked into the door of Hoskins Restaurant just before closing. Hoskins, which had been in business since 1948, had tables and booths with red seats in front of them on the left side of the restaurant. The hostess showed them to a table on the right side of the room divider where they were seated. They were as proud as two big old peacocks. Their waitress who was a friendly little white-haired lady in a blue dress came over bringing them a couple of glasses of water. She informed them of the specials in a beautiful southern drawl perfected by years of use.

"You said that Salisbury steak comes with mashed potatoes and gravy and two vegetables?" Dion asked.

"Yes. And either Tea or coffee," the waitress answered. "You can choose the vegetables from the list on the board over there."

"That sounds good to me. I'll have the greens and the pinto beans," Dion said.

"What would you like to drink?" The waitress asked.

"I will stick with water," Dion replied.

"I'll have the Salisbury steak too. But, I want green beans and French fries. I'll have sweet tea to drink," Tea said.

"Man, this is the life," Tea proudly said when the waitress was gone.

"You are so right. This is big. Think about all of those poor people back there working today," Dion responded with an equal amount of pride over being at OD.

In a matter of less than five minutes their waitress was back saying, "Fries," in a questioning voice as she sat a plate down in front of Tea. Then she announced, "Pinto beans," as she sat the other plate down in front of Dion.

While they slowly ate their lunches, they overheard the conversation between two men sitting at the table beside them toward the north wall. One said to the other, "Harold is going to have a band at the Spanish Galleon tonight. That'll be the first time that has ever happened. I'm going. You in?"

As they walked out the door of Hoskins Restaurant, Tea asked Dion, "Did you hear what those two were saying in there? There's going to be a band at the Spanish Galleon tonight. Fat Harold is really stepping out. We have to be there!"

"Indeed sir. It's three-ten. I think it's important for us to go the beach and have a drink or two. I'm going with or without you. What do you think?" Dion said.

"That's a good plan," Tea answered. "We will have time to have dinner and be at the Spanish Galleon by eight-thirty or nine. I'll bet you Harold will be surprised to see us!"

The happy campers filled two cups with ice. They poured

themselves a big drink. Tea had to add his Coke. They parked beside the pavilion in the horseshoe at the end of Main Street. They walked out onto the beach behind the pavilion strutting as proud as kings. They stood with drinks in hand watching the women who were still out.

"That girl in the red bathing suit is the best looking girl I ever saw!' Tea said pointing at a young lady ten to fifteen feet away. Then he said without missing a beat, "Actually, that one in the blue bathing suit looks even better! Man, this is great! Look at all these beautiful women!"

They stayed on the beach drinking until about seven. During that time they went back to the car for one refill. "Let's go over here to the Boulevard Grill and get a hamburger." Dion said.

"I'm up for it," Tea answered. "Let's put the cups in the car."

They did. They thought they were behaving like natives.

At eight forty-five Tea said, "I've waited long enough. Let's go to the Spanish Galleon."

"I guess it is about time," Dion answered.

The Spanish Galleon was located on the northeast corner of the intersection of Main Street and Ocean Drive. It was a large building with an arcade in the front facing Ocean Drive. In the middle of the building was a bar. Behind that on the ocean side was a large open concrete floor with a roof over it that served as the primary dance floor. Just outside the concrete floor lay the sand dune. If you walked beyond the concrete floor you were going to get sand in your shoes. At high tide, if you walked a few yards beyond the dunes, you were going to get your feet wet because you would be in the greenish-blue water of the Atlantic Ocean.

When they entered, the place was already jumping. There

were probably one hundred and seventy-five to two hundred people in there drinking beer and mingling. Some were dancing the Shag to the jukebox.

"You remember that the Spanish Galleon only serves beer," Tea said to Dion.

"Yes. Lamentablely, I do remember that. I think that's a shame. Some liquor would be real good thing about now. But I guess is not too hard to go out to the car to get a drink when I need one," Dion said.

"I'm going to go over to the bar and get me a beer," Tea announced.

Dion motioned toward the bar, "Go ahead. I'll wait right here."

Tea came back with a beer in his right hand. "This is going to be fun. The band is going to start playing very shortly. Hey, who is that beautiful blonde with the incredible body? That's what a real woman looks like. Man, she can shag too."

"I have no idea, but I plan to ask her to dance. I'll let you know when I come back." Dion said.

He started moving in the direction of the stunning lady. When the next song started he made his move. He beat at least one other guy to her. "Would you like to dance?" He asked as he quickly extended his left hand toward her.

"Yes, thank you. I would," she said as she accepted his hand into her own.

"You are extremely attractive and a great shagger. What is your name?" Dion said as they settled into the dance.

"Thank you. I'm Nancy," she replied.

"I'm Dion and it is a pleasure to meet you,." he said before she could say anything else.

"Where are you ladies from?" Dion asked. He nodded to the girls she was with.

"We're from Anderson in the western part of the state," she said. "I have never seen you here before. Where are you from?"

"I'm from St. Umblers, North Carolina." Dion answered.

When the dance ended, Dion thanked Nancy and returned her to friends.

"Thank you. I enjoyed the dance. Save another for me," she said.

"I will. I'll look forward to that," Dion said.

He returned to Tea and reported on the beautiful young lady. Dion did save another dance for her; however, she was in such great demand that she was asked to dance every song before he could get to her. She stayed on the dance floor all night.

At a little after nine the band appeared on the northwest corner of the concrete floor. They had six young men playing instruments and a female lead singer. However, though mediocre in skill, they were entertaining. Dion and Tea wandered through the crowd. Each of them shagged aperiodically with this young lady or that. Dion danced with three young ladies from the OD area. Their names were DeRhonda, Tommie Lynn and Sonja.

Most of the audience, which had by then grown considerably, was having a good time. Dion noticed three rough-looking young men standing in the sand just off the concrete floor who did not act happy. They were all three drinking PBRs' and talking excitedly to each other with a scowl on each of their faces. As they became more animated in their discussion, they took turns pointing toward the band. They were drinking their courage twelve ounces at a time from those PBR cans.

The time came for the band to take a break. While the band was out, the jukebox played. The concrete dance floor was full on almost every song.

Dion saw the band start back toward their instruments and microphones. Out to the corner on his right eye he saw the three men who had been drinking the PBR's move toward the band. "Tea, you'd better come with me. I think there is a possibility of trouble."

"What are you talking about?" Tea asked.

"You see those three moving toward the band. They have been standing over there drinking PBR's all night. They stand out like a sore thumb in here. None of them has been dancing and none of them has talked to anyone other than the other two. They sure look like rednecks and trouble to me," Dion said over his shoulder as he started toward the band.

"I'm sure you're right. I'm right behind you." Tea responded as he too started toward the band.

When they were still a few steps from the band, one of the three PBR drinkers reached toward the singer. He grabbed the microphone and shouted at her in an angry voice, "Give me that and you get out of here!" Everybody in the Spanish Galleon heard him. Everybody started to surround the band.

At that moment, Fat Harold arrived. "Hey! Just what seems to be the problem here?" He asked the young man holding the purloined microphone.

"Harold, we don't cotton to no niggers singing in here," the young man holding the microphone answered. "It's just not right. We just can't have that."

Dion spoke up, "Harold, I don't see any niggers in here, do you? But if you do see any niggers in here, either black or white, I'll help you throw them out. All I see is a young lady trying to entertain us. And I think she is doing a pretty good job." Dion was indicating that niggers came in black and white versions. Nigger, around St. Umblers and probably a large portion of the South, was a demarcation of attitude as opposed to race or color. He was accustomed to both blacks and whites calling each other "nigger." In general it was said in jest. One had to say "Nigger" as a statement of hatred or disdain for it to be a slur to either race. It might be said to a white person or a black person and have the same connotation.

One of the other two said to Dion "You stay out of this. You ain't from around here anyways." As he was making his speech, he was putting up his fists as if he were ready to fight.

"I saw you listening to The Tams and The Drifters while the jukebox was playing at the break. You didn't make any fuss about them. They are as black as this young lady," Dion countered.

"That's different. They wuzn't in here breathing the same air as us. That there nigger is," the apparent leader said.

At that point Harold looked at the leader and said, "We are not having any fighting in here. We want everybody to have fun, but it's necessary for you to act like somebody your mother would be proud of when you're in here."

Dion took off his tie. He walked over to the young singer. He reached out to place the tie around the young lady's neck. The singer was a little nervous and drew back slightly from him even though she knew from his words and his mannerisms that he was not a threat. She also knew that he did not agree with the redneck aggressors.

Dion tried to calm her by saying, "Just relax. All I'm going to do is put this tie around your neck to show that you are one of us. You have shown courage by performing here. You're pretty good. I hope you will continue." She was still tense but she let Dion put the tie around her neck.

Tea walked over taking off his tie which he too offered the young lady. Nervously she allowed him put his tie around her neck. The combination of their actions seemed to calm her down. At the same time it seemed to defuse most of the tension in the crowd. Not another word was spoken. There was no need. The situation was under control.

Fat Harold said to the three, "Is this settled? Can we go back to having a good time now?"

"I reckon if you and everybody else can put up with it, then we can for tonight," the guy who seemed to be the redneck leader said with resignation in his voice. "Let's go get a beer." The three went to the bar and ordered themselves fresh PBR's.

Harold said to them, "This one's on me, but never again. You are not to come back unless you can have fun without having a confrontation," as he handed their money back along with three cold PBR's.

The band resumed playing. They played the rest of the night without further incident. The confrontation was forgotten as soon as the music resumed. Even the three rednecks with the PBR's appeared to relax and enjoy the band and the evening.

Dion and Tea were leaving the Spanish Galleon when it closed. "Harold, where can we get a good cheap place to stay tonight?" Dion asked Fat Harold as they walking out the front door where he was standing.

Harold pointed diagonally across Ocean Drive to a small side street, "There is a nice guest house halfway down that street. They are reasonable if you can wake them up. They probably have a room. He is a shrimper so he might be up getting ready to go out. He might even be gone already. She stays home and runs the rooms. Some people say she drinks a bit and that it is sometimes hard to get her up. If that doesn't work, there's Floyd's two streets farther down. Thanks for your help tonight. I thought for sure we were going to have trouble with those three. They will be back tonight and they will be fine. They are good old boys who thought that they were doing everyone a favor."

They went to the house that had been pointed out by Harold. Mr. Rice was up already as Harold had said he might be. He rented them a room for two nights for four dollars each per night.

They slept late the next day. They arose and had a hair of the dog to get them going. After eating lunch at Hoskins, they started drinking seriously for the day. "Ah, to be drunk and shaggin' at OD! It wont anything any better than this. The Lake is in there but there wont no other place that has a chance," Tea said.

That night they walked the short distance to the Galleon. They shagged to the jukebox which played without interruption. Many of the people who were there the previous night were also back. They recognized many of the faces. They were in turn recognized. They saw the three from the confrontation the night before. They talked to them. There was no animosity between them. As Harold had told them, those guys turned out to be pretty good people.

Dion danced frequently with DeRhonda, Tommie Lynn and Sonja. He also danced with others of the young ladies there. He tried to dance with Nancy, but once again, she was in such demand that she was on the floor every song.

The next day they returned home as victorious warriors. They had been to OD a couple of times before but that time they felt they had conquered OD.

CHAPTER TWENTY-SIX

WALKING UP A TWO-WAY STREET

"WE ARE ON OUR WAY to the Lake tomorrow night for a big blow out. I'll pick you up at six if you want to go," Cosmo said to Dion as he stopped his car in front of the Gas Company.

"I only want to go if the sun comes out tomorrow or if it does not. I'll be ready. I'll be wearing my best yellow shirt and khaki pants," Dion said.

As promised, Cosmo showed up at six. They went to pick up Tea then Cherry before Connie Sue. After which, they stopped at the ABC store. They made their purchases and stopped for supplies at the convenience store. They commenced drinking on the way to the Lake.

They were among the first people to arrive. Others from St. Umblers came in later. There were Harry and Neil with Robert. Just before they were ready to enter, Toney dove up. Toney was by himself because he had to be in Raleigh with his grandfather during the day and had told his friends he wouldn't be back in time to go with them. Others came later. The Drifters were the musical attraction.

The Drifters were putting on quite a show. Everyone was

in a great mood. People were shaggin' everywhere one looked. In fact, there were so many people shaggin' that it was almost full combat dancing. No one seemed to mind.

Dion danced with quite a variety of women. Cosmo on the other hand had spent the entire evening making mooneyes at a single young lady. He was determined to gain her attention and her favor. Cosmo was still intent on losing his virginity. He was so consumed by his desire to enjoy her delights that he was salivating like a dog in heat. She had welcomed his companionship and responded in kind. *This could be the moment*, Cosmo thought to himself.

It wasn't until break time when they went outside that they realized how hot it was inside. When they opened the car, Dion was able to see that his fine yellow shirt was wet with perspiration. He said to Cherry and Connie Sue, "Is it as hot in there as I think it is? I didn't even notice until I came out here. This little bit of breeze feels really good."

While they were not perspiring as Dion was, they each responded in the affirmative that they too found it very hot inside. They were merely glistening as Southern Belles do in the heat. They too found it quite refreshing to be outside where it was significantly cooler.

"I was so hot I thought I was going to die," Connie Sue said in her tantalizing high-pitched voice.

Toney, Robert, Neil and Harry joined them. There was small talk about how good the entertainment was. The consensus was that The Drifters were as good that night as any one had ever seen them.

Cosmo and Tea made their way to the group. Cosmo walked up to Toney and whispered something in his ear. Toney nodded affirmatively in response to whatever Cosmo said to him.

"I told Tea on the way out that I have a date tonight. You're going to have to ride home with Toney. It's okay with him," Cosmo said.

"You are welcome to ride with me," Toney said.

"There's room for one of you to ride with me. Don't you know?   Would one of you like a ride with me?" Robert said.

Dion thought for a moment in the silence after Robert's comment. He decided Robert was a safer driver than Toney. "I'll ride with you Robert," Dion said.

As Dion was making his comment to Robert, Harry started taunting Cosmo about his date. "A date! Woo! Woooo! Woooo! A date! Cosmo has a date!" Harry teased in a loud playful voice as he bounced up and down pointing both index fingers toward the ground as he did. Harry's antics overshadowed Dion's response to Robert. Few in the group heard what Dion said.

"When are you leaving on this mystical date?" Dion asked.

"As soon as y'all go back inside. She has gone to tell the girls she rode with that I'm taking her home," Cosmo beamed with pride.

"Aren't you going to at least introduce us to her?" Neil asked.

"There wont no way that that's going to happen," Cosmo answered.

"There might be some things we need to tell her about you. Don't you know?" Robert teased.

Cherry moved up beside Cosmo and said in a sexy pleading voice, "Why Cosmo, Connie Sue and I thought you would take us on a date tonight. We were hoping you would take us home. Weren't we Connie Sue? You can leave them here or they can ride home with Toney."

Connie Sue caught on to Cherry's tease. She too moved beside Cosmo and smuggled close to him on the other side. She put her left arm around his waist and looked up at him and said in a come-hither voice, "Yeah, Cosmo. How about it? Cherry and I want some of you tonight big boy! You never pay us any attention and that just drives us wild."

Cherry moved in closer on Cosmo's left side and started playing with the hair on the back of his head with her right hand. "Can you handle a threesome big boy? Connie Sue and I are ready for you. We are eager to go. Your talk about a date has us all hot and flustered. Why don't you take us instead of her? We are a sure thing and you don't about her." Cherry said.

"We can make you happy. We know what you want big boy! Can she make you as happy as we can?" Connie Sue jested.

The attention from the girls had Cosmo completely flustered. He straightened his brown framed glasses on his face. He tried to assume his most macho look. He said, "You girls cut that out. This is serious. I have a date tonight. You wont serious about what you were saying."

Cherry backed away from Cosmo. She put her right hand over her heart and said, "Cosmo I wanted you badly. I have never been scorned so badly in all my life. I'm just going to die!"

Connie Sue clung to Cosmo even more tightly. "I'll never let you go for another woman Cosmo. I want you! I'm going with you . . . big boy! I'm yours!"

"Now Connie Sue you turn me loose! I'm serious! I have to go!" Cosmo said in a macho tone. Connie Sue did turn him loose as she broke into a laugh. Cherry joined her. Cosmo was off to find his date.

The group went back in after the break. Cosmo disappeared

with his mysterious date. The Drifters were going strong again after the intermission. Dion went back and shagged the night away. He danced periodically with Cherry and Connie Sue. Tea and the others spent most of the time wandering around talking to people and listening to the band. That was a wonderful evening to be young and carefree. Those times and those emotions were fleeting; they had no chance of lasting indefinitely. If they could have done so and if they have been wise enough, the group from St. Umblers would have bottled the magic of that evening.

Closing time relentlessly pursued them. It inevitably caught them. Robert and his passengers arrived at his car first. Dion hopped in with them. They turned left and then drove past the entrance to the pavilion on the right. They were on their way to St. Umblers.

Some ten to fifteen minutes later Toney and Tea arrived at Toney's car where Cherry and Connie Sue were waiting. Toney and Tea were both totally plastered. Connie sue was also pretty much wasted.

"You three are seriously drunk. Toney let me drive your car home," Cherry said.

"No, I'm not too drunk to drive," Toney said.

"What if you get stopped? You're sure to get a big ticket," Cherry argued.

"If I get stopped, I've got a wad! I can get us out of it," Toney answered with bravado.

"Toney you are drunker than me, and I'm too drunk to drive. Why don't you let Cherry drive your car?" Connie Sue said.

"Tea, help us here. Help us get Toney to let me drive. I'm afraid he'll have a wreck and we will all get hurt," Cherry said.

"Toney are you okay to drive?" Tea asked.

"Tea, you know I'm alright. I can drive. I'll get us home," Toney answered.

Tea staggered to the shotgun position. He opened the door. He said over his left shoulder, "Toney's alright. He can drive us home. Let's get in and get going."

Cherry and Connie Sue reluctantly assumed spots in the backseat. Toney maneuvered under the steering wheel in the driver's seat and closed his door. He turned left from the parking lot to go to St. Umblers. They had traveled less than 15 minutes before Cherry and Connie Sue heard Tea snoring in the front seat.

"We had better talk to Toney to keep him from joining Tea's chorus," Cherry said.

They started up a conversation in hopes of keeping Toney awake in order to minimize the potential for having an accident. Even at that Toney was all over the highway. Toney was lucky that there was no highway patrolman on the route home that night.

"Toney find some Beach Music on the radio," Connie Sue said. Toney fiddled with the tuning knob on the radio until he found some Beach Music.

"Toney slowdown to drinking speed," Cherry said. Toney slowed down to forty-five miles per hour as instructed.

As they entered the last curve in the road before getting to St. Umblers, Willie Tee of New Orleans' song "Walking Up a One Way Street" came on. Cherry reached over the seat and punched Tea on the left shoulder. She said, "Tea wake up, you don't want miss this."

Ironically, Robert was depositing Dion at his house as Willie Tee's song played. Robert had already dropped Harry and Neil off.

Tea responded with surprise but tried to hide the fact that

he had been asleep. "Wow! Would you listen to that? I don't have that music! While he is not our Willie T. from Burlington, this Willie Tee can really sing that song." He started pumping his left fist in the air to demonstrate that he was alert and in control of himself.

"Connie Sue, I'm going to take you home first. Then I'll take Cherry home. After that I'll take Tea home before I go home," Toney said.

"Wait a minute! What about Dion? Where is Dion?" Tea said with alarm.

"Where is Dion?" Toney said with equal alarm.

"We must've left him at the Lake. Toney, we have plenty of time to take the girls home, come back and wait here at the intersection for Dion to come walking up the highway. The sun will be up before he can get here," Tea said.

They took the girls home and went back to the intersection to wait for Dion to come walking up the highway from the Lake.

"I don't know how I could have been stupid enough to leave Dion at the Lake. He would never do that to me. I think we should drive back and pick him up," Toney said.

"No, we can't drive back. If we did, we would never spot him. We have to wait right here for him to come walking up the highway. He has to come right by here in order to get home," Tea argued.

That logic sounded good to Toney. "Okay. We'll wait right here," Toney answered.

"Let's move right over there to see him better," Tea said.

"Okay," Toney answered. However, when he turned the key in the ignition, nothing happened. There was not even a noise.

They sat in the car for about half an hour to forty-five minutes. Then they paced around the car. Toney opened the trunk and pulled out the tire tool. He said, "I'm so stupid. I would give a wad to have Dion here. I should never have left him!"

"Unfortunately, I don't think a wad will help us right now," Tea said.

Toney started swinging the tire tool and smashing out the windows and windshields of his classic dark blue fifty-five Chevy. The more he swung the angrier he became. The angrier he became, the harder he swung. In less than fifteen minutes, he had knocked all the windows out of his car. Tea stood quietly and watched.

When Toney had finished, Tea said, "There's a car coming up the highway. Let's flag the driver down and ask him if he saw Dion walking this way."

They both stepped up to the side of the highway and started waving their hands over their heads. The car slowed and started to pull over. They recognized that it was Cosmo's car. Cosmo stopped. A huge smile came over his face when he recognized Tea and Toney. When he saw the carnage that had been Toney's car he asked with astonishment, "What in the hell happened here?"

"I left Dion at the Lake. We're waiting here for him to come walking up the road to get home," Toney said with a air of despair.

"I just drove ten miles of the way he would come and I didn't see him anywhere," Cosmo said.

"He'll show up about daylight. It's your fault, Cosmo. You and your hounding! If you hadn't been gung ho on the date thing, we would have all come back together just as we had gone. We would all be in bed by now and Dion would be home in bed too," Tea said.

"Wait a minute. He said he was going to ride back with Robert. I heard it. Didn't you hear it? I'll bet he's already home in bed," Cosmo said.

"We can go to Robert's house. His bedroom is at the end of the house and he sleeps with the windows open. We can tap on the window and ask him if he brought Dion home without disturbing anyone else, "Toney said.

"We need to find out. If we go to Dion,'s house and try to wake him up if he is there, we will disturb everybody in the house. If he's not there, we will still disturb everybody. I don't want to wake his father up," Tea said.

"I guess I'll have to drive, huh," Cosmo said.

Without further discussion, Cosmo drove to the block where Robert lived. "You'd better stop about two houses down the street and we will walk to Robert's window," Toney said. Cosmo complied. They walked to Robert's window.

TAP. TAP. TAP. Robert heard a slight repetitive noise at his window. "Who's there?" Robert said.

"Did you bring Dion home from the Lake?" Cosmo whispered.

"Who are you?" Asked a sleepy Robert who was as of yet unable to focus on the voice or the words he was hearing.

Cosmo tried again speaking a little louder, "Did you bring Dion home from the Lake?"

The voice was beginning to register with Robert. "Cosmo is that you?"

"Yes. Tea and Toney are also out here with me," Cosmo responded.

"Sure, I brought Dion home. He said he was going to ride with me. And so he did. Don't you know?" Robert said.

"Thanks man! You did real good. We're going home," Tea said with deep relief.

"Cosmo, if you could drive me home, I'll get my car later today," Toney said.

"No problem. I'll drive you home before I take Tea home. I'll be home before daylight," Cosmo said.

"I guess we won't see Dion walking up a two-way street after all," Tea said.

CHAPTER TWENTY-SEVEN

SLEEPING IN THE COLD

JANUARY WAS EXCEPTIONALLY cold that winter. It was so cold in St. Umblers one Friday that some of the Lake regulars decided to go to OD for the weekend. Dion, Tea and Mike rode with Cosmo. Phil, Neil and Robert traveled with Harry. They thought it would be significantly warmer than being at the Lake on Saturday night. It had been so cold and windy at the Lake the previous Saturday night that it distracted significantly from some of their rituals. That weekend was expected to be somewhat colder. They were right. It was warmer than it was at the Lake, but not as much as they had hoped.

They arrived in OD around eight-thirty that evening. "Cosmo pull into the parking lot of that service station on left on the corner of Hillside and Main Street," Dion said.

Cosmo stopped in front of the service station. Harry followed.

"It's much colder here than I thought it would be," Cosmo complained.

"Yeah, I wasn't expecting it to be so cold," Tea echoed.

Mike, who had just returned to the area, said through his

sheepishly shy grin, "It would freeze the balls off a brass monkey."

"Let's go around the corner to Rice's guesthouse to get us a room. We can get one room for sixteen dollars a night. We can put as many people in it as we want to," Tea said.

"I've heard you talk about Rice's guesthouse. If we get a room there, it would only cost us four dollars apiece for the weekend. I vote we go for it," Cosmo said.

No one objected. They went to Rice's to get a room.

"I'll do the talking. They'll recognize me," Tea said as he headed for the door. Tea knocked. Mrs. Rice opened the door. "Hello, Mrs. Rice, do you remember me?"

"Yeah, I remember you," grumpy Mrs. Rice said.

Tea looked back at the car," Ms. Rice we need a room for tonight and tomorrow night. Do you have one available?"

"I can let you have the one on the front East corner. It's a pretty big room, but I don't know if all of you can sleep in there. But if you want it, it is sixteen dollars a night."

"That would be just great. We'll take it," Tea answered.

"I'll have my money upfront thank you," Mrs. Rice said waiting with her hand stuck out.

"Just a minute. I'll get the money," Tea said as he turned and started toward the car. He walked between the two cars and everybody handed over four dollars each to pay for the room.

Tea walked back to Mrs. Rice. "Here's the money."

"Here's a key to the front door. We don't have no key to the bedroom," Mrs. Rice said.

They unloaded their belongings and took them inside with Tea leading the way. As soon as they had put their things down, they broke out the liquor.

"Hey we are behind here," Tea shouted! "We'd better catch up fast!" He held up the red label vodka bottle saying to Dion,

"Are you ready?"

"Mark it and hand it here," Dion answered.

"Hold on. I want to go first this time," Tea replied.

Dion sighed and dropped his shoulders in inpatient resignation saying, "Okay, but hurry up. You are taking too long already."

Tea removed the cap and threw it in the trashcan. He turned up the bottle and began to drink with an accompanying guzzling sound. Harry and Neil both stood there with their eyes lighting up becoming as big as the main serving plates at an all-you-can-eat buffet. "Wow! Wow wee!" Neil said in total amazement.

Everyone except Cosmo and Mike, who had seen the spectacle before, watched in shock as Dion reached over and pulled the bottle down from Tea's mouth saying, "You have had enough. I'll take care of the rest." Dion turned up the bottle and consumed the rest of the vodka.

Mike broke the ensuing silence, "I'm going to The Barrel and have me a beer in a few minutes. Anybody else wanta go?"

They all agreed that they would go along to The Barrel. Dion added the caveat, "I'll go for a while. Then I'm going over to the Galleon. I'm going to dance some instead of drinking at the Barrel all night. Anyone who wants to come along is welcome."

"Can we at least finish our drinks before we go?" Harry asked. "I'm pretty thirsty right now and this is tasting real good."

Mike answered, "Sure, but hurry up. You need to save some for tomorrow anyway."

Within ten minutes, they had finished their drinks. They set out on the two-block walk to the Barrel. There were a few people, mostly men, at the Barrel. They were drinking beer or playing pool. The group from St. Umblers joined them. All of them but Dion ordered a beer. They sat talking among themselves and occasionally interacted with people who were already there.

About forty-five minutes later Dion said, "It is time to go to the Galleon for some shaggin'. Anybody coming?" Almost in unison, they followed Dion a block down the street to the Spanish Galleon.

The jukebox was playing as they went into the Galleon. They stayed there until closing. Some were dancing. Some were drinking. Some were talking. Some were doing all of the above. Dion found Tommie Lynn and Sonja. He danced with the two of them most of the night.

When the Spanish Galleon closed, they walked to Rice's. Tea fumbled with the key before the front door was finally unlocked. They laid out their sleeping arrangements. Four slept lying across the bed and the other four slept on the floor. They agreed that the next night they would reverse positions.

They were awakened during the night by a loud rumbling noise. As they looked around, they soon recognized that it was Tea snoring. They rolled him onto his side on to get him to stop. They returned to their sleeping position. They managed to sleep fitfully between Tea's snoring episodes. Each time he awakened them, one would roll him from his back onto his side.

The next morning at around ten they gave up trying to sleep. Tea was still sleeping but the rest made him get up as punishment for keeping them awake. "The bed was obviously too soft for Tea," Cosmo said in disgust. "That was the worst night of sleep I think I ever had."

"Cosmo, check to see if there's any glass in that hole over there," Mike said as he pointed to the dingy beige drapes that were in front of the window.

Dion laughed, "Did any of you hear that train that kept rumbling through? It couldn't make up its mind where it was going but it sure made a loud noise."

"Oh, that was Tea. He's as big as any train that comes through here I'm sure," Harry said in a low gravelly voice before he giggled.

"It wont possible that it was Tea," Cosmo joked.

"No sir. We'd have heard him if it had been Tea," Neil added with a laugh.

"Tea, how are you doing this fine morning?" Mike asked.

Before Tea could speak, Dion said, "You mean the snoring king? He's alive but without permission."

"Thank you," Tea said with a sheepish grin.

Mike turned the conversation to a serious note, "We can joke about that snoring all we want. The plain truth is that if you do it tonight you're going to have to sleep outside. The rest of us need a little sleep too. There was damn little of it last night thanks to you."

"Alright, alright, message received," Tea said. "Now can we go get some breakfast? I'm hungry."

"Good plan," Mike said. "Hoskins is waiting for us. Hopefully we will not have to wait in line at this time of day."

"One of the nice things about staying here is that we can walk everywhere that we want to go. We can walk to Hoskins and stop at the three red dot store on the way back. I think some more liquor is in order," Tea said.

They walked to Hoskins where there was no line and had breakfast. They stopped at the ABC store and restocked their liquor supply on the way back. They were back in the room around twelve-thirty. They pulled out their liquor and started drinking.

"I have heard Jan say that you should not drink brown

liquor before noon. I guess it's okay since it is twelve-thirty,"
Dion said. "I'm going to have some anyway even if I misunderstood her starting time."

Each of them seemed to think drinking brown liquor was
okay at that time of day. Drink brown liquor is what they did
for the rest of the afternoon.

Around six they began to talk about being hungry. "What
do you say we go to the Sunset Grill or the OD Arcade to get
something to eat?" Mike slurred.

"I vote for the OD Arcade. I think it has the best hamburgers. We can get them with a beer. We can eat on the porch and
watch people walking on Ocean Drive," Tea said.

As there were no dissenting opinions, after showering and
changing clothes, they walked to the OD Arcade. With eight
of them and one only bathroom showering was a lengthy affair. It took them in excess of two hours to accomplish getting
dressed. They made Tea wait till last because he always took
the longest as he was determined to have every hair precisely
located on his head before leaving the room.

They sat on the porch unfazed by the chill in the air and ate
their hamburgers like royalty. They could have been the finest
and most sophisticated British Royalty; they felt that important to themselves. Oh those beers, those must have been the
best beers ever made. The beers matched the view. They
watched a continuous stream of young beauties walk by. They
tried to make conversation with each and every one as they
passed. Some responded to them; some did not. But it was
great fun.

Some time past ten Tea said, "We'd better move over to the
Spanish Galleon. I know Dion wants to go dancing. I'd enjoy
doing that myself."

They followed three particularly attractive young ladies toward Main Street. They struck up a conversation with the girls and found that they too are going to the Spanish Galleon. The girls told some of them their names but the next day none of them could remember the names.

Some of them danced with the two shaggers in the group. On their way out they spoke to Fat Harold. While they were in the Spanish Galleon a fine mist had started to fall. They walked back to Rice's through the cold, damp air and went to bed.

Only half an hour or so had passed before Tea started to snore again. Dion and Mike rolled him onto his side. They lay down and went back to sleep themselves. In a few minutes the unruly concert awaked them again. That time the noise woke everybody. Dion and Mike rolled Tea him onto his side. "That's his last chance," Dion said to Mike.

"Yes, next time he's out the door," a sheepishly mischievous Mike grinned.

In less than five minutes, there was another window-rattling snore. "That didn't take long did it?" Dion asked rhetorically. "Let's get him out of here. Who's going to help me?"

Mike, Neil and Harry stepped forward each saying, "Me."

"Grab hold," Dion said as he reached down and grabbed Tea's hair. Mike, Neil and Harry grabbed his arms and belt. They pulled him out the door of the room and through the front door of the house. They pulled him across the front porch and onto the steps. When his head was over the sidewalk Dion put his head down and released his hair saying, "This should be a good spot."

Cosmo had walked out onto the porch. He watched as they put Tea down. "It's cold and wet out here. He could catch pneumonia and die."

"He'll be all right most of him is still under the porch over hang," Dion replied.

Mike snickered and laughed out loud as he said, "At least we can get some sleep."

Around four-thirty, Tea woke up. Shivering thermogenesis had set in. His teeth were chattering. It took him a moment to realize the fact that he was cold. In fact, he thought, *I have icicles forming on my chin. That the fine mist has become a light rain and it is really cold.* He stood up and straightened his neck which had been crooked because the side of his head was on the ground while his side was on the steps. He was sore where his body had been laying on the edges of the steps. He shook like a dog to get as much of the moisture off as possible. Because of the anger building in him, he failed to realize he was getting wetter.

He vowed to have his revenge. *How could anybody think of doing this to me? I'm going to show them. They've messed with the wrong guy this time.* He stormed into the house. He reached across his body and opened the bedroom door with his left hand. He gave it a mighty shove expecting to wake up the group with the noise of the door hitting the wall. That didn't have the effect that he thought it could have because there was a padded doorstop just beyond it that prevented it from making a loud noise. He tried the door one more time grabbing the knob in his right hand swinging it as hard as he could to close it. Unfortunately for him Neil had rolled over. His foot was in the opening and blocked the door from making an exploding sound. Neil yelped softly. Tea reached over with his left hand and turned on the light switch. He screamed in red-faced rage, "Who put me out there in that cold rain? It's a miracle I didn't die! I could have frostbite, but y'all wouldn't care! I'm going to kick somebody's butt! Now who did it?" He was jumping up and down shaking his fists.

Dion sat up in the bed and calmly said, "You were snoring!"

That answer completely defused Tea. He thought to himself, *Who am I to argue with that kind of logic?*

Mike attempted to stir the pot on the situation a little more, "You can stay in here if you're quiet or you can go back outside and sleep if you are going to snore."

"It seems to me you have a very simple choice to make. Sleep here quietly or go outside and make all the noise you wish. Now turn out that light! It's making almost as much noise as you are," Dion said authoritatively.

Tea chose to sleep inside. He slept on his side the rest of the evening and into the morning when they arose. There was no more snoring that night. There would have been serious consequences for such an outburst. When they arose, they went home to St. Umblers.

CHAPTER TWENTY-EIGHT

FAT JACK'S EXPLODES

Dɪᴏɴ, Tᴇᴀ ᴀɴᴅ Mɪᴋᴇ went to OD on a Wednesday for a long weekend. Tea arrived for Dion a little after six that afternoon. Then they went to get Mike. "Boy this is really going to be something! Four nights in OD," Mike said with a big grin as soon as he sat down in the backseat of the little green Tempest.

"I'm really looking forward to this myself. I have had to work some really long hours the first three days of the week to be able to get a break," Dion said.

"Yeah. We are going to be doing some partying. We will be the kings of OD. Let's stop and get some barbecue on the way out of town," Tea said. They went to Herbert's where each ordered a chopped barbecue plate with coleslaw.

"We had better fortify our supplies on the way. You know the ABC stores close at dusk in South Carolina," Mike said.

"Okay. We will pass right by one if we go this way," Tea said pointing east.

"Fine choice! Go that way. I want to go ahead and buy all my liquor now so I won't waste the money on eating later," Mike said.

They agreed that was a good plan. When they reached the ABC store on their way, they all went in. Each bought his own liquor for the weekend.

They started east toward to Clinton and US701 south again. Tea said, "It's too bad that Cosmo didn't come with us. I know he'd have a big-time."

"You know Cosmo is not leaving his new woman to go to OD. He is afraid she wouldn't be there when he returned. We have seen Cosmo get those big yellow moon eyes over girls before. I think this is different though; those eyes are bigger than ever and his decisions are more out of character than ever. I think we are soon to be in store for a wedding. Can you imagine that? One of our crew being married?" Dion said.

"I think The Gator is right up there with Cosmo. It looks like there'll be another wedding in the near future. It looks like there is no way to avoid it this time," Tea said.

"I had better have a drink. You're depressing me with all his talk about marriage. It's up to the three of us to keep the tradition alive and the parties going," Mike said.

Dion and Tea decided to join him in having a drink. They arrived at OD a little after nine-thirty. "I'll drive around to Rice's and can get a room. We'll leave the car there and walk where we want to go," Tea said.

They went to Rice's and rented a room for four nights. They cleaned up some before going out around a quarter till eleven.

Tea was in the bathroom. He had left the door half-open. He was busy staring at himself in the mirror fixing his black hair so that every strand was perfectly located.

"Tea, you're looking as good as ever… and that's a shame!" Dion quipped. Mike joined Dion in a rousing laugh at Tea's expense.

Tea left the door open. He was enjoying being the center of attention.

They partied hard that night.

When they woke up the following morning, Mike said, "I have to brush my teeth. I have enough film to shoot *Gone With the Wind* on them!"

Friday night Dion and Mike were ready to go out significantly earlier than was Tea. "Dion let's go out on the beach and have a drink or two while we wait," Mike said.

"I'm for it. Let's go. I'm going to make me a drink in this thirty-two ounce cup. I'll have plenty of time to drink it before Tea is ready," Dion said.

"I'm mixing one right now myself," Mike said.

"Tea, we're going to walk down to the beach at the end of the horseshoe. You can find us there when you're ready," Dion said.

With that Dion and Mike were off. They stood out on the beach drinking and swapping war stories. They had both finished their drinks before Tea showed up.

"How nice of you to join us. Where did you get that ugly black shirt? You are just in time to buy us a beer at the Spanish Galleon," Mike said letting out a little giggle.

"Let's go to The Pad and have a drink first. There's plenty of time to go to the Spanish Galleon later," Tea said.

Mike held out his left arm toward Tea saying, "Go ahead twist it. See if you can make me go to The Pad."

"You are such a smooth talker. You talked us into letting you have your way. Don't count on that happening again," Dion said as he winked at Mike.

They went to The Pad. Tea and Mike had more than one beer.

"I'm ready to go to the Galleon and do some shaggin',"

Dion said. They left The Pad and started walking north along Ocean Drive toward the Spanish Galleon.

"Let's stop at Fat Jack's on the way. We haven't been there yet this weekend. There might be some fun to be had there," Mike said.

They did. Mike walked up to the bar to order a beer. "What do you have on draft?"

"You're too drunk for me to serve you a beer," the bartender said.

"I would like two draft beers," Tea said to the bartender.

"I'm not going to serve you either. And your other friend might as well not ask because I'm telling him in advance that I'm not going to serve him either. All of you are too drunk," the bartender said.

Mike reached over to the bar and picked up an empty mug. He switched it from his left hand to his right. Before anyone could move, he had drawn it back and thrown it at an illuminated beer sign behind the counter.

Tea picked up another mud and threw it into another beer sign behind the counter. Patrons were darting out the doors. The bartender jumped down behind the bar to protect himself from the flying glass. Mike threw another mug into the mirror. Tea grabbed a bar stool and threw it into the glasses that were sitting upside down on the shelf behind the bar.

"We'd better get out of here quickly! Follow me!" Mike said. He headed out the door with Tea following.

"Wait a minute! Where're you going? We have to take Dion with us," Tea said, balking while they appeared to be running blindly into the dark.

"If there is anybody in OD who can take care of himself, it is Dion. I don't know where he is. He's going to be alright. We're going out into the ocean to hide," a frantic Mike said.

They heard police sirens as they ran toward the ocean. They waded out to their waists. "Come on we are going out to our necks. That way they are less likely to see us when they shine their lights out here. I had to do this to get away in San Diego once. The police are too lazy to come after us out here even if they see us." Mike informed Tea.

"You're crazy. They will wait for us to come out and then arrest us. We will get soaked for nothing. We will have to spend the night in jail in our soaking wet clothes that's all this will get us," Tea said in a worried tone as they continued to wade out to deeper water.

"We are going to walk north parallel to the beach once we get out there. The police will lose sight of us anytime a wave comes in. It's time to turn north," Mike said.

"Yeah, I just know they will. We'll be dead. We'll drown when the waves wash over our heads. I'm having a hard time seeing you at times," Tea said as he turned north.

"This is way easier than it was in San Diego," Mike said.

"That probably has a lot to do with the fact the water in the Pacific Ocean is much cooler than in the Atlantic Ocean," Tea said.

Mike rewarded his insight by replying, "Yeah. How did you know that? I nearly froze my ass off in that cold water."

"Don't you think that the San Diego police know how cold that water is? That's why they didn't go in after you. The police here won't be deterred by cold water. They'll just wade out here and get us." Tea said.

They saw a couple of flashlights shining out toward them from the shore. Then they heard one policeman say to another, "If those fools are crazy enough to be out there in the ocean like that, then I'm going to let them go. You're on your own if you want to go get them."

"Nope. I'm not that crazy. I'm with you," the other policeman said. The policemen stayed on the beach looking for them for a few minutes. Then they went to their cars and left.

Mike and Tea came back a little closer to shore but continued to walk north. "I think we'd better stay out here and keep walking for another fifteen or twenty minutes to make sure they're really gone. I don't see them, but they could come back at any minute," Mike said.

"We'd better get out of here soon I'm about to lose my shoes. They are full of sand and water! This is awful walking! It might have been easier to get locked up," Tea growled.

"You are just being a damn wimp! Quit whining! Cowboy up a little bit. You are going to make it out of here just fine without being thrown into jail," Mike teased.

They continued walking for about twenty minutes. "I think it's safe to go back to shore now," Mike said as he started walking toward the beach.

"It's about damn time! I'm ready to get out of here. I want to go take a shower and change clothes!" Tea said. They walked out onto the beach. "Let's sit down and rest a few minutes," Tea demanded.

"Oh, come on wuss. We can be back to Rice's in less than ten minutes. Then you can get that shower you're talking about," Mike urged Tea.

Okay but I'm sure I'm going to have to throw these clothes away. No cleaner can get these things clean," Tea said.

They walked to Rice's to clean up. Dion came in. Tea and Mike exchanged stories of their escapes with Dion.

Mike had been correct in his assessment that Dion could take care of himself. He had walked out the door in a group of strangers. He walked to Ocean Drive with them. Then he nonchalantly started walking north planning to go to Rice's.

"I changed my plan quickly when there was a police car coming up the street out front here at the same time that one was coming up Main Street and there was one coming from each direction on Ocean Drive. I saw the lights of several cars behind me that were headed north on Ocean Drive so I stuck out my right thumb to try to hitch a ride. The first car stopped and picked me up," Dion informed them.

"What happened then?" Mike interrupted.

"I opened the passenger door and asked the driver where he was going. He told me he was going to Cherry Grove. I told him that was great because that's where I was going. He told me his name was Tim. We were talking and I found out that he knows Donnie Ray from the Lake because he has been dating Deborah who grew up living behind Donnie Ray in Roseboro."

Tea had ducked into the bathroom. When he came out, he only heard part of the last sentence. "Who were you talking about that knows our buddy Donnie Ray?" Tea asked.

"It was the guy dates Donnie Ray's former neighbor. He picked me up when I was hitchhiking. He drove me to Cherry Grove," Dion answered.

"So is that it? Is that all happened?" Mike asked.

"It turned out that Tim was going to a pizza place in Cherry Grove. He was going to pick up a pizza. Then he was going to go on to Little River. He told me that the restaurant delivers pizzas. I told him a pizza sounded pretty good. He told me that I could buy a pizza, have it delivered and I could ride with. He told me he had done that one time. I bought one and had it delivered here. I came with it," Dion concluded his story.

"You just saved me the trouble of asking you about that pizza," Mike said.

"It might not be a good thing to go out back out tonight. I say we stay here and let things settle down tonight. I think it will probably be safe to go back out tomorrow night as long as we don't go to Fat Jack's," Dion said.

"By the time we finish getting cleaned up, it will be almost closing time anyway," Mike agreed.

"I'm wore out from walking in the ocean with twenty pounds of mud in my shoes. I almost lost them two or three times," Tea said.

They ate pizza and drink liquor. They talked about the mighty and awful deeds that they had done in the past. They forecast the great and wonderful things they would do in the future. Their talk turned girls until they decided to go to bed.

"If your shoes are dry and you have all the sand out of them, you are welcome to come shaggin' with me at the Galleon," Dion said as he prepared to go out on Saturday night. He made his comment with a giggle as it was clearly a dig at their misadventure in the ocean the night before.

"I'll never get all the sand out of my shoes. They're not fully dry yet either. I'm not even sure that I can tell that they're brown they're so wet. Mike it's a good thing for you that it was me out there with you and not Cosmo. Because Cosmo would be threatening to keel you right now because of his wet, sandy shoes," Tea said.

"Quit whining. My shoes will be fine for the evening," Mike said with a laugh.

They went out and shagged the night away. They had a great time. Dion was the only one wet that night. That was the result of sweating from his almost nonstop dancing. Dion shagged with a number of different young ladies that evening. He spent most of his time shaggin' with Sonja, DeRhonda or Tommie Lynn.

Mike and Tea busied themselves drinking beer. They made a point of staying away from the bar however. They each danced occasionally with various partners.

CHAPTER TWENTY-NINE

CHERRY AND THE LARD BUCKET

THE PARTY STARTED at an old abandoned farmhouse just outside the city limits of St. Umblers. There was also an old barn on the property. The property was used for a while as another place to gather before a new adventure to the Lake was to begin. It was a great place to meet. There was light traffic on the two roads which intersected at the corner of the property. It was closer to town and to the Lake than the fraternity house. It was considerably closer to the nearest ABC store. A successful dash could be made to that ABC store by leaving by nine minutes until nine. On the other hand, twenty-ish year olds gathered there surely looked out of place to anyone passing.

They gathered there to prepare for going to the Lake. The characters on that particular evening included among others Dion, Tea, CJ, Cosmo, Patricia and Cherry. They had a few strong drinks and listened to Beach Music on the car radio. There was the ritual of seeing who could tell the biggest war story from their previous trips to the Lake. When it was time to go there was often a caravan of four to five cars that began the well-traveled journey of approximately five miles to the

ABC store. That night there were four cars in the caravan. From there it was on to the Lake.

Tea's car transported five that night. It was a good thing that Tea who was by far the largest of the group was driving. Cherry rode shotgun. Dion and Dare sat on either side of Connie Sue in the back seat.

Mr. Lee who ran the ABC store was a North Carolina state employee. He knew his patrons. By the time they walked in a number of nights, he would already have bottles lined up in order of repeated past purchases. They included a fifth of red label Smirnoff vodka and two pints of Lord Calvert for Dion and Tea. There might be a fifth of Rebel Yell for Toney. There would be a fifth of Gold Keg, Rocking Chair or Old Mr. Boston for Cosmo. After a stop at the grocery store they were off through the country to Spivey's Corner, the future home to the national hollering contest. The journey continued to the Mingo Community and Williams Lake Road to the Lake. The trip took about thirty-five minutes. It was made longer than the distance would normally dictate because of their standard forty-five mph drinking speed. Drinks were being mixed in both cars and not one drop was spilled. An intoxicated driver needed to be very careful with the human cargo he or she was carrying.

The Showmen were making sure that according to the promise of their song that it would stand that night.

"Hey, there's Walt from NC State over there," Tea shouted. They knew Walt through his previous visits to the Lake.

They had initially been introduced to Walt by Reese who met him at NC State. Walt was a slender young man who was in the engineering program at NC State. He was about five foot, eight inches tall. He wore plain black framed glasses typical of the studious engineering type. Walt was a fine person and a fine gentleman.

"He's a good old boy from Aurora. Let's go talk to him," Dion said. They walked over to where Walt was talking to several of his college buddies.

Walt extended his right hand to Tea and said, "How are you tonight? You've been drinking a little have you?" Walt pivoted a quarter turn to his left and reached out his right hand to shake Dion's. "How's number one tonight? Where is the rest of couple number one?"

"I'm doing just great WW. How were you? How are things up there at Moo U.?" Dion said.

"I'm studying hard every day just to get by. I'm looking forward to graduating soon. I think I have a job lined up with a paving outfit after graduation." Walt said.

"That sounds great. Are you going to make a lot of money? I wish I were graduating soon, but I still have too many classes to take," Tea said.

"Dion, who are you dancing with tonight?" Walt asked.

"There is no one in particular that I'm dancing with tonight, WW. I have been dancing with as many of the ladies as I could. And that's kind of fun. It's interesting to experience the difference in the ladies' dancing styles," Dion said.

"Have you seen old Reese around tonight?" Walt asked.

"No. Reese has been scarce around here recently. I haven't seen him in several weeks," Tea answered.

"Walter, where's that Linda girl you speak so highly of?" Dion asked.

"I really haven't seen much of her lately, but I think she is probably in Raleighwood. I don't think she has ever been to Williams Lake," Walt said.

"I think you really like that girl, don't you WW?" Dion asked.

"Yeah. I do!" Walt said in a playful voice mimicking a man from the deep country.

"Are we going to see those scandals flying across the floor tonight?" Dion asked.

"I don't think you are going to see old Dubya Dubya dancin' tonight," Walt answered with a laugh.

"Not even if that beautiful long-legged red head came over and asked you to dance?" Dion asked as he pointed toward a young lady close by.

"I think I would have to reconsider right away," Walt answered.

They continued their general banter for three or four minutes longer. "I've had a break and cooled down a little bit. I think I'm going to dance some more. Walt, it was good to see you," Dion said.

He turned and walked away toward a very attractive young lady with ear length black hair. When Dion reached the young lady, he respectfully held out his right hand and said, "Would you like to dance?"

She smiled sweetly and said, "Thank you I would."

"My name is Dion and I'm from St. Umblers. What is your name and where are you from?" Dion said.

She flashed a soft smile at him that was filled with perfectly symmetrical white teeth. Dion had never seen such a pretty teeth.

"My name is Betty Jo. I live in Sanford," the lady replied.

"You are beautiful and you have the most perfect set of teeth I have ever seen," Dion said with a slight red-cheeked blush.

"I noticed you were looking at my teeth. I'm fortunate that I work for a dentist and he has put in lots of work to make my teeth perfect. He has made them as beautiful as they are," Betty Jo said.

Dion lost track of the number of songs they shagged to but it must been at least five or six. As they came off the dance floor after the last of those songs Betty Jo said, "I'm sorry but I must leave now. The group I came with is ready to go home. We have to leave early in order to be home before curfew."

"May I walk you to the car?" Dion said.

"That would be most delightful," Betty Jo said.

Dion extended his right elbow to escort her to the car. Betty Jo put her left arm into it. They started out the door and down the steps. At the bottom of the steps Betty Jo said, "We parked in the extra parking lot to the left."

Dion turned left. As they walked he turned his face to Betty Jo. "I'd like to see you again sometime if that would be possible."

"I would like that," Betty Jo said with a shy, pearly-white smile.

"Then please tell me how I can get in touch with you," Dion said with a huge grin on his face.

"The name of the dentist I work for his oddly enough Dr. White. You can call me at the dentist office. The number is 555-1585. Dr. White is very generous about letting us use the telephone. You call me and I'll tell you how to get to my house. Please don't wait too long to call," Betty Jo said.

"I'll call you Monday if that's okay with you," Dion said.

"Perhaps we could go out with my friends Rusty and Kathy," Betty Jo said.

"Is that by chance the same Rusty that I know at Campbell? He's from Sanford. He's a math major," Dion said.

"I don't know, but he drives a souped-up, two-door coupe Plymouth Barracuda," Betty Jo said.

"Is it dark green with a stick shift?" Dion asked.

"I think so," Betty Jo said.

"Does his family have small show dogs?" Dion asked.

"They do," Betty Jo said.

"We have to be talking about the same Rusty," Dion said.

They arrived at the car that Betty Jo was riding in. Dion turned and faced Betty Jo who had turned toward him. He said, "Thank you for a lovely evening. It was a great pleasure getting to know you. I enjoyed shaggin' with you. Meeting you was serendipity."

"It was wonderful. What a fortunate accident it was. Don't forget to call me Monday," Betty Jo said with a smile.

Dion leaned over and kissed her gently on the lips. Then she responded in kind. Dion straightened up and started walking back toward the pavilion. He turned and said, "I will not forget to call you Monday!" Then he went back into the pavilion to enjoy the remainder of the show.

As the group gathered at Tea's car to depart for St. Umblers, Wayne and CJ came walking up with Dare. Wayne said, "I'd like to give Dare a ride home, but there isn't enough room for everybody."

"I rode down with Wayne and his group, if it's OK, I'll ride home with you Tea. Dare can have my spot in Wayne's car," CJ said.

"Sure, it's all right," Tea said.

"We have a bucket of beer on ice that you can have if you would like it. It you don't want it we are going to throw it away because we're afraid to drive home with it open in the car," Wayne said.

"If there's beer to be drunk the night is not over," CJ chuckled.

Wayne went to his car and came back with a big shiny galvanized lard bucket full of beer, ice and water. There was also a bottle of cheap red wine in the bucket. "Here it is," he said as he handed the bucket over to Tea.

"We'll take good care of it," Tea said. Tea looked at Cherry and said, "The only place I know to put this is on the floorboard in front of your seat."

"That will be okay," Cherry said.

Dion, Connie Sue and CJ filled the backseat. Cherry sat in the front passengers' seat. Tea set the lard bucket on the floor to the right of Cherry's legs and closed the door. They left for St. Umblers.

"Cherry, you are styling girl. That lard bucket's the fashion accessory every woman who love to have. Why, it will go perfectly with any outfit." Connie Sue deadpanned.

"You are the height of fashion." Dion said.

Connie Sue elbowed Dion in the arm. They let out rolling laughs.

"Cherry I would have one of those beers if you would pass it back here," CJ said after Tea had closed his door.

Neither Dion nor Connie Sue normally drank beer, but they decided to join in.

"Hand me one too," Dion said.

"Me too," Connie Sue echoed.

"Yeah I'll have one. How about you, Cherry?" Tea said.

"I don't think I'll have a beer," said Cherry who rarely drank more than a sip or two.

They drank two beers each on the way to St. Umblers.

Tea turned down Elon Street, a side street off of Main Street. As he passed the second intersection a car pulled in behind him. A few feet later the car turned on its flashing blue lights.

"Tea go slow so we have time to give Cherry these bottles and she can put them back in the lard bucket," Dion said.

It turned out to be a fortuitous thing that out of character for her Cherry was wearing an ankle length green floral print dress that night.

"Cherry slide that bucket up under your dress," CJ said.

As Tea turned on his right turn signal, they scrambled to

hand Cherry the beers that they were drinking for her to put them in the bucket.

Tea stopped the car in the parking lot of the old baseball diamond. He looked in the rearview mirror and could see empty liquor bottles lying up behind the backseat in front of the rear window. "There's going to be trouble," Tea said.

The policeman approached the car. He leaned over beside Tea and said, "Y'all are out kinda late tonight, ain't you?"

"We didn't think so, officer," Tea said.

"There's been vandalism round here the last few nights. Y'all know anything about that?" The policeman asked.

"No, sir, officer. We've just come from Williams Lake. We haven't even been in town until about three minutes ago. We're on our way home. If we see any vandalism going on, we'll come find you or go to the Police Department to report it," Dion said from the backseat.

The policeman stood silently beside the car for what seemed like hours even though it was only fractions of a second. Finally, he said, "I think it'd be best if y'all go on home now."

"Yes sir" Tea said with relief.

The policeman took about two steps back toward his car. He suddenly stopped and turned back toward Tea's window. He leaned back down to the window and said, "What are all them empty bottles doing back there behind the backseat?"

"What bottles officer?" Tea asked nervously.

"Them liquor bottles. I can't imagine why they'd be back there if y'all weren't drinking. Did you drink that liquor tonight?" The policeman asked.

"Oh no those have been back there for weeks and weeks," Dion said. Dion picked up one that was without a cap and handed it out the window to the officer, "You can see that it has been back there long enough that there aren't even any drops left in it. See it is completely dry. If we had drunk that tonight there would still be a few drops in the bottle."

"I reckon you have a point there young man," the policeman said. "Now git on home with you."

The policeman drove away.

They all looked at Cherry whose teeth were chattering.

"What is the matter with you up there?" CJ asked Cherry with a giggle.

"I'm so cold with his bucket against my legs that I didn't think I could stand it much longer," Cherry complained. Cherry slid the bucket from under her legs back to the right side of the floorboard.

"Let's have a beer! After all as CJ said earlier, there's beer to drink, the night is not over," Tea said.

"We can sit right here and finish it off in this parking lot," Dion said.

They sat there and drank the rest of the beer. Then Tea drove each of them home before driving himself home.

"I may have a really great date Friday night. Is it possible that I could drive your car if it works out?" Dion asked Lado.

"Do I know this wild woman?" Lado asked.

"I don't believe you have had the pleasure of making her acquaintance," Dion said.

"Where does she live?" Lado asked.

"She lives in Sanford," Dion said.

"She must really be something if you are willing to drive all the way to Sanford. She has got to be some kinda of fittin'?" Lado said.

"She is special!" Dion said.

"OK. You can take my car. I'll ride with Thomas and Phil," Lado said.

"Thanks," Dion said.

Dion was good to his word. He called Betty Jo from the lab phone on Monday afternoon. It was all he could do to wait until the afternoon because he was trying to avoid appearing too eager.

"Betty Jo, this is Dion from the Lake, I mean Williams Lake. How are you today?" Dion said.

"I'm glad to hear from you. I have been looking forward to your call," Betty Jo said.

"I know you have to get back to work so I'll only keep you long enough to ask you to go out with me on Friday night," Dion said.

"I would love to," Betty Jo said.

"I'll speak to Rusty and see about double dating with he and Kathy. Then I will call you back," Dion said.

"Great. Goodbye for now," Betty Jo said.

"Goodbye," Dion said. He was so excited that he did not even know that he had hung up the phone.

Dion set out immediately to find Rusty. Rusty normally parked in a different parking lot than the one the students from St. Umblers and the surrounding area used. Dion went through the Student Center on his way. He saw one of Rusty's friends there. He did not know his name, but he had seen him and Rusty walking around campus together a number of times.

"Have you seen Rusty recently?" Dion asked.

"No. But I think he is in class now. He should be out in about five minutes. I expect he will go to his car to drop off his books because his next class is not for two hours," the other student said.

"Hey, thanks. Do you know if he is parked in the lot he normally parks in?" Dion said.

"Yes," the other student answered.

"Thanks again," Dion said. He set off to Rusty's car. He was standing beside the car about two minutes before the end of class. He waited for about fifteen minutes before he saw Rusty approaching.

"Hello, Rusty. How are you?" Dion said.

"This is quite a surprise. I don't normally see you around here. I normally only see you around the Math Building and Chapel. Is there something going on I should know about?" Rusty said.

"Actually, there is. I think you know Betty Jo," Dion said.

"If you mean Kathy's friend Betty Jo from Sanford, I know who she is. I don't really know her. Why do you ask?" Rusty said.

"I met her Saturday night at Williams Lake. We danced and I asked if I could take her out sometime. To my great pleasure, she answered in the affirmative. She suggested that we might be able to double with you and Kathy. I asked her out Friday night and I told her I would talk to you about the possibility. Do you think we could work that out?" Dion explained.

"Kathy and I would love it. What time are you to pick her up?" Rusty said.

"I told her we would set a time after I talked to you. I can drive. I'll have my brother's car," Dion said.

"Come to my house approximately six o'clock. You can meet my folks and the dogs before we leave. Tell Betty Jo we will pick her up about seven. We will pick Kathy up on the way. She will probably be more relaxed under those circumstances than she would with two men she doesn't really know. I'll drive because I know where she lives and where we will go," Rusty said.

Rusty wrote out directions for Dion to get from Campbell to his house.

"I'll come directly from the lab to your house. How long will it take to get there?" Dion said.

"You should easily make it in under thirty minutes," Rusty said.

"That is great! I'll see you then," an excited Dion said. They shook hands and Dion floated back over to Cosmo's car to get the book for his next class.

Dion called Betty Jo again that afternoon and told her the arrangements he had made with Rusty.

Friday came slowly but it inevitability arrived for the excited Dion. He was wild with anticipation. He showed up at Rusty's a few minutes after six. He met Rusty's parents. Rusty drove them to pick up Kathy. Finally, they arrived at Betty Jo's house. Dion bounced from the back seat of Rusty's car. He looked like Dr. J taking off from the free throw line and landing at the door in one step. He knocked twice and stood back a respectable distance under the porch light to allow himself to be recognized and to allow the light green screen door to open without hitting him.

Betty Jo came to the door. She was wearing a short red dress. "Hello. You're absolutely stunning," Dion said.

"Thank you. I'm glad to see you too," Betty Jo said.

"Are you ready to go?" Dion asked her as he offered his right elbow to escort her to the car with a beaming smile. She accepted.

"Yes. I have waited all week for tonight," she said.

"Me too. Me too!" Dion said. He was so smitten by how gorgeous she was that words momentarily failed him. He helped her into the back seat.

Rusty and Kathy argued frequently during the evening. Dion and Betty Jo enjoyed each other's companionship. That fact seemed to make Kathy more agitated. The closer Dion and

Betty Jo became, the more Kathy grumbled and complained.

They arrived at Betty Jo's house before her midnight curfew. Dion walked her to the door. "I had the most wonderful time enjoying your company. I'm sorry that Rusty and Kathy were at odds," he said in a low voice.

"I think Kathy was envious of the fact that we had such a good time and were having so much fun. It seemed to make her angrier at Rusty that they were in a feud," Betty Jo said.

"I would like to see you again. Next time I think just the two of us. Would that be suitable?" Dion said.

"I think that would be perfect," Betty Jo said.

"I'll call you soon," Dion said.

"See to it that you do. I'll be waiting," Betty Jo said.

Dion returned to the car. Rusty drove Kathy home. Then on the way back to Rusty's house Dion said, "Thanks for doubling and thanks for driving."

"I'm sorry that Kathy and I were not having as much fun as you and Betty Jo. I think Kathy was jealous of the chemistry between you and Betty Jo." Rusty said.

They arrived at Rusty's house. Dion said, "Thanks again man. Goodnight."

"Good night and drive safely. Make sure you don't speed going out of town. The police have a speed trap going on every weekend night," Rusty said.

CHAPTER THIRTY

WHO DID YOU SAY SHE IS?

TEA PULLED HIS CAR into the front yard at Rice's Guesthouse. Dion, Mike and Toney followed him to the house. They went in to talk to Mrs. Rice about renting a room.

"Hello, Ms. Rice. We're back. We'd like to get our regular room for tonight and tomorrow night if we could," Tea said.

"Of course you can Tea. The room is all made up and ready for you. Here are two keys. It's good to see you. Dion, Mike how have you been?" Mrs. Rice answered.

"Everything has been just great. Thank you for asking," Dion said.

"Just fine," Mike added.

"You know we will take good care of everything Mrs. Rice," Dion said.

Mrs. Rice looked at Toney. Toney staggered a step or two toward her. He reached into the right front pocket of his pants and brought out a roll of bills. He held it up toward Ms. Rice with his right hand and said, "I got a wad. I'll pay for the room." He reeled off a few bills and handed them to Mrs. Rice to pay for the room.

"You don't have to pay for the room until you're ready to leave," Ms. Rice told Toney while he was holding the money out between them.

"Okay. We will wait until we ready to leave to pay," Toney said as he pulled the money back.

Tea and Mike each took a key to the room. It really didn't matter who took the keys. They planned to leave the door to the room unlocked as they always did.

They retrieved their stuff from the car. Since it was too early to eat dinner at five, they decided to have a drink or two while they were getting cleaned up.

"I'm ready for dinner. You two have already taken drunk," Dion said at seven-thirty.

"We didn't take drunk by ourselves sir," Tea said.

"Let's go eat! I'm starving to death!" Toney said.

"I'm going to the OD arcade and have one of their fine burgers and a beer on the porch. I'm going to do some girl watching while I eat, "Mike said with a mischievous grin.

It was an easy group to get along with. Mike's motion was unanimously accepted without discussion. Mike led the way and the other three fell right in behind him.

"There sure is some fine scenery out here tonight. That girl with the black hair down to her shoulders is the best looking girl I've ever see," Tea marveled as a scantily clad beautiful teenage girl walked toward they on the sidewalk.

"She is attractive, but don't you think she's a little young for you?" Dion asked.

Toney looked at her and said in a low gruff voice, "If they're old enough to bleed, they're old enough to butcher! I'm going to show her I've got a wad!" He pulled his roll of bills from the right front pocket of his khaki pants. He held it out toward the girl as she passed. To Toney's disappointment, she appears to ignore both his gesture and his words.

In a minute or two, a blonde with big boobs came along. She wore a mid-thigh length gray jumper with a long sleeve white shirt underneath. She had long flowing hair. It was cut into three sections by her shoulders. The biggest bunch lay quietly on her back. The other two smaller, but approximately equal, partitions graced the front of her shoulders. They fell invitingly to the nipples of her large breasts. The length of her hair made it too heavy to defy gravity and curl. It had a hint of a turn inward on each side toward the center of her chest.

Tea stood and pumped his fist in the air and said, "How about that blonde? She's the best-looking girl I've ever seen! I'd love to talk to her. I bet she would kiss me."

Tea spotted another young lady in a bright yellow miniskirt coming toward them. She was a petite five foot three to five foot four. She looked to be size zero to size two. Her most prominent feature was her long brown hair that was full of huge wavy curls. The big, wavy curls that flowed through her hair to her waist spread it all the way across her back looked like a cloak on her tiny body.

"She is definitely going out to party. That skirt is way too short to wear to school." Toney said. Then he shouted at the young lady in a gruff deep voice, "I've got a wad."

"Wow! Look at that cutie! She's a real beauty. She is the best looking woman I have seen on this beach." Tea said excitedly.

"Tea, any woman on this beach who would talk to you would instantly become the best looking woman here," Mike said as he scrunched himself up and folded his hands backward while pressing them down. Those actions were accompanied by his mischievous little laugh.

"Mike, you've set the requirements too high. The truth is any woman who does not run from Tea becomes the best looking woman on the beach," Dion said with a laugh. Toney and Mike joined the lighthearted laughter at Tea's expense. They continued the banter as they ate their burgers.

"I'm going across the street to The Pad," Mike said. They arouse in unison and walked to The Pad.

"There is Tim who gave me a ride the night of the Fat Jack incident. The lady in the blue bell bottom pants is Deborah from Roseboro." Dion announced. "Do you remember her from the Lake?"

"She's a real beauty," Tea said.

"Come with me and I'll introduce you to them," Dion said to his friends.

"Deborah, Tim this is Tea, Mike and Toney. This is Deborah and Tim,"

Dion said.

They exchanged pleasantries and made small talk for a few minutes. They heard the start of "Part Time Party Time Man" in the background. "Deborah and I are going to go dance to this song," Tim said.

"We'll see you later," Dion said to Tim. He nodded goodbye to Deborah.

They hung around The Pad for another hour or so. Dion and Mike did some shaggin'. "There are no women that are especially interesting here tonight," Mike said.

"How about we go to the Spanish Galleon?" Toney said.

They went. A few minutes later, Tommie Lynn came up to Dion. She threw her arms around him. As she hugged him, she lifted her head slightly in order to French him in the left ear.

"Wow! Was that what it looked like?" Tea asked Dion.

"I don't know. What did it look like?" Dion answered.

"It looked like that beautiful girl with the silky black hair

French kissed you in the left ear!" Mike said with a sneaky laugh as he went into his best mischievous posture.

"Who is that girl? She is definitely the best looking girl I ever saw," Tea said.

Tea, Toney and Mike had never met Tommie Lynn during any of their previous trips to OD though Dion had danced with her often. They had never really paid her any attention because she was skinny before. Her body had beautiful curves. She had filled out from girl to woman.

"That my friend is no girl. That is a beautiful, sensuous woman!" Dion said.

As soon as the next song started, Dion went over and asked Tommie Lynn to dance. They shagged to several songs before Dion excused himself and walked away.

He danced two songs with Page. Page was a beautiful little pixie about five feet two inches tall who wore her brown hair at chin length. She was made up entirely of grace, smiles, laughter and energy. She could shag. Page was much lighter on her feet and quicker than most of the women. She could immediately follow any move. She and Dion were magic of the dance floor. Any time his friend came to OD and Dion was there he thought he had to dance with her.

After their second dance that night Dion said to her, "Page, you are my favorite dance partner of all time."

"I just try to keep up," she said.

"Girl you do better than keep up. You are just simply the best shagger that I have ever seen. I love to dance with you," Dion said.

Page's face turned bright red from the compliment. They touched hands and went their separate ways.

Dion spotted Nancy from Anderson. He made an effort to reach her to ask her to dance. He was too slow as he was beaten to the prize by another of Nancy's admirers.

One of Nancy's friends saw the disappointment on his face. "We came with Nancy and we get to stand and watch as you men fall all over yourselves to dance with her. It is like we don't even take up space. No one sees our faces. All the men are trying to win favor with "The Queen of the Beach" as we have started calling her. She will get to dance every dance and we'll watch almost every single one."

Dion could see why she was the Queen of the Beach. The title fit. She was regal. That face and body undoubtedly turned heads on the beach all day. Then she held court on the dance floor all night.

Nancy's friend went on "I'm glad that we will go home Sunday. May be the four of us will get noticed when we get back there. Did you know that we picked up a guy who was hitch-hiking on the way here last Saturday and he has stayed with us all week?"

"I did not know that. Has he helped you with the lifting and chores?" Dion managed to utter. His pause and trembling response gave away the fact that he was caught off guard and more than a little uncertain how to respond to that question.

"Yes. But nothing else has happened," another of Nancy's friends added quickly as though trying to dispel any thoughts that they were easy girls.

Dion had not even considered such a thought. He knew from their behavior and demeanor that these were proper young ladies. The Queen of the Beach could have had her pick of those in attendance if she were easy. Her four friends were attractive enough that if they were inclined, they too could have easily picked up a guy. These young ladies were typical of those in attendance. They were innocent, fun-loving ladies. You had to respect that innocence. "I'm certain that all of you have behaved in a manner that your mothers would approve of." He said. When Nancy was captured for another dance before getting back to her friends, Dion excused himself and moved away from the young ladies from Anderson.

Dion spent the majority of the rest of the night talking to and shaggin' with Sonja. Mike danced a few songs, but he spent most of the night drinking beer with Tea and Toney. As they started to leave at closing time, they saw Tim and Deborah. Tim was scalded.

"Whoa! That Tim has taken serious drunk. He's blasted!" Toney said.

"I have never seen anybody who can get as drunk as Tim and still be on his feet," Dion said. He continued, "I'm going to go over and see if I can give Deborah a hand."

Dion walked over to Tim and Deborah. "Hello. May I be of any assistance?" he asked.

"Dion we had a good time tonight, didn't we? By the way, what is your name?" Tim stuttered as he put his right hand around Dion's shoulders.

"This is your friend Dion. Don't you remember?" Deborah said to Tim. Then she turned to Dion and said, "I think we have it under control. The car is just right there."

Tim leaned over and whispered into Dion's ear, "There is something I want to do for me when you tell this story. You tell them it was me. You tell them I did it."

"Okay. We'll see you later," Dion said as he left them to rejoin the others.

The four walked to Rice's. The majority of the conversation during that walk was about Tommie Lynn whose name the other three still did not know.

"I noticed that you didn't introduce us to the girl who French kissed your ear," Tea said.

"That is private stock boys. You may drool at will. You will not get any closer than that. She is picking me up tomorrow night for us to get better acquainted," Dion said.

"I wondered why you didn't do more about her approach tonight," Mike said.

"Patience makes things better," Dion said with a sly look of satisfaction on his face.

"Where are you going?" Toney asked.

"That information is classified above Top Secret and you are not cleared to know. You never will be for that matter. You have no need to know even if your were cleared," Dion said. Even in the dim light of night one could tell by the gleam in his eyes that he was proud of his current stature among his comrades.

"Do you need a wad? Because if you do, I've got a wad and you can have it!" Toney asked.

"No thank you. But I appreciate the offer," Dion said.

They arrived at the Rice guesthouse. Even before they reached the door, they could hear the TV blaring in the living room. They looked inside to see Mrs. Rice apparently passed out. Mr. Rice had already gone out to the shrimp boat.

Mrs. Rice was sitting in the green and brown floral print armchair. She had one of her arms on each arm of the chair with her hands out in front of her. Both palms were turned upward. Her head was laid far back onto the low back of the chair. She was slouched down into the chair in a reclining position. The fabric of the chair was worn where her elbows and her head were resting.

"You see that empty Scotch bottle beside her right arm? I'll bet that why she is in that chair. We have thought she enjoyed a nip in the past. Now we know for sure," Mike said.

Toney was dancing around the chair. As he did shallow

knee bends and pointed both index fingers at Mrs. Rice, he said, "If Harry were here, he would be going Woo! Woo! Woo!"

None of that disturbed Mrs. Rice.

"Leave the poor woman alone! Let's get into our room after we turn down the TV," Tea said.

Mike turned the TV down. They went into their room and went to bed.

The next morning Mrs. Rice was up and stirring when they awaken. No mention was made of their discovery earlier that morning.

They enjoyed a typical Saturday at OD. That afternoon they cleaned up and dressed. They went to the Boulevard Grill and had grilled cheese sandwiches with mayonnaise. While they were ordering, Dion absented himself with a stealth maneuver. They did not notice that he was gone until their food arrived.

"Where is Dion's grilled cheese?" Toney asked.

"Where is Dion?" Tea asked with alarm in his voice.

"He was right between us," Toney said.

"Where is he now? That is the important question," Tea said.

They had completely forgotten that Tommie Lynn was picking him up. They had never known when or where.

"He can take care of himself. He always finds a way to do that. Waitress, bring me another cold beer. Let's eat and go shaggin'," Mike said. After they finished eating, the three of them went to the Spanish Galleon.

About eleven-thirty, Dion and Tommie Lynn arrived at the Spanish Galleon. On their way in someone pinched Dion on the butt. He turned and was surprised to see only Kathy close enough to have been the culprit. "Kathy I didn't know you cared. I'm flattered."

"You pinched me. I pinched you back so you would know how it feels," Kathy said.

"I would never think of doing that. I respect you too much," Dion said.

Kathy's face turned flame red with embarrassment as she thought about what Dion had just said. "I didn't think. I know you would never do that. You are too much of a gentleman. I'm sorry," she said.

Dion reached over and pulled Tommie Lynn to his side. "Tommie Lynn my assailant here is Kathy. Meet Donnie Ray. Kathy, Donnie Ray this lovely lady is Tommie Lynn," he said. They exchanged pleasantries for a few minutes. The pinching episode was forgotten.

Dion and Tommie Lynn moved into the crowd. They came upon his friends.

"Where have you been?" Tea asked in a concerned voice. Then he saw Tommie Lynn. At that moment, he remembered that Dion had told them that he was being picked up by the unnamed beautiful young lady with the silky black hair. In fact, all three of Dion's friends remembered at that moment.

Dion did something out of the ordinary; he left without introducing Tommie Lynn to his friends. He did it to pique their curiosity. He wanted Tommie Lynn to be as big a mystery to them as possible. After they walked away he said, "Tommie Lynn, please forgive me for not introducing you. It was intentional. They will talk about you and ask me your name for days to come. I did it to make you the mystery woman," he said.

"Thank you for explaining. That was clever," Tommie Lynn said with a laugh.

Dion and Tommie Lynn went to the floor to shag to the next song, "Nip Sip." They stayed away from Dion's three friends for the remainder of the evening.

It wasn't long after "Nip Sip" until they ran into Tim and Deborah. "Tommie Lynn, this is Deborah and Tim. Deborah and Tim meet Tommie Lynn," Dion said by way of introduction. The four of them talked through a song or two before Dion excused Tommie Lynn and himself to go to dance.

At the conclusion of the song, "Green Eyes," Dion said to Tommie Lynn, "Tim can be drunker and remain standing than any person I have ever seen!"

"He certainly does seem to have a talent for that. Unfortunately, it is a talent for which there would appear to be virtually no demand," Tommie Lynn laughed.

"Let me introduce you to Larry and Patrice," Dion said. He gently took her left hand in his right and walked her over to the corner where a couple and a lady stood.

When they approached the ensemble, Jan, dressed in her normal black, said to Dion as she hugged him and kissed him on the cheek, "Hey, baby. She is gorgeous!"

"Tommie Lynn, these nice people are Jan, Patrice and Larry. Jan is from Virginia Beach and Larry and Patrice are from Kannapolis. We see Jan from time to time at various partying venues. Jan, Patrice and Larry meet Tommie Lynn. Tommie Lynn is from the local area," Dion said. They exchanged hugs with Jan and Patrice making sure to include Tommie Lynn. Larry joined in without reluctance.

Patrice was a short energetic young lady. She was quite attractive. Her two most striking characteristics were her vibrant red hair and effervescent personality. Both were brightly displayed that night.

Larry was a handsome slender young man with a mustache and a small black goatee to match. He too had a dynamic personality highlighted by his dry sense of humor and laugh.

Patrice looked at Tommie Lynn and said sincerely, "You are such a pretty lady."

"I take that as a real compliment coming from some one as beautiful as you," Tommie Lynn responded.

The group talked and laughed until closing time. "We are going to be on the beach tomorrow. You are welcome to join us. We will be right down in front of the pavilion," Patrice and Jan said to Tommie Lynn as they parted.

After Dion and Tommie Lynn walked away, Tommie Lynn turned to Dion and asked, "Are all of your friends as nice as the ones I have met tonight? Are they always as friendly as they were tonight?"

"You saw them as they are. You met the type person I want to be my friend. If you are with me, you are their friend too. It cuts both ways because I readily accept anyone they are with," Dion answered.

"I'm not ready for the night to end yet. Are you?" Tommie Lynn said.

"No. I definitely am not ready to leave *you* yet," Dion said.

"We can go up to the house were I'm staying on the ocean in Cherry Grove. You can meet some of my girl friends and maybe some of their dates" Tommie Lynn offered.

"Okay! Deal!" Dion said.

They went.

Tommie Lynn drove Dion to Rice's a little after three. When Tommie Lynn stopped the car, Dion looked longingly into her eyes, "I want to kiss you now."

"What is stopping you?" she said.

He softly tossed her hair for a few seconds then he gently took her face into his hands and applied the slightest pressure to bring their mouths together. It only took a little pressure because she was eagerly awaiting his approach. She leaned into him. Their mouths met with great mutual satisfaction. They kissed a long tender goodbye before he exited the car. Despite their yearnings, they avoided ravenous contact. That was a passionate kiss that revealed their desires and respect.

"Goodnight. I have had the time of my life with you tonight. I was proud to be with you. I want to see you again. I will call you," Dion said as he opened the car door.

"I too had a great time. I cannot wait to see you again. Goodnight," she said.

Dion closed the car door. Tommie Lynn drove back to the house on the beach in Cherry Grove. Dion heard the TV as he stepped in the front door. He went to the bedroom door expecting to find his friends sound asleep when he opened it.

"We decided you two had gone over to Dillon to get married," Tea said.

"Couldn't blame you if you had. That was some gorgeous woman. I'm with Tea on this one. She may be the best-looking woman I ever saw. She's a knockout. What did you say her name is?" Mike said.

"We could not find a preacher or a justice of the peace to perform the ceremony at such a late hour." Dion laughed lightly. "Why are you still up?"

"We had to make sure that woman didn't rape you. That is the first time I ever saw you in a situation that I had any doubt you could handle on your own. I'm volunteering to help with that babe," Mike said.

"Thanks for your concern," Dion said.

"There is no mystery about why you were with her. She looks almost exactly like Susan. She is the same height. She has the same body. He has the same silky black hair. Their faces look very much alike. We know how beautiful you think Susan is and how much like her," Tea said.

"Just a coincidence, my man. Just a coincidence," Dion said.

"She was some kind of good-looking in that crème colored short dress and that matching Philadelphia lawyer's jacket that was slightly longer than the dress. That jacket went all the way to her knees," Mike marveled.

"Who did you say she is?" Tea asked.

Dion smiled.

CHAPTER THIRTY-ONE

HOME! SWEET HOME?

CHERRY, GATOR AND GLORIA were riding with Tea to the Lake. Gloria had gone to concerts with various members of the St. Umblers group, but that was her first trip to the Lake. It proved to be quite memorable. Gloria loved to party hard even at her young age. She was daring and bold long before she should have been.

Gloria was several years younger than Tea and The Gator. She was about average height with brown hair which he wore in pigtails that fell to about shoulder length. Her voice often seemed a little loud but that was because she was excited. She wanted to have a good time and to be accepted. While she wanted to have a good time, she would not compromise herself. Her morals were proper.

They were about halfway to the Lake before Cherry asked, "Where is Dion tonight?"

"I'm not sure. I tried to call him today but I never did get an answer. It is not like him to miss going to the Lake," Tea said. "I wonder what happened to him tonight myself."

They arrived at the Lake before The Embers started playing.

Tea parked the car. They talked and drank beside the car until they heard The Embers begin to play. Then they went inside. They were ready for some entertainment and some fun.

They had no sooner paid their dollar each and gone inside than they saw the answer to the question Cherry had posed in the car on the way to the Lake. There was Dion shaggin' with a beautiful black haired lady. Dion was beaming from ear to ear. It was obvious that he was quite pleased with his companion. Her face was glowing from contentment and happiness. She was wearing that magnificent white-toothed smile. It lit up her whole face. She was radiant.

"Why that sly devil Dion beat us here. That is one good-looking woman that he is dancing with," Tea said.

"That's that Betty Jo girl from Sanford that he was dancing with a couple of weeks ago. She seemed to be very nice the night they met. He sure does seem to like her. And she seems to like him too," Cherry said.

"I wonder who he rode with. Let's go over and talk to him," Tea said.

"Dick, I'd leave him alone for right now. They seem to be really into each other," The Gator said as he squinted through his left eye to see them.

"The Gator's right. We should leave them alone. He is such a gentleman that if he is actually with her, he will come over and introduced her to us," Cherry added.

They did not approach Dion and Betty Jo. Instead, they found themselves a place to dance and hang out. Once again, Cherry proved to be a sage. Dion brought Betty Jo over to introduce her.

"Betty Jo I'd like you to meet Cherry, Gloria, Gator and Tea," he said as he pointed to each of them when he called their name. Then he continued by turning his face toward

Betty Jo and said, "This is Betty Jo; she's from Sanford. She is a rare find. She is beautiful and is blessed with a great personality. And to top it all off the girl is a great shagger."

They each in turn said hello. Each made sure to welcome her to the group and to the Lake. After about three or four songs Dion and Betty Jo left to dance.

"I don't think Dion has even been drinking tonight. He must really like that girl," Cherry said.

"I think you have it right, Dick," Gator said in a growl.

It was just another fun night at the Lake until The Embers took a break around nine-thirty. Tea and the other three who rode with him went to his car for a drink. Dion and Betty Jo did not join them. They were in the parking lot to make a drink and get in the mood. Tea and Gloria were drinking straight from the bottle. Some men whom Tea did not know stopped and made an issue of Gloria drinking straight from the fifth of Lord Calvert. They actually were considerably more interested in Gloria then they were in Gloria drinking straight from the bottle. They were hoping that they could start conversation to attract her attention.

Tea took a big shot from the bottle as the strangers watched.

"May I have that bottle?" Gloria asked. Tea handed her the bottle.

One of them said, "You cannot drink that straight."

Tea saw that Gator was mixing a drink. He said, "Gator will have some Cocola left after he mixes his drink. I'm certain he would be willing to let her chase the liquor with his Cocola."

By then, Tea had figured out that they were more interested in Gloria than how she drank. He told them, "Gloria is with me and she can drink from the bottle if she chooses to do so."

"I could drink the whole damn fifth without turning it down if I wanted to," Gloria said.

There it was. The salvo had been laid out before everyone. It was not going anywhere! By then, more people had gathered around as they had heard what sounded like a confrontation. That brought on the big dare.

"Let's see you drink that straight from the bottle with nothing but a chaser," one of them dared Gloria.

"Hand me the bottle," Tea said to Gloria. Tea took the bottle and took a big slug from it.

"We didn't want to see a guy drink the bottle. There is nothing unusual about that. We want to see the girl show us she can take a big slug right out of the bottle," another said.

That brought on more dares from the crowd. Someone stuttered, "Let's see the girl take a big drink." Another said, "There's no way!" Someone else said, "We're wasting our time waiting to see her drink because she can't do it." A female voice was heard saying, "Come on, girl. Show them you can do it!" There were other comments which were not easily understood, but the majority of them expressed great doubt that Gloria could chug a big swig. The bystanders were getting either restless or bored.

"Tea, hand me the bottle. Gator, may I have your Coke please," Gloria said.

Tea handed Gloria the bottle. There was at least a fourth of the fifth left. Gloria took a swig of Coke and a deep breath. She turned the bottle up. She held her breath while she emptied the bottle. She drank every bit of that except a small amount that was running out the side of her mouth and dribbling down her chin. Then she chased the liquor with a big pull on the Coke. She held her head back and let out a big laugh. It was the kind of laugh that only she deserved to produce at that moment. She yelled like a champion at the finish of a big race or some other athletic event.

"Way to go Dick!" The Gator cheered. He really had no idea that Gloria could do it.

"I guess you showed them, girl," Tea shouted with excitement.

Cherry was unprepared for what she had just seen. Neither was anyone else. "Are you all right Gloria?" Cherry asked in astonishment.

"I'm just great. I guess I showed all of them! Didn't I? Gloria said with a gleam in her eyes that could be seen even in the dim light of the parking lot.

There was loud clapping and shouting of cheers from throughout the crowd. One accurate forecaster said, "They'll be sorry that she did that very soon. She's going to be one sick little girl!"

Indeed, they were soon going to find out that they really wished she had not shown her newfound drinking ability quite so well. They went back in to dance and for a while, Gloria was the star of the show. Some of the witnesses gathered around to watch her. However, that came to a quick end when she became so drunk that she was flopping around. She was falling down on the floor drunk.

The group was soon on the way back to the car. Tea gathered Gloria and started for the car. It was not to get her another drink. Gloria was done for the evening. In fact, she did not make it all the way to the car before she lost the coordination required to walk.

Tea stretched her out across the front seats. He stayed there and held her head held her head until she was settled.

"Thank you! Thank you!" Gloria said repeatedly.

Tea was wondering why she was not mad. He should have stopped her from accepting the dare. He was thinking, *She's no fun at all now.* He began to wonder, *How in the hell will I explain her condition to her mother and father.*

He was also bemoaning the fact that he was down to the back-up pint of liquor behind the wheel. He thought to himself, *That is another reason I should not have let her drain the damn fifth.*

Gloria was soon out cold. Tea went back in to the pavilion but that was no longer fun.

"Tea, you know you must not leave Gloria alone in the car because there are so many dogs here who would try to take advantage of her in her current condition. Go back to the car and take care of her," Cherry ordered.

As Tea approached the car he could see that sure enough there were assholes already around it. As Tea opened the door to check on Gloria, she tried to sit up. He encouraged her to lie back down. Again, she said "Thank you!"

It was a good thing that Cherry came to the car. "Go get The Gator. We need to take Gloria home," Tea said.

Cherry found Gator. They loaded the car. Tea started for St. Umblers.

"We've got to take Gloria home, but we will not go straight to her house. We will try to get a little food into her to see if that will sober her up some," Tea finally said.

"It sounds like a good plan Dick," Gator said.

"How are we going to get her into the house without waking her mother and father which will get her in trouble?" Cherry asked, ever the voice of sanity.

"The Gator will take Gloria to the door and explain that she is sick. Therefore, we brought her home a little earlier than normal. We should get there before one," Tea said.

"Like hell I am Dick. You helped to get her that drunk. You take her to the door. I don't want them mad at me," The Gator said.

Tea and The Gator argued over the issue of who was going

to take Gloria to the door until they were about a block from her house. The Gator was drunk himself. He finally relented and agreed that he would take Gloria to the door and leave her there after Tea offered him ten dollars for the effort. Tea stopped the car in front of Gloria's house. He stood beside the driver's door in order to let The Gator climb from the back seat. The Gator went around the car and helped Gloria, who was still too drunk to walk by herself, out of the front passenger seat. Tea sneaked back into the car.

The Gator carried Gloria up the sidewalk and the steps in front of the house. Almost as soon as they were on the porch, Gloria's mother opened the front door. She was shocked to see The Gator.

Gloria's mother said indignantly as she frantically rushed out to take her daughter from The Gator."Young man what are you doing with my daughter? What have you done to my precious little girl? Give her to me. I don't know you. You leave here at once."

"Tea paid me ten dollars to drop her off at home. I'm only doing this because he's a friend," Gator said.

The Gator went back to the car. He folded himself into the passenger's seat. "Let's get out of here, Dick," he said as he slammed the door.

"What did her mother say?" Tea asked.

"Dick, she asked me what I was doing with her daughter," The Gator said.

"What did you say?" Tea asked.

"I told her that you paid me ten dollars to drop Gloria off at home and I was only doing I because you're my buddy,"

"You would have been a real buddy if you had just dropped her off and kept your big mouth shut," Tea said.

To which Gator responded, "Dick, I told you that I didn't

want to take her to the door. I warned that you I didn't want them to think it was my fault."

"Oh. Sometimes the truth hurts," Tea said. "I should have taken her to the door myself. I should have apologized for the fact that she put away that much whiskey. This appears to be another story without a happy ending"

Tea turned the car around and headed in the opposite direction to take the others home. As they were stopped at the stop sign at the top of the hill, Dion came driving along in Lado's car approaching from their right. He turned left and stopped beside them.

"Did you get Gloria home without difficulty?" Dion asked.

"No. It was an ugly scene at Gloria's house. Boy, where in the world were you? Of all times to be missing, this was when we really needed you. It was too much for Gator and me. You could probably have pulled it off. Thanks a lot for not being there," Tea said.

"Tea caused me to take on trouble that belongs to him by having me take Gloria to the door Dick. Dick, just be glad it wasn't you. You would be in trouble with her mother too," The Gator said.

"Why don't you park Lado's car over by the school and ride with me and The Gator to take Cherry home," Tea said.

"Okay," Dion said. Dion turned the car around and drove a half a block in the direction he was originally traveling. He stopped the car behind the spot where Tea had stopped his car. He joined the others in Tea's car.

"That Betty Jo is one good-looking woman. She's very friendly too. I like her. Are you planning to see her again?" Cherry said as Dion sat down.

"She is special isn't she? I certainly hope I have the pleasure and the honor of escorting her again," Dion said.

"Dick, did you drive all the way to Sanford get her and then drive to the Lake?" Gator asked.

"Gator, I did just that," Dion said.

"I guess you do think she's special," The Gator said.

Dion moved his left leg. When he did, his left foot kicked something on the floor. He reached over and picked up a pint of Lord Calvert. "What's this? I think I have found a treasure. I believe someone needs to drink it. I guess since someone has to do it that responsibility falls squarely on me," Dion said. Before anyone could say a word, he had opened the bottle and taken a big pull.

"Not so fast and free with my liquor," Tea said.

"I'm taking it slow alright," Dion said. With that, he took another big pull.

At that moment, Tea stopped his car in front of Cherry's house. Everyone said their goodbyes and Cherry went into the house. Tea nosed the car down the street.

"Dick I want a drink of that liquor," Gator said as he reached toward Dion for the bottle.

"Gator, hand that to me first," Tea demanded.

"You are crazy, Dick. I'm taking a drink first," Gator said. He took a big drink. The Gator started to hand the bottle to Tea. When he extended his arm, Dion was quick enough to intercept the bottle. He took another big drink from the bottle.

"We saved you some," he said to Tea as he handed over the nearly empty bottle.

"It is all gone! There are only a few drops left! You are terrible to drink my liquor like that!" Tea yelled.

"Glad to be of service, sir. Since I wasn't at Gloria's house, I drink this liquor to make up for not being there to help. I am certain you would have done the same for me. I provide the service free of charge," Dion said.

"Dick, I'm glad we were able to help you out," The Gator said with a big laugh.

"Thanks. But, don't ever try to help me again. It's bad enough that Gloria will never be going to the Lake with us again. Then you two down my liquor in about two minutes. I'd rather tackle a bunch of rattlesnakes than you trust you with my liquor," Tea said.

Needless to say they did not pick Gloria up to go to the Lake again. Her parents would not hear of it. However, Gloria did make it back to the Lake after she was off restriction. In fact, she went a number of times, but always, with other people.

CHAPTER THIRTY-TWO

UNAVOIDABLY DETAINED

Dion came home from work on a Tuesday afternoon to find a very official looking envelope had arrived in the mail. He quickly opened it and read it digesting the contents. He was excited by what he saw. He put the letter away.

That night he went driving around with Cosmo, Mike and Tea. He told them, "I have an interview for a job close to OD on Saturday at ten a.m. Would any of you like to go? We would leave on Friday morning and spend the weekend there."

"I cannot go. I have dates on Friday and Saturday nights," Cosmo replied.

"I have to work Friday and into Saturday afternoon. We're behind because we haven't been able to paint in the rain. This summer job is getting to be a pain. But I need the money," Tea lamented.

"I'll go," said Mike who was fairly recently back in town and was not working.

"I'm going to be able to use my brother's car since he's away. I will pick you up at ten Friday morning. We will put the top down and be on our way to OD," Dion said.

"You're going to need somebody to watch out for you on Saturday night. I'll drive down right after I get cleaned up after work," Tea said.

"I guess you know where we will be staying," said Dion.

"Yes, I'm sure I do. I'm sure I'll find you in one of three places. You will either be at Rice's, the OD arcade or the Spanish Galleon," Tea answered.

"That would just about do it," Dion responded.

Dion picked Mike up Friday morning as promised. They were on their way to OD. "If we wait until we get there, we can have lunch at Hoskins," Dion said.

"Deal," was all Mike had to say.

They arrived at Hoskins at about fifteen minutes before one. They each had one of the lunch specials. When they were through eating, they set off down Main Street to the liquor store. They soon had their supplies.

"We have time to go on the beach and have a few drinks and watch the women go by," Dion said. "There should be plenty of them out today since it is the middle of the summer."

"That ought to be good for a few hours," Mike answered.

They did. They stayed out there till about five-thirty or a quarter till six when most of the bathing beauties had left. They went around to Rice's and rented a room for two nights. They went inside and cleaned up. Afterward they sat and had a drink or two.

At about seven-thirty Dion said, "Let's go to the OD Arcade and get a cheeseburger and some fries."

"Do they sell beer?" Mike asked as an intended funny rhetorical question. "If they do we can get one and sit out on the front porch while we eat and watch people passing. We may see some interesting young ladies."

"You are such a smooth talking devil that you have talked

me right into it," Dion said with a laugh.

They left for the OD Arcade. They sat on the front porch and ate. After they had had a couple of beers, Mike said, "Let's go over to the Boulevard Grill and have another one." They walked diagonally across the street to the Boulevard Grill. They ordered a beer apiece and took a table by the front window to drink them.

Once the beers were gone Dion said to Mike, "Let's go over to The Barrel for a few minutes and then go to the Spanish Galleon to do some shaggin'." They walked out of the Boulevard Grill onto Ocean Drive. When they reached the center of the street a policeman hailed them.

"You're supposed to cross the street at the intersection," he said.

"We were just going right there to The Barrel," Mike answered.

"A wise ass, huh? You think you're real smart don't you, punk? You rich boys think you can come here and get away with anything. Well, you are wrong," the policeman scowled. "I'm going to show you who's smart. You two have been drinking and you're drunk. I'm arresting you for public drunkenness. You are going to get to spend the night in jail. See how you like that! Still think you're such a wise ass? Both of you come with me." With that he led them around the corner to a police cruiser. He opened the back door and motioned for them to get in. They quietly complied.

He drove to the OD jail. He opened the backdoor and motioned for them to get out. They climbed out slowly onto the black asphalt surface of the parking lot. He motioned to a door behind them. The two turned around and preceded the policeman through the door.

"I have arrested these two for public drunkenness on Ocean

Drive," the policeman said to the officer behind the desk. "We're going to lock these wise asses up for the night. They can pay to get out tomorrow morning."

The officer behind the desk said to them, "Let me see some ID's please." They each handed him their respective driver's license. At that time the arresting policeman turned and walked back out of the building. "What did you do to piss off Mr. Happy?" the man behind the desk asked.

"I don't know but it sure didn't take much. Maybe it was the polite smile we gave him when he walked up to us on the street. I never said a word to him. And Mike only told him that we were going to The Barrel and indicated that it was shorter to cross the street there in front of the Boulevard Grill than to go to the intersection," Dion answered.

"We normally just watch to make sure that you don't get hit by a car and leave you alone as long as you're not making a nuisance of yourself," the man said. "But somebody's put a bug up his shirt and it's been biting him all day. I'm sorry but since he arrested you, I must lock you up. You just happened to be in the path of the wrong policeman at the wrong time."

He wrote down Mike's personal information. He handed Mike's license back to him. He started copying Dion's information from his license. He stopped and looked at Dion before saying, "You will be happier here than you would have been at the old jail. Your uncle, Joe, built this jail for us because he said the old jail wasn't good enough for him to be thrown into. Did you know anything about that?"

"No, sir. I didn't know it thing about that. My uncle's money has never done me any good because I've never seen any of it. In fact, I have only seen my uncle twice. I doubt I would recognize him if he were standing here," Dion responded.

The officer finished Dion's information and returned his license. "I have to take you back to a cell now. Follow me. I'll be here until eleven if you need anything. I get replaced at that time by another officer."

"I do need to make my one phone call tomorrow morning," Dion said to the officer as they walked down the hall.

"You tell the morning officer after he comes on at seven. He will let you use the phone. Here is your cell. I hope it's not too uncomfortable for you," the officer said.

At eleven that night, the night clerk came in and said hello to the boys. He seemed to be a nice enough, but unfortunately for him by then the boys were getting tired of being in the cell. They became loud and noisy. They stayed that way until the morning clerk came in.

The morning clerk informed them, "You pay your twenty dollars each and I'll have you out of here by ten."

"I need to make my phone call at about eight-thirty, please," Dion said.

"Hell, if I were you, I'd make that call before I paid the twenty dollars," the clerk said.

"Will you still have us out of here by about ten if I do that?" Dion asked.

"I sure enough will," the clerk answered.

At eight-thirty the clerk came for Dion, "If you need to make that call, you come with me."

Dion looked at him and said, "Thank you. I definitely need to make that call!"

The officer took him to a small room in the corner of the jail. He opened the door and motioned inside to the telephone. Dion closed the door behind him. He picked up the phone and dialed the number which he had learned for Mr. Willis. He heard the phone ring on the other end. After the third ring he heard Mr. Willis say "Hello."

He responded calmly, hoping that his calmness would help him achieve a positive result, "Mr. Willis, this is Dion. Can we change our interview to this afternoon? I'm sorry to ask that but I have been unavoidably detained and will be late getting there."

"I suppose that the fine. But when will you be here?" Mr. Willis asked.

"I can be there any time one or later that would be convenient for you. Just tell me what time I should be there and I'll be there. I really appreciate your being understanding and accommodating," Dion said.

"We're really interested in having you. We don't normally do interviews on Saturday anyway. I didn't schedule anything else for today in case we run late. Why don't you come at two o'clock and we will take as long as necessary to conduct the interview? Would that work?" Mr. Willis said.

"Yes, sir. That would be absolutely wonderful. I can stay until tomorrow if we need to talk that long. I'll see you promptly at two o'clock, not a minute later," Dion said. "Goodbye." When Mr. Willis said goodbye, Dion hung up the phone.

The clerk came back for him when Dion opened the door to the telephone room.

"We are ready to pay the twenty dollars so that we can get out of here. I have a job interview this afternoon," Dion said.

"Let me get your buddy and I'll take your money. Then I'll do the necessary paperwork before you can leave," the clerk said.

"Here it is," Dion said as he forked over a twenty-dollar bill to the clerk.

"Here's mine too," Mike grinned and said.

The clerk took their money and soon had the paperwork

completed to release them. He escorted them to the door say-ing, "I don't want to see you in here again."

Once they were inside Rice's, Dion relayed the phone con-versation with Mr. Willis to Mike.

"That's the damn coolest thing I ever heard," Mike re-sponded. "You deserve a medal or some kind of award for pulling that one off. That's just way cool calling from jail to reschedule a job interview because you were unavoidably de-tained. Yeah, I guess, unavoidably detained because you were thrown in jail for public drunkenness."

Dion cleaned up and left for the interview wearing a coat and tie as expected. He was five minutes early for his inter-view. Mr. Willis said to him, "Dion, it's a real pleasure to meet you. Please come into my office so we can talk?"

They talked for three hours. "Mr. Willis, it's been my pleas-ure to talk to you. I really appreciate your flexibility today. I am sorry that something came up that I could not avoid," Dion said as he left.

"Okay, tell me how it went." Mike said when Dion opened the door to their room.

"I guess it went okay. It was no big deal," Dion answered.

"I mean did you get the job?" Mike continued.

"Let's have a drink to celebrate. I start the second week in September." Dion said.

"You know, you're too much. You get thrown in jail for public drunkenness one night. You have to call the next morning to delay the interview that they scheduled especially for Saturday morn-ing to accommodate your schedule. You get the job which requires public trust and you act like it was nothing, I'm drinking this one and the next one and the next one to you. You are now officially my hero. Way to go man. Way to go. Wait till Tea gets here. Here's to you," Mike said as he lifted his glass toward Dion.

Tea arrived considerably later than he had hoped. He arrived in OD at about eight. He went first to Rice's Guesthouse to freshen up for the night. Dion's brother's car was sitting in the front yard. He knocked on the door.

Mr. Rice answered the door, "What can I do for you?" Then he recognized Tea. "Won't you come in, Tea? Dion said you'd be coming. He and Mike are staying in that room," he said pointing to the room on his right. "It was the same room you are normally in."

"Have you seen them recently?" Tea asked.

"They left about an hour ago."

Tea said over his shoulder as he entered the bedroom, "Thank you. I'm sure I'll find them shortly." He went in and freshened up. About eight forty-five he went over to the Boulevard Grill and had dinner. He went to all the usual haunts trying to find Dion and Mike. At about eleven fifteen when he had not yet found them, he decided he was going to the police station to report them missing.

Tea walked into the Police Department thinking he was going to file his report. When entered the front door, he saw Dion and Mike in front of the clerk's desk.

"What are these two fools doing here?" The clerk asked the young policeman.

"I brought them in for public drunkenness. They were drinking on the beach and singing at the top of their lungs. They were being a nuisance," the policeman said.

"Did they kill anybody?" the clerk asked.

"No," the policeman said.

"Did they rape anybody?" The clerk demanded.

"If they did, I don't know about it," the policeman said.

"Did they hurt anybody?" The clerk asked.

The young policeman looked puzzled. "No."

"Did they steal anything?" The clerk asked the policeman with an upset tone.

Once again the young policeman answered, "No." Then he added, "They were just drunk is all I know."

"You get them out of here right now and you forget that you brought them here tonight. Those two nearly worried me to death last night," the clerk demanded of the young policeman.

"Okay." the young policeman said.

At that point the clerk turned and saw Tea. "How long have you been standing there?"

"Just a couple of minutes, sir." Tea answered.

"I guess you could see that I'm in a bad mood from that conversation. What do you want anyway?" The clerk growled.

"I just came to report those two missing," Tea pointed toward his friends.

"You know those two? If you do, you get them out of here and you see to it they never come back to my jail again," the clerk demanded.

"Yes, sir," Tea said.

Dion and Mike left with Tea. After they were in the car, Tea shouted at them, "What have you idiots been doing?"

Mike started the response, "You ain't gonna believe this shit! I don't even believe it myself and I've been there. Let's go shaggin' and we will tell you the story tomorrow."

They went to the Galleon and danced until closing time.

Mike told Tea the full story the next morning before they left OD. Mike had been correct. Tea didn't believe the story as told.

"Let me make sure I have the story right. You come down here, get drunk and get thrown in jail for public drunkenness on Friday. You raise so much hell that you worry the clerk all night. You have to get up and call from the jail to reschedule your interview. You have the interview and get the job. You celebrate and get drunk again. You get arrested again. Then the clerk won't let you in the jail because you made so much noise the night before that you worried the Hell out of him. Is that pretty much the way you say it was? And you expect me to believe you did all that in two days? When we tell this story in the future only an idiot will believe it! Everyone will just say that wont possible. Tea said.

"That's about all of it. There's nothing you didn't capture," Mike said.

"That is close enough. It was really no big deal. The clerk just happened to be there when we decided it was time to go shaggin'. We wanted out of there to go. He was just totally un-cooperative on the matter. We were as determined to go shaggin' as he was to keep us there," Dion added.

"Why the Hell did you keep it up all night? Even after the clubs had closed? You could not go shaggin' then." Tea said.

"It became a point of honor. But we did get some shaggin' done after hours." Dion replied.

"Dion and I took turns singing, mostly Tams and Drifter's songs. While one would sing the other danced with the cell door's knob. We did some fine shaggin' all night long," Mike said.

"Now I know how you worried the clerk so. It was your damn horrible singing. I don't blame him for not wanting you back in there and take a chance you would do that again all night. I could not put up with a night of that either. You tortured the poor man." Tea bemused.

Dion broke out, "Under the boardwalk, down. . ."

Mike started, "Nip Sip. . ."

"Stop it. Stop it! Your killing me! Stop it! The Rices will never let us stay here again if you keep that up." Tea pleaded.

Dion and Mike continued without hesitation for a few more words each before they both had to stop because they had broken into a fit of laughter at Tea's pleas.

CHAPTER THIRTY-THREE

LAST NIGHT AT THE LAKE

THE LAST NIGHT AT Williams Lake for some of the St. Umblers regulars actually began months earlier with a trip to Raleigh. The purpose of that trip was to see Otis Redding (Mr. "Try a Little Tenderness") perform. Cosmo, Cherry, Gloria and Tea were ready for a night filled with fun. Gloria had left her house with some other friends. Her mother had not forgotten that Tea and The Gator brought her home drunk. Gloria's mother would not have let her leave with either Tea or The Gator regardless of anyone else who was in the car. Gloria rode with them from the Gas Company where several cars gathered to caravan to the concert. On the way to Raleigh, they prepared themselves with a little vodka and some Lord Calvert. That concert happened only months before Otis Redding was killed in a plane crash.

Otis Redding, who was one of the ultimate live performers of all time, was on fire that night. He was great. Tea and friends were putting on a show in response. They were down on the main floor of the venue. At one point in the performance Gloria was sitting on Tea's shoulders waving both hands in the air. The group caught Otis Redding's eye. He announced to the audience that he was going to come down and introduce them "to a group that knows how to have a really good time!" He even encouraged them to sing along with him on two songs. That was ugly. They did not know the words and were unable to carry the tune with him. Nevertheless, they tried. What a night they had. They had had their fifteen minutes of fame that night.

On the way out of Raleigh, they made an unscheduled stop for Cosmo to get a ticket for running a red light.

Later in the evening, they were informed that their good friend Glenn was undergoing something that resembled a breakdown. When they reached Glenn, they learned that he had been at the show. He sat high in the arena with his young pregnant wife of a few months. After he took his wife home, Glen left her to go drinking. That activity led to the amateur misdiagnosis of a breakdown.

"Glenn, what are you doing leaving your wife home by herself at this time of night?" Tea asked.

"I'm despondent because I was sitting up in the auditorium tonight watching you fools down there having fun. I was wishing that I could have been down on the floor with you. I realize that those days are over forever because I'm married. I feel that my youth has been cut short," Glenn said.

A few months later on a lovely starlit Saturday night in the summer of sixty-eight, the whole St. Umblers contingent was at Williams Lake to see Willie T. and The Magnificents.

Willie T. also preformed his interpretation of a number of Beach Music hits. Few people at the Lake knew and less cared that they were not seeing the Willie Tee who made those songs famous. Willie T. provided fine entertainment.

There was a new guy singing that night. He did the warm

up and sang during Willie T.'s break. No one in the audience was familiar with the newcomer. He was having trouble connecting with the audience. He decided that he should do a tribute to Otis Redding. No one was happier that "(Sittin' on) the Dock of the Bay" had made it to number one on the chart than those who had recently gone to see the Otis Redding concert. The tribute turned out to be a fiasco. The audience started booing him. "Why don't we go up there and ask him to stop his terrible tribute?" Phil asked.

"Good idea," Tea responded. They walked to the stage to discourage the young man.

"My friend here met Otis Redding several months before his plane crash. We are all sad about his death. In fact, Charles and George over there," Phil said pointing to his left, "went down to Georgia to go the funeral. More of us would have gone had we been able to. We are disappointed in your tribute. We appreciate that you have tried, but it is not working. We would like you to stop your tribute. Please go back to your own music."

The young man announced, "It has come to my attention that some people here don't appreciate my tribute to Otis Redding. However, feel that I must do it. I'm going to continue to sing this set."

His next song was worse than the first. Though his inspiration was admirable and he had the heart, he was far short of having the vocal talent to sing Otis Redding's songs. He was a member of the vast majority; there were only a few people with the ability to sing those songs properly. More booing ensued. Charles and George were among the loudest.

"We have to stop this disgrace," Tea said.

"Okay!" Phil said. He started back toward the stage. Phil and Tea went onto the stage.

"Please stop your tribute. It's bad. There's no polite way to say it. You can hear the boos. It is upsetting the crowd. Please stop and do something else. Please," Tea pleaded.

Tea and Phil left the stage again.

The man was upset and confused by then. Looking back at the episode it is clear that he did not know what to do. He paused for a few pressure packed seconds before he told the audience, "I must continue my set to my soul mate."

"We have asked him and we have begged him to stop and he continues the tribute. We'll have to take things in our own hands." Tea said.

"Let's go! We need to pull him off that stage to shut him up," Phil said as he pumped his fist toward the stage.

Tea and Phil went to the front edge of the stage. They grabbed him by the legs and the arms. They pulled him off the stage. He landed knees first on the floor with a THUD. Pulling him from the stage took some effort as he was easily six foot three.

That stopped his tribute. It elicited some boos and some cheers from the divided audience. Tea and Phil felt good about their actions as they only heard cheers. The euphoria did not last long. Several workers escorted them to the office.

They told Tea and Phil, "You have upset some people. We have had a number of them complain about your antics. You must leave for the evening to cool off. What you have done is a bad thing. We will not tolerate such actions. Go home now; this all be forgotten and behind us by next week."

They left the building without going back inside as ordered. However, they had to wait for their respective rides to leave. They probably would have, if they had a ride. Their rides did not know at time that they were expelled for the remainder of the night. Once out of the building Tea and Phil reflected on the event. Too much time frequently leads to calamity. It did that time.

Phil finally broke the sentence, "You know we actually did a good thing by stopping that terrible tribute. That singer was the one that should have been thrown out,"

"We surely were mistreated in this. We should find a way to get even," Tea said.

"Excuse me. I have got to go to the bathroom," Phil said.

Phil came out about two minutes later carrying a commode. He threw it on the steps leading into the building. That inspired Tea. He went into the restroom. There was water everywhere on the floor. It was still bubbling up from the opening left by the removal of the commode. He came out with a sink that he pitched onto the steps beside the commode.

When Phil saw Tea's action, he reentered the men's room. He looked around and saw another commode. He ripped that commode off the floor. The men inside just stood there stunned as they watched him. He came out with the commode. Phil, always polite said, "Excuse me ladies" to a group of young ladies who were gathered outside the entrance to the pavilion. He threw the commode onto the steps beside the sink and commode that were already there.

Once again, Tea was moved to action. He went to remove the other sink to throw on the steps. It would only be justice to have matching pairs.

Afterward, both were thoroughly soaked but feeling much better. They went to the parking lot to wait for their friends to leave for St. Umblers. Phil immediately wandered off toward the pavilion. Tea sat quietly.

In a few minutes, someone came to the car to fetch Tea. The messenger said, "Tea, the owners want to see you. Phil is already in the office. They are going to arrest him for the damage done to the bathrooms."

Tea went to the office. He heard The Magnificents playing through the office wall. Robert and Wyman Honeycutt along with several of the staff were in the office with Phil. Robert had been at Campbell College with Dion, Cosmo and Tea. They considered Robert a friend.

Robert asked Tea, "What happened?"

"You have commodes and sinks on the steps. You must've pissed somebody off." Tea said.

By that time, Dion had heard of the proceedings and went to the office. Tea and Phil recounted the Otis Redding tribute incident.

The conversation became a little testy. Some of the staff wanted Tea and Phil arrested; they were ready to press charges. Robert was calmly resisting that sentiment.

Dion stepped forward and told all present including the young singer whose tribute had been at the heart of the incident, "Tea and Phil asked the young singer to stop. The crowd had asked the young man to stop the tribute. It was a bad act. Tea and Phil begged him to stop on their second trip to the stage. There's a lot of blame to go around here. That young singer deserves some of it to land on him."

Willie T., who had been standing in the background listening, said, "I too was embarrassed with both the idea of the tribute and the quality of the performance. I should have stopped it. I didn't because I thought my young friend deserved a chance to mature."

Because of Dion and Willie T.'s intercessions, Robert had listened patiently to everyone. He showed great restraint and business acumen as he said, "No charges will be pressed. It'll be expensive to repair the damage. We needed to remodel both bathrooms anyway; this provides the impetus. We will take care of the necessary repairs. We've turned the water off in the men's room and will stay open unless we get complaints about the bathrooms since it is getting close to closing anyway. The guys will go to the woods. We have to be concerned about the young ladies, but their bathroom is okay," Robert said.

The room fell silent.

Robert hesitated before saying quietly, "Tea, I hate to do this to a friend but you and Phil are banned from the property indefinitely. Dion go on back inside and enjoy yourself if you can."

Dion had met the charming Julie, earlier in the evening. He was disappointed in the punishment that befell his friends, but decided he was going to dance with Julie while the opportunity existed. After all, he might never see her again. He was understandably taken by her beauty and charm. Julie was tall. At five foot eleven she was taller than the other young ladies and many of the young men. She was a novice to the Shag. That was no impediment to enjoying dancing with her. She was eager to improve her dancing skills. She was quite intelligent which generated stimulating conversation.

Julie had three distinctive physical features other than her height. Her brilliant orange-red curls fell several inches below her shoulder. It shone so that it appeared to be almost translucent. Her smooth skin was as white as porcelain. And she had tantalizing green eyes.

Julie was witty and self-confident, almost to the point of arrogance.

Dion enjoyed every minute of his time with her that evening. As was inevitable, the evening ended. "Good evening, fair damsel. It was indeed a pleasure to meet you. I hope that we meet again," Dion said.

"I'm almost certain that you know I would like to see you

again," Julie said with a beautiful coy smile. Her smile made her entire face glow in the dim light.

Indefinitely banned from the Lake. That was the ultimate punishment. It was tough because they lived to see the bands and be with friends. Not to mention the girls. They loved the Shag. They would have to go in other directions to enjoy those things.

While the ban was not stated as being for life, it had the *de facto* effect. Reese had already yielded to conscience and responsibility. Dion would not return for reasons unrelated to the ban. He soon left for his job near OD. Tea probably would have returned without the ban. Cosmo made two simultaneous trips to the Lake that night. It was his first trip in months. Ironically, it was also his last. Cosmo was in love. He was soon to be a married man. He would obtain that stability he had sought.

A car full of uncharacteristically quiet campers left for St. Umblers.

Dion and Tea went to other venues before Dion moved to South Carolina, but they never found a greater love for fun, friends and the dance than they found at Williams Lake. Cosmo was settled. Williams Lake would live within them forever. The memories helped to keep them young.

Others from St. Umblers continued to enjoy the Lake; some were there the night it closed.

CHAPTER THIRTY-FOUR

THE YOUNG BUSINESS MEN

IT WAS A LAZY HOT, muggy Friday. That afternoon provided no indication that it would be any different from any other Friday in St. Umblers. Cosmo's bachelor party was scheduled for Saturday night prior to his pending wedding on Sunday. That party was limited in attendance primarily to family. Some of Cosmo's friends decided earlier that week that they were going to have a surprise blowout party for Cosmo on Friday night to celebrate the occasion. The attendance list for that party was more diverse. They rented two connecting rooms on the top floor of a two-story motel near St. Umblers for the party.

Each participant other than Cosmo had an assignment in the preparation for the party. CJ and Toney had the assignment to fill one of the bathtubs with beer and ice. Harry was to pick up Neil and Phil. The three of them were to get snacks and eats for the party. Robert was to pick up Charles, Cosmo's soon to be brother-in-law. The two of them were to get some moonshine for the party. It had been arranged for them to get it from Charles' neighbor. Dion and Tea were responsible for most of the liquor. They had picked up four half gallons and a few fifths and pints on Thursday night. More importantly, Dion and Tea were to get Cosmo to the motel without him discovering the plan.

Dion and Tea had picked up the keys to the rooms up earlier in the afternoon. They had given CJ the key to one room. He was to see that everyone was in that room when they arrived with Cosmo. CJ had made contact with everyone else before they left St. Umblers to let them know the room number. The others were in place before six-twenty.

Tea and Dion arrived at Cosmo's house before six-thirty. They had planned a quiet night for Cosmo's consumption. After they were on the road, they told Cosmo that there were four women having a party in the motel. "They asked Tea and I to find somebody else to bring to their party," Dion deadpanned to Cosmo as they drove through St. Umblers. "I think they would have liked us to be at least four, but we couldn't find anybody who wanted to party. So it's the three of us."

Cosmo was not quite sold by the story. Thinking something was up, he asked, "When did you two see these girls?"

"We met them Tuesday night while we out riding," Tea said.

"How come I don't know about this? Who else did you ask to go? Why did you wait until the time of the party to ask me?" Cosmo persisted, still skeptical.

"We asked CJ and JW right after we talked to the girls. We didn't ask you sooner because you are about to be a married man. We thought that you would be with your future bride until we heard that she was going out with the girls tonight. We knew you would be true to your intended. We still expect you to do so, but help us out a little here as a last great act of friendship. We really want a chance to get to know these ladies. We'll only be there a little while," Dion answered in an attempt to sell their story.

"We asked Lado, Phil, Toney and Robert Wednesday. We ran out of time to ask anybody else because they wanted us to bring some liquor and we had to go get it last night," Tea said.

"You know everybody already had something going on," Dion said.

"Why did they invite the two of you? Boy, if my bride finds out, I'll be in big trouble. I think you'd better take me back home," Cosmo said.

"I guess they didn't know anybody else who could get liquor. We promise you that no one, especially your future bride, will find out. We will take the liquor, talk a little bit and be out of there before you know it. Tea and I'll follow up another time," Dion said.

"I see, what they really wanted was some liquor. They'd be okay with anyone who would bring liquor to their party. I'm not buying them any. You'll have to buy all the liquor if we're going to take any," Cosmo said.

"I'm certain you are correct Cosmo. We've already bought the liquor and it cost a wad. Who knows, Dion or I just might get lucky someday as a result of your help. We really need to get the liquor there. Help your old friends out," Tea added.

Cosmo was sold on the idea. However, he added, "That's good because I'm not spending any money on these wild women. I'm engaged and proud of it. I'll be faithful to my love."

"Thanks, Cosmo, you are a true friend. We'll help see that you don't do anything wrong or get into any trouble. No one will know a thing," Dion said.

They went to Tea's and picked up the liquor from where he hid it behind the house. They drove to the motel. When they arrived at the motel, they led Cosmo to the room. Dion opened the door. They went in.

"This room is empty! Hey, you had a key to get in. How did you have a key? Where all these wild sex starved women, you talked about? I knew there wont gonna be any women." Cosmo ranted.

WHACK! WHACK! Two loud knocks sounded on the connector door from the other side. There was a muffled, "Shut up! You are making too much noise over there," coming from the other side.

Cosmo bristled. "Are you going to make me shut up?"

"You bet I am. You just open that door. I'm going to whip you sorry ass, you prick," came back from the other side.

"You had better pack a lunch because there are three of us," Cosmo challenged.

"I'm going to get you asshole. Come on. Open the door or are you scared?" the voice on the other side of the door said.

"Cosmo, you have made me a prisoner in this conversation. Are you ready to back up your mouth?" Dion interrupted. "I'm going to open the door and we will see what happens next."

"Don't you dare open that door," Cosmo said in a pleading voice. "There could be a bunch of them. I bet it's a trap. Then what would we do?" Cosmo had forgotten about the four women.

Dion was reaching for the door as Cosmo spoke. When he grabbed the door knob, Cosmo said in a pleading voice, "No, don't open it. I'll stay quiet."

"Too late," Dion laughed at him as he yanked the door open.

Phil, who had been the voice, led the charge into the room. Cosmo was already ducking and covering his head before the door was completely open. He did not see who had come through the door. Phil saw Cosmo and could not resist saying, "Alright who is the asshole who was challenging me through the door?"

They could not maintain their composure any longer. They broke out into a rambunctious series of laughs.

Only then, did Cosmo uncover his head and look up. He said with a wry smile on his face, "I knew it all the time. I was as playing along with it so you could have fun. I knew it was a surprise party. What else could it be? I knew there wont no women."

The first of the ladies arrived around seven. There were Cherry, Connie Sue, Charlotte, Anne and Charlene. About fifteen minutes later Debbie, Beth and Betsy came onto the scene. Cosmo was the center of attention. He was in heaven or as close to it as he had ever been, but he was true to his intended bride.

The party was in full swing. They had brought a stereo and some records. They were playing Beach Music at the top of the stereo's volume. They were eating. They were drinking. Some were dancing. They were all talking and most were talking at the top of their lungs in an effort to be heard over everybody else. They had opened the doors to the rooms to allow easy access, influx and egress.

That continued until about ten. The manager came up to one of the rooms. He said politely, "You people are making way too much noise. You're disturbing the other guests. Please get quite." No one responded to his comments. No one even noticed he was there.

He knocked on the door and said more forcefully, "You people are making too much noise! You're disturbing the other guests! Please get quite." He was still ignored.

Toney happened to be standing nearby. The manager walked over to him and shook him by the left arm to get his attention. "Sir, I have to ask you people to get calmed down because you're disturbing all the other guests. You're making too much noise."

Toney let out a yell to the other occupants, "The manager says we're making too much noise and that we have to be much quieter."

When the group quieted down the manager said, "Now please keep the noise down. If you don't, then I'm going to have to ask you to leave."

Toney said to the manager so everyone could hear, "We'll keep quiet if we want to."

The manager was irate. He said, "That does it! You people have to get out of here. I'm going to give you thirty minutes to leave or I'm going to call the police."

"We're going to need some plastic laundry bags to gather stuff up in," CJ said.

"You can come to the office and I'll give you some," the manager answered, feeling pleased that he had rectified the problem.

"Well we're not leaving here until we get our money back. It wouldn't be right for you to throw us out and keep our money," Dion said calmly.

"Money back! What money?" The manager huffed.

"The money for these two rooms. That's what money. We're not leaving without the money for these two rooms. You either give us the money back or we're staying. You can call the police and we will to," Dion said.

The manager looked around and said, "This place is a total mess. There are cheese snack crumbs and potato chip crumbs all over the floors and the beds. It'll take the cleaning crew hours to clean this up. I'm not giving your money back."

"I guess that settles it. We're staying. We will check out in the morning as scheduled," a defiant Dion said.

"Okay. You come down to the office and I'll give you some plastic bags. When everything's out of here I'll give you your money back," the manager conceded

CJ went with the manager and came back with plastic bags. They used the bags to empty the bathtub of ice and beer. They gathered everything and took it to the cars.

"What are we going to do now?" Harry asked while they waited for Dion to come out of the office with the money.

"This would be a good time to go find another motel. Don't you think?" Robert said.

"That's a very good idea. We can use the money that Dion is getting to pay for two rooms somewhere else. That's pretty good since we didn't pay for the rooms to begin with. We'll let this motel pay for us place to stay because of the inconvenience," Tea said.

Dion came out of the office grinning from ear to ear.

"He's got a wad!" Toney said as he saw the money Dion was holding up in his left hand.

"There is another motel right across the street. It looks just like this one. Let's go over there and get two rooms," Tea said.

The girls decided they were going to go home. They would have had to have leave within thirty minutes anyway.

They drove across the street. Dion and CJ went into the office to talk to the manager. "Sir, we'd like to rent two connecting rooms for tonight," Dion said.

The manager looked at them and responded, "Do you think I'm crazy? I already heard about what you did across the street. The manager over there called me as soon as you were in your cars. I've just been sitting here watching for you come over here. There is no way I'm renting you any rooms tonight or any other night for that matter."

Dion and CJ went back out to the cars. They informed the group, "The manager will not rent us rooms here. Our friend across the street already called him."

CJ said, "I know we can get rooms at the Americana Motel. The rooms in the old motel are almost like this. Its two stories and all the rooms open to the outside. Let's go there. When we get there the rest of you stay out of sight and Dion and I'll go in and get two rooms."

They went to the Americana Motel. Once again Dion and CJ went in to talk to the manager. In a few minutes they came out with Dion holding up keys in one hand and a few dollars in the other.

"We made a small profit on the transaction," Dion told them when they were in the rooms.

The party was underway again. They talked about girls. There was no other subject so natural for them to talk about as girls. Next, they told war stories primarily about their exploits at the Lake and at the beaches. Their war stories were actually fish stories without the fish in that each time they told a tale it became bigger and grander and more detailed. Unfortunately, each time it was told it became subject to a degree of loss of accuracy. By the fourth or fifth telling of a tale, it was difficult to tell which parts were true and which were embellishments. On that particular evening, their tales were centered on Cosmo. That was as it should have been. It was Cosmo's time.

Tea told the story of the night Carol had offered Mike that she would do each of them for two dollars apiece. Tea told about how Cosmo was trying to secret Carol to himself in hopes of scoring with Carol and about how Cosmo had defended Carol's honor telling everyone else, "She wouldn't do that. She's not that kind of girl!" That was followed by the events at Carol's house after the Lake. He recounted how they had left Dion under Carol's bed while the rest of them rode down the highway a short distance to wait for him. He mimicked how Dion had come running down the highway to the car after Carol and her boyfriend slipped into the bed thinking they were alone and had become quiet passionate. His highlights were accurate. His details were sometimes embellished.

Toney when into detail about Cosmo taking the seltzer tablets at Carolina Beach. He told them that Cosmo was quite drunk when he decided he needed the tablets. He tried to reproduce Cosmo's expression and protruding stomach after Cosmo had plopped the tablets dry. He described Cosmo fizzing. "Cosmo had to have his stomach pumped out at the hospital to get relief." Toney made sure that everybody knew that Cosmo missed at least half of the trip to Carolina Beach with Reese.

Dion recounted the story of Luray and Cosmo's attempt at sex in a packed car. He explained how he, Mike and Patricia came to be in the trunk. They decided they would be more comfortable and have more room if there were less stuff in the trunk. He elaborated on the three of them through throwing things such as the carjack out of the trunk. He described to them how the spare tire bounced and bounced and bounced on the highway behind them when it was jettisoned. He informed them about how Tea had called for Ralph and Buick from the front seat. When Ralph didn't show up with the Buick, Tea had thrown up into the backseat all over Cosmo who was about to score with Luray. He spoke of Luray throwing Cosmo against the roof of the car. Dion mocked Luray pouring the liquid out of her shoes to be able to put them on. "Instead of putting then on, she threw them away in disgust.

While the car was stopped to clean up some of the mess, Mike, Patricia and I stayed in the trunk and continued our party. They did their thing. We did ours."

Next, they heard the story of Steve in the dryer from Robert. Robert touched briefly on the excruciating looks on Steve's face and the screams he emanated. His story was mostly from his interpretation Cosmo's point of view. There was Cosmo, ever the peacemaker, initially trying to keep from putting Steve in dryer. Robert reminded them that Cosmo had tried to talk the others into getting Steve out early in the cycle. Finally, he described how Cosmo was afraid that Steve would be injured and they would be responsible. Robert said, "Cosmo was afraid Steve was going to die in the heat." According to Robert, Cosmo actually was afraid that he personally was going to get in trouble over the incident so he tried very hard to make them take Steve out of the dryer before it stopped. He spoke of Cosmo's relief when Steve crawled from the dryer without serious injury.

Neil went into how he was amazed one night while traveling with Cosmo. Neil said, "I was in the car after drinking beer with Cosmo, Dion and Tea. We were traveling along Railroad Street in the dark when Cosmo said that he had to pee. Cosmo stopped the car. He turned off the lights. We closed the doors to turn of the interior light. Cosmo said he was going to set the world record for peeing. I think he must have because he wrote Cosmo ten times in the dirt. I have never seen anything like it."

"Cosmo, you are such a pig." Toney said.

"Yes, he's the Guinea Pig of World Records." Dion said.

"Wait, you've got to hear the one about Cosmo's date with Joan Dale on her birthday. He didn't have any money and was afraid to face her. He picked Dion, Toney and I up. He didn't tell us about the date. We thought we were on the way to the ABC when he turned left into Joan Dale's yard. She was stunning when she came out dressed in a white dress with pink trim. It was obvious from her appearance that she expected to be taken out and shown off. Her face expressed more than surprise to see three escorts in the car. Cosmo went up to her and managed to stutter something like Happy Birthday. He used as an alibi a line about us not having a ride to the Lake and he couldn't stand to leave us stranded. Then he asked her to go back in to get some money from her mother because he was running a little short. She went back in the house. We started betting on whether would come back out or not. She finally did. She had changed into more causal clothing. She was still beautiful. She even had money. Joan Dale said she would just be one of the boys. She told Cosmo not to consider that night a date. We had a great time. She was such a good sport. Fine woman that Joan Dale," Tea said.

After a brief lull, a poker game had broken out in one room. Dion, Toney, Warren, Robert and Neil sat down at the table to play. Phil and Charles were watching. They had played a few hands while the others migrated to the other room continuing to tell their war stories. To a man, they were drunk.

About one a.m. there was a single loud knock on the door of the room with a poker game. "I guess that's the manager coming to tell us we're making too much noise. Robert since you closest to the door would you get it please?" Dion said.

Robert went to the door. He opened the door and jumped back shouting, "Whooa!" They looked over and saw that there was a large group of black men at the door starting to enter. They had no idea who these men were or why they were at their room. Charles grabbed one of the quart jars that was still partially filled with moonshine. He took one step and threw it hitting one of the men right on the nose. The jar exploded when it made contact. Blood spurted from the man's mouth, nose and lips. Pieces of broken glass and rivulets of moonshine went flying everywhere. Blood began to pour from the man's face from a number of places where he had been cut. The man staggered backward into his allies.

Phil, a broad strong man, grabbed one of the half-gallon bottles of liquor. He rushed toward the door and hit one of the attackers squarely beside the head with it. POW. The man fell instantly to the floor outside the door. Blood ran across his bleeding head.

At the same time, Dion rushed the door and knocked one of the men back into the second-floor safety railing. He hit the guy in the stomach with his right fist. When the man bent over in pain Dion landed a vicious blow to the assailant's face with his left knee. Blood exploded from the man's nose. The man's head recoiled as he was knocked upward and backward. The man's head hit the metal railing with a THUD! That sent him unconscious to the deck.

Tea came running out the door of the other room. He had an empty half-gallon bottle in his hand. He hit the first perpetrator he saw in the temple it. That sent the man sprawling to the deck in front of the door to that room. He followed by landing a hard right to another's jaw staggering the man. A jab to the nose knocked the man down as his blood gushed. He managed to scrabble off the landing by staying low.

The startled attackers began a hasty retreat to the stairs.

Dion looked over the railing and saw four of the aggressors below the room around cars parked by the motel. He rushed inside and grabbed one of the easy chairs. He took it to the railing and threw it down onto the group of men below. The chair hit one of the four causing the others to scatter.

The men who had started the brawl were running into the field behind the motel. Dion, Tea, Phil, Robert and CJ were giving chase. Charles and Harry were watching the three attackers who were still down on the deck upstairs.

At that moment, four Sheriff's cars showed up. The deputies stopped them. The deputies said they had been called by the night clerk who had been beaten up by the gang of attackers.

"What happened here?" one of the deputy sheriffs asked.

The revelers recounted the story. "There are still three of the attackers upstairs on the deck," CJ said.

"Go back to your rooms and wait for us because the excitement is over," another deputy said.

As they started back to their rooms, they looked around and realized that Cosmo and Neil were unaccounted for.

"Has anybody seen Cosmo or Neil?" Tea asked.

No one could remember seeing them during the foray.

"They must still be upstairs in the rooms. Let's go have a look," Phil said.

Two deputies went upstairs with them. One of the deputies arrested the three intruders who were still out on the deck. The other went inside with to assist in the search for Cosmo and Neil. Neither of the two was visible upon entering the rooms. They soon realized that both the bathroom doors were closed.

Dion walked to the bathroom of the room where the poker game had been going on. He knocked on the door saying, "Cosmo, Neil, are either of you in there? You can come out; the excitement's over."

Neil, who was one of the two or three biggest of the group, unlocked the bathroom door. He walked out with a sheepish look on his face. He threw out quickly, "I had to use the bathroom." That brought quite a roar of laughter from the rest of the partiers.

"You must have shit your pants when you saw those guys at the door, huh? You had to go clean yourself up did you?" Harry said. He doubled over laughing.

In the meantime Tea had gone to the door of the other bathroom. He opened the door and walked in. When Tea pulled back the shower curtain, Cosmo sat shivering on top of the beer and ice that filled the bath tub. He held his head down and offered whoever was there an unopened beer with his right hand. They enjoyed a robust laugh at Cosmo's expense.

The deputies returned as they promised. One of the deputies informed them, "Those men had already beaten up the night clerk. One the staff held three of them at bay in the boiler room by swinging the fire axe back and forth. Further, they had attacked people in four other rooms. They had assaulted the occupants and stolen a number of valuables including money. It is a good thing y'all reacted quickly before they could get on you. Their numbers were of little value to them on the landing. In fact, they probably worked to their disadvantage in the confined space. Including the ones who were downstairs, there were about twenty-five of them. Thanks to y'all getting those three, we know who most of the others are and we're going to round them up. Goodbye and have a good night. Enjoy your party, but don't go out driving."

The local paper described the assault on the motel by a group of thuds. It stated that the hooligans had been routed by an unsuspecting group of young businessmen who were meeting in two rooms at the motel. It said that only the quick actions by the agile young business averted more damage by the perpetrators who had reigned havoc on the motel's staff and clients.

CHAPTER THIRTY-FIVE

CAVE WOMEN

IN THE FALL, Dion moved to his new job near OD. The Lake was becoming a part of his past as opposed to continuing to be a part of his active present and future. His trips to the Lake were a part of history. They were largely replaced by trips to OD which were increasing in frequency.

He had changed. The Lake had changed. His friends had changed. Cosmo and The Gator were both married to fine ladies. He became a regular in places such as The Pad, The Barrel and the Spanish Galleon. He made new friends in the area, both male and female.

One of those new friends was Ted. He had gone to college with Ted but had never really spent any time with him so he knew little about him. They had run into each other several times in the math building. Ted and Dion had graduated together. Ted had grown up on a farm near Dion's new place of employment. Ted was too a new employee there. He and Dion had started work on the same day. The two of them became friends right away. They began to do a variety of things together. Most of the time they spent together was going to the clubs in OD and to parties.

Ted was a fine young man. He was a year or two older than Dion. All the ladies thought him to be quite handsome. His short hair was a shiny blonde color. He was only about five feet, nine inches tall. He was slender and probably weighed one hundred and fifty to one hundred and fifty-five pounds. He was not exactly the classical physical specimen. He was clearly not the challenger for Mr. World or Mr. Universe. However, he had worked hard on the farm all his life and his wiry body was well defined. He was strong for his size.

One morning when they arrived at work Ted approached Dion. "The volunteer fire department is having a grilled chicken dinner for a fundraiser on Saturday. They need some help cooking. I'm going to help. I told them you might be willing to help. What do you say? A large percentage of people from the surrounding communities will be there and I'll bet it will be fun. You'll get to meet a lot of people from all around. It will be a regular social event. Are you game for it?"

"I'm free on Saturday. What time is this event?" Dion said.

"You'll need to be at the fire department at about three to help set up and get ready to cook. We'll start cooking around five. We'll be there until cleanup is over, probably around ten-thirty or eleven," Ted said.

"It sounds like a fine opportunity. Would you want to go to OD afterward," Dion said.

"It's a deal. You help with the cooking and I'll go to OD with you after we are through cleaning up," Ted responded.

When Dion showed up at the fire department at five minutes till three on Saturday, Ted was already there with his father. Dion walked over to Ted and his father saying, "Private Dion is reporting for duty. What do I need to do order to be most productive?"

"We need to move this grill over there under that shade tree so we won't get so hot while cooking. Perhaps you could help us do that. Then if you're willing, you could clean the grill while Ted and I get the charcoal and wood together." Ted's father said.

"Yes, sir. That's fine with me," Dion said.

One of the other volunteers arrived then. The four of them moved the big black grill, which had been made by cutting a barrel in half and putting hinges on it, under the big leafy green oak tree. As soon as it was moved Dion, set about his assigned task of cleaning the cooking surface on the grill. He used a heavy stiff bristled metal brush with a handle about three feet long to accomplish the task.

While he was cleaning the grill, four other volunteers had shown up to assist with the preparations. Some of them were putting barbecue sauce on the chicken. Others were busily getting the beans in a pan so that they could be cooked on the grill. One slight gentleman was struggling by himself to set up the boiler to make chicken bog.

"May I help you with that, sir?" Dion asked.

"Yes, young feller. I would really appreciate that. This here contraption is a might awkward. But it does a right fine job once it's together," the gentleman replied with a deep South Carolina drawl.

Dion helped the gentleman set up the support rack under the tree eight to ten feet from the grill. Then the two of them connected the gas bottle to the burner in the support rack. Afterward, they put the boiler on top of the rack.

"You act like you have used one of these things before," the gentleman said to Dion.

"No sir. I never have actually used one myself but I've seen them used before. I'm a big fan of chicken bog. I think it beats barbecued chicken every time. I'll be happy to help you get the chicken bog going," Dion said.

"Young feller, I liked that a whole heap. If you git this here boiler filled up to about here with water, I'll turn her on. Then we can git the chicken cut into little pieces while the water's boiling," the gentleman said.

"Yes, sir. I'll find a bucket," Dion replied as he set off to find said bucket. Dion returned with a bucket full of water. After several trips he had the boiler full to the level that the gentleman had indicated.

After the gentleman lit the flame under the boiler he said to Dion, "You make right smart help but you ain't from around here are you?"

"No, sir. I came here from St. Umblers over in North Carolina. It's a couple of hours away." Dion answered.

"It looks like your folks learned you pretty good manners. I bet they're right proud of you," the gentleman said.

"I hope they are," Dion said. Then he said in an attempt to change the subject from himself, "If you tell me where the rice and sausage are, I'll get them and bring them over here to the boiler."

"They're over there in that pickup truck sittin' by the highway," he replied as he pointed at an old beat up blue pickup.

"I'll be right back," Dion said as he turned and started walking toward the pickup.

When he returned, Dion helped the gentleman finish cutting up the chicken. It was Dion's turn to ask the gray-haired gentleman about himself. "Are you originally from around here?"

"I've been in these here parts all my life. I was born and growed up in a house about three miles down that way. When my wife and I was married, we built a house right across the highway from her folks were lived. That was about a half-mile from the house I growed up in. Me and the Missess have been there over forty years. We ain't ever been more than fifty miles from home. We've always had everything we needed right here. We didn't see no need to go anywhere else. Our youn-guns growed up in that house. Now they come and bring their little ones sometimes. We've just been real happy there. We shore nuff ain't going no wheres now," the old gentleman proudly responded with a gigantic sparkle of happiness in his eye. There was a man who didn't need much in the way of material possessions. There was a man who had priceless pos-sessions.

"That's a really fine story. You are a man to be envied," Dion said with sincerity.

"The water is boiling. Let's put in the chicken, sausage, rice and seasoning. This chicken bog'll be ready in plenty of time for dinner," was the response from the man who wanted to di-vert attention from himself. They added all the ingredients to the water and stirred vigorously. At that point the old man turned the heat down on the boiler.

"I'll come back and help later if you need me. But I had bet-ter go over and help with cooking the chicken as I promised I would do," Dion said.

"That'd be jest fine. Thank you. I have this here under con-trol. I'll keep stirring and adding water to get it good and thick. The rice will get real tender too. It was a pleasure to meet you young feller," the old gentleman said as Dion started walking toward the grill.

Once at the grill, Dion saw that the chicken had all been covered with barbecue sauce. The fire had been lit. It was just a matter of waiting for the coals to cool enough to begin cook-ing.

Dion heard someone behind him say in a Southern drawl, "It's time to break out the beer now that all the preparations for cooking have been made." Someone's right hand reached around Dion silently offering him a twelve-ounce longneck brown bottle.

Dion took the bottle and twisted off the top. He started sipping the beer. He really didn't care much for the taste of beer. There would be a number of other beers passed to him before the night was over, but that was to be his next to last beer for the evening.

Someone else brought out a quart jar of homemade hooch. The jar was passed around for the workers to sip. That hooch was smooth. The return of that jar to Dion's lips would be welcomed. It or other jars like it showed up on several occasions. That was an unexpected benefit of helping with the fundraiser.

"I'm ready to start cooking chicken whenever you would like." Dion said to Ted's father.

"We'll let you and Ted be in the first shift. We will trade shifts about every half-hour to keep from getting so hot standing over those coals all night. That okay by you?" Ted's father said.

"Yes, sir I'm your man. That's a plan that I can handle quite readily. I like being first," Dion said.

Ted looked at Dion with a smile and said, "Time to for us to cook."

When they went to the grill, the beans were already on and were getting warm. One of them was on each side of the pans of beans. Dion and Ted each picked up long forks and started placing chickens on the grill surface. In order to get the chickens on the grill surface they would puncture a piece of chicken with the tines. They lifted the chicken and placed it on the grill. They withdrew the tines. When it was time to turn the chicken they would again insert the tines into the meat and turn it over.

Cooking chickens was hot work but it did not demand constant attention. They were able to talk and joke. They were able to carry on conversation with others who happened to pass by. While they were taking their first turn at the grill, some of the ladies from the community brought in pans of coleslaw and potato salad. One brought a huge pan of rolls.

Shortly after Dion and Ted had finished their first rotation at the grill members of the community came in and began to eat. "Dion do you want to eat now or wait till after our next turn cooking?" Ted asked.

"I'm eager to try that chicken bog. I suspect it's the best thing here. We can get some now. We can eat chicken, beans and coleslaw later. What do you think?" Dion asked.

"That would be just great with me," Ted said.

They ate chicken bog and then went back to work cooking more chickens. "That was really good. If there is any left at the next break, I think I'll have some more," Dion said.

"It was good but we can't eat it all just because we're working here. We have to leave most of it for the paying customers," Ted said.

"Good point. In that case I guess I'll just have to be a paying customer. Then it doesn't appear there would be any objection to my eating more chicken bog," Dion said.

"I guess you have the answer to that dilemma," Ted laughed.

At their next break, Dion paid for a plate. He went straight for the chicken bog and ate his fill. Later he ate a few beans and some coleslaw. But he did not try the barbecued chicken. One wonders if that was his commentary on his own cooking.

They finished cooking about nine-thirty. The beer and hooch moved through the volunteers quite freely while they were cleaning up. By the time they were through around ten-thirty, Dion and Ted had both become a little tipsy.

Dion turned to Ted. He said, "Preston is having a party tonight at his father's house in OD. We should go by the clubs and find us a couple of dates to take. Everyone who will be there will already have dates. Preston is spending the night there and he's invited us to stay. He has two spare bedrooms he said we're welcome to use."

"It would be nice to see Preston. I haven't seen him since graduation. How did you find out about this party anyway?" Ted responded.

"He called night before last and invited me. When I told him about our cooking job he asked if I would tell you about the party. He said to make sure you know that you're invited to spend the night." Dion said.

"Do you really think we will be able to find some women as dirty and grimy as we are? You know it will be after eleven before we get there. If we find any, they are probably going to be pretty hard favored," Ted said.

"I guess it's worth a try. We don't have anything to lose. We don't have any women now," Dion said.

"You're right. We have nothing to lose. Besides as you get drunker and the hour gets later the women start looking better anyway," Ted said.

They set off on their quest to find a couple of dates for Preston's party. Ted was driving. "I have a jar with some hooch. I think I'll have a drink. Would you like some?" Dion said.

Ted, who was giddy, answered, "You'd better not drink that hooch without letting me have some. If you even try that, I'll leave you at OD."

"Yes, Mr. Driver. You first," Dion said. Dion handed Ted the jar with the lid removed. Ted took himself a big pull before he handed the jar back to Dion. Dion followed his lead. They passed the jar back and forth until it was empty just before eleven some five miles before they reached OD. By the time they alit from the car, they were bobbing and weaving.

Dion and Ted went patrolling the clubs to find dates for Preston's party. As they went into each club they surveyed the situation. They were striking out everywhere they went. It seems that all the ladies were already escorted. After a couple of hours of searching, they came upon two young ladies who were by themselves. Their normal selectivity filters had been destroyed by alcohol and desperation. Dion and Ted started up a conversation with the two young ladies.

"May we join you," Ted asked politely as he and Dion approached.

"Sure, honey," one answered in a deep backwoods drawl. The other nodded.

Had Dion and Ted been thinking straight they would have realized immediately that at least that young lady was from the country and they were probably rednecks. Instead of making such recognition, Ted asked with an alcoholic slur, "Are you ladies from around here?"

The short answer was, "No." The young lady who answered expanded, "We live about thirty-five miles the north of here toward Wilmington." Her response confirmed the fact that they lived in the country.

None of that mattered anyway as Ted said, "We're going to a party at a friend's house. Would you ladies like to join us?"

"That would be something. Us at a high-fluting party," answered one of the young ladies.

The other young lady put her left arm around Dion's waist and said, "Why sugah, that just sounds like the most fun. We would love to go. I'll be your date sugar. Come on now let's go." If it were possible, she spoke in an even more rural drawl than the first young lady.

The other young lady said to Ted, "That leaves you and me, Honey."

As the group started toward the door, Ted said, "We have been invited to spend the night. We would like you to stay with us."

"We hardly know you. We'll just have to see about that. You ask us later. You hear?" Ted's date said.

They stumbled into Preston's house. The party was still going strong. They knew many of the guests. They were greeted by questioning smiles as they entered. Preston was the consummate host. All the necessary introductions were made among the guests. He, assisted by his beautiful date, tried hard to make the four late comers feel welcome.

"Ted, how are you? I have not seen or talked to you since graduation." Preston said.

Ted worked hard to answer that everything was good and that he was happy to see Preston again.

"Please come in and join the fun. There is liquor on the kitchen table and beer in the refrigerator. Dion, you know your way around. Show Ted where things are. Help yourselves to whatever you want. Fix your dates drinks too." Preston continued.

"Thanks ever so much Preston," Dion answered. "We will be back in a couple of minutes. Ted, ladies come with me to the kitchen." He staggered toward to the kitchen with Ted and the ladies in tow.

After they were in the kitchen Preston's date asked, "Do you think it wise to let them drink anymore? They're already plastered."

"I think they are going to need to get drunk enough to pass out in order to best get through the night. Otherwise, something bad might happen to them. I'm going to encourage them, all four of them, to drink as much as they can," Preston answered.

"They are going to hate themselves tomorrow anyway. Drinking may be their safety net," Jeff piped in. "Let 'em get really bombed. I mean the passing-out you can't move variety"

"Let's help them with that." Preston's date said.

"I'm in. I know they would do the same for me," Preston said.

That sentiment was echoed as the consensus of the guys in the room. The ladies were not sure that was the best choice, but they decided to acquiesce. Every time that the glass of one of the four approached empty, one of the men in the room refilled it.

The strategy worked. The partiers finally put Dion and his date who were both totally wasted in a bed sometime around three. They put Ted and his date who were asleep in the bed in the other spare bedroom.

About ten Dion was awakened by an urge to go to the bathroom. He was still high from the night before. He started to move before he realized someone's arm was across his chest and had him pinned to the bed. He looked to his left and saw what appeared to be a body with a very fuzzy looking face. He squinted to focus better. then he realized that it must be a female because of all the long stiff brown hair that was protruding everywhere. When he looked closer, he was startled by the female's appearance. She was in her early twenties, but indeed, she had been hard-favored by the fates who handed out beauty. Her lone obvious redeeming visual feature was that she was far from being nondescript. He let out a loud SCHREEH! He pushed the arm away and jumped out of the bed screaming in horror as he did. The woman moved only slightly in response to the commotion.

Then he remembered Ted. *Ted must be in the other guest bedroom. I have to go find him so we can leave. There is a monster in here and I have to save us.*

He stumbled down the hall as quickly as he could to the other guest bedroom. He threw open the door without knocking. He went over to the bed yelling, becoming ever more frantic as he continued, "Ted, wake up! Ted, you've to get up! We have to get out of here! There is a monster in my bed! Hurry up!"

For the first time, he looked at the bed in front of him. He saw Ted with his arms wrapped around a woman whose face was down on the pillow. She had her right arm draped over Ted's chin. Ted was unable to move. Ted and the woman where awakened by Dion's yelling. The woman rolled over and looked at him. He was still yelling, "Ted, you have to hurry so we can get out of here! There is a monster in my bed."

When she moved, Dion was finally afforded a good look at the woman beside Ted. She was easily twice his size. She was three to four inches taller than Ted. She probably weighted at least two hundred and fifty pounds. She was lying there in the nude beside Ted. For all Dion knew she might have been in the mood for Ted. The lady was missing several of her teeth and they were black spots from decay on some others. Her face and body showed serious wrinkles. In her case, they were the result of excessive weight, not age. She appeared to be at least sixty years old even though she was probably in her late twenties.

The woman pulled the covers of the bed over her as quickly as she could when she realized Dion was looking at her.

After a few seconds when Dion finally absorbed the impact off the picture of the woman in the bed, he went from being frantic to suddenly laughing. He was laughing so hard that he had to sit down in the middle of the floor at the end of the bed. Then he was laughing so uncontrollably that he started rolling on the floor.

Dion's noises woke the other three people in the house. Preston and his date along with Dion's date stood in the doorway behind him.

"What is so funny that you are lying in the middle of the floor rolling and laughing in your underwear?" Preston asked.

Dion composed himself slightly before trying to answer. While he did, he held up his left hand as an indication for them to wait for his response. After fifteen to twenty seconds, Dion said, "I came to warn . . ." Dion fell back into his uncontrollable laughter pointing at the bed in front of him.

"Dion, please control yourself and tell us what is going on," Preston's date said in a smooth, calming voice.

Dion composed himself. It took only about five seconds before he looked and pointed at Ted. Then he said, "I came to warn Ted . . ." he was again overcome by laughter that left him rolling on the floor.

Ted was out of bed and had put on his pants. He walked over to Dion and put his hand on Dion's shoulder. "Calm down and tell us what you're trying to tell us," Ted said.

Dion was able to compose himself enough to tell the story. "I came in here to warn you about the monster in my bed. Then I saw what was in bed with you. She was really scary. I found that extremely funny," he said in a voice loud enough for everyone else to hear. He broke into a full body laugh but it was less consuming than his previous laughter. It would be an understatement to say that no one else appreciated the humor.

"You have been such a fine gentleman up until now. Why the sudden radical change," asked Dion's date in an angry voice from the door where she was standing.

"I'm sorry ladies. This is just quite ironic in light of a conversation Ted and I had last night. Please forgive me for my behavior. It was just too much of a coincidence," Dion pleaded.

"I think I should drive these ladies back to their car," Preston's date said in a very kind and understanding voice.

"I think that would be the best thing for all. Would you be so kind? You can take my car," Preston said. Preston handed his date the car keys. The women left without another word being said.

The three of them talked about the previous evening. They spend most of their time talking about how Dion, Ted and dates came to be there.

"Ted, I think if I were you, I wouldn't drive through that town for a long time. Especially, not in your current car. I told you about what happened to Chuck's car after the pig party. That could happen to you too," Dion said.

"They will be looking for you too. If I were you, I would get down in the floorboard anytime I was passing through there. I think I'll do that even if I'm driving," Ted said.

The three men had a hearty laugh at that.

Preston's date came in. The conversation turned to other topics. Dion and Ted were soon organized.

"I'm sorry that I put you in an awkward position this morning. I embarrassed myself as well, I accept full responsibility for my actions," Dion apologized again to Preston and his date for his behavior before they left. His contrition was genuine.

EPILOGUE

Dion, Cosmo and Tea had made their final visits to Williams Lake. They moved on. Responsibility engulfed them. They had left Williams Lake, but the Lake had not left them. It will stay with them the rest of their lives. Truly, Williams Lake was once the center of their universe.

When one occasions upon people who frequented the Lake, their eyes light up as they think back to their memories. The women will often giggle as they remember an event. The men normally stand taller and more erect as they become lost in momentary nostalgia. Each of them has stories they are eager to tell. Those stories are magnificent and grand.

The cast may not have actually been as depicted in the tales relayed herein. However, those stories represent who they have become because they tell those stories of themselves. More importantly, they accept those stories as true. Who is to be as brazen and bold as to claim to know the perfect truth? Truth over time hides in the corners and darkness of memories and eventually under the dust that we become and survives us. Truth comes in as many colors as there are in the light spectrum. It is uniquely attenuated to accommodate our individual quirks of vision. We each see truth through the filters of the sum total of our personal experiences.

Only a small fraction of the story has been told. It is now a part of you. It is no longer the sole domain of the characters to whom you have just been introduced. Is it for you to decide if it is fact or fiction. Legend or lie. You choose, but understand that your answer may be different from that of others. Especially, those who were there and know or think they remember the truth.

Your answer may rest in a question posed by Gita, the female lead, to Dubin, the male lead, in Scott Turow's excellent book *Ordinary Heroes*. That book has World War II as its backdrop. The backdrop could have been Williams Lake. Gita wisely queried "Who are we but the stories we tell about ourselves, particularly if we accept them?" That question is relevant here.

You own these stories along with the youth turned adult who lived them. Williams Lake is now and will continue to be a part of your life. Williams Lake may not have been at the center of your universe, it may never be, but it will go with you everywhere you go from this moment forward. Take it with you as proudly and as humbly as the characters in the stories. The question has not been posed to those characters, individually or collectively, but for some of them those memories may yet today be the center of their universe. It may always be that way.

WHERE ARE THEY NOW?

As A RULE, the most prominent members of this group are highly educated. They have been quite successful in their chosen professions. They have in common that they went into the service of the public. The majority served as employees of the state of North Carolina.

Dion started as a decorated science teacher. He left academia after a relatively brief stint to become a scientist of some reputation. He worked primarily in the United States defense industry. He was happily married for almost thirty years.

Cosmo went to work in the service of the people of North Carolina until he recently retired. That wedding Dion had forecast on the way to OD two nights before Fat Jack's did take place soon after their last trip to the Lake.

Tea became a distinguished educator in North Carolina. He was at the time of this writing still serving the people of his state as an educator.

The Gator also became quite an educator. He has since retired and has enjoyed retired life. True to the prediction The Gator was also married to the young lady he was dating at the time of the Fat Jack episode. As of this writing he is still happily married to that young lady.

Neil is a prominent attorney with a thriving private practice. He has continued to be one scary driver; the fact that he drives big cars makes him more so.

Cherry has worked for the state of North Carolina as an auditor. She has been happily married for many years.

Connie Sue became an excellent nurse. More importantly, she became a model mother who had to overcome tragedy. She recently remarried.

Phil later, followed in the footprints of St. Paul, and became a man of the cloth. He, like Paul, had certainly tasted the other side of life first. He knew of which he spoke when he warned from the pulpit.

Harry worked for the state of North Carolina prison system before retiring.

Reese worked for the state of North Carolina in the prison work program. He has since semi-retired.

Glenn became an accountant.

Carol has her own business.

Patricia became a teacher.

Gloria became a teacher and married the Mayor.

Experiencing marriage is something that the group has in common. The results have been mixed. Some have had long, happy marriages.

Some of the players have gone from this life. Others have had significant brushes with death. The grave is awaiting the survivors. If anything is carried over from this life, there is a good chance that Williams Lake will be with them wherever they go. If that is true, you can expect the remaining characters to carry the memories of growing up including Williams Lake.

Williams Lake was once the center of the universe.

THE HISTORY OF WILLIAMS LAKE

WILLIAMS LAKE is a vastly different place today than it was during its glory days in the late Sixties. Little of the Williams Lake Pavilion has survived. Portions of the open shelter and the collapsing, decaying cypress timbers of the pavilion can be seen through a cluster of loblolly pines and brush. There is no water in the lakebed. A rapid buildup of water from Hurricane Fran broke the fifty-foot dam in two in 1996. Trees and shrubs have shot up from the bottom of the empty lake in the years since.

Williams Lake was frequented by shaggers and partiers in the late Fifties and throughout the Sixties. Back then, the old dance hall was jumping with life. It was full of young men and women who loved to dance and periodically were lucky enough to get an opportunity to find a little romance. There were soldiers there looking for a good time away from the strict regimen of the military. There were the young who were being forced into coming of age rapidly in what was a tumultuous time in our history. They danced a variety of different dances including the "Twist." But mostly they danced the Shag. The youth who frequented Williams Lake were primarily hardcore shaggers.

Williams Lake, or at least what remains of it, was and is in the Mingo community in the northwestern part of Sampson County. It was about thirteen miles from Dunn, about eighteen miles from Clinton and roughly twenty-one miles from Fayetteville.

"Right in the middle of nowhere," Robert Honeycutt was quoted by Michael Futch as saying of Williams Lake's location. Right in the middle of nowhere was an appropriate location. Honeycutt operated Williams Lake for four plus years in the late Sixties. Williams Lake was at its zenith. During that time, popular rhythm-and-blues acts played shows by the water on Wednesday and Saturday nights for a time. After that it was open on Saturdays and holidays. Williams Lake thrived as a dance spot for the young who wanted to escape the realities of life. They went there to party, seek the opposite sex and dance. They came to this remote community by the carloads.

The Lake benefited from it location in the triangle subtended by Dunn, Clinton and Fayetteville. People who could dance went to Williams Lake. It drew people from Dunn, Clinton, Fayetteville, Smithfield, Selma, Four Oaks, Roseboro, Salemburg and Benson as well as other small towns. There were regulars who came all the way from Carolina Beach. People from as far away as Charlotte came especially to see the Tams. There were often people from Raleigh and North Carolina State University there.

Even after some thirty-five to forty years have past, Williams Lake remains a memorable haunt for aging shaggers who surfaced in the early years of the eternal Beach Music scene. Beach Music is part of rhythm and blues. National music stars such as Martha Reeves and the Vandellas and Jackie Wilson entertained the young on many nights here. Regional favorites such as the Embers, The Tassels, the Fabulous Five, the Swingin' Medallions, Gene Barbour and the Cavaliers and the Tams played as young people shagged the night away. Khakis and Weejuns were standard fare for the guys. Few wore socks. As a gathering place,

Williams Lake changed over time. Its local history spans from a time preceding the Civil War to the early Seventies.

The physical lake existed before Clayton G. Williams was born. He was the Sampson County farmer who built Williams Lake into a recreational facility for neighborhood families, local church and school functions. People swam there when the water was warm enough. Others fished. Williams added the dance hall and a lunchroom during the Forties, people started to spend their evenings there.

Civil War veteran Joel Jackson has been credited with building Williams Lake. It has also been said that it was James Jackson, Joel's father, who oversaw the creation of the body of water. Sometime in the first half of the nineteenth century, prior to the War Between the States, the lake was established. Its water was used then to power a sawmill. The exact dates of the lake's construction have been long since been lost to the appetite of time. A mill house operated on the same site.

At some point in time the original dam broke. That date was also lost to us. It may have been during the Civil War. The saw mill and mill house collapsed and were destroyed.

Clayton Williams was the eldest of seven children. When Clayton Williams married, he was given a piece of the farm that included the empty lake. He had the dam repaired and a new grist mill and diesel engine-powered saw mill were built. He was said to have cut all the trees out of the lake and burned them.

When the locals began to trade with Williams, they started to go swimming in the twenty-acre lake. It was the center of local activity. There was no mall to go to. Transportation was severely limited. If you wanted to find out what was going on in the area, you went to the mill. Clayton Williams built a little store to serve his captive audience. That became successful because it was the only place around get provisions.

As the years passed, Williams Lake expanded. A concession stand which featured hot dogs was built. When World War II broke out Williams landed a job as a carpenter on Fort Bragg. He added a dance hall by the lake. He encouraged the soldiers to come to Williams Lake to have a good time. They did. The little dance hall was successful. Once it was successful, he no longer wanted the soldiers as they were a risk to cause trouble.

The actual lake had a diving board in the deep part and a couple of slides. A small section of the lake by the shelter was fenced off for little children. It was the playpen. Until the Sixties, admission was free. For a time, there were rental boats on the lake. Students from the old Mingo School would have picnics there.

While Williams operated the lake during the days of segregation, it was for whites only. Drinking was officially forbidden, but it went on. Guys would slip out to their automobiles and drink a beer before coming back in. Mr. Williams tried to keep it straight. Mr. Williams was reputed to ask people coming in if they had been drinking. If one were honest, and said "Yes, sir, Mr. Williams. I have," he was denied entry. If he said, "No, sir, Mr. Williams," he was admitted no matter how drunk he was. Mrs. Lillian Williams was the bouncer because they thought no one would hit a woman. It worked.

That was before the bands started playing dates at Williams Lake. During this Williams-run period, couples danced to a jukebox. Williams opened the business on Memorial Day and ran it through Labor Day.

In 1965, Robert Honeycutt started leasing the pavilion. That became "The Lake" to many young people in the area. Honeycutt who was twenty-two at the time was a student at nearby Campbell College in Buies Creek. Honeycutt had played saxophone in a band in high school.

Williams, who was aging and was not making money, told Honeycutt that he wanted to close down the lake's operation. The live bands were killing his jukebox business. Business was so poor that Williams closed before the end of the summer season in 1964. The young people wanted to hear bands not jukeboxes. Honeycutt figured that he could make a go of Williams Lake by also offering live music.

Williams Lake entered its last successful era in 1965 after opening the Wednesday night following Easter with Bob Collins and the Fabulous Five out of Greensboro. Bob Collins and the Fabulous Five were best known for their hit song "If I Didn't Have a Dime (Little Jukebox)." Bob Collins and the Fabulous Five had the best-blended sound of any band around at the time. All the instruments were blended except the saxophone which was played by a tall, skinny red head.

For the next five years, the operation was profitable largely because it enjoyed word of mouth advertising from its faithful following. Robert Honeycutt charged one dollar for admission except when really high profile bands were performing there.

It became notorious for fights for a time. The participants were frequently the same from week to week. Though there were fights, the vast majority of those going to the Lake were never involved in one. For every fight, at least one was averted.

The great showman Jackie Wilson played Williams Lake once backed by the Cavaliers. Billy Stewart's jazzy pop rendition of Gershwin's "Summertime" had charted in *Billboard's*

Top Ten when he gave a Wednesday show at the Lake right in the middle of nowhere. Pop-soul singer Mary Wells performed at the Lake. So did Barbara Lewis. Martha Reeves and the Vandellas did a show there. The Drifters and The Platters graced the stage of the Williams Lake Pavilion. The Tams were perhaps the most popular attraction at the Lake. The Tams would arrive shortly before it was time for them to go on. There were so many cars there that they had a tough time finding a place to park. It was common that somebody would have to move a car so they could park. Though most of the performers were black, they were well received by the all-white crowds who filtered into the pavilion.

Honeycutt's run ended New Year's Eve 1969. A few others tried their luck at moving Williams Lake into another successful era. The little pavilion with its once wildly popular dance floor closed for the last time in the early Seventies.

The property has left the Williams family. Clayton Williams, who built Williams Lake into a recreational attraction and dance hall, died in 1971. Today the pavilion lies in a state of near collapse. A blanket of green moss has spread over the cement steps that served as the front entrance to the pavilion. Williams' old house across the road from the empty lake has remained occupied.

Time and the elements have treated the structure harshly. Nature is always seeking maximum entropy. Man-made structures are produced to stave off entropy. They must surrender to nature at some point. The little dance hall will finalize that surrender.[2]

AN INTERVIEW WITH
ROBERT HONEYCUTT

ACCORDING TO ROBERT HONEYCUTT, "Williams Lake was on Williams Lake Road in the northwestern part of Sampson County. It was about twelve miles from the closest towns, Dunn and Salemburg. It was about eighteen miles from Clinton and about twenty-one miles from Fayetteville."

Honeycutt operated Williams Lake the last half of the Sixties. That was the period when the Lake was at its zenith. Honeycutt brought popular rhythm-and-blues acts to the pavilion by the water. There were initially bands on Wednesday and Saturday nights in 1965. Honeycutt only had bands on Saturday nights and holidays after that. Williams Lake thrived as a dance spot for teenagers who wanted to escape the realities of life. They went there to party and dance. They came by the carloads. The success was more improbable due to a fact pointed out by Honeycutt, "We could not sell alcohol." He went on to say, "We didn't let drunks in."

Honeycutt paid Mr. Williams one hundred dollars a week rent for the pavilion on a week-to-week basis. Mr. Williams told Robert that he was going to take the lake back after Labor Day of 1965 so that his daughter could run it. Robert called the

Jokers Three, through whom he booked his bands, and told them not to book bands for others for Williams Lake as he was considering building a new facility. "My bluff worked," He said. When the Williams family was unable to book bands, Mr. Williams allowed Honeycutt to continue the operation. Had the Williams family, who only had a phone number for the Jokers Three taken from Honeycutt's posters but no personal contacts with them, been able to book bands, there undoubtedly would have been a different story to tell about Williams Lake.

"Mr. Williams had operated the pavilion for thirty-three years since 1932. His first jukebox was powered by a generator as there was no electricity in that part of Sampson County at the time," Honeycutt said.

Mr. Williams added French doors to the façade of the pavilion over the lake the first winter. That was to allow them to be closed during the winter for heating and to be opened during the summer for cooling. Even so, everybody who danced and most of those who didn't left with their clothes wet from perspiration during the summer months. The pavilion had a floor that was 33' x 107'. That included the bandstand which was twenty-four to twenty-seven feet wide. Both the men's and women's bathrooms were single stall facilities outside the pavilion until the winter of 1966. Three new stalls where added inside for the ladies. Both of the exterior bathrooms were converted to a single men's room.

Honeycutt knew a little about music as he was a musician himself. "I played the saxophone in a band called The Flames in high school in 1958 and '59." He was also influential in helping Gene Barbour, his college roommate and a future member of the Cavaliers, secure a position as lead vocalist with the Shakedowners. Because of his musical experience,

Honeycutt knew good bands and good musicians when he encountered them.

Honeycutt was an accomplished shagger. "I didn't know that the name of the dance was the Shag at the time. When I went somewhere else and asked a lady if she could dance, I always asked if she could do the dance from Williams Lake. Or I would ask if she could do the Williams Lake dance," He said. On the subject of learning to shag he said, "I wore a U-shaped hole through the rubber tile to the concrete floor of my grandfather's store near Williams Lake practicing."

When asked about the reaction of bands coming to Williams Lake for the first time in that rural setting, he replied, "There were those who were concerned about the potential size of the crowds. They would remain concerned until they started seeing the cars coming from the other side of the lake about seven. That was true of the first band to play there on Wednesday, April 22, 1965. That band was Bob Collins the Fabulous Five. They arrived between four and five in the afternoon to set up. When the band arrived I was below the dam bass fishing. I went to help them unload their equipment. Afterward we went back to the spillway and found that my cane pole had been pulled in by a large bass. Bob Collins joined me fishing and caught the largest fish he had ever caught. It was a four pound bass."

When asked about the cost of booking bands, he answered, "I paid the Fabulous Five one hundred and fifty dollars for that Wednesday night performance. I had Buddy Skipper booked the first five Saturdays that I was open. I paid Buddy Skipper one-fifty for each of those nights. That first year, 1965, I paid bands one hundred and fifty dollars for a Wednesday night and about three-fifty for Saturday night. Bands became more expensive as they began to realize the size crowds that they were drawing when they appeared in various places. I charged one dollar admission except for a few big-name attractions for whom the charge was two dollars"

On the issue of race Honeycutt said, "We had a predominantly white audience even though we never turned away a black customer and one did show up periodically. I remember two students from Fayetteville State who came one night. We told them we would let them go in to look around and see if this is what they were looking for. They went in. They came out shortly and said that it was not what they expected. They left without incident. Chester Mayfield and the Casuals the first black act that we ever booked."

Honeycutt discussed attendance. "I thought the place seemed a little empty if there were less than four hundred people in there. The largest crowd we had was in early 1969. That was over twelve hundred and fifty paid admissions to see The Tams. That was in spite of the fact that there was a big snowstorm that day. We had our smallest crowd of approximately one hundred just a few weeks later. That came on the Saturday night one week after Percy Sledge was booked here. Mr. Sledge didn't show up until eleven-thirty. We had to return everyone's money and there were over one thousand paid admissions that night." After that, crowds were sporadic. That appeared to be the beginning of the end of the Honeycutt run at Williams Lake. Honeycutt closed Williams Lake after a New Year's Eve 1969 performance.

Robert sat there with his head full of blondish white hair and said the he would like people who went to Williams Lake to know, "I'm doing well. I am in good health. I regret having given up the saxophone years ago, but I started playing again. I'm enjoying playing the saxophone more now than I did what I was young. I have a collection of five saxophones."

As for his fondest memories of Williams Lake, "I was under too much stress during those years when I operated Williams Lake to really enjoy it. I enjoy talking about it now. I get a lot more pleasure from talking about it now than I got from it then."[3]

That is as true for many who went to Williams Lake as it is for Robert Honeycutt.

THE SHAG AND BEACH MUSIC

THE SHAG HAs always been the attraction. Beach Music has been there to support the Shag. Inadvertently, the Shag has supported Beach Music. In this case, unlike the chicken and egg, we know which came first. The music came first, then the Shag. The Shag has been the nutrient that has sustained and shaped the life of Beach Music.

Unlike other music dependant social developments primarily associated with the Sixties, Beach Music didn't have a scene from which to spring. There was no primary city of development. Beach Music is the backdrop for dancing the Shag. It has always been possible to have and enjoy Beach Music without the Shag. However, the reverse has never been true. It has always been the case that the Shag was accompanied by Beach Music. The easygoing beach dances that used the name had a point of origin the beaches of the Carolinas. That appears to have happened when white kids broke the color barrier. Such activities have been reputed as early as the Thirties. The white kids convinced local DJs to add rhythm and blues to their playlists. There were no bands specifically dedicated to Beach Music during the Shag's peak of prominence in the mid-Sixties. The Shag has always been a rare cultural movement that picked its own music after the fact.

That doesn't mean there ever was an absence of a distinctive sound or feel to the music to which the Shag was danced. To the contrary, the Shag started as a lazy adaptation of the jitterbug. It has customarily been danced on beaches on nights, weekends and holiday afternoons. Shaggin' has always been done with someone of the opposite sex. Therefore, the music shaggers picked for their soundtrack had to be sunny, sexy, fun and lazy. Shaggin' has been done to songs as diverse as Elvis' "Return to Sender" and Marvin Gaye's "Sexual Healing." In general, there has always been a strong instrumental rhythmical beat which conjured up a slow shuffle and a southern soul vocal. Many of the big hits of Beach Music have been one-hit wonders. They were cherry-picked for their utility for the Shag. For shaggers it has been all about the dance. They needed music with the proper beat. They have been willing to adopt music from any genre as long as it has the requisite beat. Evidence the selection songs such as "Happy After" by the Bee Gees, "Havana" by Kenny G., "Unbreak My Heart" by Johnny Mathis, "Things Have Changed" by Bob Dylan and "Crazy" by Gnarls Barkley that have been adopted into the Beach Music fold to support the shaggers. Songs by the Backstreet Boys, Santana, the Mighty Mike Schermer Band and Cher to name a few have also served as support for shaggin'. Perhaps the most popular Beach Music song of all has been "Lady Soul" by the Temptations.

If you were in the central southeastern United States and you did the swing dance, you probably did the form known as "The Carolina Shag." "The Carolina Shag" has been the swing dance of the South! The Shag had the ability to survive without the beer and warm summer nights because its essence has been the cool guys and the hot girls. That has always been the case. It always will be.

It has been argued that the Shag was born in Ocean Drive in the late Thirties. The Shag has gained such a following that it is the Official State Dance of South Carolina. Over twelve thousand shaggers have annually attended the North Myrtle Beach "Spring Safari" of the Society of Stranders, typically in April. And almost that many have shown up to dance the Shag at the SOS September "Fall Migration" since 1980. There have been more Shag Clubs in the Carolinas, Georgia and Virginia than there have been in any other one type of swing dance club in the world.

The roots of the Shag are said to have resulted from the cross-pollination of black music and club dancers in Myrtle Beach. That was possible because of the natural openness of fun-loving and carefree groups of white and black teenagers in the Thirties and Forties. The racially myopic mainstream radio stations of the Forties in the South did not play black music. Kids had to flock to the beaches to hear it on jukeboxes were some of them had prevailed on club owners to add them.

Young men and boys left Ocean Drive at night and attended black nightclubs. They "jumped the Jim Crow rope." During that time of segregation they were allowed to watch from the balcony. They adapted what they saw and liked to their own style. Those same young men are also credited with initiating the "Beach Music" phenomenon, by convincing jukebox owners to put R&B into the playlists.

Lindy Hoppers have expressed familiarity with the "Big Apple" dance. It and its derivative, the "Little Apple," had their origins at the former Fat Sam's Big Apple Club in Columbia, South Carolina. The "Big Apple" then drifted to New York City and the Savoy Ballroom. Jazz affected the Southern style directly. The Savoy transmutations returned home to the South. Early Shaggers were called "Jitterbugs." The music was fast, and it was big band swing. The term "Shag" was first heard over a decade later. By the early Fifties, the Shag had slowed down and adopted the tempo and feel of Rhythm and Blues as its own.

In the post-WWII era, with the close of the Savoy Ballroom and demise of the big bands, the Lindy Hop lost most of its USA popularity. However, the popularity of The Carolina Shag grew rapidly in the Deep South.

That 1968 soul record by the Tams, "Be Young, Be Foolish, Be Happy," described the sentiments of Beach Music devotees and the shaggers who never seem to grow weary of dancing into the night. Shaggin' has always been about fun. Following the Shag has become a lifestyle for some. Nostalgia has been the Shag's lifeline.

Beach Music is comprised of 4/4 rhythm songs. Many of them wax smartly about the sun and the surf. At its essence have been the beach and of course girls. It complemented the drinking and partying going on. It said let's enjoy the girls and let's stay young forever. Many of the songs of Beach Music may be old, but they will always be fondly remembered. Beach Music has avoided be buried by the sands of time.

Beach Music came close to dying out on at least a couple of occasions. Its popularity faded in the Seventies when some of the beach acts stopped touring and the responsibilities of family and work kept all but the most faithful followers at home. Its popularity fell again during the middle Nineties when tougher drinking laws in the Carolinas kept some of the younger followers away from the clubs where the Shag was practiced. However, this style of light, danceable Beach Music has proven to be irrepressible just has been true of the coastline of the Carolinas where the Shag was spawned. One significant reason for that was that there is big money to be made. An affluent white audience was out there keeping Beach Music and the Shag alive into the Twenty-First century. The presence of money was unforeseen by the majority of the support structure for Beach Music and the Shag.

Though its national influence had waned by the Seventies, the industry that built up around Beach Music appears to be holding strong today. There are Beach Music clubs and shag dance associations scattered across the country. A record charting service similar to *Billboard*, *Wax Museum*, sprang up in Charlotte to chart the hottest beach songs. For a number of years Beach Music has produced its own awards similar to the Grammies, the Cammy Awards, each November in North Myrtle Beach.

Shaggers turned Beach Music into a lifestyle. Most shag dancers today are aged thirty-five to sixty-five years.

One of the primary reasons that Beach Music has survived until today was nostalgia. Nostalgia and romance provided a powerful combination. The shag world has frequently been a sort of lonely-hearts club where single, divorced and widowed people meet each other. Many marriages have been made in that crowd. Lamentably, a number of marriages also dissolved. It has reflected our society in microcosm.

Though their contributions tend to be largely ignored, Fayetteville in Cumberland County, NC, and White Lake in Bladen County, NC, made significant contributions to the growth of the Beach Music culture on the Atlantic seaboard. One was a Fayetteville band called the Houserockers. The other, perhaps the first royalty of the Shag, was a drop-dead gorgeous young lady named Claire Reavis. She was a dancing sensation who honed her steps at White Lake while hanging out with younger guys. As far back as the Thirties, Reavis was dancing at White Lake's Goldston Beach, where there was a dance hall called the White Lake Pavilion. It extended out over the water. During the war years, she would dance at the U.S.O. clubs in Fayetteville. She was given the unofficial status of "the Queen of Shag." A poster sized cheesecake picture of her has graced a wall at Duck's in North Myrtle Beach for years.

Since the passing of the royalty of the Shag no one has been since been dubbed "King" or "Queen." However, Charlie Womble and Jackie McGee have unofficially filled those positions.

A bit of explaining is due those who think of the Beach Boys and Jan and Dean when the term "Beach Music" is uttered. There music was altogether different. That music was "Beach Boy" music to fans of Beach Music. "Beach Boy" music was built around a twanging Chuck Berry like guitar riff and group vocal harmonies. That music has generally drawn scoffs from the true devotees of Beach Music.

Beach Music has generally been a group of songs that are R&B based. They have enjoyed a tempo which allowed one to do the Shag to them. One steeped in the Shag would never have considered shaggin' to "Beach Boy" music.

The name "Beach Music" is said to have originated at Carolina Beach. The young sun-tanned bunch who gathered there were perhaps responsible for the name. Naturally, they gave soul songs the name because that what they heard at the beach. The songs that were strong hits have survived and become standards. Beach Music came from black R&B. Doo-Wop from the Northeast and New York City had a strong influence on Beach Music. Many college kids came to the beach as lifeguards and heard the music on the jukeboxes. After they returned home at the end of summer, they could not wait to get back to beach and hear the music they left behind. It was essentially rhythm and blues. There were regional stars, but just often the records that they played were heard around the country.

The Sixties proved to be an explosive time for the Shag's growth and popularity. It took "Beach Music" right along with it. The older beach crowd in the Carolinas will recall such dance spots as Williams Lake in Sampson County, N.C. Raleigh had the Cat's Eye, the Varsity Club, Red's and the Embers. There was the Coachman and Four in Bennettsville, S.C. Cecil Corbett's Beach Club was between Ocean Drive and Myrtle Beach. Lake Artesia was in Clinton. Faison, N.C. was home to the warehouse

The dance evolved from the jitterbug and the jump blues of the big band jazz era. It is said with good reason that the Shag originated in Seabreeze. Seabreeze was a tourist resort for blacks across the Intracoastal Waterway from Carolina Beach. Blacks did what was called the jitterbug. The Shag was essentially the jitterbug that white people slowed down. Then they added cool to it. The dance in its purest form is true improvisation.

Boys were drawn to it by the abundance of beautiful women. The renegade debutante has always been the big draw for the guys of shag. It has been a man's dance. Man, not woman, gave birth to the Shag. The coolest girls have always gone for guys who could and would shag. Aging shaggers have continued to slow down the dance, but has retained the characteristic of having the man lead. The youth who shag today along with a few of the more spirited oldsters have kept the fire and fury of the early Shag alive.

In 1949, Jimmy Cavallo and the Houserockers of Fayetteville were playing their brand of R&B for crowds all over North Carolina. During that year, they had a residency in Carolina Beach at a dance club called Bop City. The band drew huge crowds of dancers. It has been called the beginning of Beach Music. There would be kids in the crowds from towns all over North Carolina. The Houserockers may have been the first white band ever to cover songs by black artists the way Elvis would do later. By 1950, the Houserockers had disbanded.

Though it was grounded in rhythm-and-blues, the Beach Music scene in the Carolinas has always been a part of white America. Make that Southern white America. In the glory years of the Fifties and Sixties, crowds of Southern belles and peg-pants kids wearing Weejuns without socks came together for good times. They came to fraternize. They came to party. But mostly they came to dance the Shag. That generation has aged, but for the most part the Beach Music scene has remained mostly a white affair. Some blacks have periodically showed up and they are readily accepted. If you were buck-toothed, or tall, or fat or thin or had a mole between your eyes, none of that mattered if you could dance. If you danced, you were accepted in spite of your shortcomings. In the beginning, Beach Music was pure soul. Laying the foundation to the summer soundtracks of these pimply white kids was black R&B. Music with a dance beat performed live by dancing, harmonizing men in gaudy neon jackets and pants so tight that it appeared that something had to give; fortunately, no such occurrence was known to occur.

OD serves as the touchstone for the many shag dance associations and clubs in existence across the Eastern United States today. Some disbelieve the notion that the Shag and Beach Music are dying out. Their thoughts have actually been that the reverse is occurring. They have reasoned that we have yet to see the peak. There have been good reasons to believe that such a trend is possible. What many people have failed to realize is that the Shag and Beach Music are all over the country. Outside the Carolinas, Georgia and Virginia little pockets have been found all over the country. Those pockets of fans add up. The movement has benefited from the Internet. *Affectionatos* have started to connect with each other in cyber space.

Shaggers Hall of Fame brick "pavers" with the names of shag clubs and enthusiasts engraved in them have been placed in some of the sidewalks and parking areas of North Myrtle Beach. The Shagging Hall of Fame Museum has been spread out along some of the walls of the Ocean Drive Resort Hotel, Fat Harold's and the Spanish Galleon. Plaques of the inductees from each year were hung from the walls, with their fond remembrances of the beach and their contrasting photos from past and present framed for all to see.

Beach Music has been reputed to have turned sixty years old in 2005. That assessment was because *Billboard* magazine announced in 1945 that *"Swing is dead; bands are out and vocalists are in."* The same year "Beach Music" emerged on one jukebox at the beach; spreading rapidly to "jump joints" along the boardwalk, then to other saloons and restaurants along the East Coast.

Local bands, often termed "Beach" bands, left their hometowns and joined the Beach (and frat party) circuit in the late Fifties. Harry Deal and the Galaxies first played the Myrtle Beach Pavilion in 1960. The Pavilion at Atlantic Beach near Morehead City, N.C. didn't have live acts until approximately 1960. The Sixties were explosive for the growth and the popularity of Beach bands. In the Seventies, many disappeared; while others shouldered the "Rock" mantle for a few years.

There has long been a standing debate on the actual birthplace of the Shag. That debate has stirred a significant number of arguments. Most have been friendly. Some have been otherwise. It has been generally agreed that it was born on the East Coast of the Carolinas. There are a number of claims as to the specific location. Some say the Shag originated at White Lake. Many have claimed it originated at Carolina Beach. And, not surprisingly, there has been the claim it originated at Ocean Drive or OD as it was popularly known among those who went there. North Myrtle Beach on the Grand Strand has wrestled squatter's rights as the home of the Shag because the Shag and Beach Music have been such a big tourist business in the area. At Carolina Beach about sixty miles north of North Myrtle Beach on the North Carolina coast the once flourishing Shag and Beach Music scene has largely disappeared.

The bottom line was that the Shag was pretty much about being at the beach, cold beer and the freedom of little boys of all ages looking for little girls of all ages. It was equally about little girls looking for little boys.

As far as the Shag world was concerned, Carolina Beach was to many the place to be in the early and mid Fifties. As a shagger and Beach Music fan if you were unable to get into the Plaza, you were going home. Shaggers from that era were eager to be standing on the second floor of the old Ocean Plaza Ballroom at the corner of Harper Avenue and Carolina Beach Avenue North. The uniform for the male weekend Beach Music fan was a long-sleeve blue shirt, khakis and shiny brown Weejuns without socks.

Many people who frequented the North Carolina tourist town in the Sixties will recall the "Ring the Bell with the Hammer" carnival attraction that was once across the sidewalk from the art deco Ocean Plaza. It like other things from Carolina Beach's heyday has changed including the boardwalk itself. There are those who claim that the Drifters' 1964 hit song "Under the Boardwalk" was penned here. It would have been written about the original boardwalk. During high tide, the water lapped under the wooden boardwalk. A concrete sidewalk has long since replaced the original wooden one. Today the boardwalk sits up safety behind a high berm. The berm makes it impossible to see the ocean from the current boardwalk. The old amusement rides, the Tilt-A-Whirl, the Ferris wheel, the Bullet and the hobbyhorse are long gone.

Through all the changes to Carolina Beach, the Ocean Plaza, which was among the last remaining beach pavilions, stood until the summer of 2006. It had a history that dated to 1946, the year after World War II ended. It approximately coincides with the demise of the swing era. That was where some future husbands and wives met. Mr. and Mrs. Gene Reynolds, "Ma and Pop" Reynolds, built the Ocean Plaza. They first opened it on Memorial Day in 1946. Bill Grassick and his Orchestra were the musical attraction that day. The building was being considered for nomination to the National Register before it was razed in the summer of 2006.

The Ocean Plaza was the last surviving building that housed the clubs from what many call the heyday of the Shag and Beach Music. The Lumina at Wrightsville Beach is no longer there. The Pavilion at Atlantic Beach, Morehead City has long been gone. Spivey's at Myrtle Beach is gone. Sonny's at Cherry Grove is long gone. The Ocean Plaza was the last one left.

It's was a little weather-beaten, but the building appeared to be in good shape before its demise. It withstood the fury and ravages of Hurricane Hazel in 1954. It has recently endured the battering winds from five hurricanes. It was unable to withstand the rules of economics.

If you ask almost anybody of age here, they will tell you that it started here. They will tell you this is the birth place of the Shag. They maybe right. They may just be biased.

"Welcome to North Myrtle Beach, Home of the Shag" is splashed across a cream-colored water tower looming over the town. A counter argument is that the Shag started around '47 or '48 at OD. At that time, Ocean Drive was nothing but a dirt road. That was even before The Pad was there. The lack of facilities in Ocean Drive at the time has served as a principal reason why the Shag could not have started there.

An old house on Ocean Boulevard with a pretty fair hardwood floor, The Pad, was known for its cheap beer and the old R&B selections that played on the jukebox. The Pad opened on July 4, 1955. That was the year after Hurricane Hazel brought devastation to the pavilions, the piers and the familiar dance haunts along the Carolina coast. The Pad's long run at the beach ended Jan. 28, 1994. It gave way to the tools of demolition and was razed that year. In its place came The Barrel, but that gray, wooden establishment closed recently. It stood empty across the street from the Boulevard Grill. It had shards of broken beer bottles littered on the sidewalk out front until it was torn down in 2003. Among other hangouts, there was Sonny's Grill which was another juke joint and one that has been likened to a poor man's version of the old Spivey's Pavilion before Hazel.

The third location that has made a strong claim to being the birthplace of the Shag is White Lake, N.C. Young people gathered at the White Lake Pavilion on Goldston Beach early in the history of the Shag. Unlike the beach areas, the White Lake claim does not appear to have been tied to guys going to the dance halls of the black community. It like Carolina Beach, has relinquished its hold on the Shag and on those who have kept the Shag alive over the years since its birth. Its popularity waned in the Sixties. White Lake has lost the majority of its early following to time. These facts have not diminished the validity and value of White Lake's claim to being the place the Shag was born.

The identity of the true birthplace of the Shag is buried with its forefathers. Perhaps that happened as a blessing to the progeny of the Shag. That fact has provided us and the shaggers of the future an opportunity to have fun discussing the matter.[4]

THE PERFORMERS
(IN THE ORDER THEY APPEAR)

THE ENTERTAINERS were from Kinston, North Carolina. They were the reincarnation of the Sunsetters Combo. That rebirth had occurred in 1965. They performed at Williams Lake on a number of evenings. They also played with some regularity at The Pavilion at Atlantic Beach. They performed at fraternity parties primarily at UNC and NCSU. They entertained in some other venues in eastern North Carolina.

The Entertainers occasionally drifted outside eastern N.C. to the western part of N.C. and to neighboring states. They recorded several songs. "Mr. Pitiful" and "I Want to be Your Everything" were recorded in 1966. In 1967, they cut "Be Me" and "I Want Someone."

The Cavaliers were a well-known and established band out of Dunn, N.C. under the management of Harry Driver. In 1965, the group added Campbell College student, Gene Barbour. Mr. Barbour had previously been with the band known as the Shakedowners. He paired with N.C. State band members Donald Hobson and Billy Wellons anchoring the group that produced "Nobody." "Nobody" is one of the most sought after recording from the legendary JCP catalog. Original copies of the 45-RPM recording of the song routinely produce bids exceeding $600. There favorite place to play in those days was Williams Lake. They later played regularly at the club named for them in Ocean Drive, S.C., The Cavalier Club.

Gene Barbour was the roommate of Robert Honeycutt, who operated Williams Lake from April of 1965 until the end of 1969, in the Kitchen dorm at Campbell the fall semester of 1964. The two of them and another young man occupied a trailer just off the Campbell campus the spring semester of 1965.[5]

The Monzas were started in 1962. They were the first of several Beach Music groups to be established in the Burlington, North Carolina area. Throughout most of their existence of **The Monzas** venues included the frat houses of the Atlantic Coast Conference Colleges, those of the Southeastern Conference and clubs in the Carolinas. They performed at a number of private functions. They were the first group in that era to use two female vocalists. Each of them was more than capable of carrying lead vocals on a number of songs which became crowd favorites. In the mid Sixties they became the first regional band to have a record released which was picked up by a national label. Their song "Hey I Know You" was produced by Wand Records. It had become a huge regional hit on its own prior to Wand. They released "Instant Love," a single written by Billy Carden who was the lead singer at the time, in 1969. Over the course of nine years, there were over a dozen extremely talented musicians were members of **The Monzas**.[6]

Maurice Williams is one of the most extraordinarily durable figures in the history of classic rhythm-and-blues and rock 'n roll. He wrote the song "Stay" which became one of the classic singles in the history of Beach Music. It was a number one hit after its release on Al Silver's Herald label weeks of October 17 and 24, 1960. "Stay" was part of the 1987 *Dirty Dancing* soundtrack that sold over twenty million copies worldwide. Williams has remained active as a performer, recording artist and songwriter.

Maurice Williams was born in Lancaster, South Carolina circa 1940. He demonstrated musical talent at a very early age. He started learning the piano from his older sister in the late '40's. By the time he was ten years old he was having friends from elementary school over for informal jam sessions at his house. Williams had sung in church, but his interest lay more in popular music. In 1953, he and some friends formed a group that they called **The Royal Charms**. They played school events and talent shows. They won several talent shows. Naturally, they acquired a local following before they were booked for a paying gig at the Veterans of Foreign Wars post in Lancaster. Williams wrote two songs that year. Both "Little Darling" and "Stay" were to have pivotal effects on his life and the group's history.

The Royal Charms loved performing. As one would expect, they were popular around Lancaster. However, their prospects were limited around Lancaster. Their first real break came in 1956 when a Nashville disc jockey put them in touch with Ernie Young, the head of Excello Records. Williams won an audition over the phone. The band had to raise money around Lancaster to make the trip to Nashville in December.

Young altered "Little Darling" somewhat. He gave the song a calypso beat. He also insisted on **The Royal Charms** changing their name. Young happened to like flowers; therefore, he selected the name **The Gladiolas** for the band.

"Little Darling" by **The Gladiolas** was released by Excello in January of 1957 and was a rhythm & blues charts hit. It rose to number eleven in a four week run in the early spring of that year. It was less well received on the pop charts. It stayed on the chart for eleven weeks but never went higher than forty-first after that. A version of "Little Darling" recorded for Mercury by a white Canadian group called **The Diamonds** rose to number one on the pop charts. It sold more than a million copies. It became a definitive "do-wop"-type single.

Williams accepted **The Diamonds'** version because Young had set example for honesty that was rare in the record business in those days. Young left **Williams** with full rights as songwriter instead of "buying" them away for practically nothing. It was a decision that was to earn Williams a large sum of money staring at the age of seventeen.

Williams was a serious student. He earned a music scholarship to Allen University in Columbia, South Carolina. He turned the scholarship down because he was doing so much in music. He chose not to interrupt his career.

The Gladiolas kept performing. They did a tour through the west once before returning to South Carolina. After their return, they were they became a heavy favorite among fraternities, playing often for those at the University of South Carolina. At the end of 1958, the band decided against re-signing with Excello. That meant they had to give up their name which was owned by Young. They had to re-establish themselves under a new moniker. Band member Dion Gore reportedly saw a German car called a Zodiac. The band took its name from that car. They were **Maurice Williams and the Zodiacs**.

The Zodiacs grew to nine members. In 1960, the band started working with Al Silver of Herald Records in New York and producers Phil Gernhardt and Al McCullough. The band was to provide demos. **Williams** pulled out the other song he had written in 1953. He brought "Stay" to Silver.

Maurice Williams and The Zodiacs signed with Herald. "Stay," sparked by a great falsetto from Shane Gaston hit number one that fall. "Stay" sold over a million copies. It became the biggest hit in the history of Herald Records. Over the years, "Stay" has sold over ten million copies around the globe. A number of other artists including the Four Seasons, Jackson Browne and Chaka Khan have all reached the top twenty with their renditions of "Stay".

The Zodiacs recorded "I Remember" on the Herald label. It was a modest success reaching number eighty-six on the pop charts. It failed to register on the rhythm & blues chart. They tried again with "Come Along" in the spring of 1961. "Come Along" climbed to the eighty-third position on the pop charts, while failing to make the rhythm & blues chart.

In the mid-Sixties **Maurice Williams and The Zodiacs** teamed with the New Orleans-based production team of Marshall Sehorn and Allen Toussaint. Sehorn and Toussaint lead the band to record **Williams'** "May I." The song was good. It suffered the misfortune of being licensed to Vee Jay at the wrong time in Vee Jay's history. Vee Jay was then the most successful Black-owned record company of the day. Bad luck had Vee Jay fall into bankruptcy within days of the record's national release. "May I" was unable to over come that set back. "May I" reappeared on the Dee Su label out of New Orleans. That rescued it physically from being lost. "May I" has been certified a million-seller by the RIAA even though it never managed to appear on any chart. "May I" became a modest top forty hit when performed by Bill Deal & the Rhondells. The band later released records on Atlantic, Sea-Horn, and

Scepter, including "Return" with **Gladys Knight & the Pips**.

Maurice Williams and the Zodiacs were still a major draw in the south especially in their native state. Throughout the seventies and eighties **Williams** led various incarnations of **The Zodiacs** on oldies tours, primarily on the Beach Music circuit in the Southeast.

Maurice Williams has remained an active performer on the Beach Music scene. He has been inducted into the South Carolina Music and Entertainment Hall of Fame and the Beach Music Hall of Fame in Myrtle Beach.[7]

The Catalinas have been one of the most popular bands ever to come out of the Carolinas. The band has been known for their recordings, their thousands of live performances including many concerts and the antics in their very lively shows. **The Catalinas** have been one of Beach Music's best and most popular, along with being among most durable groups. The band held its first practice session in the chorus music room of Myers Park High School in Charlotte, North Carolina. The date was January 15, 1958. Seventeen years later in 1975, they helped revitalize the Beach Music genre with the smash hit "Summertime's Calling Me." The band has held a special place of esteem among Beach Music bands. It was 1980 before the band followed with the *Summertime's Calling Me* album which included single releases of "Dancin' Romancin'," "Facts Of Love" and a remake of "You Haven't The Right." They have worked continuously on dance and show material. They have covered the Southeast with live performances.

The Catalinas band began work on another album at Studioeast in Charlotte in 1989. The album, Line Up, enjoyed a quick start with the release of a double sided hit. "They Call Me Mr.

Bassman" and "Whatdja Do That For," both made the Top Forty chart. **The Catalinas** have continued to perform into 2008.[8]

Arthur Alexander wrote several famous soul songs in the Sixties. Those songs were stories of inconstant love and private gloom. His biggest hits were covered by entertainers that are more famous. The Beatles covered "Anna" and The Rolling Stones recorded "You Better Move On." Arthur Alexander introduced the word "girl" as in "I wanna tell you girl..." to his lyrics. This was a great convenience to John Lennon and others thereafter. Other high profile artists who have covered **Alexander's** songs include The Bee Gees, Dusty Springfield and Tina Turner. He has also been covered by The Tams, The Fiestas and The Drifters. British R & B bands were raised on Alexander's original versions of "Where Have You Been" and "A Shot Of Rhythm And Blues." The Beatles recorded "Where Have You Been" and "Soldier Of Love." **Alexander** sang his precise geometric songs with a dark and wholly individual intensity. His personal vocal renditions were often quite underrated.

Arthur Alexander Jr. was born on May10, 1940 in Florence, Alabama some five miles from the Tennessee River. The Tennessee River separates Florence from Sheffield and Muscle Shoals. The rural community echoed to the sounds of down-home music. **Alexander** came from a family of musicians. His mother and sister sang in church. His father played gospel songs on the guitar. He was known to use the neck of a whiskey bottle for a slide. On Saturday nights, Alexander Sr. played the blues in the juke-joints in and around Sheffield.

While in the sixth grade, **Authur Alexander Jr.** joined a gospel group, **The Heartstrings**. The other members were older than him. As a result, they performed without him when they played outside the local area. After leaving high school, he worked as a bellhop in the Holiday Inn in Sheffield.

In 1958, **Alexander** and Henry Lee Bennett wrote "She Wanna Rock" with Tom Stafford and Rick Hall. It was published under the banner of FAME (Florence Alabama Music Enterprises). Stafford took the song to Decca in Nashville where it was recorded by the Manitoba-based singer, Amie Derksen in April 1959. The following year Stafford and **Alexander** wrote "Sally Sue Brown," which he recorded in Stafford's studio. On that occasion, Stafford took the tape to Memphis where Judd Phillips released it under the name of **June Alexander** because **Arthur** was known as **June**, short for Junior, at that time.

Rick Hall bought a tobacco warehouse in Muscle Shoals. He lined the walls with egg crates and installed a four-track recorder. It was there in the summer of 1961 that **Alexander** recorded "You Better Move On." He was the first of the off-the-beaten path black entertainers that were so important to the development of Beach Music. The flip side was "A Shot Of Rhythm And Blues." Rick Hall enticed Noel Ball to sign a tape-lease deal. Ball produced "You Better Move On." It was a hit reaching number twenty-four on the charts in 1962.

In Ball's hands, **Alexander's** recordings took a more commercial turn which paid off handsomely. "Where Have You Been," a Barry Mann-Cynthia Well song, reached the top 60. "Anna," which was composed by **Alexander** himself, became a third "Hot 100" hit. It was his only Top 10 R&B hit. "Go Home Girl" peaked at No 102 in January 1963.

In April 1966, **Arthur Alexander** went to Great Britain. He appeared at the Ram-Jam Club and the Flamingo. He suffered from a less than immediate rapport with the reserved Brits.

He recorded "(Baby) For You" under a new contract with Monument's Sound Stage 7. Sound Stage 7 persevered for four years; however, it is said that **Arthur Alexander** was unprepared for success. It is not publicly known why that was true as neither he nor any of his associates have ever talked about his problems.

A return to Muscle Shoals brought forth a pop hit on Buddah with "Every Day I Have To Cry Some." It climbed to number forty-five on the charts in 1975. His renaissance was short-lived. He appeared on Music Mill in a tribute to Elvis in 1977 and shared a Koala album with Carl Perkins in 1979.

Arthur Alexander died of a heart attack in 1993 at the early age of fifty-three. He had recently begun a comeback. He had completed the album, *Lonely like Me,* before his death. That album was the punctuation of the talented, but often troubled individual's career.[9]

The Tassels was an early beach band formed in 1962. After the summer of 1964, they began calling themselves **The Mighty Tassels**. Their membership rooster boasts of some of the greatest musicians to ever play the Beach Music genre. In 1967, the six-member band merged with two former Swingin' Medallions and became The Pieces of Eight. Williams Lake and the Castaways were two of their favorite places to perform.

The Tams was formed in 1952 in Atlanta, Georgia. Although such an early origin suggests longevity, it was not until 1960 that the group emerged with a single on Swan. Then dubbed **The Tams** (derived from their wearing of Tam

O'Shanter hats on stage), they added another member before signing with Bill Lowery, an Atlanta song publisher and entrepreneur. Among those already on his books were Joe South and Ray Whitley, two musicians who would work closely with the group. "Untie Me," a South composition, was recorded at FAME and leased to Philadelphia's Arlen Records. The song became a top twenty US R&B hit.

In 1963, Lowery secured a new deal with ABC Paramount. The Tams' first single with the record company, "What Kind Of Fool (Do You Think I Am)," reached the US top ten and established a series of Whitley-penned successes. His compositions including "You Lied To Your Daddy" and "Hey Girl Don't Bother Me" were ideal material for Joe Pope's lead and the group's polished harmonies.

After 1964, the group preferred Atlanta's Master Sound audio. South and Whitley continued their involvement, writing, playing on and producing various sessions. In 1968 they produced another hit with the bubbling "Be Young, Be Foolish, Be Happy," which peaked on the *Billboard* Rhythm & Blues chart at twenty-six. It reached the UK Top 40 in 1970. By the end of the Sixties their mentors had moved elsewhere while the Master Sound house band was breaking up.

The Tams moved to 1-2-3 and Capitol Records where a reissue of "Hey Girl Don't Bother Me" became a surprise UK number one in 1971. Their association with the Shag, a dance craze and subsequent Eighties film secured a further lifeline to this remarkable group, giving the group a UK top thirty hit with "There Ain't Nothing Like Shaggin'."

The Tams were still popular in the Nineties. They recorded "Flesh and Bones" with Jimmy Buffett and joined them on the "Beach House on the Moon Tour." **The Tams** began the new millennium by debuting their new album *Steppin' Out in the*

Light with guest artist, G.C. Cameron of The Spinners featured on "Walkn' Dr. Bill."

The Tams have recorded thirteen albums and have been performing for over forty-five years. The band's first hit "Untie Me" was recorded in 1962. They have had 1 platinum and two gold records. They were featured in "Top of The Pops." They have traveled all over the globe performing.

The Tams have been featured in such magazines as *Gold Mine*. They have a long history as pioneers in the music industry. They have been inducted into the Georgia Music Hall of Fame, the Beach Music Hall of Fame and the Atlanta Hall of Fame. They were elected Outstanding Black Musical Group and voted the Eighties Beach Band of the Decade.[10]

The genesis of **The Men of Distinction** was in 1963. A group of teenagers in Dunn, North Carolina asked Harry Driver for advice about a band they were trying to get going. Harry soon had them assembled under the banner of **Gene Barbour and The Cavaliers**. Through Harry's connections in the music industry they became the backup band for many big-name entertainers when they played in the Carolinas.

The war, police action or whatever it was that was taking place in Vietnam, soon impacted the band. Its personnel changed. Some members left and returned. By 1970 the band was new. It consisted of members of the original **Gene Barbour and the Cavaliers** and some new members. Those new members came from another band from Dunn, The Tymes, which had imitated **The Cavaliers** since its inception. Gene Barbour continued on his own. Standing outside at Williams Lake one night when the band was performing there Harry Driver named the new band **The Men of Distinction**. The name was regularly shortened to "**The Men**" by their fans.

They adopted a driving visual performance. They took on the horn-heavy style of nationally popular groups such as Blood, Sweat & Tears, Chicago and Earth, Wind & Fire. They continued their repertoire of Beach Music playing the works of The Tams, The Four Tops and The Impressions as well as other groups. Then they wandered from their roots and tried other musical genre.

Responsibility came creeping onto the scene. **The Men of Distinction** were lost for some fifteen years. "**The Men**" fire was rekindled at a birthday party in 1995. They scheduled a performance for December the next year to celebrate Harry Driver's sixty-fifth birthday. That was the beginning of the resurgence of **The Men of Distinction**.

Harry Driver died unexpectedly on March 11, 1998. He was sixty-six at the time. Harry who has been called "The Father of the Shag" was gone. He left a huge void in the band. The band had to go on. **The Men of Distinction** changed their name to **Harry's Band** to honor him. They have continued to practice the craft under the name **Harry's Band**.[11]

Larry **Billy Stewart** was a distinctive and influential R&B vocalist whose stuttering delivery and word-repetition technique borrowed liberally from the jazz practice of scat singing. Born in Washington, D.C., in 1937 Stewart began singing publicly with his mother's group, the Stewart Gospel Singers, as a teenager. He made the transition to secular music by filling in occasionally for the **Rainbows**, a D.C. area vocal group. While he was with the **Rainbows, Stewart** met several future music stars including a young talent named Marvin Gaye. Bo Diddley has been credited with discovering **Stewart** playing piano in Washington, D.C. in 1956. Diddley invited him to be one of his backup musicians. That led to a recording contract with Bo Diddley's label, Chess Records. Bo Diddley played guitar on Stewart's 1956 recording of "Billy's Blues." Later **Stewart** signed with Okeh Records. He recorded "Billy's Heartache" on that label. He was backed by the **Marquees**, another D.C. area group which featured Marvin Gaye.

At Chess in the early Sixties, Stewart began working with A&R man Billy Davis. He cut a song called "Fat Boy." He expanded his repertoire with his recordings of "Reap What You Sow" and "Strange Feeling." **Stewart** hit both the pop and R&B charts big in 1965 with the songs, "I Do Love You" and "Sitting in the Park." His improvisational technique of doubling-up, scatting his words and trilling his lips made his style unique in the Sixties.

Stewart recorded the LP *Billy Stewart Teaches Old Standards New Tricks* in 1966 in an attempt to appeal to a wider audience. The first single released from that album was **Stewart's** radical standout interpretation of the George Gershwin classic "Summertime" from *Porgy and Bess*. "Summertime," which became his signature song, reached the top ten on both the pop and R&B charts that year. The follow-up single was Billy's remake of the Doris Day hit "Secret Love." It narrowly missed the top ten on the R&B chart.

Stewart continued to record throughout the remainder of his brief life. His life was tragically cut short on January 17, 1970, just two months prior to his 33rd birthday, when the car he was driving plunged into the Neuse River near Smithfield, North Carolina killing him and three members of his band.

Billy Stewart was inducted into the Washington Area Music Association Hall of Fame in 1982.[12]

At an early age **Martha Reeves'** voice possessed an earthy, direct quality that distinguished her from other female singers. Her voice bore the righteous fervor of gospel and the flinty edginess of rhythm & blues. Those characteristics combined with Motown's stylized pop-soul approach produced an exciting sound. **Martha and The Vandellas** recorded a classic run of singles in the mid-Sixties. Most of the songs were composed by the songwriting Team of Brian Holland, Lamont Dozier and Eddie Holland. **The Vandellas'** hit streak included what may be the definitive Motown anthem, "Dancing in the Street," in addition to such danceable blockbusters as "(Love Is Like a) Heat Wave," "Nowhere to Run" and "Jimmy Mack."

Martha, who had ten younger siblings, began singing with the **Del-Phis** in 1960. She was discovered in 1961 at Detroit's fabled Twenty Grand Club by Motown's Mickey Stevenson. She was invited to drop by the Motown "Hitsville" compound the next day. Initially, she did secretarial work in the A&R department and sang background vocals on records by the likes of Marvin Gaye, most audibly, on "Pride and Joy" and "Hitchhike."

Motown founder Berry Gordy soon offered **Martha's** group a recording contract of their own. **The Vandellas** got their name by combining Detroit's Van Dyke Street with the first name of a favorite singer, Della Reese. **The Vandellas** were Rosalind Ashford and Annette Beard (later Sterling). Betty Kely replaced Sterling in 1964, and Lois Reeves (**Martha's** younger sister) replaced Kely in 1967.

The trio had their first hit with Holland-Dozier-Holland's "Come and Get These Memories." However, it was the irresistibly upbeat "Heat Wave" in the summer of 1963 that made **Martha and the Vandellas** one of Motown's vanguard acts. Another symbol of summertime, "Dancing in the Street" which was co-written by Mickey Stevenson, Marvin Gaye and

Ivy Joe Hunter was a smash hit in 1964. It went all the way to number two in the face of the British Invasion. **Martha's** insistent alto cut through the punchy horns, driving bass line and funky rhythms to deliver a timeless message to the youth of America: "Summer's here and the time is right for dancing in the street. . ." The song's anthemic qualities have much to do with its call for youthful solidarity, with "music, sweet music" bringing a generation together. It was heard everywhere. The song has become a cult hit. It has been covered by the Grateful Dead, Van Halen, David Bowie and Mick Jagger among others.

Martha and the Vandellas recorded throughout the Sixties for Motown's Gordy label, charting twenty-four R&B hits, and became one of the company's most successful touring acts. As female artists at Motown, they were outshone only by Diana Ross and the Supremes, with whom they competed for resources and attention. **Martha and the Vandellas** left Motown in 1971 when Motown moved out west. They performed a farewell concert in Detroit. **Martha** embarked on a solo career with the big-budget album *Martha Reeves* in 1974. **Martha and the Vandellas** regrouped toward the end of the Seventies, and the group received a boost when the Motown 25th Anniversary TV special, which aired in 1983. **Martha and the Vandellas** continued to perform, enduring as one of the most visible reminders of Motown's glory days.[13]

The O'Kaysions recorded their biggest hit song "I'm a Girl Watcher" in 1968 on a small North Carolina label. The record became a regional hit. It was picked up by ABC Records before becoming a national hit that same year. "Girl Watcher" was listed in the top 10 for over two months and listed in the Top One Hundred for six months.

Wayne Pittman, an original member and manager of the group continued **The O'Kaysions** audience appeal by performing favorite selections from the Sixties, Seventies & Eighties throughout the Southeast. Talent and energy coupled with experience combined to keep them a fresh look on the music scene. Those attributes made **The O'Kaysions** one of the most sought after groups in the country. Variety and versatility has long been the emphasis of **The O'Kaysions**. The band has been made up of trumpet, saxophone, drums, rhythm guitar and keyboards sections. Their vocalists have dazzled a wide range of audiences with versatile selections from Beach Music and Top Forty favorites. **The O'Kaysions'** immutable style that has responsible for their beach classic, "I'm a Girl Watcher," enduring over the years. **The O'Kaysions** have remained popular as recently as 2005.[14]

Mary Esther Wells was born on May 13, 1943 and died on July 26, 1992 She has been credited with being the founder of the world famous "Motown Sound," **Mary Wells** was considered not only one of the best female singers in the music industry; she was also a vital part of the success of the prestigious label. Wells' early years were not easy. As a small child, she suffered a bout of spinal meningitis, which left her temporarily paralyzed, with loss of hearing and partial blindness in one eye.

When she returned to good health, **Wells** suffered the hardship of having to learn to walk for a second time. She was always grateful, however, to regain her hearing and sight. As a talented teenager, **Mary Wells** auditioned for Berry Gordy's Tamla Records as a songwriter, but instead received a contract to be a performer. "Bye Bye Baby," a song written by Wells, was recorded on Gordy's new label, Motown Records. In 1961 the song became a hit. **Wells** stayed with Motown for five years.

During those years with the help of producer and songwriter Smokey Robinson, **Wells** made several recordings. Her intimate and assertive voice, mixed with a soulful urgency, gave **Wells** a distinctive sound. Three major singles, "The One Who Really Loves You," reached number eight in 1962, "You Beat Me to the Punch" reached number nine in 1962 and "Two Lovers" which achieved a number seven ranking in 1962, along with tours of the U.S. and Europe, turned her into one of the most popular singers in the Motown stable.

In 1964, **Mary Wells'** career reached a significant peak when her song, "My Guy," made it to number one on the pop chart. It was one of the year's best selling recordings. She also sang duets with Marvin Gaye. One of those duets, "Once Upon a Time," climbed to number seventeen in 1964. The Beatles declared **Mary Wells** their favorite American singer, calling her "their sweetheart," and invited her to England to tour with them. Upon her return to the states, the Beatles sent **Wells** several compositions to be released on their next album. In return, **Wells** recorded an album entitled Love Songs to The Beatles.[15]

James Brown was born **James Joseph Brown, Jr.** on May 3, 1933 in Barnwell, South Carolina. He has been one of the most influential musical figures in America. He was a prolific singer, songwriter and producer. **Brown** was a significant force in the evolution of gospel and rhythm and blues into soul and funk. He has also left his mark on numerous other musical genres.

Brown began his professional music career in 1953. His thrilling live performances and a string of smash hits skyrocketed him to fame in the late Fifties and early Sixties. In spite of various personal problems and setbacks, he continued to score hits in every decade through the Eighties. In the Sixties and Seventies, he was a presence in American politics. He was especially recognized for his activism on behalf of African Americans and the poor.

Brown is recognized by a wide range of primarily self-bestowed professional titles. He has been known for his shouting vocals that drop and rise in emotion along with tone and for his frantic high-speed dancing. His song, "How Do You Stop," has become one of the great shag songs in the Beach Music genre.

Unfortunately, **James Brown** passed away on Christmas day, 2006.[16]

"Tradition" is defined as "the handing down of a belief, legend or custom from generation to generation." The **SWINGIN' MEDALLIONS**, a tradition out of Greenwood, S.C., are a true living definition of the word according to one of their promotions.

As the headliners of the Original Coors Beach Party, the **SWINGIN' MEDALLIONS** bring their high-energy party style performance to the delight of audiences of all ages. Their act and their music is indeed timeless. The eight-member group is led by John McElrath, founder of the original band. Today's **SWINGIN' MEDALLIONS** has featured a five-piece horn section and has effectively blended the sounds and music of yesterday and today. Their diverse song list has made them overwhelmingly popular with college audiences and mature rock and rollers throughout the Southeast.

The band became famous in 1966 with the release of their million seller, "Double Shot of My Baby's Love." "Double Shot" remains the signature song of the group today. The song, in fact, demonstrated its own timeless popularity as the cast of the hit television show Ally McBeal sang along with the original **SWINGIN'MEDALLIONS** recording in an October 1998 episode. Bruce Springsteen labeled it "the greatest fraternity rock song of all time". "Double Shot" was followed by Top Forty hits, "She Drives Me Out of My Mind" and "Hey, Hey Baby." Although membership of the group changed over the years, the popularity of their show did not. They became known in the talent industry as "The Party Band of the South" a tag that the group has proudly advertised.

In 1993, the nationally syndicated columnist Lewis Grizzard wrote, "Even today when I hear the **SWINGIN' MEDALLIONS** sing "Double Shot of My Baby's Love," it makes me want to stand outside in the hot sun with a milkshake cup full of beer in one hand and a slightly drenched coed in the other". The **SWINGIN' MEDALLIONS** are Yesterday and Today! Even in the new millennium, they have continued their own timeless tradition. They have become a true Southern Institution![17]

The Pieces of Eight featured one of the great horn sections of any band known to Beach Music in the Sixties. Their predecessor was **The Tassels** from Raleigh, North Carolina. **The Tassels** was an early beach band which was founded in 1962. After the summer of 1964, they called themselves **The Mighty Tassels**. Their membership boasted of some of the great performers in Beach Music history. Two members of the original **Swingin' Medallions** joined six **The Tassels** in late 1966 to form **The Pieces of Eight**. That group stayed together just over a year and were replaced by other excellent musicians and showmen. The band had a full itinerary until late 1970 even though more than two dozen musicians had ridden on their old Greyhound. The 1968-1970 incarnation of the **Pieces of Eight** who became the **Bits & Pieces** in early 1970 were recruited by Ron Simpson, a member of the third **Pieces of Eight** of the mid-1970's, also known as **The Missing Pieces**, to reform in 2002 as the **Pieces of Eight**. **Kenny Helser** is a minister in the Sophia, N.C. area as of this writing.[18]

The Drifters helped create soul music with their gospel style vocals. After Clyde McPhatter was fired by the Dominoes, Ahmet Ertegun of Atlantic Records encouraged him to form a group. McPhatter discovered the others who became members of **The Drifters** singing at the Mount Lebanon Church in Harlem, New York. **The Drifters** were as popular for their choreography as for their vocals. During their first year, McPhatter and the Drifters recorded "Money Honey," "Such A Night," "Honey Love" and "White Christmas."

McPhatter was drafted into the Army in 1954. After McPhatter's departure, George Treadwell, **The Drifter's** manager, hired Johnny Moore to become the group's new lead singer. The Moore led Drifters had a hit with "Ruby Baby."

The group's fortunes diminished. That fact along with the fact that the members were complaining about wages, caused George Treadwell who owned the name to fire the entire band in June, 1958.

Jerry Wexler, Atlantic A&R man, recognized the value of **The Drifter** name. He convinced Treadwell to apply the name to a brand new group. Treadwell heard Benjamin Nelson, who became Ben E. King sing. Treadwell hired Nelson and his group the Crowns. He renamed them **The New Drifters**. **The New Drifters** with Ben E. King as lead tenor was even more successful then the original **Drifters**. Songwriters Leiber and

Stoller wrote the group's first record "There Goes My Baby," a number two hit, in 1959. Orchestral strings, gentle Latin rhythm and King's yearning romantic vocals became the group's trademark. **The Drifters** produced other hits. They were "This Magic Moment," "I Count the Tears" and "Save the Last Dance for Me." King left the group to pursue a solo career in October, 1960.

The Drifters enjoyed their greatest hit making period with Rudy Lewis as the lead vocalist. **The Drifters** had major pop and rhythm and blues hits provided by Brill Building songwriters over the next two to three years. These included Carole King and Gerry Goffin's "Some Kind of Wonderful," "When My Little Girl Is Smiling" and "Up On the Roof." Doc Pomus and Mort Shuman's "Sweets For My Sweet" was also a hit. Barry Mann and Cynthia Weil wrote "On Broadway" and "I'll Take You Home."

Lewis died in the summer of 1964 and early **Drifter** Johnny Moore took over the lead for the group's final pop hits "Under the Boardwalk" and "Saturday Night At the Movies." **The Drifters** continued to record into the early Seventies. Around 1972, Johnny Moore with a new group of **Drifters**, moved to England, toured the clubs and cabarets, and signed with British Bell, for whom they had a series of British hits through 1975. Several different groupings of **Drifters** perform today. Johnny Moore died in London on December 30, 1998 at the age of sixty-four.

Ben E. King reemerged in 1974 with the hit "Supernatural Thing" and later recorded with The Average White Band. After his popularity waned, he rejoined **The Drifters** for European Tours in the early Eighties. Ben E. King enjoyed renewed popularity with "Stand By Me" the title song to the movie under the same name in 1986. He later recorded songs for the EMI, the Manhattan, and the Ichiban labels.

The Drifters were inducted into the Rock and Roll Hall of Fame in 1988.[19]

The Showmen have been renowned throughout the world for their anthem, "It Will Stand." The original name for the group was **The Humdingers**. **The Humdingers** were formed by General Norman Johnson who was known as "Cricket" for the insect at the time. General Norman Johnson (born 23 May, 1943) was the lead singer. They came together in the mid-Fifties in their hometown of Norfolk, Virginia. In 1956 they recorded for Jesse Stone at Atlantic, but those four songs which were done after the style of Frankie Lymon were never released to the public.

They became **The Showman** in the late Fifties. That was because Joe Banashak in New Orleans picked up on the outfit. He insisted on the name change.

After a brief session in Washington DC with Allen Toussaint at the helm, Banashak summoned the group to the Crescent City in May 1961. Eight soundtracks were produced. The first release was "Country Fool" on the A side and "It Will Stand" on the B side. As was often the case with classic rock 'n' roll, it was the B side that caught the public's ear. "It Will Stand" peaked at number sixty-one at the end of 1961. That was strange when the later reputation of the song is considered. However, the impact was sufficient to get the combo on the road touring.

The follow-up single "Fate Planned It This Way" had "The Wrong Girl" on the B-side. Both were summarily unsuccessful. Another session was scheduled for them and seven new tracks were cut. Three singles saw the light of day on the Minit label in 1962/1963. All three were unqualified failures. The Showmen became disillusioned. Joe Banashak had gone into temporary retirement. The members of the band split up. After

Liberty Records acquired the Imperial/Minit catalogue, they reissued "It Will Stand" in 1964. Again, it became a hit all be it a lesser success. That time it only went to number eighty.

In 1965, the group re-emerged on vinyl with Swan Records. There were three singles issued on that label. They proved that **The Showmen** were attempting to move with the changes in musical direction.

In 1968 lead singer Norman Johnson, left the outfit and formed the Chairmen of the Board. They recorded for Invictus Records. Invictus Records was a label set up by Holland, Dozier and Holland after they split from Tamla Motown. The group had a huge hit with "Give Me Just A Little More Time." It went all the way to number 3 in 1970. "Give Me Just A Little More Time" was followed by five other chart entries. General Johnson left and went out on his own in the late seventies.

The Showmen remained intact for some time. Leslie Felton took over as the lead vocalist. They disbanded in the early Seventies. In the late Eighties, General Johnson reformed both The Chairmen of the Board and **The Showmen**. In the Nineties, both bands were working along the southeastern seaboard area. They worked primarily around the Carolinas. The Chairmen of the Board has continued into 2008. They have had another frequently requested hit in the Beach Music arena titled "It Ain't What You Do (It's The Way That You Do It)."[20]

The Embers have been called Beach Music's most enduring band. They have been wowing audiences since 1958. They have continued going strong in 2007. Bobby Tomlinson, one of the original members of the band, is one of the most consistent performers in the history of Beach Music. Jackie Gore was the primary voice of **The Embers** from 1958 to 1994. They have continued to turn out great recordings reminiscent of one of the genre's standard bearers, "I Love Beach Music," which was released near the halfway point in their career in 1977. "I love Beach Music" is undoubtedly their signature song. There are those who credit with them with starting what has become true Beach Music in a park in Raleigh, North Carolina in 1977. Others however, will tell you Beach Music is more appropriately dated back to 1945.

Over the years, **The Embers** have played for a diverse clientele in a myriad of locations. They have performed for presidents, princes, students and bankers. They have opened for the Rolling Stones. They have done commercials for Budweiser. They have played at The Olympics. They even played at an inauguration for Bill Clinton's Presidency. They appear equally at home either at the beach or in the city. Their music has been enjoyed by many on recordings and in concert. They have been inducted into the South Carolina Rhythm & Blues Hall of Fame.

The Embers have had an unusual history for a rhythm and blues band. They have outlived the disco, punk, new wave and hip-hop music eras. They also survived their stint as businessmen when they operated the Embers Club in Raleigh. They have continued to take the stage as one of the most tightly knit and entertaining bands to grace the Beach Music scene into 2007. They have remained popular for almost fifty years.[21]

Otis Redding, Jr. was born in Dawson, Georgia in 1941. He owed his musical style to his Baptist Minister father. At the age of five **Redding's** family moved to Macon, Georgia. He began his career as a singer and musician in the choir of the Vineville Baptist Church. **Redding** attended Ballad Hudson High School where he member of the school band. He was determined to help his family financially. As a result, he dropped out of high school and went on to work with Little Richard's former band, the **Upsetters**. He began to compete in local talent shows. After winning first place in fifteen consecutive shows, **Redding** was banned from future competitions.

In 1959, **Redding** sang at the Grand Duke Club after his exposure in the church choir. **Redding** joined Johnny Jenkins and the **Pinetoppers** in 1960. He participated in the "Teenage Party" talent shows sponsored by Hamp Swain on Saturday mornings initially at the Roxy Theater and later at the Douglas Theatre in Macon.

Redding toured the United States, Canada, Europe and the Caribbean. His concert tours were among the biggest box office successes of any touring performer of his time. He was nominated in three categories by the National Academy of Recording Arts and Sciences (NARAS) for recordings he made during 1967. 1968 was scheduled to be the **Redding's** greatest year to date. He had appearances slated at such locations as New York's Philharmonic Hall and Washington's Constitution Hall. **Redding** was booked for several major television network appearances including The Ed Sullivan and The Smothers Brothers Shows. There was also a planned television special starring Redding.

In 1970, Warner Brothers released an album of live recordings from the Monterey International Pop Festival, June 1967, featuring **Otis Redding** on one side and Jimi Hendrix on the other. That record is evidence that the hip white audiences, better known as the "love crowd," were enjoying **Redding** right along with the black audiences for whom he had routinely played. His combination of energy, excitement and showmanship allowed him to reach and connect with audiences all over.

Johnny Jenkins and the **Pinetoppers** drove to Memphis, Tennessee for a recording session in October 1962 at Stax Records. The session was not going well, so Jim Stewart, Stax co-owner, allowed Otis to cut a couple of songs with the studio time that had been booked. Those songs included "These Arms of Mine" which was released in 1962. That was the first of his hits including classics "I've Been Loving You Too Long," "Respect" and "Try A Little Tenderness." Nine months later he was invited to perform at the Apollo Theatre for a live recording.

"The Dock Of The Bay" was unlike anything he had ever written. It was influenced by Redding's admiration for the Beatles' classic *Sgt. Pepper's Lonely Hearts Club Band* album. **Redding** spent a week on a houseboat in Sausalito when he was performing at San Francisco's Fillmore West Theater in the summer of 1967. He undoubtedly spent time "sittin' on the dock" looking out at the bay and the lights of San Francisco across the Bay. It is easy to understand the source of **Redding's** inspiration for the song, "(Sittin' On) The Dock Of The Bay." It was recorded just three days prior to his death. The song posthumously went on to become Otis Redding's biggest hit and his signature work. "(Sittin' on) the Dock of the Bay" reached number one in the nation in the spring of 1968.

Michael Bolton later released **Redding's** "(Sittin' On) The Dock Of The Bay" for his first single release from his album *The Hunger* and took it into the nations' Top Twenty in1987.

In September 1987, Atlantic Records released *The Otis Redding Story*, a two volume record set, featuring **Redding's** hits and some of his most unique songs such as "Pain in my Heart" and "Satisfaction." In 1995, Atlantic Records released *The Best of Otis Redding* which was a two record set including many of his most famous songs.

Redding met his wife Zelma Atwood in 1959. They were

married in August 1961. They had three children: Dexter, Karla and Otis III. Demetria was adopted after his death. In 1965, he moved them to "The Big O Ranch" in Round Oak, Georgia. The ranch was named after "The Big O" himself.

He was the President of his own publishing firm, Redwal Music Co., Inc. **Redding's** prowess as a businessman led him to form his own label, Jotis records, in 1965. In addition to his many business interests in the fields related to music, **Otis Redding** was engaged in other business interests in his native state such as real estate, investments, stocks and bonds.

It is impossible to forecast where **Otis Redding's** career path might have taken him had he not been killed when his twin-engine Beechcraft crashed into Lake Monona in Madison, Wisconsin on December 10, 1967.[22]

Willie T. and The Magnificents were a favorite at fraternities and clubs throughout the south in the Sixties. **Willie T. and The Magnificents** performed the standards of the more famous entertainer, Willie Tee, who recorded the songs "Thank You John," "Walking Up A One Way Street" and "Teasing You." Many who saw them thought that they were seeing and hearing that Willie Tee. However, **Willie T. and The Magnificents** were from Burlington, North Carolina, not New Orleans, Louisiana – home of Willie Tee.

BOB'S ALL-TIME TOP 40
BEACH MUSIC SONGS

SELECTING MY PERSONAL top 40 favorite Beach Music songs of all time from the hundreds that I love was extremely difficult. You will notice I cannot count because I picked 48 of my top 40. Picking the top 20 – 25 without putting them in order was relatively easy in comparison to picking rest. Putting them in order was another matter. I put them in an order based on how I felt the day I did built the list. I have changed it several times since. The order varies from day to day. The order did not mean much in as little as a few minutes. The list was reasonably accurate as of April 19, 2008. I think!

Now you know something about what I like in Beach Music. Anyone can argue that I have left out a large number of truly great songs. I agree. However, I don't believe that anyone can successfully argue that any of these songs falls short of greatness.

I suggest that you select your own Top 40, or 48, even if you don't put them in order. I hope it is an easier task for you. However, if you are a true Beach Music fan, I doubt that it will be an easy undertaking for you either. Good luck and happy list making!

SONG TITLE	ARTIST
Happy Ever After	The Bee Gees
How Do You Stop	James Brown
Stay	The Temptations
I Don't Do Duets	Patti LaBelle & Gladys Knight
Queen of the 88's	Kelly Hunt
Unbreak My Heart	Johnny Mathis
Just for You	Solomon Burke
Shakin' the Shack	The Fantastic Shakers
Things Have Changed	Bob Dylan
Wish I Didn't Miss You	Angie Stone
In The Mood	Bobby Jonz
A Place In My Heart	Liz Abella
Crazy	Gnarls Barkley
Wrapped Up, Tied Up, Tangled Up	Carpenter Ants
Lonely Drifter	Kenny Helser & The Pieces of Eight
Zing Went The Strings Of My Heart	The Attractions
A Quiet Place	Garnett Mimms
If I Didn't Have A Dime	Bob Collins & The Fabulous Five
Hold On To The Blues	Lonnie Givens
Dixie Moon	Mark Roberts with CWB
Love Buys Love	Solomon Burke
Something Said Love	The Impressions
Just Ask The Lonely	The Four Tops
Lady Soul	The Temptations
Havana	Kenny G
Twisted	Mark Hamilton with Santana
Meet W/Your Black Drawers On	Gloria Hardiman W/Prof's Blues Review
Used To Be My Girl	The O'Jays
Beverly Hills Boogie	The Fantastic Shakers
Talk It Over	Grayson Hughes
Ms Grace	The Tymes
It Won't Always Be This Way	The Men of Distinction

Waitin' On A Sunny Day	Bruce Springstein
Ain't No Big Thing	Gene Barbour & The Cavaliers
Any Day Now	Chuck Jackson
I'm Blue	Jackie Jackson
What You Do To Me	Carl Wilson
I Just Called To Say	Teddy Pendergrass
How Much Longer	Delta Farr
It Started With A Kiss	Hot Chocolate
Well-A-Wiggy	The Weather Girls
Somewhere O The Rainbow /	
Wonder World	Cliff Richards
Some Enchanted Evening	The Temptations
Hoocie Dance	Barbara Carr
Blueboy	John Flogerty
Too Late Too Soon	Jon Secada
Memory	Menage
39-21-46	The Showmen

REFERENCES

1. From an interview with Wyman Honeycutt in July 2006

2. After "Right in the Middle" of Nowhere by Michael Futch published in the Fayetteville Observer (N.C.) August 3, 2003

3. From an interview with Robert Honeycutt on August 17, 2006

4. After works from the pens of Robert Fontenot, Bo Bryan and Michael Futch.

5. After www.heybabydays.com/Cavaliers

6. After www.heybabydays.com/Monzas

7. After http://www.mauricewilliams.com/musicNEW.cfmx)

8. After http://en.wikipedia.org/wiki/The_Catalinas

9. After http://www.alamhof.org/alexand

10. After The Encyclopedia of Popular Music Copyright Muze UK Ltd.

11. After the cover for the CD, *Harry's Band*

12. After http://en.wikipedia.org/wiki/Billy_Stewart

13. After www.rockhall.com/hof/inductee.asp?id=203

14. After willisblume.com/bands/okaysions

15. After cmgww.com/music/wells

16. After http://en.wikipedia.org/wiki/James_Brown

17. After www.partybandsusa.com/Swingin'Medallions

18. After www.heybabydays.com/Tassels

19. After www.history-of-rock.com/drifters

20. After www.rockabilly.nl/references/messages/showmen

21. After www.heybabydays.com/Embers

22. After www.otisreading.com/biography